THE BRANDENBURG GRADUATES

Owen Sela is a British author who lives and works in North London. Celebrated for his fast-paced thrillers – *An Exchange of Eagles* was an immediate bestseller – he has rightly been called 'one of our most talented storytellers' by Len Deighton. *The Brandenburg Graduates* is his third novel to be published by Fontana, and he is currently working on another.

Available in Fontana by the same author

Triple Factor
The Kremlin Control

OWEN SELA

The Brandenburg
Graduates

Fontana/Collins

First published in 1986 by Fontana Paperbacks
8 Grafton Street, London W1X 3LA

Made and printed in Great Britain by
William Collins Sons & Co. Ltd, Glasgow

This is a work of fiction. All characters and commercial
institutions in this novel are wholly imaginary, and are
not intended to bear any relation to any real person or
institution, alive or dead.

This is for
Ramesh and Kokila,
true friends

CHAPTER ONE

Moscow. November

The old man lay on the large bed connected to life by a series of rubber tubes. He looked in surprise at the white ragtag of snow streaming past the window. He'd been with Ylena at the dacha by the Black Sea. It had been summer and they'd been walking together towards the headland beyond the bay. He still felt the warmth of the sand against his feet. Staring at the snow he realized it was November and that he was in his bedroom in the Kremlin, that he hadn't been back to the dacha in two years and that Ylena was dead.

He looked away from the window to the far end of the room where he could just make out the pale figures of nurses in starched uniforms and doctors in dark suits. They spoke in muted voices as if he were already dead. He closed his eyes and was with Ylena again. The warm sun made his blood stir. The voices faded into silence.

He shivered as he felt the wet snow drive into his face and trickle down the tiny opening between his scarf and collar. Now he was standing triumphantly above the Lenin mausoleum while in front of him the Red Army marched in gorgeous phalanx, stepping high and striding proud, their gleaming boots springing from the cobbles of Red Square. As the soldiers marched they slapped their arms flat across their chests and turned their heads to him, to him, Nikolai Berezin, Siberian peasant and Supreme Leader of All the Russias.

Had that only been a week ago? His arm still felt stiff from the effort to keep it raised and immobile. The others, Iakir, Gushenko, Lemekhov, Aliyev, were all his age and must have suffered similarly. He wondered about the younger ones,

7

Timochek, Alyushin, Borodin, Ivanov, the next generation of leaders.

He would outlast them all, Berezin thought. He had a peasant's blood and a peasant's strength, and unlike so many of the others had not damaged his constitution with alcohol, cigarettes and wild living. His mind drifted to the red and green Politburo Committee room. Gushenko was the one who had angered him and brought on the attack which now crippled him; Gushenko with his constant demands for ever larger appropriations for his nuclear counter-strike force and his beloved Army.

As soon as he could move, Berezin decided, as soon as he could get out of bed, he would finish Gushenko. Gushenko and his supporters were yesterday's men. The era of the Cold War was over. The two most powerful nations in the world had no alternative but to live in harmony. That was his policy. That was the policy his predecessor Kuznetsov had come to accept at the end.

Berezin felt his face flush as he remembered Gushenko's taunts. Coward! A man not fit to lead the Soviet Union! A man only capable of opening bottles of mineral water and turning up Kuznetsov's hearing aid!

In the twenty years Berezin had been Kuznetsov's friend, secretary and confidant, Berezin had frequently opened bottles of mineral water, turned up Kuznetsov's hearing aid and asked translators to speak louder. But he and Kuznetsov had been one. And without Nikolai Berezin, Kuznetsov would not have become the great and wise leader who had presided over Russia's destiny for twenty years.

Gushenko was wrong! The Army was wrong! He would control the Army and all their Gushenkos. As soon as he could move, as soon as they let him out of this vast bed —

He became aware of a young physician standing over him. He must have groaned without knowing it. 'How do you feel, Comrade Chairman?'

Berezin tried to talk, but the words clotted on his tongue.

'Good.' The young man had a sharp, intelligent face. Obviously a very clever doctor, otherwise one his age would never have been on the Kremlin detail. 'How bad am I?'

The young man smiled. 'For someone your age, very good.'

Berezin smiled, satisfied. 'Peasant constitution. That's what it is. A peasant's constitution.'

'Yes, of course.' The doctor's smile grew encouraging. 'You'll be well soon. A matter of weeks. But you must rest. You must have plenty of rest.'

'What's been happening? Who's in charge?'

'Everything is running satisfactorily. Marshal Iakir and Comrade Aliyev are filling in for you. There have been no problems.'

The Chairman sank back against the pillows. Iakir and Aliyev. That was good. They would not make any dramatic changes. And they would hold the line against Gushenko.

The doctor was holding a syringe against the light, carefully ejecting all the air from it. He turned to Berezin and rolled up his sleeve. 'Everything is under control, Comrade Chairman,' he said softly. 'There is nothing for you to worry about.'

The Chairman felt himself floating again. He was back in the dacha with Ylena. The doctor was bending over him. He had nice hands with long, sensitive fingers and a firm, kindly grasp. The Chairman relaxed. He would be all right. He would live.

And then he saw the gold chain and tiny medal on the doctor's wrist, a medal on whose face was emblazoned the letter M enclosing the smaller letters, OR and US.

The Chairman stared in horror. He had seen that symbol years ago when he had been an adjutant to Marshal Stalin. It was the sign of the Izgoi! But the Izgoi were no more!

The Chairman tried to sit up but already his heart was like a football, its hollow, irregular beat filling his ears. There was a knifing pain across his chest that made it impossible to breathe. He gasped and sank back on the pillows, staring wildly at the doctor. He heard voices and the urgent rush of feet.

The Izgoi, he thought, helplessly. Impossible!

An orchestra in black tailcoats played Tchaikovsky as Director of Special Investigations, Anatoly Karelin, filed slowly past the catafalque where former General Secretary Berezin lay amid wreaths and flowers, with row upon row of medals pinned to cushions below his feet. At his head were three furled flags of the Soviet Union and beside him soldiers with downcast eyes and red armbands edged in black.

Berezin's embalmed body was dressed in a black suit with a white shirt and black and red striped tie. His face was like alabaster, drained of colour and distant in death. Berezin had been a weak man surprisingly strengthened by his office. Elected as a stopgap, he had in three years imposed his own personality on the Kremlin and done what Kuznetsov had not been able to do in twenty years. Berezin had stopped the military. He had diverted resources to increasing the living standards of the people. He had taken the first steps towards meaningful, peaceful co-existence with America.

Karelin walked to where Berezin's widow and two sons sat to the left of the coffin. He shook their hands and murmured brief condolences before walking towards the line of men standing on the right. Russia's new young leader, Valentin Timochek, stood in the centre of the group, flanked by Marshal Maxim Iakir and party philosopher Pavel Aliyev, the two most senior members of the Politburo. Beside them, their distance from the leader designating their importance, were General Gushenko, Foreign Minister Lemekhov, KGB Director Valichek, Komsomol Chairman Alyushin . . .

Karelin stood to attention and bowed slowly. The autopsy report had revealed an unusual amount of succyl choline in Berezin's body, an amount that could have been a natural by-product of Berezin's heart condition, or the result of an unnaturally administered injection. Karelin raised his head and looked slowly along the line of men. Which one, he wondered, and why?

CHAPTER TWO

East Berlin. January

The two cars, their tyres fitted with snow chains, clanked their way across the Alexanderplatz. At two o'clock in the morning the square was deserted except for the sentries stamping their feet by the entrance to Party Headquarters. Only a few rectangles of light glowed in the building. It was the start of the New Year and not many Party officials were working late.

Three men smothered in heavy overcoats clambered out of the cars. A light still burned in the office of President Dietmark. Huddled together they hurried past the guards into the building.

That afternoon President Dietmark had suffered a defeat in the Politburo, a minor defeat, true, but any defeat was a matter for concern and fresh planning. Now he pored over the personnel files of Party officials, trying to ascertain who was loyal and who was not. Absorbed in his work he did not hear the sound of the cars or the approach of the men until his secretary entered his office. 'I am sorry to disturb you, Comrade President, but Comrade Blucher is outside with General Kork and Colonel Eidemann. They insist on seeing you immediately.'

The Deputy Secretary of the Party, the Commander in Chief of the Army and the Head of Special Forces! It had to be a crisis of some sort. But his staff knew he was working late, and news of a crisis of such magnitude would already have reached the Alexanderplatz. Hiding his incomprehension, Dietmark said, 'Show them in.'

Blucher came in first, young and darkly handsome, wearing as usual a sharply cut imported overcoat and a silk scarf. Behind him Kork and Eidemann lumbered with measured tread, bear-like in their badge-studded Army greatcoats. All three men ignored his offer of chairs and stood in a row before his desk. Dietmark felt a tremor of uncertainty.

'We have come about the meeting of the Politburo this afternoon,' Blucher began.

'That meeting is over,' Dietmark said. 'Everything that had to be decided, was.'

'Except one thing,' Blucher said. 'At the meeting you opposed the acceptance of West German loans. You opposed the proposed rapprochement with West Germany.'

'That is correct.'

'And you were defeated.'

'The issue was unimportant,' Dietmark said.

'My colleagues on the Central Committee do not think so. Neither do our friends in the Army. The question of cooperation with West Germany is a fundamental part of the foreign policy of the Democratic Republic.'

'I do not see it that way,' Dietmark snapped.

'That is why my colleagues wish me to inform you that they no longer have confidence in your leadership.'

'Our future lies with preserving the Revolution – '

'And exporting it.' Blucher smiled thinly. 'My colleagues would appreciate your discreet withdrawal from the leadership of the Party.'

Dietmark looked from Blucher to Kork and Eidemann. The fact that they had chosen to accompany Blucher meant that not only was the Army supporting Blucher, but they were confident that Blucher himself had enough support. Dietmark said, 'If your colleagues wish to make changes they should use the proper democratic processes. Please ask your·colleagues to summon a meeting of the Central Committee at which the whole question of leadership could be discussed.'

'Such a meeting will only arouse unnecessary controversy.' Blucher paused for effect and added, 'It will confuse the people and do great damage to you and your reputation. I'm sure you appreciate, Comrade Dietmark, that public censure

12

must be followed by public punishment. That is something my colleagues wish to avoid.'

'Who are your colleagues?'

Blucher handed Dietmark a letter.

Dietmark saw Blucher had a majority of two. But it was a majority he could shake. Konstanz, Fleck and Tippet were beholden to him. He could fight Blucher. He could — 'My resignation will not find favour with the Russians,' Dietmark warned.

'The matter has already been discussed with Soviet Resident Primakov,' Blucher said. 'General Primakov confirms that it is not the policy of Soviet Russia to interfere in the internal matters of another country.' He pointed to the phones on Dietmark's desk. 'You may telephone him if you wish.'

Dietmark did not bother. 'And if I agree to do what you and your colleagues want?'

Blucher smiled. 'A guarantee of peaceful retirement on full pension, a life-time tenure of the Presidential residence in Harz, undiminished honour and prestige . . .' Blucher pushed some papers across the desk to Dietmark. 'It's all there, Comrade. All you have to do is sign.'

Moscow. Easter Sunday, 30th March

Easter came early that year and with it the first hint of Spring, skies of limpid blue with clouds as thin as thistledown.

At the General's estate outside Moscow, Easter was celebrated with an ancient ceremony pre-dating even that of the Orthodox Church and afterwards the participants sat down to breakfast in an old, timbered dining room decorated with geometric symbols and abstract variations of the letter M. The General sat at the head of the table before plates decorated with gaily painted eggs and the initials XB. His companions ranged in age from the early twenties to the mid-fifties and the General knew each of them like he knew his own children.

There was Mikhail Gamalrik, Head of Directorate K and Viktor Alksnis of Special Service II; Lieutenant Colonel Ranov, Deputy Head of Moscow Army Command, Andrei Lyko, Director of the KGB's Third Directorate, the General's son who commanded the Army's Special Task Force, Vaslav Svyatoslav, Commmander of the Warsaw Pact Defence Forces, Dimitri Kuryakin from the Ministry of Supply, Ivan Trushin from the Central Committee Secretariat, Albert Mironov from the Finance Ministry, Viktor Chermassov from KGB Procurements . . . every one, in effect, a son.

The General had fostered each of these men, he had supervised their education and ensured they were brought up in the right way. It was the General who had decided upon the schools they had attended, the subjects they had studied and the jobs they had taken. It was the General who had arranged for their patrons and their privileges. Each and every one of them owed their lives to him, and would sacrifice those lives instantly upon his command. Each man present was one of the chosen, the best of the elite, a leader of countless others safely hidden in the web of Russian society. And all of them were waiting, waiting for the word.

The General raised a golden goblet. 'Today,' he said, 'we celebrate more than the rising of Christ. Today we celebrate the birth of a new world.' He looked over the goblet at the men gathered round the table. 'I have heard from our brothers in Germany and in America. Everything has been finalized. We start to move now. In exactly thirty-one days we will achieve the ancient dream of our forefathers.'

He drank. 'To the sign and the symbol, to the everlasting, ever present ONE. *Kristos Voskres*! Christ is risen!'

The men raised their glasses. '*Voistine Voskres*! He is truly risen.'

The general hurled his goblet against the wall. He had waited nearly fifty years. And now he thought, just thirty-one days. For the General, the thirtieth of April could not come too soon.

14

CHAPTER THREE

Yuri Orlov woke up wondering if his soon to be former wife was at that precise moment in bed with Oleg Polyakov. He'd seen them together when he'd been on home leave in December; noticed how their glances found each other and the casually practised way they'd danced at Sergei's New Year party. Oleg was Galina's former coach, and Galina had said they were just good friends. Yuri hadn't believed her. There was, Yuri thought, only one reason for a heterosexual Olympic coach to spend so much time with a female ex-athlete.

He opened his eyes to the grey early morning light. The figures on his bedside alarm clock, an elaborate device he had bought from Hausers in the Marienplatz and which contained a radio, cassette player and recorder, proclaimed 6.17. Last week, Galina had written wanting a divorce. She had also enclosed the appropriate papers, Galina, who in all her life had never been able to complete an electoral registration form without help.

The phone rang. Yuri pressed it to his ear. 'Orlov,' he said, huskily.

The voice at the other end of the line said, 'Greetings.'

Greetings indicated an important message from the Special Investigation Directorate. Yuri was instantly fully awake and switched on the recorder he had wired to the phone.

'This is Pavl,' the voice said. 'Pavl, from the Commission.'

Pavl was Anatoly Karelin, Yuri's former tutor at the

Moscow Foreign Intelligence School and present Director of Special Investigations.

'Munich is to be terminated,' Karelin said. 'I repeat, terminated. Call me back on 1313 when you have done so. 1313, that is thirteen repeated twice.'

Yuri felt the phone grow cold in his hand. Thirteen was the ultimate sanction, named after Department Thirteen, the former assassination bureau of the KGB. Karelin was ordering him to terminate the Munich operation and, if necessary, kill the agents.

Yuri had killed before. But those killings had been official, and the victims had been the enemy. In Munich he would be operating against his own people. 'I am a Line PR officer,' Yuri said. 'I am not concerned with Active Measures.'

'You are now,' Karelin replied. 'I am ordering you to stop Munich.' In a gentler tone, he added, 'There is a lot at stake, Yasha. Hundreds of innocent lives.'

Damn Karelin, Yuri thought. He had transferred to Political Intelligence to get away from decisions of life and death. Then he thought, hundreds of people dead and maimed. He could not allow that.

Karelin asked, 'You'll take care of it then?'

'Yes,' Yuri said. He put down the phone and sank back on to the bed wishing he had never got involved with Frederich Mohler.

In the late sixties, Professor Frederich Mohler had been among the first university lecturers to encourage students to burn their books and take to the barricades. Since then, his writings and exhortations from various professorial chairs had encouraged five of his students to die in terrorist shoot-outs, and numerous others to find revolutionary fulfilment in long jail sentences, or a lifetime on the run. A week ago, a frightened and disillusioned Mohler had come from Frankfurt to meet Yuri.

They had dined at the Haxnbauer. Over veal shank, smoked pork and a fine Pflaz wine, Mohler had told Yuri that

16

the KGB were mounting a short, sharp, vicious campaign of terrorism in West Germany, directed by a former Tupamaro, Nino Valdez. 'If they are slaughtering Germans, we must know why,' Mohler had said. 'Terrorism without purpose achieves nothing.'

Yuri had told Mohler that KGB support of terrorist activities had been specifically proscribed by Russia's new leader, Valentin Timochek.

'Valdez' people were behind the murder of the American NATO commander in Duisburg,' Mohler had said.

'Didn't the Revolutionary German Army claim credit for that?'

'The RGA does not exist,' Mohler had said. 'It is a fiction created by Valdez.'

Valdez, Yuri thought, was an unlikely candidate to spearhead a campaign of terror. He had escaped from Argentina five years ago and settled first in Scandinavia and then West Germany. He'd been adopted by the KGB's Directorate K and relegated to providing support to other, more active groups. Three years ago Yuri had worked with Nino Valdez. He recalled a short, pudgy, unprepossessing man, whom he had categorized as insecure, over-reliant on orders, and over-anxious.

'The KGB was not involved in the murder of the American,' Yuri said.

Mohler had looked sadly at Yuri over his glasses. 'You know,' he had asked, 'or you think?'

'And you? Are you guessing or do you know?'

Mohler had moved his glasses back to the bridge of his nose. Looking boredly past Yuri, he'd said, 'The two cars were driven by Chico Perez and Juan Angelito.' The American NATO commander had been killed on an autobahn, his official car sandwiched between two stolen BMWs and riddled with bullets from three separate Kalashnikovs. 'The gunmen were Gunther Stachiowak, Rolf Ennslin and Valdez himself.'

'How do you know all this?' Yuri had asked.

Mohler had simply stared. 'Now you tell me, what is Moscow planning?'

'It is not Moscow,' Yuri had said.

'It is Moscow,' Mohler had insisted. 'Moscow is turning us into political delinquents.' His narrow face had become flushed, his wispy grey hairs grown damp across his forehead. Mohler had said, 'We are indulging in terror without any defined political objectives, we are committing atrocities without purpose.'

'What do you mean?'

Mohler had told Yuri that on the second Monday after Easter, over a hundred pounds of explosive was going to be planted in Munich railway station, timed to cause maximum damage, maximum outrage, maximum mutilation and maximum loss of life. 'There cannot be any justification for such an atrocity,' Mohler had said. 'Moscow has got to tell us why or stop it.'

'How will the explosion be controlled?' Yuri had asked.

'Remotely, by radio.'

'The source of your information?'

'A former pupil with experience in these things, who'd never heard of the RGA. He discussed it with me because he had a crisis of revolutionary conscience.'

'And what did you advise him?'

'Nothing I said had any effect. He had read my books.'

'I need names,' Yuri had said. 'Times, places.'

'The only name I have is my former student, Wolfgang Raspe. The time is Monday morning. The ostensible object, to kill as many NATO soldiers as possible returning from weekend leave, the truth, to kill and maim as many people as possible. After the bombing a statement will be issued, claiming that as long as there are foreign troops on German soil, no one will be safe.' Mohler had paused and asked, 'The destruction of NATO is an end desired by Moscow?'

'Not in that way,' Yuri had said.

'But I am told that the orders come from Moscow. Can you get back to Moscow? Can you have Moscow investigate?'

'I shall want to know everything,' Yuri had said.

Yuri showered and shaved, hoping the noise would not disturb Vasili Ogarov with whom he shared the apartment in Schwabing. Normally, KGB officers were expected to live within the Residency or in Soviet-monitored apartments. But Yuri and Vasili were both political intelligence officers, whose cover required a certain distancing from the Residency, and whose work called for easy, rapid and discreet contacts with outsiders. So under the new regulations made by the former British double agent, Colonel Philby, now a Director of the KGB, they lived in Schwabing, away from the Residency.

Officially, Yuri worked for the Sixth Department of the KGB's foreign service, the First Chief Directorate. His work normally consisted of making contacts, of collecting and disbursing information, of running agents and preparing analyses of political and economic intelligence. Unofficially, he worked for Anatoly Karelin and the Special Investigations Directorate which investigated foreign penetrations of the KGB and the dereliction of duty by Party officials.

Mohler had told him the bomb was planned to go off at eight o'clock that Monday morning, when the rush of people returning from the weekend would be tightly mixed with the crowds coming in to Munich for work. The control location was an apartment on Gollier Strasse, in the complex of one way streets south of the station. Mohler had told Yuri there would be two men controlling the explosion, Raspe and one other, who Mohler believed was from the East German SSD.

The SSD had been created by and worked closely with the KGB. It was logical that if a section of the KGB was defying Timochek's directive, they would involve the SSD. But why, Yuri wondered, would the SSD agree to be involved? Russia still exerted considerable influence over East Germany and no SSD Director would want to incur the wrath of the leader of the USSR. Yuri sighed and hoped Raspe and the East German would be reasonable. He walked to the small safe by the wardrobe and took out his gun.

Line PR personnel abroad were forbidden to carry arms. But because emergencies rarely took account of bureaucratic procedure, Yuri had always kept a private weapon. The gun was an American Colt Python, more powerful than the KGB standard issue Makarov, and for which ammunition was more readily available in Munich. He checked the mechanism, put the gun in its holster, fitted the holster beneath his arm and went out of the apartment.

CHAPTER FOUR

The apartment block on Gollier Strasse was wide and gracious, with a lattice of wood-shuttered windows and a huge wooden door opening on to a central courtyard. Undoubtedly, like most of the area around the railway station, it had been pulverized by Allied bombs, but there was no way of telling that now. The apartment block looked as if it had always been there. It was as if the war had never happened.

Yuri studied the names by the bells. There were thirty-two apartments. While Mohler had told Yuri the address, he hadn't known the apartment number. Yuri jabbed his finger on the caretaker's bell and kept it there. He heard the scrape of slippers on a concrete floor and the sounds of bolts being drawn. A sleepy old man with tousled white hair peered through a slot in the wooden door.

Yuri held out a fifty-mark note. 'I'm sorry for disturbing you. I have just driven from Berlin to collect two friends who recently moved here. We're driving to Switzerland this morning.' He looked helplessly at the row of bell pushes. 'I cannot find their names.'

The money disappeared through the wooden grille. The caretaker said, 'They must be the two men who moved in last week. Apartment twenty-seven.' He opened a small door for Yuri to enter.

Yuri stepped on to a brick-floored verandah which ran the circumference of the building. In the middle was a small garden with a palm tree and a fountain. Apartment doors led off the verandah and on each side were flights of concrete stairs.

'Second floor,' the caretaker said. 'On the right.'

Yuri went up the stairs.

The apartment house was just coming to life. Sounds of traffic from the street filtered through the thick walls. There was an inviting smell of coffee and fresh bread. Yuri approached apartment twenty-seven, cautiously.

He placed his ear to the door and listened. No sound other than the usual creaks of floorboards and expanding wood. He eased the gun in its holster and knocked.

'Who is it?'

'Message. From the Centre.'

A large, bloodshot blue eye peered through a crack between the door and the jamb. Yuri glimpsed the edge of a straggly blond beard and a heavy-set frame. Wolfgang Raspe.

'What message?'

Yuri held up his KGB workpass. 'I'm not going to deliver a message from the Centre in public.'

Raspe moved away from the door and opened it. Yuri stepped inside quickly. There were two of them, Raspe large and unkempt by the door, the SSD agent standing in the middle of the room before a small attaché case placed on a low table. Raspe carried a gun loosely in his hand. Mohler had warned Yuri that Raspe was unpredictable.

Unlike the SSD agent, a slim, balding man in his early thirties, with the calm, compact air of a professional.

Beside his attaché case was a Walther PPK. Yuri looked the man directly in the face. 'The operation is aborted,' he said.

'Can I see your confirmation, Captain?' the man asked, calmly.

'The order comes from the office of General Secretary Timochek himself,' Yuri said.

The man pointed to the phone. 'In that case why was the cancellation not made through authorized channels?'

'I don't know why my superiors do things, Comrade. I simply do as I am told. And I advise you to do the same.' Yuri shrugged and added, 'I was woken up twenty minutes ago and ordered to get here and tell you that the operation has been cancelled.'

The man said, 'Excellent, Captain. You have carried out your orders.' He turned his attention back to the case.

'My orders were to see the operation aborted.'

The man looked up at Yuri. 'Whose orders, precisely, Captain?'

'Timochek's personal assistant in the Kremlin.'

The man reached for the phone. 'I'll check this personally with Moscow.'

Yuri reached casually into his jacket, replacing his work-pass. 'I have a telex here,' he said softly. Then moving much more quickly, whipped out the Python. 'Get away from that phone,' he shouted and stepped back to cover both men. 'This is my authority,' he said, tightly. 'Now whoever you are, get the hell out of here.'

He kept his eyes on Raspe as he spoke. Raspe's gun came up.

'Don't!' Yuri cried. He saw the gun being levelled at him. Mad, fucking revolutionary! Yuri fired.

Raspe spun with the force of the shot. Blood spurted high up on his chest and streaked the wall. He slid along the wall in a marionette's dance and collapsed.

The SSD agent opened the case. As Yuri had surmised, a professional. 'Leave it,' Yuri snapped. 'And get the hell back to East Berlin.'

From the belly of the suitcase a knob protruded. The man's hand flashed high over it. 'Leave it,' Yuri shouted again.

The man's hand swung down.

Yuri fired.

Yuri rushed up to him. The SSD agent was dead. He went over and looked at Raspe. Raspe was dead too. Quickly he searched the body and took out a wallet from Raspe's jeans. An ID described him as twenty-eight years old and coming from Bremen. The wallet contained 2000 marks, two credit cards and a slip from the Dresdner Bank confirming the receipt of $10,000 from Skorpion SA of Vaduz, Liechtenstein.

All the SSD agent had was a billfold with five thousand dollars worth of German, French, Swiss and American currency. A true professional, Yuri thought.

He became aware of a faint whispering from the case on the table. Inside was a small radio with a panel of glowing LED lights. Slipping a glove over his right hand, Yuri picked up the phone, dialled emergency and asked for the Police. 'This is not a hoax,' he said. 'About a hundred pounds of explosive have been placed in Munich railway station. It is controlled by a radio device in Apartment twenty-seven at Gollier Strasse 320. It is timed to go off in the next five minutes. Get the Bomb Squad. NOW!'

He replaced the phone and ran down the stairs.

The stairway was empty. So also the verandah. The smell of coffee, mingling now with that of fresh bread and frying bacon was much stronger. From one apartment a radio blared. Yuri reached the foot of the stairs and hurried towards the front door. The door yawned open, and Vasili Chernov of Directorate K, rushing through the doorway, stopped.

'Orlov! What are you doing here?'

Chernov was a squat, heavily built man, with a face in which tiny eyes, squashed nose and gap-toothed mouth all seemed too close together. He came from Simbirsk, and like most Directorate K personnel had graduated from the KGB's domestic service, the Second Chief Directorate. Like most officers with his background, he viewed all foreigners as hostile, dissident and probably Jewish.

'Everything's been cancelled,' Yuri said, silently berating himself for not anticipating a KGB observer.

'On whose authority? Who's been giving you orders, Orlov?' Chernov looked suspiciously up the stairs.

'There's no one there,' Yuri said. 'The man from the SSD and the other one, they've both gone.'

Chernov thrust his hand into his overcoat pocket. 'Get back up there,' he growled.

Chernov was carrying his Makarov unholstered in an overcoat pocket. Just like a peasant from Simbirsk, Yuri thought, wishing he'd thought like a peasant himself, and had his own gun out. 'There's no one there,' he repeated. He backed slowly up the stairs.

'Turn around and hurry up,' Chernov snarled.

Yuri did as he was told.

From behind him Chernov asked, 'Who gave you orders to cancel the operation?'

'The Kremlin,' Yuri said, thinking if one had to lie, one might as well make it a big lie.

'This has nothing to do with the Kremlin,' Chernov grunted. 'You fucking around with the CIA, Orlov? Or licking some German's arse?'

'All I know is what I was told. My orders came from Timochek's personal assistant.'

Chernov grunted in disbelief.

Yuri knew he had to do something before Chernov took him. They reached the top of the stairs. Out of the corner of his eye, Yuri could see Chernov three feet behind him and to his left, hand thrust firmly into his overcoat pocket, too far away to be surprised, and a damn sight too close to miss with the Makarov. Unless something happened, Chernov was going to end up ferrying him back to his own funeral.

Yuri stopped before the apartment door. The smell of

cordite seeped through the wood, so strong, Yuri felt certain Chernov must smell it. 'They've gone,' he said.

Chernov moved into the doorway, keeping his body between Yuri and the hand in his overcoat pocket. He raised his free hand and knocked.

'You see,' Yuri said. 'They've left.'

Chernov knocked again.

'There's no one there,' Yuri said.

Shouldering Yuri aside, Chernov reached into his pocket, took out a key and fitted it into the lock. Working awkwardly with his left hand he turned the key and pushed the door open. Chernov gasped with shock and horror. His gun hand jerked in his overcoat pocket. His squat body started to turn towards Yuri.

Yuri swung his arm forward and smashed his elbow into Chernov's gut. With a soft explosion of escaping air, Chernov gasped and doubled up. Yuri brought his elbow up into Chernov's face. Clenching his fist, Yuri hit Chernov in the stomach again, followed with a chop to the side of the head, swung Chernov into the room and jabbed him viciously in the body.

Chernov's hand came away from his pocket in futile defence. Yuri hit him again. Chernov's hand pressed against his middle. Beneath the solitary streak of red, his face was white as plaster. Yuri whipped out the Python and jabbed it against Chernov's chest. With his free hand, he dipped into Chernov's pocket and took out the Makarov. 'I told you,' Yuri said, 'It's over.'

From outside the apartment came the high-pitched scream of police sirens.

'You fool!' Chernov gasped. 'You don't know what you've done.'

'Never mind. When I get you back to the Residency you can tell me.' Yuri pocketed the Makarov and stepped back.

The wail of sirens grew louder and more insistent. Yuri said, 'We'd better get out of here before the police come.'

Chernov's mouth worked spasmodically. His jaws tightened. There were tears in his eyes. Suddenly, he hurled himself past Yuri and threw himself on Raspe's body.

'Don't be a fool, Chernov,' Yuri shouted, whirling and covering Chernov with the Python.

Chernov's hand scrabbled for Raspe's gun.

'I killed both of them,' Yuri shouted. 'Don't make me kill you.'

Chernov took the gun, sat up and turned.

Yuri cocked the Python. The scream of sirens filled the room, reverberating against the walls.

Chernov lifted the gun to his mouth and pulled the trigger.

CHAPTER FIVE

Yuri drove back towards Schwabing. He reckoned he had about an hour in which to find out what Chernov had been doing before the Residency was informed of Chernov's death and everything became official. At the end of the Barer Strasse he turned down a side street and stopped before the apartment complex where most of the Residency staff lived.

He used his Special Investigation pass to get into the building, took the elevator to the second floor and knocked on the door of Vladimir Petrov's apartment.

Vladimir Petrov was the head of Directorate K in Munich and Chernov's superior. A man in his mid-fifties, he had spent most of his career with the Scientific and Technological Directorate in Moscow. Munich was his first foreign posting, and it was rumoured that his transfer was the result of someone in Personnel confusing Line K, which was how Scientific and Technological Officers were described, with Directorate K which was very different.

Petrov was a mild, professorial-looking man, with a bony face, silver hair, rimless glasses and pale-blue eyes that peered out ingratiatingly at the world. He opened the door, dabbing at the corner of his mouth with a napkin. He smiled happily as he recognized Yuri. 'Come on in, Yasha. We were just having breakfast. Have you eaten?'

Yuri followed Petrov into a small, neat lobby with coats and umbrellas on a stand and everything else tucked away in cupboards. There were prints of Moscow and Leningrad on the walls and a large black and white photograph of Valentin Timochek. Yuri said, 'I want you to come with me to the Residency.'

'Why? What's happened?'

'Chernov's dead. I want to check his office.'

'Dead! How?'

'I'll tell you on the way.'

Petrov dabbed at his face with the napkin and removed the rest of the egg. 'You want some tea?'

'There's no time for that.'

Petrov reached into a closet and took out a light raincoat. 'I have to go to the Residency,' he called to his wife.

'You haven't finished your breakfast.'

'Never mind. I'll get something at the Residency.'

'Take your raincoat and hat. It's going to rain this afternoon. And you know what happens to you when you get wet.'

'I catch cold,' Petrov muttered and took a hat from the stand. Throwing back his head he called, 'I've got my raincoat and hat. I'll see you when I get back.' He looked round confusedly and stuffing the napkin into his pocket joined Yuri in the corridor.

On the way to the Residency Yuri told Petrov what had happened. The news and the fact that Yuri worked for Special Investigations had a subduing effect. 'I know nothing about any of this,' Petrov said. 'Nothing.'

'Didn't Chernov work for you?'

'Yes. But he was very much his own master.' Petrov smiled apologetically. 'I am still the new boy in Munich. In fact, I don't even know why I was posted here.'

Because someone in Moscow had wanted a dupe in charge of Directorate K, Yuri thought. He asked, 'If you weren't running Chernov, who did?'

'I don't know. Chernov reported to me and I reported to Moscow. Moscow sent me orders and I passed them on to Chernov.'

'What orders did you receive from Moscow regarding the bombs at Munich station?'

'There were no orders for that. All the orders I received were routine, about contacts, payments, meetings and reports.'

'And nothing to do with today? Nothing to do with an escalation of terrorism?'

Petrov shook his head. 'No. Very definitely, no.'

Chernov's office in the Residency was small, neat and clean. There was a modern, oak-veneered desk, a vinyl-covered office chair, two chrome and plastic visitors' chairs, a cheap brown carpet. On the desk were plastic-framed photographs of Chernov's family, his wife who looked in her mid-forties, a boy and a girl who looked about nine and eleven. By the desk was a fireproof filing cabinet with a combination lock.

Yuri and Petrov started with the desk drawers. There were the usual office supplies, four unclassified intelligence reports, two paperbound books and a file of letters to his wife. There were also a notebook and a diary. Chernov had adhered scrupulously to regulations. Everything to do with his work was locked in the filing cabinet.

Petrov had the key but not the combination. Yuri checked the blotter on the desk and the drawers. Then he said, 'Try his birthday.'

Petrov twisted the knob. Nothing happened.

Yuri looked through the file of personal letters and said, 'Try his wife's birthday, twenty-third February 1938.'

Petrov did and opened the cabinet. The files inside were marked with coloured tabs which, Petrov explained, designated areas of Directorate K's responsibility; yellow was for foreign intelligence personnel, red for terrorist organization, green for the affairs of Soviet citizens abroad.

There were two yellow-tagged files which recorded a few contact meetings on which no further progress had been made. The red-tagged terrorist files contained information on groups, meetings, payments, exchanges of information, press cuttings and intelligence summaries. There was nothing on Valdez or the bombing at the railway station.

The Soviet personnel file covered staff at the Residency, the Trade Mission and the commercial agencies. Chernov had had no information on Yuri. There was nothing on Valdez, Centrale, the escalation of terrorism or hundred-pound bombs. As Petrov said, nothing but routine.

At the back of the cabinet was a grey folder marked: FINANCE. Inside were neatly typed statements of accounts and stapled bundles of receipts and vouchers. Yuri passed them on to Petrov. Petrov said the payments were routine.

In the last envelope was a statement from the local Deutsche Bank in the name of Trepart SA and showing a balance of 7212 DM. All the withdrawals on the statement were marked: Cash. All the payments in had come from Skorpion SA.

'I know nothing about this,' Petrov cried. 'We have no bank accounts here. We draw all our requirements from the Residency, and then account directly to Moscow.'

Yuri went through the rest of the envelope. Pinned to the back of an invoice Petrov did not recognize was the carbon of a typewritten note.

Nino,
Here is $50,000, the balance for D'burg. $30,000 is for

you, Stachiowak and Ennslin, the rest for the cars you say you had to have destroyed.

D'burg had to mean Duisburg, Yuri thought. According to Mohler, the American NATO commander had been killed near Duisburg by Valdez, Stachiowak and Ennslin, and Yuri recalled that the cars used in the killing had not since been traced.

Tell Raspe that I have arranged his money directly with Skorpion.

That fitted too. Skorpion had paid Raspe $10,000.

Tell him there must be no more argument, that Munich must proceed as planned. Nothing can be allowed to stop Munich or us.

I am also sending you the money ($2,000) for the van. This must be acquired, kitted out and tested as soon as possible. Everything must be ready by the third week in April AT THE VERY LATEST! We are in the countdown period now. The final act takes place on the 28th and by the 30th we will have succeeded.

The note had been dated two weeks ago and signed with a flamboyant initial M, within whose frame were the letters OR and US. Yuri passed Petrov the note. Nino was obviously Valdez, and Chernov, a methodical man, had kept a copy of the note as evidence for his controller in Moscow. 'What's going to happen in the third week of April?' he asked. 'What is taking place on the twenty-eighth? What will be completed by the thirtieth?'

'I don't know,' Petrov replied. 'And I know nothing about these payments.' He peered closely at the note and looked up at Yuri, shaking his head. 'I don't believe it,' he said, softly. Then in a louder voice, 'It's impossible! It's not true!'

30

'What is it? What's wrong?'

Petrov held the note out to Yuri. 'That signature is the sign of the Izgoi.'

'Who're they?'

'An ancient secret society going back to the beginning of Russia. I thought Stalin eradicated them.'

'Obviously not completely if Chernov is still running bank accounts for them.'

Petrov came closer to Yuri and looked anxiously into his face. 'If the Izgoi survived Stalin,' he said, hoarsely, 'if the Izgoi are behind today's bombing and planning further acts of terrorism, then it means they have regrouped and reorganized and are on the march again.'

Yuri stared suspiciously at Petrov. There was a heightened colour in his cheeks and he was blinking furiously. 'How do you know all this?'

'My father used to be the Chief Archivist at the Russian Academy in Leningrad. Everything about the Izgoi is in a file called *Zemschina*. My father said that when Stalin moved against them, he found Izgoi everywhere, in the Army, the NKVD, even in the Politburo.'

'What do the Izgoi want?'

'Power, I suppose, to rule Russia — I don't know. What is significant is that if they are moving now, their people are already in positions of influence.' Petrov looked round and lowered his voice. 'They are already everywhere. If you're going to do anything about this, Yasha, a word of warning. Trust no one, however important. And be very careful.'

Two words of warning, Yuri thought, and both probably too late.

Yuri left the Residency and drove to the post office on Agnes Strasse where he placed a call to Karelin. After three rings there was a busy tone. Then the phone rang again. A voice said, 'Party Organizing Commission.'

'The Deputy Chief Organizer, please.'

'Do you have his extension?'

'23478.'

The line went dead. Sixty seconds later, Yuri heard Karelin say, '23874.'

The transposition of figures was the correct acknowledgement. Yuri said, '1313 has been executed. Munich has been terminated.'

Karelin said, 'Well done, Comrade.'

'There was a third party present. He was dealt with in the same way.'

'Do you have any other messages?'

Which meant Karelin had been told the line was clear and Yuri could speak freely. Yuri told Karelin about Raspe, the SSD agent and what had happened in the apartment, about Chernov, the letter and bank statement and the connection to Skorpian SA and the Izgoi.

Karelin said, 'I want you to get after Valdez right away. Confront him with Skorpion and the Izgoi. Find out who in Moscow he is loyal to.'

'Valdez is in Frankfurt,' Yuri said. 'I'm in Munich.'

'So go to Frankfurt.'

'And let Valdez kill me?'

'You're more likely to get killed if you stay in Munich. In the next hour or so Chernov's real masters will know of your involvement, and they will want to stop you.'

Yuri felt a shiver run down his spine. 'It might be better if you recalled me to Moscow,' he said.

'Not yet. Our best chance is to find them before they know who we are, what we are doing and how much we know.'

The line crackled momentarily. Yuri said, 'You mean before they find out who I am, what I am doing and how much I know.'

Karelin said, 'Same thing. One for all, all for one. That's Communism.'

'Dumas said it first,' Yuri snapped. 'And D'Artagnan had friends.'

'So have you, Yasha,' Karelin murmured. 'So have you.'

Yuri put down the phone, paid for the call, went to his apartment and packed.

CHAPTER SIX

In Moscow, Director Mikhail Gamalrik drove anxiously along the Sadovoye Kol'tso looking for the signs that would direct him to the M10 and Sheremetyevo Airport. 'We can't allow anything to go wrong now,' he told Alksnis crouched uncomfortably beside him in the front passenger seat of the Zhiguli. Munich was four hours ahead of Moscow and it had been lunch time when he'd had a phone call from a worried and anxious Vladimir Petrov informing him that Vasili Chernov had taken part in an attempt to bomb Munich railway station and that Chernov and the terrorists were dead.

'The first thing you must do is put a blind on the local police,' Gamalrik said. 'Then deal with Petrov. His stupidity is no longer an asset and he knows too much.'

'Do we know exactly what happened this morning?' Alksnis was a big man, very tall and completely bald. The smooth, tightly stretched skin of his face looked like wax poured over stone.

'Only what Petrov reported.' Gamalrik tugged at his half-framed glasses and swerved the car towards the M10 exit. He hadn't driven for years and the only reason he was driving now was that it gave him an opportunity to talk privately with Alksnis who was flying to Munich.

'For goodness' sake, be careful,' Alsknis cried. 'We've had enough bad luck today.'

Gamalrik concentrated on driving till they were on their way out of Moscow. He told Alksnis all he knew about

Munich. 'You'll have to handle Orlov very carefully,' he finished. 'Orlov's one of Karelin's people.'

'What do we know about Orlov?'

'Presently a Line PR officer, Political Intelligence, a ferret.' Gamalrik told Alsknis Orlov had been born the year Stalin died. His father had been an Army officer and both his parents had been killed in a train crash when Orlov was two. Orlov had been brought up by his grandfather, General Vyssorian Orlov.

'The hero of Minsk?'

'The very same.'

Orlov must have had a lonely and difficult childhood, Alksnis thought. 'Why didn't he join the Army?'

'I bet the General would have loved to know the answer to that.' Gamalrik told Alksnis that in 1970 Orlov had won a scholarship to Moscow University, where three years later he had been recruited into the KGB. Orlov had spent a year at the Moscow Foreign Intelligence School, then after a short spell at the Centre, had gone as a field agent to the Bosporus and then to America, England and Europe.

'Unusual,' Alksnis remarked, 'to have spent so much time away from Russia.'

'Karelin's always liked to keep his stars outside Russia,' Gamalrik said. 'He believes it encourages independence of mind. But I think the real reason is that Karelin is able to control his agents with less interference from the Centre.'

'And Orlov was one of Karelin's stars?'

Gamalrik nodded. 'According to the record, one of the best. His only fault seems to be a resistance to discipline.' Gamalrik slumped in his seat as they stopped at a traffic light. 'Three years ago, he transferred to Line PR work.'

'And how did Karelin react to losing one of his stars?'

'Oh, Orlov's never left Karelin. Karelin is like the father he never had. Orlov's always worked for Karelin. They're like this.' Gamalrik held up two locked fingers. 'Orlov's a specialist on Germany. As soon as he finished his present tour, he was to be given the run of the German desk.'

'So why did he interfere?'

'Because Karelin ordered him to.'

'How did Karelin know about Munich?'

'You'll know that when you've broken Orlov.'

'Do I bring Orlov back?' Alksnis asked.

Gamalrik shook his head. The lights changed and he forced the Zhighuli into gear.

Blackie's Bar was dark and smoky, and at that time of the day, the counter was crowded. Allison Maynard peered through the murk until she saw a figure waving at her from a cubicle at the back.

Ray Pollard was a balding, plumpish man in his mid-thirties, with large smoke-lensed glasses and a defiant wisp of moustache. His small fingers were nicotine-stained and there was a crumpled pack of Gitanes on the table in front of him beside a smouldering ashtray and a glass of beer.

'I'm Allison Maynard.'

'I know. Ray Pollard.' He eased himself out from behind the table. He was a good two inches shorter than Allison. 'What will you drink?'

'White wine,' Allison said. 'The drier the better.' Pollard went to the bar. Allison sat.

Allison Maynard was Deputy Director of the Financial Administration Agency, a Treasury department formed two years previously to combat economic sabotage. Last Wednesday, all the television stations and Washington newspapers had carried the story of how she and Agency Director Brad Drewett had foiled a KGB plot to acquire a manufacturer of strategic software in California's Silicon Valley. On Friday Ray Pollard had called and said he worked at the Federal Reserve Bank and that there was something about the Barynin Bank of New York Allison ought to know.

Pollard had said he could only meet her after work and had suggested Blackie's Bar in Georgetown, a discreet distance from where they both worked. Brad Drewett had warned her the man might be a crank, and Allison had thought someone might be playing a joke on her. Nevertheless she was curious and decided to go. 'How will I know you?' Allison had asked.

'I'll know you,' Pollard had said. 'I've got your picture from the paper.'

Allison had wondered if it was the picture from the *Enquirer* which had displayed a lot of thigh and a headline saying MODESTY BLAISE T-GIRL FOILS KGB.

Pollard came back with her drink. He had taken off his tie and his dark-blue office suit was well worn. He took a gulp of beer and asked, 'What do you know about sovereign loans and LDCs?'

'Sovereign loans are loans made to countries or national corporations,' Allison said. 'LDC is banking shorthand for Lesser Developed Countries.' Allison knew that in the past twelve years the amount of loans to LDCs had increased from $90 billion to $700 billion, and that now there were more than thirty countries who could not honour their obligations. Sovereign loans to LDCs was a subject that made bankers instinctively reach for Alka-Seltzer.

Pollard looked vaguely disappointed at not being able to explain sovereign loans and LDCs to her. 'You know about cross-defaulted loans?'

Allison nodded. Cross defaulting was a process where if a borrower defaulted on one loan, all the other loans made to the same borrower were called in.

Pollard took another pull at his beer and lit a cigarette. 'If you were a banker would you rush to buy millions of dollars' worth of sovereign LDCs?'

'I'm not a banker,' Allison said.

Pollard sighed. 'Barynin's are heavily into sovereign, cross-defaulted loans,' he said. 'Here.' Giving a furtive glance round the bar he reached into his inside jacket pocket and brought out a set of accounts.

Allison looked at the figures. They were dated a week

previously and showed that nearly sixty-five per cent of Barynin's reserves consisted of sovereign loans. Also in the last three months Barynin's had borrowed heavily from other banks.

Pollard placed a nicotine-stained finger over a group of figures. 'Barynin's have lent everything they've borrowed on three-month revolving credits.'

'What's wrong with that?'

'Two things.' Pollard hissed as he spoke and his breath smelt fetid. 'The first is that while Barynin's lending is on a three-month revolving basis, Barynin's borrowings are on three-day call. The second is that the companies Barynin has lent to have little in the way of assets. They are all located abroad in tax havens.'

'You think someone is using the companies as a front to collect the loans and then disappear?'

'All I know is that Barynin's are breaking every rule in the book. They're borrowing short and lending long. They're lending without an asset backup. They have most of their reserves in an unsafe and not very easily realizable investment. And their liquidity ratio is way out of line.'

Barynin's sounded like a basket case. 'What's the Fed. doing about this?' Allison asked.

Pollard threw up his hands in disgust. 'If you will pardon my French, sweet fuck all. That's why I came to you.' Pollard explained that he had reported the matter to his Section Head, who had told him that Barynin's problems were only temporary and that any publicity, investigation or disclosure would only aggravate Barynin's problems and risk starting a large-scale banking collapse.

'I took the matter up with Division,' Pollard said, aggrievedly. 'Then last Thursday, Cowdrey Berle, the headman himself, sent for me and told me to lay off. Barynin's were sound, he said. Their problems were temporary and were already being alleviated. My scrutiny had not gone deep enough and he was satisfied there was nothing for the Fed. to worry about.'

'But you obviously think there is.'

Pollard nodded and drank some more beer. 'There's something else,' he said, 'which may explain the cover-up.' He put his glass down and looked triumphantly at Allison. 'Barynin's are Russian.'

Allison stared thoughtfully at him. After the Silicon Valley affair she could well believe that the KGB had infiltrated the Treasury.

CHAPTER SEVEN

It took Yuri six hours to drive to Frankfurt. He concentrated on traffic, on the sound of his tyres, on the sloping bonnet of his BMW, on anything except the fact that he had killed two men and watched a third man kill himself. Regret is the deathwatch beetle of the soul, Karelin had said. Never think about the bad things afterwards. Yuri left the autobahn past the less distinguished business area north of the city centre, and drove to the tarted-up suburb where Mohler lived.

Mohler was watching a television newscast of the Munich incident. According to the report, the police had been summoned to an apartment in Munich's Gollier Strasse, where they had found three dead men and bomb detonating equipment. Bombs had been found in the main Munich railway station, and all trains in and out of Munich had been delayed for some five hours until all three stations had been searched and pronounced safe. An intensive police search was underway for the person who had killed the bombers, and the police had a description of a man in his mid-thirties who had been at the apartment shortly before the men were killed.

Mohler looked from the television set to Yuri. 'Who was the third man?'

Yuri shook his head in mystification. 'I don't know. It looks as if Moscow decided to intervene directly. They asked me to come here and talk to Valdez.'

The narrow, irate features of Siegfried Lothar, the German Christian Socialist coalition government's Finance Minister, appeared on the screen. With a finely controlled display of outrage, Lothar called upon the German cabinet to consider means of controlling this new wave of terrorism, and to eradicate its cause — the presence of foreign troops on German soil — which was shameful to many people in Germany.

'A windbag,' Mohler pronounced. 'What he should have emphasized was the revolutionary aspects of — '

'Where can I meet Valdez?' Yuri asked.

Mohler coloured at the interruption. 'I'm not sure. I mean, I haven't really been in touch — '

'Where did Raspe meet with Valdez?'

'I don't know.' Mohler looked back at the television screen, where they were showing pictures of blanket-clad bodies being carried out of the apartment on Gollier Strasse. He turned off the television saying he had seen that before. Then he added that Valdez usually dined at a Pekingese restaurant in Saschenhausen, called the Yangtse. 'You'll need a mortgage to eat there,' Mohler said, and mentioned that Valdez now travelled. everywhere in a black Mercedes limousine accompanied by a coterie of Argentinian bodyguards. 'Be careful, Yuri,' he warned. 'Valdez' people are killers.'

•

The room had no windows. Its walls were covered with something that looked like the grey cardboard cartons you took eggs home in. The carpet was thick and felt curiously solid. The only illumination came from a screened bank of lights set into the ceiling. Alksnis sat behind the bare wooden table and watched Vladimir Petrov struggle to keep himself erect on the small bench in the centre of the room.

For the fifth time Alksnis had Petrov tell him what had

happened. Orlov had come to Petrov's home and told Petrov that Chernov and two terrorists had attempted to set off a bomb at Munich railway station, that the terrorists had been killed and that Chernov had committed suicide. Orlov had then asked Petrov to accompany him to the Residency where they had examined Chernov's effects.

'How did Orlov find out what Chernov and the others were doing?'

'He didn't say.'

'Didn't you ask him?'

'No . . . I suppose I was too shocked by his news to think properly.'

'What did Orlov say about the other men?'

'Nothing.'

'Did he say who killed them?'

'No.'

'What did you find in Chernov's office?'

'Routine letters and papers, evidence of meetings with contacts, intelligence summaries, records of payments. There was nothing concerning the bombing at the station.'

Alksnis thought Petrov was either stupid or clever enough to act very stupid. In any case he hadn't told Alksnis anything new. 'But you discovered something else?'

'Orlov did. A bank statement and a note.'

'Where are those documents now?'

'Orlov took them.'

'With your authority?'

'He didn't ask specifically. If he had, I would have agreed.'

'What was in those documents?'

'The bank statements were in the name of a company I hadn't heard of before. There were a number of receipts and payments and a balance of some 7000 DM.'

'Tell me about the note.'

'The note had to do with certain payments, the purchase of a van and certain events occurring later this month.'

'What events?'

'The note didn't say.'

'Who were the payments to?'

'I don't remember any names except that of the recipient of the note. He was called Nino and some of the money was for him.'

'What else do you remember about the note?'

'It was signed by a symbol I recognized as that of the Izgoi.'

'What do you know about the Izgoi?'

'I know that it is an ancient secret society that was destroyed by Stalin. That's what my father told me. He was the Chief Archivist of the Russian Museum in Leningrad.'

'What was Orlov's reaction to the note and the bank statement?'

'I don't know. Orlov didn't say anything.'

'How did he look?'

Petrov thought for a moment. 'Usual. Normal. I mean he did not react in any way.'

'Did he say why he wanted the bank statement and the note?'

'No.'

'Perhaps he wanted to show them to someone, someone in Special Investigations?'

'If so, he didn't say.'

'Are you sure about that?'

'Positive.'

'How well did you know Orlov?'

'Not well. We occasionally shared a table in the cafeteria . . . once or twice we had a game of chess. He seemed a pleasant young man. I liked him.'

'Did Orlov mention going on a trip?'

'No.'

'Did he mention going anywhere?'

'No.'

'Do you know where Orlov is now?'

Petrov shook his head.

There was nothing more he could find out from Petrov,

Alksnis thought. Any more information would have to come from Orlov. Where *was* Orlov? No one had seen or heard from him since he'd searched Chernov's office.

Alksnis rubbed his cheeks with his palms and thought about what Orlov had found. He'd found bank statements. He'd found a note from Chernov to Valdez signed with an Izgoi symbol. It was logical to suppose that Orlov had gone to Frankfurt to meet with Valdez. If so . . . Alksnis got up, walked to the small office next door and telephoned Frankfurt.

Valdez was not at his home. Alksnis was given the phone number of a Chinese restaurant in Saschenhausen where Valdez was expected in the next half hour. Alksnis put down the phone and returned to the interrogation room. He might as well deal with Petrov.

He sat down behind the table, took a bottle from a drawer and poured out two shots of vodka. 'I didn't realize the time,' he said. 'How do you feel? You must be quite tired.'

'A little,' Petrov said.

'Would you like something to help you rest?'

Petrov laughed half-heartedly. 'I think after all this, I shall sleep without difficulty.'

'It is essential you sleep well,' Alksnis said. 'I may require you to return with me to Moscow tomorrow morning. And I want you fresh.' He gave Petrov a narrow smile. 'I know how trying these interrogations can be.'

Petrov asked, 'Am I being removed from my position?'

'No. We just want to get to the bottom of this business.'

Alksnis took a small vial from his pocket, slipped two small pills into one of the glasses and pushed it towards Petrov. 'Drink this, Comrade. It'll make you feel better.'

'What? Why?'

'It is essential you rest. This will help you sleep.'

'I assure you, I shall sleep all right. I shall be — '

'Comrade Petrov,' Alksnis snapped. 'I have just given you an order.'

42

CHAPTER EIGHT

Saschenhausen was south of the river, a combination of raffish suburb, restaurants and folksy weinstuben serving Epelwoi, a local drink made from apples, and usually served with a funeral wreath of green leaves, indicating the drink's sharp unpleasantness rather than its alcoholic potency.

The Yangtse was in a street leading up from the river. Beside the restaurant, a well-lit alleyway led to a parking lot. Above the restaurant door was a small sign in yellow neon. Its windows were screened from the street with blinds decorated with fragile paintings of bamboos, reeds, flying birds and Chinese peasants. The Yangtse was discreet, expensive, and exclusive; the ideal eating place, Yuri thought, for a well-heeled terrorist.

Yuri sat in a bar opposite, ate smoked pork, drank beer, and waited. Around eight o'clock he saw a black Mercedes limousine pull up outside the Yangtse and disgorge Valdez and a party of four men. Yuri watched them enter the restaurant. He paid his bill and when he reckoned Valdez' party had settled down, went out of the bar and crossed the road to the restaurant.

'I want to talk to you,' he said loudly, as he approached Valdez' table.

The largest of Valdez' men got to his feet. Good suit, big shoulders, swarthy skin and a dark moustache. And too big around the hips to do much pushing around, Yuri thought. Valdez looked up warily from his crabmeat and asparagus. He was fleshier and better dressed than he had been in Berlin three years ago, and behind the thin-rimmed, blue-tinted glasses, Yuri saw his brows piece together in a puzzled frown.

'Who the hell are you?' Valdez asked, no doubt reckoning that five to one were good odds.

Yuri felt a hand descend on his shoulder, a warm flutter of breath as the Chinese restaurant owner apologized to Herr Valdez. Yuri took out his Special Investigations ID and dangled it before Valdez' tinted spectacles.

Valdez' eyes moved from the workpass to Yuri's face and back again. He spoke through a strained smile. 'I remember you. Berlin wasn't it? The Kurt Brehm case?' He extended his smile to the Chinese floor manager. 'It's all right. We're old friends.'

Yuri felt the weight on his shoulder ease, heard the Chinese drift away. Valdez said, 'Sit down, Captain Orlov. Meet — '

'Outside,' Yuri said. 'I want to talk to you outside. Alone.'

'Don't be silly, Captain. Now that you're in Frankfurt, enjoy yourself. You won't get a meal like this back in Moscow, you know.'

'There are three men from the Centre who want to talk to you,' Yuri snapped. 'And they want to talk to you alone. Now.'

The bodyguard who had stood up at Yuri's approach asked, 'Shall I get rid of this pisspot, Nino?'

Without taking his eyes off Valdez, Yuri said, 'Try that, sonny, and you won't even see the truck that hits you.' He nodded to Valdez. 'Go on, Nino. Tell snake hips here that none of you are big enough to fuck with the KGB.'

Valdez said, 'Ask your friends to join us.'

'My friends have no wish to eat this bourgeois swill.'

Valdez' glance darted from Yuri's face to the workpass. He got to his feet. 'It's all right, Chico,' he said to the bodyguard. 'We're all friends. Order some roast duck and bean sprouts for me.' He nodded to Yuri. 'Let's go.'

Outside Valdez became less controlled and more voluble. 'What the hell do you think you're doing?' he demanded. 'Who the fuck do you think you are? You people may think you own me, but let me tell you — '

'Later,' Yuri said, steering Valdez through the illuminated alleyway into the parking lot. 'You'll have plenty of time.'

'Who am I meeting from the Centre?' Valdez asked.

'A Deputy Director and another bigwig. They flew in from Moscow this afternoon.'

'Because of Munich?'

'I guess so.'

'Look, I didn't organize Munich. Munich was handled by Raspe.'

'He fucked up. And you fucked up.'

'What's your involvement?'

'I'm just a messenger.'

'Why couldn't you people just ask for a *treff*, or come into the restaurant like civilized people?'

'You know Russians,' Yuri replied, dropping two paces behind Valdez. 'Very uncivilized.' He took out the Python and jabbed it hard into the middle of Valdez' back. 'Get over to the blue BMW in the second row. The rear door is open. Get in.'

'What? Who — '

'Move your arse,' Yuri said, and jabbed Valdez again in the back.

Valdez got into the car and sat immobile. Yuri, still covering him with the gun, slid in beside him.

'Where are the others?' Valdez asked.

'There are no others,' Yuri said. 'They sent me because I'd already met you. Moscow wants your balls for Munich.' He placed the barrel of the gun against Valdez' temple.

'Christ, man! Munich wasn't my fault! I had nothing to do with it. And even if I had, no one can guarantee results. Not even the KGB!'

'Munich should never have happened,' Yuri said. 'Politburo Directive 3243 specifically prohibits acts like Munich.'

'I know nothing about that,' Valdez grumbled. 'I just do as I'm told.'

'Who tells you, Nino?'

'The KGB of course. Who else d'you think?'

'Who in the KGB? Is it the Centre or Frankfurt?'

'If you're that fucking important you wouldn't have to ask.' Yuri flicked his fingers into Valdez' eye.

'Shit! Man!' Valdez twisted away, hands flashing up to his streaming eye. His glasses fell soundlessly into his lap.

Yuri slammed Valdez' head against the car door. 'The next time I'll pop out your eyeball like a cherry. So tell me, who gives you orders? Who ran Munich?'

Valdez crouched and pressed his hands to his face. A trickle of shiny wetness glistened on his fingers. 'Chernov,' he muttered.

'Who runs Chernov?'

'I don't know.'

Yuri said, 'Tell me about the plans, about what happens next. Tell me what's going to happen in the third week of April. What's happening on the twenty-eighth?'

'I know nothing about any of that.' Valdez took his hands away from his face and blinked wetly at Yuri. His right eye was red and weeping.

Yuri pressed the gun barrel below Valdez' eye. 'Tell me what you know.'

'I don't have any details.' Valdez' voice was high-pitched and whining.

Yuri picked at the flesh below Valdez' eye with the gunsight.

'They're planning more incidents like Munich, perhaps the killing of a politician or a couple of Americans.'

'Why?'

'I don't know.'

'What's the build-up for? What's happening on the thirtieth?'

'I don't know. If anything's going to happen then, no one's told me.'

'Tell me about Skorpion,' Yuri said.

Valdez blinked at him in surprise.

'Skorpion who paid Raspe and Chernov. Skorpion who funded Trepart SA.'

Valdez' glance steadied. He started to speak and stopped. He said, 'Skorpion is your outfit, man. Hausmann is your conduit.'

'Who's Hausmann?'

'The lawyer who runs Skorpion.'

'Skorpion is nothing to do with the KGB,' Yuri said. 'Munich was nothing to do with the KGB. You're free-lancing, Nino. Your controllers are freelancing. We know you. We want them.'

Valdez sniffed and put his glasses back on. 'I think you're the one who's freelancing, Orlov. You're the one who doesn't seem to know his arse from his elbow. I work for the KGB, man. My orders come from the highest levels. So why don't you get that gun out of my face, go back to Moscow and find out who's giving the orders.'

Yuri cocked the gun. In the silence the click was harsh and very audible. Yuri said, 'Chernov is dead. I have orders to kill you if you don't cooperate.'

Valdez went very still. Then he said, 'You'll be very foolish to do that.' He forced a smile. 'Don't you see there's been a mistake, that some people in the Kremlin have got their wires crossed. Tomorrow they'll realize what's happened and cancel the order to kill me.'

'Tomorrow will be too late,' Yuri said. 'We're both Communists and don't believe in afterlife, so I'll say it now. I'm sorry if there has been a mistake.'

'You're crazy to shoot me,' Valdez shouted. 'Crazy! I was only doing what I was told to do. I was only doing what the KGB ordered me to do!'

'Who in the KGB?' Yuri demanded. 'Was it Directorate K? You said the very highest levels. Who is it? Alksnis? Gamalrik?'

Valdez nodded.

Yuri jabbed the gun into Valdez' cheek. 'Tell me about the

47

Izgoi? Tell me about the funny signature on Chernov's note to you. Tell me why the Izgoi financed Munich.'

'Fuck off,' Valdez said.

Suddenly there were shouts from the alleyway, the sight and sound of men running into the parking lot. 'Nino!' they shouted, 'Where are you, Nino?' The group broke up among the cars.

Yuri prodded Valdez with the gun. 'Quiet,' he said. 'I will shoot.'

Someone shouted, 'Nino! Phone!' Someone else cried, 'There they are. In the blue 525.'

The man who had tried to assault Yuri in the restaurant appeared ten feet from Yuri's door, partly covered by the boots of two cars. There was a Walther PPK in his hand. 'We know all about you, Captain,' he cried, levelling the gun at Yuri. 'Come on. Get out of there with your hands up.'

'What do you know?' Yuri asked, jabbing his gun against Valdez' nostrils.

'You betrayed Munich, you bastard. You wasted Raspe.' The man laughed harshly. 'You're finished now. We've got you.'

'You're being snowed,' Yuri said. He prodded Valdez. 'Tell him.'

Valdez gurgled.

'You're the one that's being snowed,' the man cried. 'You're the one the KGB want killed.' He raised the Walther.

Yuri pushed Valdez away and whipped the Python round. As the bodyguard clapped both hands to the butt of the Walther, Yuri fired.

The man spun upwards and backwards, hit the bonnet of a car, slithered and hit the ground with a dull thump. Valdez elbowed Yuri in the ribs, flung open the door and half threw himself, half fell out of the car. From somewhere among the row of parked cars to the left a man shouted, 'Come on KGB, get out of there! We have you covered!' A bullet smashed through the rear window in confirmation.

Yuri leapt out of the car and threw himself to the ground. Shots ricocheted as he crawled underneath one vehicle, then another.

'Munich wants you, KGB,' a man shouted. 'Your people want you back.'

Another voice cried, 'We know who you work for, Captain. The CIA.'

'Get the bastard!' That was Valdez.

On hands and knees, Yuri dragged himself underneath two more cars. The firing stopped. Yuri thought eight more cars to the end of the row, and then what. He passed beneath one more car. The next car was a low-slung English sports car. No way he could crawl beneath that. With his gun pressed to his face he waited.

Directly in front of him where the rows of parked cars ended was a gravel path illuminated by arc lights running from the alley to the restaurant kitchen. The kitchen was busy, full of shadowy figures misted by condensation.

The men were hidden among the cars between him and the gravel path, no doubt moving around to get a better angle and a clearer view. Going forward was impossible. Go back? He looked along the row of cars at the wall, and slowly crawled back the way he had come. He reached his own car, reached up and opened the door. The noise brought a hail of fire from behind him. Yuri crouched into a ball and rolled across the space between the rows, flattened himself and crawled beneath another car. An exhaust pipe grazed his back.

Gently, he eased himself towards the wall. Four cars, all prosperous family saloons with good ground clearance. He lifted his head and risked a look. A new Opel and a white Range Rover stood right up against the wall. He calculated distance and height, drew himself out from underneath the car and crouched like a sprinter on starter blocks.

He glimpsed a movement in the first row of cars. Someone had drawn the Mercedes limousine across the alley. They thought they had him trapped.

He holstered the Python, braced himself, sprang upwards and forwards, sprinted. Behind him he heard a shout, heard the report of a gun. Then he was by the Range-Rover, slowing, kicking down, jumping.

He leapt on to the bonnet, his shoes skidding on the polished metal. The metal flexed. He steadied himself by grabbing the roof and the wing mirrors. He straightened up and leapt again.

The top of the wall caught him across the chest. His outstretched arms went up and over. He slid down and was caught by his armpits. He pulled himself up as a bullet smacked into the wall by his ribs.

Behind him the men had broken cover. He could hear their shouts, the pounding of their feet. He pulled his body over the wall, swung a leg across, paused and drew the Python.

Four cars away from him, Valdez had his gun aimed at the top of the wall. Behind Valdez the three others were still running with weapons held high. Yuri fired quickly, swivelling the Python. He heard bullets whine off metal, heard the tinny tinkling of glass, heard someone scream. He swung himself over the wall and dropped.

He fell with legs limp, allowing them to stiffen slightly as he landed, forcing his body into a forward roll that ended with him on his back in the middle of a flower bed. Quickly he sat up. No one was coming over the wall after him. Yuri got to his feet, dusted off the thick dirt of the flower bed, and hurried across the park.

He hadn't expected Munich to move so fast. He'd thought they'd be so occupied with the bombing and Chernov's death, that they wouldn't have got round to interrogating Petrov or noticing his absence till tomorrow. Someone from Moscow must have activated Munich, and Yuri wished he knew who. Anyway, the connection had been made and Munich had warned Valdez. Quite soon, Valdez' terrorist hordes would be stalking the streets of Frankfurt looking for him.

He had to get out of Frankfurt. But how? He came to a low

gate on the opposite side of the park, climbed over it and got on to the street. He thought the one place Valdez' people would never think of looking for him was here in Saschenhausen, as near as possible to the Yangtse.

He walked down the street, turned at the end and walked along the ordered river front till he came to a large, crowded beer keller. The room inside was full of people, standing at the bar and sitting in happy camaraderie at long tables. The air was thick with cigarette smoke. A juke box played an old Presley number, *Treat me Nice*. Someone should sing that to Valdez, Yuri thought. He got himself a beer and sat at one of the tables.

Hiring a car at this time of the night would be difficult, and conspicuous. He thought about trains. Trains to where? Or what about a hotel here in Saschenhausen? He became aware of a man opposite, staring at him. Yuri held the man's glance for a moment, then looked away, picked up his stein of beer and drank. When he lowered the jar, the man was still studying him.

The juke box was playing an old Supremes number. The man opposite still stared curiously at him. Yuri wondered whether to confront the man, and decided not. If the man was a drunk, or worse still, a lonely drunk, he could pick up a noisy, difficult to get rid of companion. Yuri looked away to his left at the television over the bar. They were still covering the story of the Munich bomb, the screen filled with pictures of the sheeted bodies being carried out of the Gollier Strasse apartment. Then Yuri felt his heart stop. The next picture on the screen was his own!

He stared horrified as the reproduction of his face, taken from his KGB workpass, looked out sternly across the bar. He felt everybody in the beer keller must be looking at him. He strained to hear the announcer. A Russian diplomat had disappeared in Munich that morning. The Russian Consulate stated that the disappearance had no connection with the bombing, but they were concerned that the diplomat might have been kidnapped by terrorists. The newscaster added that unattributed opinion believed the Russian might have defected.

In other words, it was an alert, but not an alert. While warning the German authorities to watch for Yuri, Munich had ordered all KGB stations in Germany to find and seize a defector!

Yuri raised his glass and found he was covering his face with the side of his hand. Cautiously, he looked around the bar. Most people were ignoring the news broadcast. No one was looking at him, except his companion across the table, who had raised his glass in silent salutation. Yuri looked away. The man might not be Valdez' but he could be KGB.

The KGB knew he was in Frankfurt. They had got in touch with Valdez and by now would have arranged a joint search and destroy operation. They would have covered all the hotels, the airports, train and bus stations. The man opposite was still staring at him. Definitely a KGB spotter, Yuri thought, and stood up. Holding his handkerchief before his face as if he had a toothache, he hurried out of the bar.

He stood hesitantly on the street outside. Remaining in Saschenhausen hadn't been such a bright idea after all. Together the KGB and the terrorists had enough manpower to cover Saschenhausen and all of Frankfurt. They would have men at the railway and bus stations, at the airport; they'd have alerted their contacts in car hire companies and hotels. He was trapped.

Yuri started to walk along the street. Behind him, the keller doors opened and the man who had been staring at him emerged. Yuri walked faster. He heard the man's footsteps accelerate and dropped his hand to his gun.

'*Mein Herr! Mein Herr*!'

Yuri decided to ignore the man. If anyone heard, they would conclude he was simply being pestered by a drunk.

'Mein Herr!' The shout was louder. Closer. A confrontation was inevitable. Loosening his gun, Yuri turned.

The man was standing a few feet away, a ring of keys in his hand, a hesitant smile on his face. Speaking in English he asked, 'You are Russian diplomat, yes?'

Yuri spoke in German. 'Who are you? What do you want?'

The man was opening the door of a grubby Volkswagen Passat. 'Come,' he said, 'I will take you to the American Embassy.'

'I don't want to go to the American Embassy,' Yuri said. 'I am German. I live near here.'

'You speak German very well,' the man replied. 'But you are not German. You are the Russian who has defected. I saw your picture on the television. There is no need to be afraid of me. I am a defector, too. I will take you to the American Embassy, or if you like, to the American Army base in Rothschild Park.'

'I don't want to defect to the Americans,' Yuri said. 'I am West German.'

'I am East German,' the man said. 'Ten years ago, I came over the wall. So we're friends, and I will take you wherever the hell you want to go.'

Whether the man was a genuine defector or not, Yuri decided he could use the man's car. 'I need to get to Heidelberg,' he said, thinking of somewhere out of Frankfurt, but not so far that if the man was genuine, he would want to refuse.

The man opened the passenger door. 'No problem.'

Yuri climbed in. The man wound the car into life and pulled away from the kerb, 'I am Erhard,' he said. 'I understand your situation. The problem with Communism is there is no freedom.' Talking volubly, he hurried the Volkswagen on to the autobahn towards Wiesbaden and Heidelberg.

To Yuri's relief, his new-found friend appeared to be genuine. He was a metal worker and since he had defected, had got his own business, rented a larger apartment than he would have been assigned in East Germany, and owned this second-hand car. He was happy and well satisfied. Life in the West was comfortable if you worked hard, he told Yuri, and there was no one telling you how to spend your money, what to read or what to think.

Yuri asked Erhard about his apartment.

It was in the West End with three bedrooms, central heating, and a large balcony. He lived there with his wife.

Yuri asked, 'There's just the two of you in the apartment?'

'Yes,' Erhard said with a hint of pride.

'Could you let me stay in your apartment tonight? I can pay. I have to get a flight to London tomorrow morning, and I am worried that if I stay in a hotel, they could trace me.'

Erhard swerved into the slow lane. 'Why didn't you ask before?' he cried.

Tuesday April 8

CHAPTER NINE

Tuesday morning. Yuri surfaced through layers of sleep. Last night, his new friend, Erhard, had brought him home. Erhard and his wife had been concerned to help a fellow defector escape and they had given him food and a bed in a clean, comfortable room. This morning, Erhard would drive him to Cologne. From there Yuri would take a flight out of Germany.

On the autobahn last night, Yuri had decided the only place he would be safe was Moscow. No one would think of looking for him there. And in Moscow, he would have Karelin's protection.

Sleepily rising through diminishing levels of greyness, Yuri heard a movement in the room, a sound that divided into a rustle of clothes, footsteps and a sharp click as the radio beside his bed was switched on.

Erhard stood three feet away from the bed. In his hand, pointing directly at Yuri, was Yuri's Colt Python.

'Erhard! What's wrong?'

As if frightened that Yuri might spring from the bed and attack him, Erhard backed to a chair by the dressing table. His florid face was troubled, the veined eyes bloodshot and hostile. 'You,' Erhard said with contempt. 'You're wrong. You abused my trust. You disgraced my house. You betrayed us.'

'I have not betrayed you or your house,' Yuri said. 'I have not betrayed anyone or anything.'

The accordion music faded. An announcer started to read the news. 'Listen, comrade,' Erhard said, raising his voice above the newsreader's. 'Listen carefully.'

Yuri listened. Because of the terrorist threat to NATO soldiers, the Chancellor was returning to Bonn that afternoon for meetings with cabinet colleagues and foreign ambassadors. Alerted by the Russian consulate in Munich, the West German police were looking for the missing Russian diplomat, Yuri Orlov, who was now thought to be connected with the RGA terrorists who had organized the bombing at Munich railway station. Abroad, French farmers were threatening to blockade roads in support of —

If Munich had called in the Bundespolizei, Yuri thought, they wanted him very badly. Never mind that he could disprove their allegations or might make damaging revelations. The main thing was that if the Bundespolizei found him, they were legally bound to notify the Russians. And then it wouldn't matter what he disproved or revealed. He would be dead.

Yuri looked across the room at Erhard. Erhard was slumped against the dressing table, his body curled into a question mark of suspicion. Yuri decided his first problem was to convince Erhard. His second, that there was little time for persuasion. Already, Erhard might have informed the police. While he calculated distances and practicalities Yuri listened for the sound of sirens and the pounding of fists on doors.

Physically, Erhard was no match for him. Except Yuri was lying down and Erhard was seated far away. He looked at Erhard's hand clasped around the gun. Erhard held the gun loosely, with a degree of unfamiliarity. Erhard meant the weapon to be used in defence not attack. Yuri decided Erhard would not fire unless threatened or frightened. Erhard, he thought, *wanted* an explanation. He *wanted* to believe that the man he had helped last night was a refugee from Communism and not a terrorist.

Yuri sat up slowly. 'I have no connection with the RGA,' he said. 'I did not organize Munich.'

'Then why are the police looking for you?' Erhard's face was clouded.

'The police are simply acting on information received.' Yuri reached for his shirt and struggled into it. 'The real question is who gave them that information, and why?'

Erhard shifted in his chair, but remained silent.

'I am not a member of the RGA,' Yuri repeated. 'Neither am I a defector. I am an officer in the KGB.'

Erhard's grip on the gun tightened. His face took on an expression of disgust.

'I work for a counter-terrorist section of the KGB which is trying to stop the activities of the RGA. That was my mission in Munich.' Yuri finished buttoning his shirt and swung his feet cautiously off the bed. 'With the gun you are now holding, I killed the two terrorists before they could set off the bombs they had planted in the railway station.'

Erhard looked uncomfortably from Yuri to the gun as if the weapon were still warm from killing. He asked, 'So why do the West German police want you?'

56

'Because they have been told to find me by the people who organized Munich.'

'Why?' Erhard asked.

Yuri got to his feet.

The gun barrel jerked upwards.

Yuri made a placatory gesture. 'I only want to get dressed.' Without giving Erhard time to disagree he stepped across to the wardrobe and took his trousers from a hanger.

'The fact of the matter is . . .' Yuri held his trousers in front of him and stepped into them, 'that Munich was organized by a faction of the KGB, contrary to the orders of the Politburo and the official policy of the KGB. Because I stopped Munich, because I now know who the perpetrators are, they want to prevent me getting that information to my superiors. So last night they issued a statement that I had defected, thereby warning all KGB stations in Germany to apprehend me. When, because of the kindness of you and your wife, they could not find me, they informed the West German police that I was implicated in the bombing.' Yuri pulled up his trousers and fastened his belt.

Erhard still looked dubious, his brow furrowed, the lines beside the protuberant nose deepening. 'The German police will not help Russians,' he said.

'Not wittingly. Not knowingly. But like any other organization they can be used. Do you know that once the German police find me, they are legally bound to notify the Russians?'

'Yes,' Erhard said.

'So you understand how badly they want me.'

Erhard frowned hesitantly. He said, 'I think you had better explain all this to the police.'

Yuri reached inside the wardrobe for his jacket. 'There are worse things than Munich planned,' he said. 'The only people who can stop those things are my superiors. If they are not stopped the consequences for West Germany will be disastrous.' He searched through his pockets checking that his documents and money were there. He pulled the documents out of a pocket. 'Here,' he said, moving towards Erhard, 'I have proof. Lists of times and places where atrocities much more terrible than Munich are planned. They are written in Russian, but being East German you would have learned — '

Still talking, he held the wad of documents out to Erhard. Instinctively Erhard's eyes swivelled. Yuri clenched the hand carrying his jacket into a fist and drove it into the bridge of Erhard's nose.

Erhard's head rocked back against the wall. The chair slid from under him. Yuri dropped documents and jacket and threw his body across Erhard's, twisted round and brought his hands up to grasp the gun barrel and Erhard's wrist. Using the barrel as a lever Yuri forced Erhard's hand back. Erhard's face reddened. His teeth bit into his lips. 'Don't fight, my friend,' Yuri whispered hoarsely. 'Don't force me to break your hand.' He levered Erhard's wrist further backwards.

Abruptly Erhard's hand went limp and he released the gun. Yuri collected it and got to his feet. 'Stand up slowly,' he ordered. 'Get your back to the wall. Now, kick the jacket and the documents over to me, gently.'

Erhard did as he was asked. The colour had drained from Erhard's face and there was an unnatural sharpness about the lines on it. His lips were dry and there was a frightened rigidity about his stare.

'I could kill you now,' Yuri said. 'If I were a terrorist, I *would* kill you now . . . But I am not a terrorist and killing would not be the way to repay your friendship.' He put the gun down on the dresser between them. 'Please trust me,' he said.

Erhard looked hesitatingly from Yuri to the gun.

Yuri said, 'Take the gun. But if you take it you will have to kill me.'

Slowly Erhard reached out a hand.

Yuri said, 'If you take the gun and kill me you take the responsibility for what happens in Germany afterwards.'

58

'And if I leave the gun?'

'Then after you've done me one more favour, I'll walk out of your life forever. There is someone here in Frankfurt who is already involved in what is going on. I want you to take me to him.'

Erhard glanced from Yuri to the gun. His hand dropped to his side. 'All right,' he said.

As they drove in the heavy rush hour traffic to the centre of Frankfurt Yuri realized it would be a long time before Erhard offered another refugee sanctuary. He had Erhard drop him off near a second-hand clothes shop where he bought a cheap but respectable dark suit and hat, and a pair of lightly tinted, horn-rimmed spectacles from a neighbouring optician's. He changed in a toilet, went to a booth and took two photographs of himself wearing the glasses.

To get out of Germany with immigration, police, Valdez' people and the KGB looking for him, he needed false documents. In other times he had known people who could have provided a false passport, but to reach them now would be to trip an alarm to the KGB, and to prowl the bars of Frankfurt looking for a forger of passports was impossible. Yuri decided what he needed was a national identity card, the document most Europeans used for travel within the Common Market and which was much easier to forge than a passport. He found a taxi outside the station and had the driver take him to the chintzy suburb where Mohler lived.

CHAPTER TEN

It was nearly noon when Mohler braked his Golf GTi outside the Frankfurt air terminal. With his new suit, hat, glasses, and the ID Mohler had procured from a forger in the Kaiser-strasse, Yuri felt sure he wouldn't be spotted.

He climbed out of the car and walked into the terminal where he joined the throng of similar, anonymous, sober-suited, brief-case clutching men waiting for the flight to Düsseldorf.

He had picked Düsseldorf because it was further from Frankfurt than Cologne and had more frequent international connnections. He had a reservation on a 1.45 flight leaving Düsseldorf for London and from there he would take a flight to Moscow the next day. It was a circuitous route, but to get on a flight to Russia he would have to produce a Russian passport or visa, and to do that was tantamount to walking into the arms of the KGB.

He heard his flight called and boarded with the other businessmen. He took an aisle seat and buried his head in the inflight magazine for the duration of the journey. Forty-five minutes later he was in Düsseldorf.

He had twenty minutes to pay for his ticket and board the flight to London. He hurried to the Lufthansa cash desk. Then it happened.

As he was turning away from the desk, a middle-aged woman whom Yuri had earlier seen scurrying from one ticket desk to another cannoned into him. Yuri was hurled back against the desk, the force of the collision flinging the glasses from his face.

'Per favore, signore, scusi! Vorrei un biglietto per Roma!'

The woman was short, middle-aged and bustling, her made-up eyes and rouged mouth wide with shock and apology. *'Mi scusi,'* she cried, *'Mi scusi!'* She picked up the spectacles and held them out to Yuri.

Yuri kept staring at the woman. Was she genuine or a KGB diversion? If she was a KGB diversion —

'I cannot miss my flight, signore. I have to be in Rome tonight.'

Yuri knew there *was* a flight to Rome five minutes after his own. The woman looked genuine enough, confused enough, and thankfully the glasses were undamaged. *'Prego,'* he said, and took them from her. He stepped aside from the counter and raised the glasses to his face.

A man was staring at him from the middle of the wide passageway, a stocky man about his own age. Yuri had met him once at the Residency in Hamburg, a low-level KGB officer called Alexei Droznin, now obviously drafted from Hamburg to help and assigned to Düsseldorf where they least expected Yuri to appear. Stuffing a rolled up newspaper into his jacket pocket, Droznin was walking quickly towards the far wall and a row of grey beehive shrouded telephones.

Yuri moved after Droznin. They hadn't expected him in Düsseldorf. They'd only sent one drone with provisions for a back up. Droznin must not make that call.

He stepped around an elderly man wheeling a baggage trolley. Droznin would be armed. Yuri wished he had not left his own gun with Mohler. But travelling with a gun in his hand baggage, even with its firing pin removed, was impossible.

Droznin had already reached the telephones. With a casual backward look he stepped into one of them, his free hand fumbling in a pocket for change. Abruptly, Yuri changed direction and moved diagonally away from the telephones, away from Droznin's direct line of sight. Droznin entered the booth and looked around, his head emerging from the booth like that of a tortoise from its shell. Then, as if satisfied, he concentrated on his phone call.

Yuri raced for the wall against which the telephones were arranged, turned and walked quickly along the wall to the row of phone booths. Droznin was in the fourth. Yuri transferred the attaché case to his left hand, and as he drew level with the booth, swung his right fist hard into Droznin's kidneys.

Droznin straightened in agony, releasing the phone, his head arching backwards, his mouth sagging open. Sliding his briefcase between Droznin's legs, Yuri stepped into the booth, left hand closing Droznin's mouth, left arm

61

supporting Droznin, right fist pressing against the damaged kidney.

Quickly, he reached under Droznin's jacket, took out the service Makarov and pressed it against the side of Droznin's belly. 'One word and you're dead,' he murmured into Droznin's right ear. He reached past Droznin for the dangling receiver.

'*Ahlo*,' a voice carolled in his ear. '*Ahlo, Ahlo*!'

'Orlov arrived three minutes ago,' Yuri said in Russian. 'He was met by two men near the Hertz desk who took him to a car. I heard them say they would drive him to Brussels.'

'What kind of car?'

'A brown Ford Capri, Düsseldorf registration.' Yuri paused for a moment and added, 'The men looked American.'

'Fine,' said the voice. 'Collect Mikhail and return here immediately.' Yuri replaced the receiver.

Droznin groaned.

'Who was that?' Yuri asked.

'My control . . . at the trade mission in Düsseldorf.'

'Where is Mikhail?'

'At the other terminal.'

'How do you feel? Can you walk?'

'I think so.'

Yuri reached down and picked up the briefcase. He clicked it open and inserted his gun hand into it. 'Come with me,' he said. 'Walk slowly and carefully. Try anything and I'll shoot you.' Holding the briefcase between them, he backed away from the booth. Droznin lumbered out after him, doubled forward, his hand pressed to his back, his face pale and sweaty.

'It hurts to walk,' Droznin gasped.

'Try.'

Overhead the loudspeakers crackled. 'This is the final call for passengers on Lufthansa flight zero five two to London. Please go to gate — '

It took him less than five minutes to dispose of Droznin and make his flight.

Allison paused in the taxi outside the two-storeyed green and white tiled building on New York's lower West Side which housed the Barynin bank. The tiles were decorated with intricate carvings, and the window ledges and door frames picked out in gold. The sign above the door was in both English and Cyrillic. Barynin's looked more like a church than a place of business. Allison got out of the taxi half expecting to see the building crowned with an onion-shaped dome.

When she'd told Brad Drewett about her meeting with Pollard, he had as she expected immediately become concerned about the sovereign loans. Brad believed sovereign loans were financial hydrogen bombs, that in the wrong hands they could destroy the American and European banking systems and severely damage the economic foundations of the West. Brad had asked Allison to get to New York and see Ellesmere Wentworth, the head of Barynin's.

Wentworth turned out to be a man in his late thirties, just about old enough, Allison thought, to be running a bank. He wore a two-piece, grey Brooks pinstripe and round, tortoiseshell glasses. His office was clubby, with overstuffed armchairs, an antique, leather-topped desk, mahogany bookshelves and gloomy hunting scenes in artificially faded oil. While he spoke Wentworth toyed with his pen, a large, gold, old-fashioned fountain pen, with a lever on the side to fill it and a large, gold M prominently displayed on its clip. Wentworth told Allison that Barynin's involvement in sovereign loans was a private business matter, and nothing to do with the FAA.

'You believe sovereign loans are good investments?'

Wentworth gave her an abstracted smile. 'Generally, yes. Of course there are some loans I wouldn't recommend . . .' He revolved the pen in his fingers, furiously.

'Why do you have sixty-five per cent of your reserves in sovereign loans? Don't you think putting so much in one type of investment is a risk?'

'A question of opinion, Miss Maynard. In any case the manner Barynin's choose to invest their reserves is nothing to do with the FAA.'

'Not yet,' Allison said and waited.

Wentworth toyed with his pen and smiled.

Allison asked, 'Barynin's have recently made substantial loans to a series of small companies located abroad in tax-advantageous countries?'

'That is possible,' Wentworth replied. 'What is more significant however is that Barynin's only advance moneys after a most exhaustive and thorough check on the borrower's financial standing and ability to repay. The fact that certain borrowers may be resident in what you describe as tax-advantageous countries is not necessarily a disqualification. I think you will find that every major bank has some borrowers resident in those locations.'

'As many borrowers as Barynin's?'

'I am not prepared to discuss specific customers, Miss Maynard.'

'Why have Barynin's recently substantially increased both their lending and their borrowing?'

'Again, Miss Maynard, that is the bank's business.'

'It is our understanding that the recent increased lending has caused Barynin's to exceed their liquidity ratio?'

'I neither confirm nor deny that. If, like any other bank, Barynin's have had occasion to exceed their liquidity ratio, then you may rest assured it has been done with the full knowledge, consent and approval of the Federal Reserve.' He leaned across the desk, smiling humourlessly. 'Banking is a business, Miss Maynard, a continuous, ongoing, living organism. It does not and cannot always fit within the constraints of abstract rules.'

'Are Barynin's in breach of any of those abstract rules?'

Wentworth shook his head. 'No comment.'

'Barynin's have perhaps committed a technical breach. Is

64

that why you will not talk to me more freely? Is there something you're trying to hide?'

'We have never done anything illegal, Miss Maynard, and there is nothing we wish to hide. However, I will not answer your questions. I will not set a precedent of discussing our affairs with any government department which feels curious about what we are doing. If you want to examine the records of Barynin, Miss Maynard, come back with a subpoena, a Grand Jury commital or a court order. But until you do . . .' Wentworth put his pen away in the top pocket of his jacket and stood up. The shiny gold M gleamed.

In the book-lined study of the Dean of Clairvaux Academy College, the red phone rang. Miles Kingdon picked it up on the second ring. 'Yes.'

It was Ellesmere Wentworth from New York. 'The FAA are sniffing around,' he said and told Kingdon about Allison Maynard's visit.

'How much does she know?'

'I don't believe very much. I think she was here on a fishing expedition.'

'And did she catch anything?'

'No. But I don't believe she will be satisfied until she does.'

Kingdon said, 'I'd better put a stop to that.'

'And talk to Berle. I think the source of Maynard's information is inside the Fed.'

CHAPTER ELEVEN

The British Airways Boeing descended through layers of soiled grey cloud and landed with a thump of wheels and screaming engines. The runway was lined with patchy snow, and as they slowed, streaks of water scarred the windows.

Yuri sat erect in his seat, his seat belt pulled tightly around his waist. His time in London had been uneventful and the check in at Heathrow had revealed nothing. No one had bothered with him once they saw he had a Russian passport.

His fingers were cold and his mouth was dry. If Munich had realized what he had done, they would be waiting for him. He wondered if they could have made a connection through Droznin. Or if they had found Mohler and broken him. He unfastened the seat belt and stood up. There was nothing to do but join the line of passengers and go into the terminal.

Inside the terminal, lines stretched everywhere. Returning Soviet citizens stood around piles of opened luggage with video recorders, books, magazines, records and cellophane-wrapped shirts strewn as if at a jumble sale. It looked as if someone had ordered a crackdown on the privileged.

Yuri stood in line and inched forward, telling himself the KGB was a huge bureaucracy that was constantly tripping over itself. Even if Munich knew he had returned to Moscow, there was a good chance their alert would not have reached Sheremetyevo.

Yuri looked around him. There were guards at the exits to the aircraft, more guards at the exit into the terminal. There was nothing he could do but move patiently in line and hope he had not been discovered.

The immigration officer was carefully checking the immediately preceding passenger's passport against a thick, red-bound book. Yuri told himself he should act calmly, with just a hint of the arrogance expected from a KGB officer. If he was arrested, he would have to leave everything to Karelin. There was no point worrying about things he could do nothing about. The thought did little to slow his racing heart.

'Passport.' The immigration officer had a two-day growth of stubble and an irritated expression.

Yuri handed over his passport and workpass.

The immigration officer peered closely at both, looked suspiciously from the documents to Yuri's face and back again. Yuri felt a tiny shiver run down his back. If there was an alert, the immigration officer would know, would hold on to the documents, would walk away and − The official stamped the passport and gave it back to Yuri. 'Luggage?'

Yuri held out his attaché case. 'Only this. I am here on urgent KGB business. They gave me no time to pack.'

'No other luggage?'

'No,' Yuri said. The official stamped a form and ushered him through.

His relief was so great, he almost ran. He forced himself to walk slowly past customs and steely-eyed guards. Outside the terminal he found a bus taking a party of exchange students to Moscow University and paid the driver a *treshka*, three roubles, to drop him off at Oktyabrskaya.

In London, Yuri had had time to think about his divorce. He'd decided to fight Galina. Galina was his wife and the mother of his son. Stefan needed a mother. Stefan was his son. There was nothing he would do, nothing he would permit Galina to do that would change that.

Before the bombing in Munich he'd been scheduled to return to Moscow, on the way, it was rumoured, to becoming a Deputy Director of the German desk. Now, he thought, perhaps Karelin could fix it for him to remain in Moscow. His working in Moscow would keep Polyakov away and he and Galina could get together and pick up where they left off. Which, he wondered, was precisely where?

Galina was twelve years younger than him, and with them the habit of marriage hadn't had time to take root. Yuri had been away too much. When he'd been back in Moscow he'd worked too hard. Between his work and an apartment that seemed perpetually full of Galina's friends, they'd hardly been together. After the first short months of constant lust, they'd drifted apart.

Their son, Stefan, had distanced them further. Galina had resented the outrage that had been committed on her body and the pain she'd had to undergo. She'd loathed the illness and the unsightliness of pregnancy. Karelin had told Yuri such a reaction was not unusual among younger women. Karelin had forecast it would pass. But in all the time since, Galina had not once suggested having another child.

The bus was an ancient Zil, its sides silvery brown with a mixture of mud and salt. Inside, there were holes in the roof and the driver shouted at the students not to smoke. He turned off the interior lights and drove as if he were in a Grand Prix. 'Turds,' he told Yuri as they bounced along in the reflected glare of headlamps. Yuri wondered if the students knew any Russian.

The heater filled the bus with solid, soporific heat. Flecks of snow danced in the yellow headlamp beams. Moscow was much colder than Frankfurt or London, and Yuri thought he needed an overcoat.

The driver stopped by the Oktyabrskaya Metro and shouted to Yuri to get off. Yuri shivered as he hurried along Dmitrova. He had a fortuitously acquired apartment in

Yakimovski Pereulok, the former property of a university classmate, who had at the time feared the rebuilding of the area would interrupt his writing.

For two years after Yuri had taken the apartment, the air had been thick with dust and pulsated with the noise of concrete mixers, diesel engines and sledge hammers. Men had worked at all hours erecting a Literary Museum and a Picture Gallery. Yuri had worried about the effect of noise and pollution on his infant son, while his classmate collected the Shokolov Prize. When the rebuilding had come to an end, his classmate was a member of the Academy and Yuri had a peaceful apartment with three rooms, its own kitchen and bath, and only a short walk from Gorky Park. Sometimes things did work out.

Yuri turned on to Yakimovski and hurried past the church of St John, the cold seeming to intensify as he stepped out of the shadow of the ornate red and white building. St John's was a working church and its paintwork gleamed, which reminded Yuri his apartment needed painting. He decided to do that as soon as Karelin cleared him with the KGB and he'd sorted out this divorce nonsense with Galina. But before that he would spend a whole day with Stefan in Gorky Park.

Yuri entered the apartment building and walked up the stairs. There was a rustle from behind the elderly concierge's door and as usual the elevator wasn't working. Yuri climbed the stairs and knocked on the apartment door.

A long moment of silence stretched out endlessly. Yuri wondered if Galina was with Polyakov. He knocked again, harder, louder. There was a faint shuffling of feet, then Galina's voice, muted and nervous. 'Who is it?'

She *was* with Polyakov. 'It's me,' Yuri said. 'Open up.'

There was a sound of bolts being drawn, of a lock being turned. Galina stood in the doorway staring up at him. There were shadows under her eyes. Her face was pale and guilty.

'Yasha,' she said in a small voice, then louder, again,

'Yasha,' standing stunned, barring his way. Yuri stepped between her and the door jamb and went in.

The living room was a mess, the sofa dragged out of its corner, books and records scattered on the floor. Galina had been partying. When they were first married their life had been a constant party, the apartment crowded with Galina's friends and always untidy. Yuri recalled how he had resented the continual mess and the constant presence of gymnasts posing before mirrors and talking about anabolic steroids. Galina and her friends had spent an inordinate amount of time talking, sleeping, eating and going to the cinema. They had played American rock and country music loudly.

From behind him, Galina asked, 'What are you doing in Moscow? Why didn't you tell me you were coming?'

Because I wanted to find you with Polyakov, Yuri thought angrily. Because I wanted an excuse to beat the shit out of that prancing trapeze artiste. He said, 'I was ordered to come back.' He hefted the attaché case. 'I didn't even have time to pack.' He stared balefully at the bedroom door. How should he play the role of the outraged husband? Should he kick open the door and attack a wilting Polyakov? Should he discover Polyakov and leave the apartment in disgust? Or should he cast them both out on to a dimly lit Moscow street?

Abruptly, he walked to Stefan's bedroom. That was why he had really come. To see his son. And while he was with Stefan, Polyakov could discreetly remove himself, leaving man and wife to talk divorce over soiled bed sheets. That was the saner way, Yuri thought. That would give him time to resolve his problems with Karelin before deciding how he, Galina and Stefan would live.

Stefan lay on his side, his lips slightly parted, his eyes fast closed. By his tousled head was the teddy bear Yuri had sent from Germany. Looking at this diminutive image of himself, that was like him, but not him, Yuri felt his heart melt. Stefan had the same dark hair and the same long, dark lashes. While Yuri had been away, his body had grown longer and leaner, shedding most of its baby fat. His son had grown from a baby into a boy and Yuri had not been present at the transformation. Yuri felt his eyes smart as he leaned over and lightly touched his son's head. He had missed so much being away. Stefan stirred, and Yuri withdrew his hand.

Galina came in quietly and stood by him. Yuri found himself listening for Polyakov's step and the sound of stealthily closing doors. 'Stefan asks about you every day,' Galina said. 'He misses you. Are you back to stay?'

'I think so.' Stefan stirred again and Yuri went with Galina to the living room. She had recovered her composure, the colour was back in her face. She asked him if he wanted anything to eat or drink.

Yuri remembered Galina and her friends only drank beer or wine. He asked for beer and wondered what had happened to Polyakov.

She brought him the beer. Yuri drank from the bottle. 'I'm not going to sign the divorce papers,' he said.

She looked pained. She reached up and placed a finger across his lips. 'You've just come back,' she said, softly. 'We can talk about that, another time.' She reached up and kissed his cheek.

Yuri said, 'I'm not losing this apartment. And I won't lose Stefan.'

'Yasha!' She took his face between her hands. 'Another time.'

Galina was shorter than him, with a stocky, firm gymnast's body, solid-shouldered and trim-waisted, with handsome, flaring thighs. In Munich, Yuri had dreamt of her twice, and now recalled the heavy, straight blonde hair blown across her sweaty forehead, her eyes screwed shut in passion. He looked at the reality and it was no different from the image. He felt a surge of desire. He pulled her to him. His woman child. His wife.

Her mouth tasted of milk, her body felt deliciously languid. She was kissing him with her eyes closed, her head thrown back. Her fingers kneaded his neck and pulled his head down to hers. Her tongue darted between his teeth.

He pressed her to him and ran his hand under her skirt. She was naked underneath the dress. His fingers caressed the cool smoothness of her skin. He brought his hand up between her legs. Her pubic hair was moist. He pulled her round towards the bedroom.

Abruptly she broke away, pushed his hands from under her and stood smoothing her dress. 'No,' she said. 'Not now.'

'What's wrong with now? Aren't you glad to see me? Haven't you missed me?'

'Yes, yes . . . but − '

'I'm still your husband,' Yuri snapped and looked past her at the bedroom door. Polyakov was still there. She had been wet *from* Polyakov, not *for* him. He pushed past her and flung open the bedroom door.

The bed was empty, the side where Galina had lain, rumpled. By her pillow was a reading light and on the counterpane a copy of Nelly Kim's biography. Yuri turned accusingly. Somehow he had been tricked.

Quietly, Galina asked, 'What have you done, Yasha? Why have you come back?'

Yuri's eyes darted suspiciously around the room, lingered on the bedroom window fastened shut against the cold, on the open bathroom door. Where was Polyakov? Irritably he told Galina, 'I've already told you. I was ordered back.'

'Earlier this evening the KGB were here,' Galina said.

Yuri whirled and stared at her. 'The KGB? What time? What did they say? How many men?'

Galina sat on the bed, her hands folded in her lap. 'What's happened, Yasha?'

'You tell me what happened.'

Galina sighed and said, 'They searched the apartment. They went through everything and they took away our letters, the ones we wrote before we were married, when I was training in Kiev and you were here in Moscow.' Galina's voice sounded tearful. 'They said you had done something terrible in Munich. That you might have defected.'

Yuri went up to her and placed a hand on her shoulder. 'I'm here,' he said, looking round the room again for something more sinister than Polyakov. He placed a hand over Galina's mouth and said loudly, 'Only a fool would think I could ever defect. If I was going to defect, I would have done so in America.' He ran his hands beneath the bedside table, and behind the bed head. He reached under the mattress and ran his fingers along the bed frame.

'Yasha, what are you — '

He gestured her to silence and beckoned her into the bathroom. He turned the taps on. 'How many men?' he asked.

'I don't know. Three, no, four.'

'What did they do?'

'They searched the apartment. They looked into everything. They even slit open Stefan's teddy bear. I had to sew it up for him afterwards. What have you done Yasha? Were you going to defect?'

Yuri took Galina's hands in his. 'You think I would leave you? Leave him?' He gestured with his head towards Stefan's room.

'I don't know what to think. You're away so much. I've never known what you really do. You — you — ' She gave a small sob and rushed into his arms.

Yuri pressed her compact body to his. 'I won't leave you,' Yuri said. 'I'll never leave either of you.' He kissed the top of her head. 'Did the men wear any kind of uniform?'

'No. They wore suits, from GUM.'

'Did they have a document authorizing the search?'

Galina nodded into his shoulder.

'What did it say?'

'Only that the search was authorized.'

'What department of the KGB was it? It would have been stated in the right-hand bottom corner of the paper?'

'I don't know, Yasha. I don't remember.'

'What else did they ask you?'

'When I had last seen you. If I had heard from you recently. What we talked about. What you wrote from Munich.'

'Did they ask you to do anything, to inform them if I came here?'

'No.'

Yuri held her to him. If they had not asked Galina to inform him, it meant the apartment was watched. He could not stay in the apartment. But where was he to go? People had no reason for wandering about Moscow at night and those who did were liable to be picked up by the Militia and the KGB. 'You don't remember which department of the KGB it was?'

Galina shook her head. 'No. I'm sorry, Yasha. I didn't know it was important.'

Yuri hugged his wife and then held her at arm's length. 'I cannot stay here,' he said. 'It would not be safe, for you or me.'

'Yasha, what's happened? What have you done?'

'It's too long and complicated to tell you now. But don't worry. It will be all right. Nothing will happen to me. Or to you or Stefan.'

'Where will you go?' Galina asked. Tears rimmed her eyes.

'There are people who will look after me. Important people. Don't worry about me. I will be all right.'

'I can't help worrying about you,' Galina said. 'I can't stand this not knowing.'

'It won't be for long. In a few days it will all be over. And I'll be back here, painting the place. The apartment needs a new coat of paint, you know.'

'How can you — you — think of the apart — painting!' Galina's face broke. Tears brimmed and ran down her cheeks. She stood with her hands by her side, letting the tears flow unheeded. More than ever she looked like the little girl he had courted.

'Don't worry,' he said. 'Everything will be all right.'

'I don't want anything to happen to you,' Galina sobbed.

'I'm sorry about the letter. It was a difficult time for me and I didn't know what to do or how I felt and things were so different then, and now you've come back.'

He pulled her to him and pressed her head to his chest. 'Don't worry about it. I'll be back soon. And we can talk. There's a lot we should talk to each other about.'

He felt her head rock against his chest. 'I know.'

He held her till the sobbing subsided. Then he said, 'I should go. I'll be in touch with you tomorrow. Give the boy a hug for me.'

She moved away from him and pressed the backs of her knuckles into her eyes. 'Be careful,' she said. 'I want you to come back.'

'Don't worry. I will.'

'I'm sorry I cried,' she said.

He tilted her head backwards and kissed her. 'When I come back we'll talk,' he said. He left her and walked quickly out of the apartment.

Huddled into his overcoat, Yuri came out on to the street and peered anxiously right and left. Streetlamps glowed in a lonely procession, light was buried in potholes. The street was empty.

He stepped out of the apartment doorway and began to walk towards Dmitrova. Leaving the apartment, he had decided what to do. He would call Karelin and arrange to be picked up. Then he would —

A car skidded into Yakimovski, pale flashes of light darting off its gleaming sides. Yuri froze, then darted into a doorway. The car roared up the street, headlamps wavering over broken pavement and yellow walls. As it neared him, a spotlight came on, raking the sides of buildings, illuminating shuttered windows and the crevices of doorways. Horrified, Yuri watched the pale-yellow dancing circle. The light reached him and stopped.

With a grinding of suspension and a shrill locking of wheels the car braked. Doors opened. Yuri broke out of the doorway and ran. At the end of Yakimovski were a few side streets, enough for a man to lose himself in if he was lucky. But Yakimovski itself was relatively straight and there was no cover. The pounding of his feet reverberated off the pavement, echoed by the sounds of pursuit. His breath began to come and go in ragged gasps. His coat flapped untidily about his legs. Sweat dampened his shirt.

'*Tovarich! Stoi!*'

Yuri had no intention of stopping. If he stopped he was dead anyway, and he might as well die moving.

A shot rang out wild and high.

Yuri kept running. He could see the massive slab of the Picture Gallery and the intersection with Maronovski. He heard the sound of a racing engine, felt the slap of wind as the car raced past him, saw it brake, swerve on to the kerb in front of him and stop.

The driver's door swung open, blocking the kerb. The driver climbed out and braced a gun on the door frame, holding it with both hands. 'Stop, Comrade,' he called. 'Or I will kill you.'

Yuri stopped.

The two men pursuing him drew level. They thrust guns into his back. The chauffeur strutted along the pavement towards him, gun still pointing at Yuri. 'Workpass,' he demanded, stopping a foot away and holding out his left hand.

Yuri gave him the document.

The driver looked down at it cursorily and said, 'Come with us.' He put the workpass into his own pocket.

'What for? I have done nothing!'

One of the men behind Yuri ran his hands quickly along Yuri's body. The other man said 'Move,' and pushed Yuri towards the car with the barrel of his gun.

CHAPTER TWELVE

The battered red Zhiguli turned into Yakimovski Pereulok and stopped outside the apartment building where Yuri Orlov lived. Two men got out, went inside and knocked on the concierge's door.

A rectangular stripe of light appeared in the gap around the door frame. There was a slurp of slippers dragging along the floor. A voice said 'Who is it?'

'Open up, Comrade. Committee of State Security.'

The concierge threw the door open. 'You're too late,' he started to say, then seeing the men were not who he expected, tried to shut the door.

One of the men caught the door and pushed it. The concierge staggered backwards into the room. The men followed him in. One of them shut the door.

'I tell you, there's no money here,' the concierge cried. 'I warn you I have connections.'

The room served as the concierge's office. There was a small desk littered with papers, a rickety swivel chair, two plastic and chrome visitors' chairs with seats that were blackened and torn, an old wardrobe, a samovar. A cast-iron radiator gurgled below a picture of Valentin Timochek. A door with peeling grey paint led to the concierge's living quarters.

One of the men waved a workpass in the concierge's face. 'We told you. We're KGB.'

The concierge stared and swallowed. He'd never seen KGB men like this before. They wore baggy trousers, sweat-hardened leather jackets and caps, open-necked chequered shirts and were unshaven. Their eyes were pure acid. He said, 'What do you want with me? I've already told you he's gone. He left about ten minutes ago.'

The men looked round the office as if memorizing every speck of dirt and every stain on the walls.

'I telephoned as soon as he came,' the concierge said.

One of the men fixed him with an icy glance. 'Who did you telephone?'

'The Sluzbha, of course. The number I was — ' The concierge walked round the desk and scuffled urgently through the pile of papers. He held out a scrap of paper. 'Here. This is the number I was told to phone.'

The man looked at the number. 'Is this your writing, Comrade?'

'Yes. But the number is the right one. I called it and the Sluzbha answered.'

The man put the paper with the number in his pocket. 'We're going to be staying here a few days,' he said.

'But there are no apartments vacant. There is a waiting list ... If you gave me a week or so, I could have a word with the Housing Committee Chairman ... I daresay something could be arranged ... I'm sure someone can be persuaded — '

'We're staying here, Comrade,' the man said. 'In this office.'

'But — but — my work, my admin . . .' The concierge looked from one man to the other. 'Yes, of course.'

'And while we're here, we want you to continue with your normal duties. If anyone asks, you will say we are trainees sent by the Ministry of Housing.'

'Yes, yes.' The concierge nodded, eagerly.

'And you will make your reports to us and no one else. Do you understand that, Comrade?'

'I report to you and no one else. Yes, I understand that.'

'Good.' One of the men walked round the desk and sat down. He tilted back the swivel chair and placed his feet on the papers. 'It's cold in here,' he said, and stuck a match between his teeth. 'Get that samovar going. We would like some tea.'

*

Yuri sat compressed between the men. They were large men and smelt of a day's sweaty work. Neither of them spoke, and one of them kept a Makarov stuck in Yuri's ribs.

They took the Ring Road past the massive colonnade at the entrance to Gorky Park and went across the Krimsky Bridge. On Zubovski, Yuri saw that the old provision warehouses were being pulled down and that Novosti had moved into the large white Press Centre building erected for the Olympics. They passed the Foreign Ministry and the Belgrade Hotel. At Gorkovo they turned left.

'Where are you taking me?' Yuri asked.

The men said nothing. They raced up Gorkovo and on to Leningrad Prospekt, back towards the airport.

'I demand to know where you are taking me,' Yuri shouted.

One of the men said, 'You'll know when we get there.'

By the Hydroproject tower they turned on to Volokolam-skoye Schosse. The Schosse led out of Moscow to Riga. So where could they be going? They passed a series of small lakes and drove into the tunnel below the Moskva Channel.

There was nothing he could do while he was in the car, with the men seated so close and a Makarov sticking into his ribs. His chance might come when they got out of the car.

If the man with the gun got out first and Yuri followed quickly, there would be a brief moment while the man turned and he would not be covered. Yuri would have a millisecond or less to surge upwards, grab the weapon, swing the man round and use him as a shield. The man had a thick neck, hard shoulders, a solid belly and weighed about 180 pounds. Swinging him round wasn't going to be easy.

They emerged from the tunnel and turned off into the Tushino housing estate. Pastel-coloured apartment buildings stretched endlessly. They drove past identical-looking blocks. Each block had its own food store and children's playground.

The driver unclipped a radio from the dashboard and spoke softly into it. They turned left, then right and stopped in front of Block 2321. Yuri tensed. The man with the gun opened the door. Yuri watched his movements. He knew it wasn't going to work, but at least he would die on his feet. He thought for a moment of Galina and Stefan.

The man slid along the seat. The driver turned and lifted his Makarov. He said, 'Get out slowly, Comrade. And don't try anything stupid.' The man beside Yuri was out of the car, already turning. Yuri looked from the gun in front of his face to the gun now levelled at him from outside the car. Yuri got out.

They shepherded him through an empty lobby and up a flight of stairs, down a drab, dimly lit corridor, lined with numbered doors. Two men came out of the last door on the right. They were big men with identical close-cropped heads, V-necked sweaters, dark trousers and ankle boots. Clutched in their bulging fists were identical Makarovs. As they neared the open door his guards left him and Yuri went in with the driver. The fuzzy skulls followed them in and shut the door.

They went through a tiny, rectangular lobby into a lounge with a sofa, two armchairs, a square of carpet, a sideboard and a television. A uniformed man rose to his feet. He had a narrow, arrogant face, thick blond curls, pale-blue eyes and a finely shaped mouth. His uniform seemed to have been tailored and there were no divisional markings on the epaulettes or collar tabs. The driver pushed ahead of Yuri, saluted and gave the officer Yuri's workpass.

The officer looked from the workpass to Yuri, then nodded to the driver. 'Thank you. You have done well. That will be all.'

The driver left. Fuzzy skulls took up positions by the door. The uniformed officer said, 'I'm Lieutenant Mark Kutsov. Welcome home, Captain Orlov.' He slapped Yuri's workpass against his palm as if it were a swagger stick.

'Why have I been brought here?' Yuri demanded.

Smooth as melted treacle Kutsov said, 'So that we could look after you. I work for Anatoly Karelin. Karelin has visitors. He will see you tomorrow.'

Yuri said, 'I want to talk to Karelin, now.'

'Karelin will see you tomorrow.' Kutsov returned Yuri's workpass and pointed at the other men. 'That's Boris and the other one is Andrei.' Boris and Andrei bared gapped, steel teeth. 'They are your minders. Ask them for anything you need.'

'Who were the others,' Yuri asked.

'Friends.'

'Why did they have to grab me off the street?'

'Force of circumstance.'

'You realize they could have killed me, that I was trying to kill them?'

'I asked them to take great care to avoid accidents,' Kutsov said. He tugged his jacket straight. 'You must not on any account leave this apartment until you are sent for. You may not phone anyone, nor may you have visitors.'

'How long does this go on?'

'Till Karelin says otherwise.'

'Am I under arrest?'

'No. Let's just say you're in our custody for your own protection.' Kutsov waved at the doors behind him. 'Your bedroom is through there. There is some food and a bottle of Clos de Vougeot 1982.' He permitted himself a small smile. 'Karelin insisted we looked after you well.' He walked past Yuri to the door. 'Have a good night, Captain. You've earned it.'

Arrogant, tight-arsed sod, thought Yuri.

CHAPTER THIRTEEN

Karelin came at eleven, accompanied by a squat, broad-shouldered man in his mid-sixties whom he introduced as Otto Dietrich, Head of East German Counter Intelligence.

Karelin's hand in Yuri's felt frail. His pointed beard was sparser and greyer than Yuri remembered and the hooded eyes were red-veined and tired. Though the morning was warm, Karelin wore a black fur hat, black woollen overcoat and silk scarf. Yuri kept hold of Karelin's hand. Karelin was ill, and overwork and chainsmoking were only part of it. Yuri was prepared to bet that Karelin hadn't eaten regularly since his wife had died eight months ago.

'Welcome home, Yasha. I'm so relieved you made it.'

'I'm glad I made it, too.' Yuri released Karelin's hand. 'How are you?'

Almost defensively Karelin said, 'There's nothing wrong with me that a little sleep wouldn't cure.' He led them briskly into the lounge.

At fifteen, Karelin had run communications out of Stalingrad. By eighteen he'd been a veteran of the Ukraine, Poland and Germany, and become adept at running intelligence networks *ahead* of an advancing army. Karelin had been part of Russia's first and most successful American atomic spy ring, he'd been the youngest and most innovative director of the KGB's Far Eastern network. It had been Karelin's Japanese operation that had identified and then planned the shooting down of America's stratospheric spy plane, the U−2.

Anatoly Karelin was a KGB legend and Yuri had thought himself privileged to have been trained by a man like Karelin, proud that he had been one of Karelin's best pupils, and that when Karelin had been transferred to the Special Investigations Directorate, he had chosen Yuri as part of his team. Most of all, Yuri was proud that Anatoly Karelin had chosen to be his godfather and friend.

Karelin sat beside Otto on the sofa and placed a small recorder on the table. He cleared his throat and said, 'Otto and I fought together in Prussia. Otto is *Alte Kameraden.*'

Which meant that Yuri could trust Otto Dietrich as much as he could trust Karelin himself.

Karelin lit a tubed, Russian *papyrosi*, coughed and said, 'Otto is here because what happened in Munich is linked to events in East Germany.'

'You mean the SSD agent — '

'Whom you killed.' Karelin stared coldly at him. Karelin had always insisted his pupils confront unpleasant truths directly.

'Whom I killed,' Yuri said.

'His name was Lieutenant Sigmund Heller.' Otto Dietrich leaned forward as if to make sure his voice would be recorded. 'Heller worked for SSD Special Operations and specifically requested the radio control device used in Munich be sent to him by Moscow.'

'Under the provisions of Timochek's Anti-Terrorist Directive number 3243, that device should not have been made available,' Karelin said. 'The transfer was authorized by a Senior Procurements officer in the Ministry of Supply called Chermassov.'

'SSD Special Operations,' Otto Dietrich said, 'is a group handpicked by and loyal to SSD Chief Ernst Feldmann. Feldmann is the personal appointee of East German President, Konrad Blucher, who you will recall, replaced Willi Dietmark three months ago. Blucher's chief allies in the take-over were General Werner Kork, Commander-in-Chief of the East German army, and Colonel Franz Eidemann, Chief of the Special Commando.'

Karelin coughed harshly. 'Now tell us everything that happened to you.'

Yuri told them of his visit to the Gollier Strasse apartment and the death of the terrorists, of Chernov's interruption and suicide. He told them what he had found in Chernov's desk and showed them Chernov's note.

'There's a file on the Izgoi called *Zemschina,*' Karelin said and scribbled a reminder to himself. 'I'll clear access to it through Timochek.' He nodded to Yuri. 'Continue.'

Yuri told them how he had interrogated Valdez and of Valdez' link with Directorate K and Gamalrik.

'Whatever's going to happen involves both Russia and Germany,' Otto Dietrich said. He told them that since his accession, President Blucher had carried out a massive re organization of the East German Communist Party. 'Trusted advisors, men with a long record of unswerving devotion and loyalty, have been pushed aside or retired. New men have taken over, men, or so former President Dietmark assures me, whose only qualification is an unswerving loyalty to Blucher.

'At the same time, according to an Army friend, the same thing is happening in the armed services. Long-serving officers are being replaced by men loyal to General Werner Kork.'

Yuri asked, 'Are Feldmann, Kork and Blucher linked to the Izgoi?'

'I don't know,' Otto said.

Karelin said, 'I've just come from a meeting with the KGB Director Valichek, the heads of Directorate K, the First Directorate and the Fourth Department.' He exhaled twin streams of smoke. 'The official story regarding Munich is that through his contacts with terrorist organizations, Chernov discovered the plot to bomb the railway station in Munich, and was killed in an attempt to prevent it.' Karelin smiled around his cigarette. 'So Chernov is a hero and you had nothing to do with Munich.

'Your abrupt departure has been explained by orders from me to pursue an investigation in Frankfurt concerning the murder of the American NATO officer. That explanation has been accepted and the KGB ordered to stand down its search for you.'

'Does that mean I can go home?'

'That would be dangerous for Galina, for you and for us.' Karelin's eyelids drooped. 'You are the most important source and the most important witness we have. I don't want anything happening to you.' He paused and added, 'Petrov's dead.'

'Dead?' Yuri felt his heart skip a beat.

'Apparently he had a heart attack soon after you left Munich. It seems that when Directorate K heard of Chernov's death, they sent a Colonel Alksnis from Special Services to find out what had happened and clear up the mess. Alksnis managed to persuade the Munich police that Chernov was not one of the terrorists. When he discovered you were not at the Residency, he put out a KGB alert for you. Petrov suffered his heart attack soon after being interrogated by Alksnis.'

'You think Petrov was murdered?'

Karelin shrugged.

Petrov was innocent, Yuri thought angrily. Petrov would never have got involved if he hadn't gone to Petrov's apartment and persuaded him to open up Chernov's office.

Karelin lit another cigarette and took out some files from his briefcase. 'These are abbreviated personnel records of Alksnis, Gamalrik, Chernov and Chermassov. I'd like you to read them now.'

Mikhail Gamalrik had been born in Moscow in 1935. At the time his father had been a Captain in the 1st Stalin Armoured Division based on the outskirts of the capital. His father had been killed in a plane crash on the 12th of June

1937 and after his father's death, the family had moved to Omsk on the Manchurian border. After finishing his primary education, Gamalrik had attended a specialist military school, from which he had graduated with honours.

Somewhat surprisingly Gamalrik had done his national service as a Political Officer attached to the 23rd Armoured Corps. Immediately afterwards, he had joined the KGB and had been a Junior Administrative Control Officer when in 1956 he had been transferred to the Second Chief Directorate in Moscow. Two years later he'd moved to the First Chief Directorate responsible for foreign affairs, then to the 11th Department concerned with liaison and penetration of East Bloc security services. After spells in Prague and Sofia, Gamalrik had moved to East Berlin where he had helped reorganize the SSD. He had then returned to Russia and worked for Service R, which reviewed all KGB operations, become Deputy Director of the 11th Department and then Director of Directorate K.

A truly impressive record, Yuri thought, and turned to Alksnis' file.

Alksnis had been born two years after Gamalrik. His father had been a Major in the 1st Stalin Armoured Division and like Gamalrik's father had died on 12th June 1937. Like the Gamalriks, the Alksnis family had left Moscow, and Viktor Alksnis had spent his boyhood in a small village near Odessa. Alksnis had attended a specialist military college, graduated with honours and joined the special army unit, which preceded the Special Task Force.

Alksnis had been a good soldier and seen action in China and Korea. In 1963 he'd been transferred to Special Task Force Headquarters in Moscow and then, three years later, abruptly resigned and joined Military Intelligence, the GRU. After five years with the GRU Alksnis had moved to the KGB where after a short spell with the First and Second Directorates he'd been assigned to Special Services where he was now a Deputy Director and held the rank of Colonel.

Chernov's father had been a sergeant in Moscow Army Command. When Sergeant Chernov had died on the 6th June 1937, the family had moved to Simbirsk, where Chernov had, after finishing his primary education, been sent to an army school. He had done his national service with the 32nd Simbirsk Infantry and then joined the local KGB. As far as anyone could tell, his duties in Simbirsk had been routine and Chernov had carried them out with routine efficiency. Then, in 1970, Chernov had been transferred to Moscow and assigned to the Sluzbha. After four years of unremarkable service he had been moved to Directorate K. Then had followed service in Bucharest and Sofia and five years in East Germany. He had returned from East Germany the previous year and been sent to Munich.

Chermassov had been born in 1930. His father had been a second lieutenant in the Kremlin Guard. After his death on the 9th June, 1937, the family had moved to Volgoda. At fifteen Chermassov had been sent to a special military school from which he had left without distinction two years later. He had worked in the Stores and Supply Section of the army, transferred to Communications, left the Army at twenty-six and joined the Ministry of Supply. In 1960 he had been transferred to Moscow, after which his career had progressed steadily. He was now Chief Procurement Officer at the Ministry of Supply complex near Kuzminski Park.

Yuri put down the files. 'I don't understand,' he said. 'Four men whose fathers were all in the Army and who all died in the same month. Four men who were all brought up outside Moscow, attended military schools, and then came to Moscow to attain important positions. Do the Izgoi – '

'We'll know about the Izgoi when we get *Zemschina*,' Karelin said. 'Meanwhile, what I want you to do is go with Mark Kutsov to Kuzminski and talk to Chermassov.'

'Why Chermassov?'

'Because we cannot get to Alksnis and Gamalrik yet and Chernov is dead. Check Chermassov's background with him and find out if he knows what is happening later this month. Check also if he is supplying any more equipment to Valdez.'

'Why Kutsov?' Yuri asked.

'Because he is familiar with the enquiries we have made and you may need support.' Karelin got to his feet. 'Kutsov heard the radio call for your pick-up and had the GRU move in and grab you.'

'Why the GRU?'

'Kutsov's father is head of the GRU.'

So I owe Kutsov, Yuri thought.

Karelin put on his coat. 'It was Gamalrik who arranged the search of your apartment and the Sluzbha alert for you. You never should have gone home. Now the Sluzbha are alleging they found illegally imported goods in your apartment.'

'I've never imported anything illegally,' Yuri protested.

'What about American running shoes, size 10?' Karelin's tone and expression were impassive.

'Not my size,' Yuri said and coloured.

Karelin looked down as if to check his coat was properly buttoned. 'Kutsov's arranged for Galina and Stefan to be looked after. Our people will be with them in your apartment building till this is over.' Still looking down he moved towards the door.

'I went to the apartment because I wanted to see my son,' Yuri cried.

Karelin turned and snapped, 'You were foolish.' He looked round the room. 'Are you comfortable here? Do you have everything you need?'

'I'd like to see Galina.'

'You know that's impossible.'

'I appreciate that. But there are . . . personal things between us that should be cleared up soon.'

Karelin eyed him carefully. Then he said, 'I'll see what I can do.' Taking Otto with him, he left.

CHAPTER FOURTEEN

Admittedly they were going downhill, but for a man in his mid-seventies the General moved at a fair clip. And still walked very erect, Mikhail Gamalrik thought, the way he had probably marched into Warsaw and Berlin. Then Gamalrik remembered the General had been Armoured Corps, not infantry.

Talking over his shoulder, the General said, 'The Politburo has accepted our version of what happened in Munich. Chernov is a hero.'

'That's the problem,' Gamalrik said, his downturned mouth settling glumly. 'I saw Karelin this morning. He believed us too.'

'What's wrong with that?'

'As Karelin pointed out, if our story is true, then there can be no reason for the alert on Orlov. He had me cancel the alert.'

'Karelin has always been a little too clever,' the General said. 'Where is Orlov?'

'Back in Moscow, I think. Last night a man called on Galina Orlov. The concierge informed the Sluzbha, but when they got there, the man had left and they found the apartment being covered by Karelin's people.'

'If Orlov is in Moscow then your problem is simple,' the General snapped. 'Find him and kill him.'

'Not so simple,' Gamalrik said. He lengthened his stride and drew level with the General. 'We don't know where Orlov is. He is being hidden by Special Investigations.'

'Doesn't he have a home, a wife and a family? Don't you have his apartment under surveillance?'

'Orlov isn't there.'

'Have the concierge inform you when he returns.'

'The concierge is now being run by Karelin's people.'

'His wife must know where Orlov is.'

'Even if she did, she wouldn't help us. And she's now being protected by the SI.'

'Doesn't Galina Orlov have a lover?'

'There are rumours she is having an affair with Oleg Polyakov, her former coach. When her apartment was searched yesterday, they found a pair of imported New Balance running shoes, size 10, too big for Orlov.'

'Talk to Polyakov,' the General grunted.

They had walked all the way from Lenin's statue at the top of Kremlin hill to the Tainitsky garden. Above them were the Konstantin and Nabatny towers, and the massive red battlements of the Kremlin. The General turned and began to march briskly uphill. *'Zemschina,'* he grunted.

'I beg your pardon.'

'Zemschina. If Orlov's back and told Karelin about Chernov's note, Karelin will have *Zemschina* opened. I want *Zemschina* and all sources to it destroyed. Every single one of them. Consult with Alksnis and Yedanov of the 15th Department and have it done at once.'

Gamalrik hesitated. 'Eliminating *Zemschina* might draw more attention to its contents.'

'Not eliminating it will reveal everything.' The General accelerated away from Gamalrik. 'By the time they discover what happened to *Zemschina*, it will be too late.' He stopped and waited for Gamalrik to catch up. 'Don't worry, Mikhail. We can afford to take risks now. Everything will be over soon.' The General patted Gamalrik encouragingly on the shoulder.

The Sea Shanty on Wisconsin Avenue had dim lighting and discreet alcoves with upholstered wing chairs. CIA Director Bill Timmins met Brad Drewett there.

Timmins was a big, fleshy man in his mid-fifties, with the furrowed face of an angry bulldog. His hair was thin and receding, his eyes were bloodshot and bleary. He sipped at a very dry Martini as he waited.

Brad Drewett had worked for Timmins. Before he had been lured away to head the Financial Administration Agency, Drewett had been a company man, had become at the age of thirty-eight, Director of the CIA's Economic Strategy Division. Once a company man, always a company man, Timmins thought as he saw Drewett enter.

Brad Drewett wondered why Timmins had invited him for a lunch time drink. He had neither seen nor spoken with Timmins since he'd left the Agency. Timmins had taken his leaving as a personal slight. For Bill Timmins there was no life outside Langley.

He saw Timmins had two glasses on the table before him, playing his usual game of remembering drinks. Drewett greeted Timmins, slipped into his seat and pushed away the glass of Californian Chablis. 'I'm into fitness these days,' he said. 'I haven't had a drink in two months.' He ordered a glass of Perrier.

They talked briefly about what had happened since Drewett had left the CIA. 'You were damn stupid to leave,' Timmins growled. 'You could have been in the Director's office with me, helping to run things.'

Drewett sipped his Perrier and smiled. 'I guess I've given up trying to run the world.'

Timmins said, 'One of your investigations is getting sensitive.' He glowered at Drewett from underneath beetling brows. 'Barynin's.'

'Don't tell me Barynin's have been investing the company pension funds in sovereign loans?'

Timmins looked at him uncomprehendingly. Then he said, 'This is serious, Brad. We've been using Barynin's as a cover.'

Drewett knew that the CIA had its own network of banks and front companies, that they only went outside that network on matters that were so sensitive they needed absolute distancing, a special kind of secrecy, or immediate deniability.

Timmins said, 'Your investigation could ruin a very important operation. We could lose people, and expose some very important sources.'

'We're concerned about Barynin's involvement with sovereign loans,' Drewett said. 'That isn't anything to do with the Company is it?'

Timmins' expression told him it wasn't. Timmins said, 'You know how these things go. You begin investigating one area and soon everything is out in the open. One pissant break-in and a President has to resign.'

'We'll be careful,' Drewett said. 'I'll call you the second we find any bodies.'

'I've been told your assistant is carrying out the investigation.'

'I'll warn her.'

'She doesn't have clearance, Brad.' Timmins finished his drink. 'Leave Barynin's alone. It's highly sensitive. And that's not only me telling you. The word comes from Sixteen Hundred. You go ahead with this, Brad, and they'll bury you.'

Drewett said, 'I still want to know what Barynin's are doing with sovereign loans.'

Timmins looked thoughtful. 'And if you know that, you'll lay off?'

'That's all I'm concerned about,' Drewett said.

'I'll see what I can do.'

Friday April 11

CHAPTER FIFTEEN

Allison tried to think why Cowdrey Berle, the officer at the Federal Reserve responsible for supervising Barynin's, should remind her so strongly of Ellesmere Wentworth. It wasn't simply the grey Brooks Brothers pinstripe — they were common enough — or the wood and antique-leather male club atmosphere of Berle's office. It was — she wished she knew what it was.

Berle gave her a toothy smile. 'What can I do for you, Miss Maynard?'

Berle had the same neutral, clipped accent as Wentworth. Allison forced herself to think of why she had come to see Berle. 'We're interested in Barynin's Bank,' she said.

A polite elevation of eyebrows. 'Why Barynin's? They're only a very small bank. If they do get into trouble, it wouldn't affect too many people.' Berle looked at her carefully. 'Is there something you know about Barynin's?'

Allison realized why Berle reminded her of Wentworth. It was his bearing and speech, the way he looked at her, the way he moved. Berle and Wentworth, she thought, had been bred from the same womb.

'I was saying, is there something else you know about Barynin's?'

'No — no.' It was impossible that Berle and Wentworth were brothers. Allison forced herself to concentrate. 'We're interested in why Barynin's have invested so much of their reserves in sovereign loans.'

'Isn't that simply an internal investment decision?'

It probably was. But banks had responsibilities to their depositors, to their shareholders and to the public. 'Do you think sovereign loans are the best possible investment? Don't you think sixty-five per cent of a bank's reserves in sovereign loans is excessive?'

'It still remains a private investment decision,' Berle said.

'Well, we — that is the FAA — want to know why. We want to know why so many loans were bought in the last three months, why the volume of Barynin's trading activity has increased, why it has borrowed so heavily, why it has lent so freely to a number of small foreign corporations based in tax havens. We want to know why Barynin's have exceeded their liquidity ratio, and what you people are doing about it.'

Berle sighed patiently. 'You sure want a lot of answers. Let's see what we can do to oblige.' He picked up a pen and began to revolve it in his fingers.

The gesture reminded her of Wentworth. She looked to see if the pen carried an emblem. It did not.

'We are fully aware that Barynin's have exceeded their liquidity ratio,' Berle said. 'They have done so with our approval.' He smiled and added, 'Liquidity ratios, Miss Maynard, are only guidelines. I'm sure you appreciate that.'

Allison nodded. 'Why did Barynin's need to exceed their ratio?'

'Barynin's are financing a scheme to release certain sums of money, a lot of it belonging to major corporations, which are presently held in various tax havens round the world. The project requires a large initial injection of capital which Barynin's have agreed to provide. Its loans are guaranteed by the owners of the tax shelter corporations, so the risk of default is minute. As the object of the exercise is to release cash, Barynin's initial investment will be repaid in full . . .' Berle consulted a leather-bound desk diary . . . 'on the thirtieth of this month. As the amount of finance required stretched Barynin for only a very short period, and the loans were categorized as first-class risks, we agreed to a temporary diminution of Barynin's liquidity ratio.'

'And the sovereign loans?'

'Your information is out of date. If you had checked with us, we would have told you that Barynin's had bought those loans on behalf of another bank and was only holding them in its own name until certain formalities could be concluded. Those loans have now been transferred to their true owner.'

'Who is?'

'The Handel Kreditbank of Zurich. It was just a normal piece of banking business, Miss Maynard.'

'I see,' Allison said, feeling deflated.

'So there is no reason for either of us to investigate Barynin's.'

'I suppose not.'

Berle got to his feet. 'The next time you get suspicious, Miss Maynard, it would be better if you talked to us first. Banks have enough problems without unnecessary government enquiries and we do not want needlessly to increase the antipathy business has for government.' He reached across the desk and took her hand. 'Good afternoon, Miss Maynard.'

A glint of gold caught her eye. She looked down and stared in surprise at Berle's cufflinks, forced herself to keep very still. Berle's cufflinks had the same curious emblem that Wentworth had on his pen.

'Anything wrong, Miss Maynard?'

Allison released Berle's hand. 'I was just admiring your cufflinks.' She slung her bag over her shoulder. 'What is the emblem?'

Berle flung out his arm and looked at the cufflinks as if seeing them for the first time. 'Nothing really. It's an old college fraternity sign.'

'Which college, Mr Berle?' They walked together to the door.

'Clairvaux Academy.' He pulled open the door.

Allison had heard of Clairvaux. It was an exclusive, old-style academy about thirty miles south of Washington. 'And the fraternity?'

Berle laughed nervously. 'It was called Ormus.'

Allison paused in the doorway. 'Did you know Ellesmere Wentworth at Clairvaux?'

'I know Wentworth of course, and I believe he is a Clairvaux man, but no, I don't recall ever meeting him there.'

Allison looked quickly at Berle. His expression was as neutral as his accent. Same college, same fraternity, same age, she thought and wondered why Berle was lying.

*

From behind the large wooden desk at which Lenin had once sat, General Secretary Timochek stared disbelievingly at Karelin. 'The Izgoi,' he said. 'I don't believe it.' He turned to Marshal Iakir who was seated at a corner of the desk. 'What do you think?'

Karelin swivelled his eyes to the grizzled face of the old warrior who had befriended every Soviet leader since Stalin. On his own Timochek would have released the *Zemschina* file. But throughout the meeting Iakir had been sceptical. And Timochek still relied heavily on Iakir and the old guard of the Politburo.

Iakir said, 'Everything presupposes the fact that the Izgoi still exist.'

'What do you think?' Karelin asked. 'You were there. Did Stalin eradicate them completely?'

Iakir sighed. 'It was one of Stalin's largest massacres. I don't believe anyone survived. But still . . .' He looked at Timochek. 'If the Director of Special Investigations believes that access to the *Zemschina* file will help him resolve his problem, I think permission should be granted.'

'I agree,' Timochek said.

Berle's lie nagged as Allison walked back to her office. Why should he lie about something as insignificant as a college and a fraternity? What was so special about this fraternity that Wentworth and Berle still carried emblems of it in early middle age? And what kind of a college was it that formed people in identical moulds? The college, she thought, would have year books, histories. She could perhaps trace a link between Berle and Wentworth. And if Berle had lied about that, then perhaps he had lied about Barynin's. And if he had lied about Barynin's she wanted to know why.

CHAPTER SIXTEEN

Mark Kutsov turned up at ten the next morning driving a red MGB with the top down. He had a long fur coat over his uniform and the car had a weak heater. Yuri huddled in his overcoat and told Kutsov summer was still two months away.

One of those naturally versatile persons who'd made good use of being privileged, Kutsov had graduated with distinction from MIMO, trained as an actor and then elected to join the KGB. He had been one of Karelin's best students, and after a year with the Sluzbha had been transferred to Special Investigations. His promotion had been rapid.

The Ministry of Supply complex was situated between the former Durasov estate and Kuzminski Park. A large, rectangular slab of concrete and glass, it stood like a beached liner in an area that had been torn down, built over and surrounded by roadways, guard posts and concentric rows of electrified wire fences.

They had to show their passes three times before they were even allowed to park, each time the guards seemingly more impressed by the MG than their workpasses. They had to show their workpasses and state their business twice more before two armed guards accompanied them in an elevator to Chermassov's office on the fourth floor.

A secretary led them to a languid young man lounging behind a desk on which were four telephones and a typewriter. In a rack behind him were reels of computer tape. He finished his phone call and looked disdainfully at Kutsov and Yuri. 'Comrade Chermassov is engaged. He will see you in a while.' In the one gesture he managed to wave towards chairs and push two slips of paper at them. 'If you will write there your names and — '

Kutsov smiled and walked to Chermassov's door. 'Don't bother to announce us,' he smiled. 'I usually enter without knocking.'

The man got to his feet. 'You can't do that!'

Yuri pushed him back in his chair and thrust an SI workpass in his face. 'We just have,' he said, and followed Kutsov.

Chermassov was a large man with a triangular face, a brush of brown hair, sagging jowls and a thick neck. He was eating a *pirozkhi*. A dribble of mince gravy ran down his chin. His eyes were large and bulbous and his mouth turned down at the corners. Yuri could imagine him frightening the life out of factory managers and small suppliers.

'What the hell — you can't come here —' Chermassov dabbed at his mouth, shoved the *pirozkhi* into a bin and reached across for his intercom.

Kutsov advanced across the room holding his workpass in front of him like a shield. The brilliant red and gold emblem seemed to convince Chermassov that if he was not among friends, at least he was not being confronted by enemies. 'What the devil do you want?' he snorted. 'Even if you're SI you can't come in here without an appointment. I have a lot to do.'

Kutsov threw himself down in a chair. 'We want to talk to you about illegal arms shipments. In particular, one illegally shipped electronic detonator used last Monday in an attempt to blow up Munich railway station. We can talk here or go back to Moscow and talk at SI HQ.' He smiled cheerfully at Chermassov.

'There's nothing to talk about,' Chermassov said tonelessly. 'Nothing leaves here without proper authority.'

'According to the Munich police the device was of Russian manufacture and American design.'

'A CIA plant,' Chermassov said. 'Everyone knows the West German police are the creatures of the CIA.'

'The serial number was EK7242098/29GBH. EK 72 is your department's reference, is it not?'

Chermassov's cheeks flushed and sweat stood out on his forehead. 'It is. But the serial number could have been fixed by anyone.'

'Perhaps we can check your records to find out what happened to the device with this serial number.'

Chermassov loosened his tie. 'That will not be necessary,' he said. 'Nothing like that has been exported since General Secretary Timochek's Directive 3243.'

Directive 3243 had only been issued in February, after the NATO officer had been killed in Duisburg. 'What about before Directive 3243?' Yuri asked.

Chermassov started. 'It is possible, but to check that will take many days. If you like, Captain, I will get someone immediately to prepare a list of shipments of this device and send it to you at Special Investigations.'

Which meant that the list would arrive in about two years. 'If such devices were shipped, who would have authorized them?'

Chermassov looked wary. 'A senior official in the KGB Department concerned.'

'And if any shipments were made after Directive 3243, whose authority would be required?'

'At least a Director's,' Chermassov muttered. He looked angrily at Yuri. 'Look here, my job is to carry out orders, not get involved in the reasons for those orders.'

Mark asked, 'Have you had any such special authorizations since Directive 3243?'

'I don't remember. I will have to check.'

'But surely such an authority would be exceptional enough for you to remember?'

'I told you I don't remember. I will have to check.'

'In that case you'd better send for the records,' Yuri said. 'Now.'

Chermassov made as if to protest, then said, 'Very well.' He spoke brusquely into his intercom. 'Now if you will wait – '

Yuri asked, 'Officially or unofficially are you aware of any terrorist activity planned for later this month in Germany or Western Europe?'

'No. Directive 3243 prohibits such activity.'

'Does the date April thirtieth have any special significance for you?'

Chermassov looked as if he had a fever. He shook his head.

Yuri asked, 'Have you ever made a shipment to a terrorist called Nino Valdez?'

'I don't remember. I don't think so.'

'Have you made any shipments to the Special Operations Division of the SSD?'

'I have, but you can't expect me to remember any specific details.'

'Have you ever dealt with an SSD Officer called Sigmund Heller?'

'I don't recall the name.'

Yuri opened the file Karelin had given him. 'Tell us something about yourself, Comrade.'

'Myself? What about myself?' Chermassov frowned suspiciously as if sensing a trap.

'Tell us about your childhood in Vologda.'

'My childhood . . . what's that got to do with anything?'

'Everything is relevant,' Yuri smiled. 'Now what do you remember most vividly about Vologda?'

'Being hungry,' Chermassov said. 'There was a war on and we didn't have enough food. After school we would forage in the forests for berries — what the devil has this to do with arms shipments?'

'At fifteen you went to a special military school. What was that like?'

'Why do you ask?'

'I was wondering why you aren't in the Army. Did you fail at the school?'

'If you must know, yes.' Then as if to justify his failure, 'Those schools were tough, you know. Most of those who succeeded went into the STF and other special regiments.

100

From six-thirty in the morning till we went to bed it was drills, military exercises, school work, special studies.'

'What special studies?'

Chermassov's expression grew wary. 'History.'

Yuri asked, 'Have you ever heard of an organization called the Izgoi?'

Chermassov looked as if he had been poleaxed. His face went pale, the sweat on his forehead seemed to congeal in small, shiny beads, his fingers wrenched at his tie. 'No,' he said. 'Never.'

The door of Chermassov's office burst open. Three uniformed KGB men rushed in with drawn revolvers. Behind them came an older man in the uniform of a Colonel. He was completely bald, the hairlessness accentuated by the ash blond of his eyebrows and the paleness of his eyes. 'Who the hell are you,' he snarled, 'And what the fuck is going on here?'

Mark stood up and came to attention. 'I am Lieutenant Mark Kutsov from Special Investigations,' he said. 'We are investigating possible irregularities in the procurement and shipment of weapons.'

'*You* are investigating! Who gave you authority to investigate anything in my division?'

Mark remained unperturbed. 'With respect sir, Special Investigations is exempt from grants of prior permission.'

'Exempt, my arse!' the Colonel roared. 'Not here, not in my division. Don't you know this is a prime security installation? No one, not even a member of the Politburo dare investigate anything here without my say-so.' He glowered furiously at Mark, recovering his breath. He rasped, 'Get your arse out of here Lieutenant while you still can. And tell Karelin if he wants to send anyone snooping around here, he'd better talk to me first. The next time I even smell one of you SI bastards, I'll shoot him.'

Mark looked questioningly at Yuri. Yuri shrugged and walked to the door.

*

Alksnis watched the door shut behind the SI men and their escort and turned to Chermassov. 'You bloody fool,' he grated. 'Why did you see them before sending for me?'

'There was nothing I could do,' Chermassov gasped. 'They forced their way in. I hit the button as soon as they said they were from SI and thought it better if I appeared to cooperate, until you came.'

'Appeared to cooperate,' Alksnis repeated disgustedly. He threw a tape-recorded cassette on Chermassov's desk. 'And what about your childhood, Comrade Chermassov? Your boyhood in Vologda? Your special education? What did you tell them, Comrade? What did you tell them?'

'Nothing,' Chermassov whimpered. 'Nothing. I kept the records from them till you came. I told them nothing that would be of use.'

Alksnis walked over to the window and opened it. He looked out as if checking that Yuri and Mark had left. 'Come over here,' he said. 'I want to show you something.'

Chermassov walked over to the window.

Alksnis pointed. 'There,' he said.

Chermassov looked. 'What?'

Suddenly, Alksnis was back in the room with a drawn gun.

'What's going on?' Chermassov asked. 'I told them nothing. I swear on my children, I told them nothing.'

Alksnis' mouth twisted in an ugly grimace. 'But they know,' he hissed. 'They know about *you*!'

He fired.

CHAPTER SEVENTEEN

From Triangle Hill Allison had a good view of Clairvaux Academy. Nearest her was a two-storey modern concrete edifice; other older buildings dotted the grounds, separated from each other by wide gravelled drives and carefully trimmed lawns. In the centre was a large playing field with football markings and goal posts and beside the main drive a small chapel with an unusual onion-shaped dome. The property was enclosed by high walls and thick woods and as Allison drove closer, she saw that the walls were spiked, the iron gates locked and flanked with warning notices. A short gravelled path off the road led to the main gate beside which was a guard house.

A burly, unfriendly looking young man in a blue uniform walked out and stood over Allison's car, staring down at her as if her car smelt of skunk. He waited for her to speak.

'I'd like to look around the college,' Allison said.

The man shifted gum to the other side of his mouth. 'Nope. No sightseers during term.'

'Is there anyone I could talk to about the college?' Allison tried an ingratiating smile. 'I'm editing a series of books on religious architecture and I saw the dome on your chapel as I was driving — '

'You'll have to write for an appointment.' The guard thrust a card at her.

'But as I'm here and — '

'Nope.'

'Look, couldn't you just phone and — '

'Nope.'

'What's so secret about the college? Why aren't visitors allowed?'

'I don't make the rules, lady. You want to look round the academy, you write for an appointment.'

'What if I were a parent?'

'You're not a parent.'

'If I were a parent would I have to make an appointment?'

'The rule is no visitors without an appointment.' With a determined finality the guard straightened up and motioned Allison to turn round.

At the road she turned right and drove past the high walls. Clairvaux Academy was more a prison than a school. She wondered why Berle and Wentworth had been educated at a prison and what kind of parents sent their children to Clairvaux. She wondered what happened to the children who were sent there. Five hundred yards along, the walls ended in forest. Allison edged the car off the road and parked.

Clairvaux looked and felt like the kind of place run by a fanatic religious sect where children were alienated from their families and brainwashed into following some crackpot philosophy. What philosophy, she wondered as she got out of the car and walked through the forest back towards the academy. When she reached the wall she decided to hell with the guard and the rules of Clairvaux Academy. She was going in.

She studied the wall. Allison was an expert on walls. At Madeira College scaling walls had been part of every student's repertoire. There was nothing difficult about this wall, especially as there was a convenient tree with an even more convenient overhanging branch. She felt a childish sense of excitement. Life was no fun if you stuck to all the rules. Grinning, she shinned up the tree, slid along the branch and dropped into the undergrowth on the other side.

She waited a moment, listening. She looked around, cautiously. No one had heard or seen her come over the wall. She rose carefully and placing her feet lightly on the dead leaves, walked quietly towards the academy. The forest was thick, and through an occasional break in the foliage she could glimpse walls and the roofs of buildings. There was no sound except for a faint rustle of wind through the trees and the sound of her own footsteps.

Suddenly to the left of her there was a massive rustling as if a huge bird were taking wing. Startled, Allison stopped and looked and thought she saw something move. She waited, rooted to the spot, feeling her heart pound uncontrollably, her breath flow raggedly through her parted lips.

104

She heard the rustling again. From behind her to the right. And the left. She veered towards the maintenance hut. The noise was coming from in front of her, behind her, to the left, to the right. She walked faster. The noise grew louder and more constant, a steady whirring like a giant beating of wings. She glanced over her shoulder. And this time she saw them. Four men moving rapidly through the trees wearing a kind of green and brown camouflage, beating at the leaves as they came after her, men whose heads were dark, shapeless blobs, without eyes or nose or hair! Allison nearly screamed.

She broke into a run. Beyond the hut was a lawn bathed in sunlight. Once she got into the sunlight she would be safe. She heard the rustling behind her grow louder, turned and saw the men running, closing up on her, those obscene shapeless blobs above their necks swivelling as they focused on her.

The hut! The lawn! People! She ran desperately towards the side of the hut, her heart thudding, her ears filled with the sinister susurration behind her. She raced across undergrowth. She jumped over a fallen branch. Foliage snatched at her clothes. Once she slipped and thought she'd turned an ankle. She hurled herself towards the sunlight and the hut.

She reached the edge of the wood, jumped across a small ditch, half fell as she landed, picked herself up, ran, arms pumping, legs bouncing off the grass, open mouth sucking air in fast, deep draughts. She saw the grass blur underneath her speeding feet, saw the roughened timbers of the hut. Then there was a rush of air, the thump of booted feet. Allison stopped and screamed as a figure in military camouflage dropped down in front of her, his face stretched and distorted behind the stocking pulled over his head.

There were staccato thuds behind her as her pursuers leapt the ditch, the pounding of boots as they closed up. She heard their ragged breathing, felt their warm breath as they surrounded her. Hands grabbed her. Obscene, insect heads silently twisted this way and that. Her elbows were pinioned behind her. The men formed a close, silent circle. She was wheeled round and frogmarched along across the lawn towards the first of the older buildings.

Their feet reverberated along the gravelled drive. They moved at the double, hardly letting her feet touch the ground. A line of boys filed out of the first building in neat pairs, all of them walking with swift purpose. They were neatly clad in jackets and ties with not a short hair out of place. Their faces were set and blank, their eyes level and peculiarly cold. The group strode past Allison without a single questioning glance. Allison twisted, looking after them in horror. These were not children, these were young men . . . robots!

Her escort raced her to the second building. As they approached it, an older man wearing a pale-brown suit emerged and stood ramrod erect on the steps. His face was deeply tanned and he had a gleaming head of tight, silver curls. The eyes were deep-set and the face moulded. He was a very big man, and for some reason Allison felt she had met him before.

He stared at her with blank hostility, then turned and led them into the building and down a long panelled corridor. The sound of the men's boots echoed against the walls. They raced passed doors with gold lettering. DEAN. ASSISTANT TO THE DEAN. SECRETARY. At the end of the corridor the man opened a door and turned. Allison was pushed past him into a small room beneath a flight of stairs.

The room had a bare wooden table and two upright chairs. It was too small for all of them and some of the soldiers waited outside. The man came in and stood on one side of the table. Allison's arms were released. Three soldiers fell into line behind her. They had removed their stocking masks, and with a start she saw that they were boys, none of them more than seventeen and all of them with that same look of blank hostility she had seen on the faces of the others.

The man said, 'Well done, you guys. Two of you wait outside. The rest of you can go.'

Allison froze. The voice and accent were Wentworth's and Berle's. The man was studying her with an angry calm. 'Who are you?' he demanded, 'and what are you doing here?'

No point telling him about college year books and student histories. 'My name is Allison Maynard. I wanted to see the academy. I was intrigued by your chapel . . .'

'We only allow visitors by appointment. You were told that by the guard. Why did you come over the wall?'

'I told you. I wanted to — '

'Don't lie, woman!' He looked as if he would strike her.

'What's so secret about this place?' Allison demanded. 'Why don't you allow visitors?' She wasn't going to let him intimidate her.

Suddenly, he smiled. 'My name is Miles Kingdon. I run this place.'

Allison recognized the name and remembered where she had seen the face. Kingdon was one of those academics who was being continually summoned to the White House to advise the President. She had seen him before on television and in newspaper photographs. Kingdon's smile widened and he extended his hand across the table.

Everything was going to be all right, Allison thought. Surprised at his sudden cordiality, she held out her hand and gasped as he grabbed it and compressed the nerve between her thumb and forefinger. It felt as if a lump of molten metal was being pressed through her flesh. She twisted and tried to pull away, fighting back a scream.

'Who the devil are you,' Kingdon grated, 'And what are you doing here?'

Her whole being was concentrated on the knob of pain that was her hand. Tears sprang to her eyes. Her face screwed up in agony. She tried to pull her hand away. 'My name is Allison Maynard,' she gasped. 'I wanted to see the academy.'

'Why?' Kingdon wrung her hand.

It felt as if her hand was being torn off. 'I told you — '

'Why?' He wrenched her hand again.

'I've met . . . met . . .' She couldn't stand the pain. 'Two of your former pupils . . . Ellesmere Wentworth and Cowdrey Berle.' Tears filled her eyes. 'I . . . wanted to see . . . their school.'

Kingdon released her.

The relief was intense. Allison found she was sweating.

'How did you meet these men?'

She was only five feet from the door. But Kingdon could easily stop her reaching it. And even if he couldn't there were the boy soldiers outside and the guards in the grounds. 'I work for the US Treasury,' Allison said. 'I am conducting an investigation into the purchase and sale of certain bank loans.'

'Go on,' Kingdon said.

'My investigations involve Barynin's Bank and the Federal Reserve Bank. Which is how I met Wentworth and Berle.'

'So why did you come here?'

'I was intrigued by their loyalty to Clairvaux, by − ' She tried a smile. 'I suppose the Clairvaux style.'

'Yes. How did you know these men were at Clairvaux?'

'Wentworth had a college fraternity emblem on his pen. Berle had a pair of cufflinks.'

Kingdon stared at her. 'Wait here,' he said and went out of the room.

Allison rubbed her hand. The space between her thumb and forefinger was sore and red. It hurt to close her fist. She tiptoed to the door and opened it. Two blank-faced boy soldiers stared impassively at her. Allison shut the door and sat, trembling. Everything about Clairvaux was strange and very frightening. She tried to fight the waves of panic rising within her. She should have told Drewett where she was going. Now Kingdon could wall her up alive for all anyone knew. Don't be ridiculous, she told herself and gripped the table tightly. No one's going to hurt you. Clairvaux may disapprove of visitors, but no one's going to shoot them.

*

Kingdon called Cowdrey Berle. 'Tell me about Allison Maynard.'

'What's your interest in her?'

'Because she's here. She came in over the wall.'

Berle gave a low hiss of surprise. He said, 'She's a Treasury agent looking into Barynin's purchase of sovereign loans. What is she doing there?'

'You tell me.' Kingdon's knuckles whitened on the receiver. 'She came here because she was intrigued by the emblems on Wentworth's pen and your cufflinks. You're idiots both of you! How many times have I told you Clairvaux is to be kept out of this. We are too close to success to allow anyone to trace a connection to Clairvaux.' Kingdon paused for a while before he said, 'I'll have to get rid of her.'

'No,' Berle said. 'That would cause more problems than it would resolve.' He told Kingdon that Allison was Assistant Director of the Financial Administration Agency and had been specially picked for the job by the FAA Director Brad Drewett.

'All the more reason to get rid of her,' Kingdon said. 'Don't you realize that if anyone traces anything back here they will find the lists?'

To Allison's relief, when Kingdon returned he appeared calmer. 'I have decided,' he announced, 'not to make a public example of your intrusion. Just this once we will not prosecute or make a public protest at unauthorized government interference. I shall however make a formal complaint to your office. Now, come with me. I will escort you off the premises.'

He walked her along the corridor and across the grounds. Kingdon said, 'One of the reasons we do not allow unexpected visitors is that our pupils train for everything here – including war. People arriving unexpectedly during an exercise could get hurt. Today, you could have been hurt.'

'Are you a military academy?'

'No. But military activities form part of our curriculum. We try to prepare our students to cope with any and everything.'

'Are the gentlemen I met typical of Clairvaux?'

Kingdon looked at her carefully out of the corners of his eyes. 'What exactly do you mean?'

'Bright, aggressive, successful, upwardly mobile.'

'We try to train our pupils as completely as possible for their vocations in the outside world.'

'And are you always so successful?'

'Our failure rate is minimal. Students are selected with great care. Our entrance standards, and by that I mean not only academic but behavioural requirements, are very high. In the academy we insist on strict discipline and hard work. Which is why you will find that none of our pupils are soft, Miss Maynard, and why we have no problems with drugs, sex, alcohol or loutishness. We emphasize not only academic excellence but physical excellence as well. *Mens sana in corpore sano*, you understand.'

'The same principles as the YMCA?'

Kingdon threw her a sideways glance. 'Not quite. We follow the principles of a Russian educationist, Vailan Ostrovensky, who himself was greatly impressed by the Spartans of ancient Greece.'

'Wentworth and Berle belonged to the same fraternity, Ormus. Does the fraternity still exist?'

'Not as far as I know.'

'They seem to be very loyal to it.' Just as she'd felt with Berle, she thought Kingdon was lying. 'They still wear its emblems.'

'Adolescent loyalties are strange things. Men are formed in those years, Miss Maynard. They often keep souvenirs of those vital years.'

'What kind of a fraternity was Ormus?'

'Quite honestly, I don't recall. College fraternities come and go like the height of hemlines or the width of trouser legs.'

'Who was Ormus?'

'Ormus was an Egyptian mystic who in AD 46 was converted to Christianity, together with six of his followers, by the disciple, Mark.'

'And Berle and Wentworth were members of this fraternity. Were they in the same class as well?'

Kingdon frowned momentarily before he said, 'Yes. I believe so.'

They reached the main driveway. Kingdon stopped and pointed to the guard house. 'One of the security people will escort you to your car. If you want to know more about the academy, please come back. Better still, ask Wentworth or Berle to bring you. We approve of visitors, Miss Maynard, but at the right time. Our curriculum is both very intensive and very extensive. We cannot have pupils being disturbed by tourists.' Kingdon turned on his heel and strode back across the grounds.

Allison watched him for a moment. The same guard who had prevented her entering approached, his hand resting casually on the butt of the gun strapped to his waist. 'This way, miss,' he said, as if he had never seen her before. 'I will take you to your car.'

Allison drove back thoughtfully. Clairvaux was the strangest school she had ever seen. And the children — she tried to imagine Wentworth and Berle marching mindlessly across those lawns, being indoctrinated with that frightening hostility and coldness. What was Clairvaux? And what were the children being taught there? And why had Berle lied about knowing Wentworth at school?

She saw the corner rushing up to her and braked hard. She felt the wheels lock, the back of the car dance, the tires yelp as she wrenched the car round. Dammit! She must concentrate. She wouldn't be doing anyone a favour if she drove off the road.

For a while she concentrated. The road to the freeway curved and switchbacked across rolling countryside. The

Fiero clung to the corners like a leech. Allison thought it was unlike any previous car she'd owned. It did not wallow and went round corners as if glued to the road. She could feel what the wheels were doing through the steering. She wondered what it would be like with more power, better handling . . .

The gleaming blob in her rear-view mirror grew into a garish jeep, college streamers fluttering from its twin radio aerials. The vehicle was travelling very fast, fishtailing round the corners with gay abandon. A kid having fun, Allison thought and wondered if she too should have a go.

The jeep was right behind her now, headlights urgently flashing her out of the way. Hold it, Allison thought. Wait till after the corner. An air horn blasted a fanfare in her ear. They hit a short straight and the jeep pulled alongside.

There was a sharp left hander at the end of the straight, and Allison momentarily lifted off to let the jeep through. But it stayed alongside. Had it run out of power, Allison wondered, and then, horrified, saw the space between them diminish.

She pressed her horn. They were inches from each other. Allison glimpsed a face looking down at her, impassively, the face of the guard at Clairvaux!

It couldn't be! She was imagining things! The jeep moved across and hit her front wing. She felt the car jolt before she heard the sound of the impact, felt her inside wheels struggle for grip on grass and adverse camber. She hit the brake as the jeep ricocheted off her again. 'Stop it!' Allison screamed. 'What are you doing?'

Abruptly the jeep braked. The lunatic had seen the corner, Allison thought. She gunned the Fiero through the gap, squeezed through, braked hard for the corner. The jeep rammed her from behind. Her head snapped back. She felt the back of the car, raised already under braking, go light and slide round. Trees, a fence, a yawning gap slid crazily before her windscreen. She saw the jeep bearing down against her door, then the rear of the car dipped, the bonnet rose, and she plunged backwards off the road.

CHAPTER EIGHTEEN

It took Allison four hours to complete police formalities, watch the wreckers lift her car from the ravine and get back to Washington. Drewett was waiting in her office. He'd been out jogging and wore a shiny, blue warm-up suit and yellow Nikes. He studied her with careful concern. 'You should drive more carefully. How d'you feel, kiddo?'

Allison eased herself on to a chair. 'Apart from this bump on my forehead, a cut on the inside of my lip and sore ribs, I feel great.'

'Want to tell me what happened?'

Allison did.

Drewett sighed softly. 'An hour ago, I had a call from the police. They wanted to know if you were . . .' Drewett tapped the side of his head, 'all there. They told me you were claiming someone had deliberately run you off the road and tried to kill you.'

'That's exactly what happened!' Allison cried. She sucked at her lip.

'If that was really so, the police are wondering why the person didn't come down the escarpment after you and finish the job?'

'And leave a body with gunshot wounds or marks of strangulation in a wrecked car at the bottom of an escarpment! And how long did the police reckon it would have taken the Clairvaux guard to climb down the escarpment, kill me and climb back up again?'

Brad nodded sympathetically. 'The guard from Clairvaux is

113

another problem. According to the police, it seems the registration number you gave them belongs to a 1982 Honda owned by a retired nurse. And no less than five independent witnesses swear that the guard was at his post in Clairvaux Academy all afternoon.'

'They checked all that so fast!' It hurt to speak quickly, and Allison felt the cut reopen. The tangy taste of blood flowed over her tongue.

'As the police would undoubtedly tell us, we live in an age of computers and instant communication.'

'It's all a goddam lie!' Allison dabbed at her mouth with a Kleenex. 'Something strange is happening out there, Brad. Clairvaux is weird. You should have seen those children! They were like zombies, like zombies programmed to hate.'

Drewett patted the pocket of his warm-up suit. 'I also have here a hand-delivered letter from Kingdon complaining that an official of this department entered the premises of Clairvaux Academy illegally and without just cause and after permission to do so had been denied. He demands an undertaking that there will be no recurrence.'

'Which of course — '

'Which of course I will give. You had no business breaking in there, Allison. Besides, Miles Kingdon is a close friend of the President. When the President was at Clairvaux, Miles Kingdon was one of his tutors.'

'Oh God!' Allison cried. Her lip bled. She pressed a wad of Kleenex to it and mumbled, 'Wentworth, Berle, Kingdon, they're all linked to Clairvaux, and Clairvaux is some kind of nucleus for whatever is happening. The President —' She flung the Kleenex into a wastepaper bin. 'And now the President himself is involved. We have to find out what is happening there, Brad. I want to know more about this fraternity Wentworth and Berle belonged to, and why Berle lied? I want to find the connection between Berle, Wentworth and the Barynin loans.'

Drewett shook his head. 'Clairvaux's off limits. The

only way you're going in there is with a court order.'

'And to get a court order we must first find out what is happening at Clairvaux. That's a catch 22 situation, Brad.'

'Not quite. We can begin our investigation at the other end. Barynin's.'

'You mean check out this tax deal they're financing.'

'No. I mean the sovereign loans.'

'But didn't Bill Timmins — '

'The CIA has nothing to do with sovereign loans.'

'But the sovereign loans have been sold to the Handel Kreditbank of Zurich.'

'Then that's where we begin our investigation.'

It hurt to smile. Allison dabbed at her mouth again and said, 'Remember you once said a Swiss banker wouldn't tell us the time from a cuckoo clock?'

Brad laughed. 'And look what happened when you started talking to them about the Silicon Valley caper. They were like putty in your hands. Just the thought of getting their hands on that body of yours turned them into panting, frenzied flibbertigibbets ready to tell all.'

'Stop it,' Allison cried. 'And give me some credit for brains.'

'And tenacity, and intuition and attention to detail. Against you, the Handel Kreditbank stands no chance.' The laughter faded from his eyes. 'You think you'll be well enough to go?'

Allison flung away the Kleenex. 'I feel better already. Let me rest up over the weekend and I'll get there Monday.'

Drewett asked, 'You still have the Apple?'

'Sure.'

The Apple was a model IIc microcomputer with a flat screen, built into a sturdy, padded carrying case and fitted with a modem, communications software, a transformer, a variety of telephone jacks and batteries. It could be operated from a hotel room anywhere in the world. Drewett had picked up two from a firm in England while attending a conference in London. He said, 'We'll use the phone only when absolutely necessary. Everything else will be sent to our electronic mailboxes. I'll give you a set of codes that will be changed every forty-eight hours.'

'Great,' Allison said. Already she was feeling very much better.

Drewett said, 'I wish I was going instead of you.'

'No way,' Allison said. 'There's no reason for you to have all the fun.'

After they'd filed their reports on Chermassov, Mark dropped Yuri back at the apartment. Yuri ate with Boris and Andrei, played chess with Andrei and looked at the Stechkins stored in the lobby. Karelin called and said he'd seen Timochek and Iakir and got access to *Zemschina*. At six o'clock a Special Investigations escort brought Galina to the apartment.

Boris and Andrei left saying they would be back in two hours. Boris left the Stechkins in the lounge. Yuri opened a dry, white Tsinandali and thought there were faint lines about Galina's eyes and mouth, that she looked tense. They sat facing each other in the lounge.

'What's going on?' Galina asked. 'What have you done? Why are you in this place with armed guards? Why can't you stay with us?'

Yuri sipped the wine. 'It's very complex,' he said. 'The situation is that I know something I shouldn't, which is why Karelin is protecting me. And as what I know isn't enough, I'm finding out more. When I've done that, I'll be able to move back to the apartment.'

Galina told Yuri that Stefan was being looked after by a woman provided by Karelin, and that word had been put around that she'd been taken from the apartment for interrogation. She said there were men watching them in the apartment building, following her when she went to work and when she went to collect Stefan from school. 'Don't you realize how this is affecting us?' she asked. 'How long is this to go on?'

'Till it's over,' Yuri said. 'People may try to get at me through you and Stefan. That mustn't happen. I won't have either of you hurt.'

'Is it fair to put us through this? Is it right to make us take this risk?'

'No,' Yuri said. 'But what's happened has happened. And both of you already are at risk. I asked Karelin to bring you here so we could talk. You want a divorce?'

She looked down hesitantly at the slowly revolving wine-glass in her hand. 'I don't know.'

'That's what you wrote to me in Munich. You sent me the papers.'

'Yes . . .' thoughtfully. 'I thought it would be best at the time with you away so much and Stefan needing a father and – '

'I am Stefan's father,' Yuri interrupted, sharply. 'Nothing's going to change that.'

'Don't snap,' Galina said.

'I'm sorry. But I want you to understand how I feel about Stefan. Nothing and no one will come between me and Stefan.'

'Don't look at me like that. It frightens me.'

'Then don't talk about Stefan needing another father.'

'All right. But you're away – What about me and you?'

'That's up to you.'

'And you. We're married to each other.'

'And we've been living apart.'

'True.'

They looked at each other in silence, not sure where to go from there. Galina asked, 'Do you love me?'

'That's why I married you.'

'That was then. What about now?'

'How do you feel?'

She smiled. 'I asked first.'

Yuri poured out more wine. 'Honest answer?'

'Yes.'

'I don't know. You?'

'I think I do.'

'Do what?'

'I think I love you.'

'What about Polyakov?'

She coloured. 'He's just a friend. A close friend.'

'How close?'

She shrugged. 'Just close. He was my trainer. He knows me very well. He helps me. I talk to him about my problems with you.'

'What problems?'

'Your being away, what you do . . . it helps to have someone to talk to.'

'Why not your mother or your sister?'

'Polyakov knows me better.'

'Karelin tells me the KGB found his shoes in the apartment.'

'Sometimes he comes round after he goes running in Gorky Park.'

'What else does he leave apart from his shoes?'

'His warm-up suit. It's just a matter of convenience.'

'How do you feel about Polyakov?'

'I don't know.'

'Do you love him?'

'No.'

'Do you want to live with him?'

'I don't think so.'

'But you've thought about it?'

Galina nodded.

'Was it he who made you fill out the divorce papers?'

'He showed me how to complete them.'

'If we get divorced, will you go with him?'

She shrugged again. 'I don't know. I don't think so.' She smiled. 'I think I love you.'

'It's a fine mess,' Yuri said. He put his arm on her shoulder.

They sat in silence. They drank more wine. Yuri said, 'We're not getting anywhere, are we?'

'I suppose not.'

The silence grew uncomfortable with a sense of time passing and nothing being resolved. Yuri finished his wine, stood up and took her hand.

She looked up at him.

'Let's go to the bedroom.'

Galina worried at her lower lip. 'What about your bodyguards?'

'There's time.'

With sudden decision she put down her glass and preceded him to the bedroom. Yuri followed, unfastening his shirt. She looked interestedly round the room, then unfastened her dress, stepped out of her shoes and swept the dress over her head. Yuri threw off his clothes and got into bed. She rolled down her panties and unhooked her bra. There were pink marks on her flesh, and a new softness about her waist and the backs of her thighs. The lassitude, after all the years of vicious training, was turning some of her muscle to fat. She climbed into bed on the opposite side and pulled the sheet over her.

Her body felt cold and stiff. There was an awkwardness about their movements as he pulled her to him. He kissed her and ran his hands along her body. He stroked her breasts and felt the tiny nipples sprout. She kissed him and played with her tongue in his mouth. He leaned over and brushed the straight blonde hair away from her forehead. He kissed her eyes and her cheeks and she pulled his face down to the curve of her neck. He felt her breath against his ear and then they moved together and she was underneath him with parted thighs, and reaching for him and guiding him into her.

He looked down at her face. Her eyes were closed, her chin tilted upwards. Her body moved in a private rhythm. He pressed her waist to him and forced her with his weight to move with him. She pulled her thighs round him, locked them, heaved rapidly.

Her mouth opened. Her eyes went tight. 'Ooooh!' she breathed. Yuri felt himself explode in an aching silence.

When Boris and Andrei returned, they were in the lounge, drinking the last of the wine. Galina looked flushed and avoided Boris' glance.

'When will I see you again?'

'Soon. I'll send word.'

She touched his hand and went to the door, nothing determined, nothing resolved.

The Colonel's uniform was one of the best quality serge and finely cut. His buttons and departmental insignia were highly polished. Beneath the peaked cap pulled low over his forehead, his face was bland and impassive.

'This is most irregular,' the Chief Security Officer said.

The Colonel looked down at the Security Officer's desk on which his workpass and the order signed by the Director of the 15th Department lay. He had very pale eyes, the colour of a fleck of cloud. 'My orders, Captain, are to collect the *Zemschina* disks.' His voice was flat and menacingly neutral. It reminded the Security Officer of a programmed robot.

'This is most irregular,' the Security Officer repeated, thinking that at two minutes past midnight there was no one he could call who would take responsibility for the handing over of the disks. He peered anxiously at the Colonel's workpass and the Director's order. Both were correctly coded and had the right security classification. The Security Officer said, 'Perhaps tomorrow morning — '

'The order says immediate,' the Colonel said. 'Immediate means now.'

The Security Officer said, 'I could arrange to have a copy sent round first thing tomorrow morning.'

'The order says original, and it says now.'

'I will arrange to have the contents of the disks transmitted to the 15th Department.'

'Captain.' For the first time there was a trace of irritation in the Colonel's voice. 'Errors are being checked. We do not want them compounded by transmission errors.'

The Security Officer sighed. 'The removal of original disks is contrary to standing orders.'

'Explain that to the Director.' The Colonel took out a small, flat notebook from his uniform pocket, and opened it to a blank page. 'Write your refusal there, sign it and put in the date and time.'

The Security Officer stared horrified at the page. 'This is not − '

'Captain! Please write.'

The Security Officer looked from the notebook to the papers on his desk. The Colonel was from the 15th Department which maintained the Archive and Registry files. He'd brought an order signed by the Director himself.

The Colonel said, 'You may telephone the Director.'

Eagerly, the Security Officer did. Then he left the room and returned with two thin-line tape canisters. The Colonel checked the titles and codings and put the canisters away in a foam-packed case. He signed the book the Security Officer gave him and entered his rank, workpass number and Department. 'Thank you, Captain.'

'My pleasure, Comrade Colonel.'

The Colonel marched briskly out of the offices of the Archive and Registry Department. In the back of his Zil limousine he opened the case, took out a canister, broke its seal and looked at the spool of tape in its neat plastic collar. He took a magnet from his pocket and ran it slowly over the outside of the tape.

CHAPTER NINETEEN

Alexander Dmitrev lived in a ramshackle dacha thirty-five miles north-east of Moscow. It took Yuri an hour to get there and another hour to find the track that led through the forest to it.

That morning Karelin had summoned him to Special Investigations Headquarters and told him the *Zemschina* files had been destroyed. Mark was helping the Sluzbha with the investigation and Karelin had wanted him to see Alexander Dmitrev, a retired archivist, who had compiled the *Zemschina* file.

'Why would Dmitrev talk to me?' Yuri had asked.

'Because you are a KGB officer in Special Investigations who is enquiring into what mistake Dmitrev made that caused the *Zemschina* file to self-destruct.'

'Why would a file self-destruct?' Yuri had asked.

Karelin had said, 'Ask Dmitrev.'

The dacha had wooden walls and a tin roof held down by stones and bricks. Beside it an ancient Moskvich rusted beneath a sheet of corrugated iron supported on four poles. Beyond the dacha was a brackish lake, its centre covered with thin sheets of dull ice. The lake was ringed with reeds and closely growing trees. Yuri parked the Zhiguli and walked carefully over the muddy grass to the narrow porch. He felt self-conscious in uniform. The porch vibrated under his feet.

An elderly woman saw him cross the window, left her ironing and hurried to the open front door. She was breathing hard as she came to it, looking with barely suppressed anxiety at Yuri's uniform.

'Natalya Dmitreva,' Yuri said, 'I am looking for your husband.'

She stared at him.

Yuri repeated the statement.

She kept staring.

Yuri noticed her eyes were focused on his lips and realized Natalya Dmitreva was deaf. He repeated his question forming the words slowly. Mrs Dmitreva pointed at the lake.

There was a tiny footpath around it. The trees looked gloomy and oppressive in the dull evening light, leaning precariously where the shore had been eroded and dipping gnarled branches into the stagnant brown water. The reeds were spiky and waist high. There were patches of crusty ice on the edges of the path. But no sign of Dmitrev.

'Dmitrev,' Yuri called. 'Alexander Dmitrev.'

With a flapping of wings a colony of ducks beat up from the reeds. There was a startled carolling of birds. 'Dmitrev,' Yuri called again. A small gnome-like figure emerged from the undergrowth about twenty yards ahead of him, holding a finger to its lips.

Dmitrev was in his mid-sixties, untidily dressed in a woollen cap, an old grey cardigan over a flannel shirt and grubby trousers stuffed into mud-stained rubber boots that reached half-way up his thighs. Dmitrev had a healthy, ruddy complexion. His eyes were bright blue and sparkling. He looked a happy man. 'What is it?' he asked.

'I want to talk to you,' Yuri said. 'One of your files self-destructed yesterday.'

'It's been five years since I retired,' Dmitrev said. 'And files don't self-destruct.'

'I still need to talk to you.'

Dmitrev said, 'All right.' He turned and led Yuri to the spot where he had emerged on to the path. 'Be careful of your new uniform,' he said, as holding aside branches he led Yuri to the place where he'd been fishing.

There was a rod leaning against a tree and there were two

lake trout in a wicker basket, with small jars of bait, a copy of *War and Peace* and a half-finished bottle of wine. No wonder Dmitrev looked happy.

He began to pack his things. Across the lake a solid red ball of sun slid into the water. The sky was slashed with pink and orange.

'It was a file code named *Zemschina*,' Yuri said.

Dmitrev gestured him to silence. 'Sit and watch.'

The sun sank lower. The light turned opaque. The forest burbled with the homing cries of birds. Suddenly a high-pitched rhythmic calling rose above the sounds of the birds and the forest, and a colony of eiders flew out of the sun in a straggling V formation, the beat of their wings growing louder as they descended among the reeds. The males were white with black bellies, the females grey. They waited till the last bird had descended, and the sun appeared to be drowning. Then Dmitrev got to his feet and said, 'Let's go. Natalya will cook the fish for us.'

The dacha was really one large wide room, with a curtained alcove in which the Dmitrevs slept. By the alcove was a wooden table covered with books and papers, with two wooden chairs tucked underneath it. In front of the table were a sofa and two armchairs covered with a faded flowered print; further along to the left, an oak dining table and four chairs next to a Calor gas stove. Beside the stove was another table with a chopping board, plates and bowls, with more cooking utensils suspended from hooks above it. There were a few shelves on the walls with dusty paper-covered books, an old radio, a few sepia-toned photographs. The place felt comfortable, lived in, content.

Natalya had already made potato soup and a salad of fresh radishes, onions and tomatoes. She grilled the fish and they ate it with the salad and black bread. Dmitrev poured vodka and told Yuri they grew their own vegetables. Yuri asked Dmitrev how a file could self-destruct accidentally.

'It couldn't,' Dmitrev said. He explained that all sensitive files had a code that had to be punched in before they could be accessed. In the case of the more sensitive files there were often two or three codes. If they were not entered in the correct sequence, the computer would either report a fault, sound an alarm or simply go dead. But the file would not be accessed.

'But don't files accidentally self-destruct?' Yuri asked.

Dmitrev explained that computer files consisted of bits of data which were stored magnetically. Files were destroyed or erased by rearranging the magnetic bits, which could be done by exposing the computer tape to a magnetic field, by a computer operator pressing the right sequence of keys or by a computer malfunction. He said that great care was always taken to prevent accidental erasure, and that in any case, a strict procedure had to be followed before any file could be erased. So if a file had been erased, it had to be carelessness, malfunction or malice. 'What happened with *Zemschina*?' he asked.

Yuri said he didn't know the details. He'd simply been told the file had been destroyed.

'That shouldn't be a problem,' Dmitrev said. He told Yuri that it was routine to make a copy of every file. 'They can recreate *Zemschina* from the backup,' he said.

Yuri said the backup had also been destroyed. Which was why they were interrogating everyone who had any connection with the file.

Dmitrev told Yuri that backups were stored separately, and if the backups too had been destroyed he should look closely at the people who had access to the store.

Yuri said, 'There is another problem. We need to know what was in the file.'

Dmitrev said, 'I can't talk about *Zemschina*. Not even to you.'

'What if I give you written authority?'

'Not even then.'

Yuri got to his feet. 'In that case, I suppose you'd better come with me to Moscow.'

'Now?'

'The affairs of State cannot wait upon your personal convenience, Comrade.'

'But — Natalya — my wife — she cannot be alone here. She is — '

'Now, Comrade,' Yuri snapped. He felt a right bastard.

Dmitrev shrank into his chair. 'Perhaps the authority, and then later . . . if I could be given notice . . .'

Yuri took out his notebook and wrote out the authority.

Dmitrev carried glasses and the bottle of vodka across to one of the armchairs and had Yuri sit opposite him on the sofa. *'Zemschina,'* he said 'contains the history of an ancient secret society called the Izgoi.'

'If it is ancient, why is it so secret?' Yuri asked.

'Because, over the centuries, the Izgoi have been involved in Russian politics at the highest level.' Dmitrev looked round as if worried he might be overheard. 'In 1917, for instance, they organized the transfer of Lenin from Switzerland and helped finance the Revolution.'

'Was Lenin Izgoi?'

Dmitrev said, 'It would be better if I started at the beginning.'

The beginning was almost prehistory, when the first Russian settlers created the Duchy of Kiev. After the dynastic wars of 1015, the succession to the Duchy was made fraternal, which meant that all brothers of the first generation were considered senior to any of the following generation. When the reigning Duke died, each brother would move his seat nearer to Kiev. If one brother died before reaching Kiev, his descendants were excluded from the succession and became the Izgoi or the excluded ones.

The Izgoi became mercenaries, and settled in various parts of Europe and the Near East. They adopted the doctrines of Ormus, a mystic who had been converted by the disciple Mark. They participated in the Crusades and the taking of Jerusalem and acquired great wealth and prestige, which in time aroused envy and fear. Following the Inquisition they

126

were driven out from many parts of Europe and fled to Germany and Russia. 'From that point onwards,' Dmitrev said, 'the history of the society loses clear definition. They appear from time to time only as forces behind events, and then just as mysteriously disappear.'

Under Ivan the Terrible and in the wars of succession that followed, they had attempted to put their own people on the Russian throne. They had encouraged German settlement in Moscow and had considerable influence on Peter the Great. They were thought to have arranged the marriage of the last Tsar to the German princess, Alexandra.

'The court of the last Tsar,' Dmitrev continued, 'gives an excellent example of the Izgoi in action. Nicholas was a weak man, dominated by his German wife who was in turn dependent upon her Izgoi friends and advisors who were both German and Russian.'

'So the Izgoi were in both countries?' Yuri asked.

'The Izgoi spread throughout Europe,' Dmitrev replied. 'They were however most influential in Germany and Russia.'

He grinned whimsically and added, 'Who knows what they might have done, if not for Rasputin.'

'Rasputin?'

'Yes, the Izgoi lost out to Rasputin. Through a so-called miraculous cure of the haemophiliac son to whom Alexandra was devoted, Rasputin came to exert a dominant influence over Alexandra and through her, the Russian court.

'In 1912, Rasputin had Alexandra persuade Tsar Nicholas to dismiss Prime Minister Kokovtsov who was the main element of Izgoi control over Nicholas. At the time, the Grand Master of the Izgoi was a Moscow banker, Zakhar Shumayev-Barynin who saw the dismissal of Kokovtsov as not only the end of Izgoi influence at court, but also the beginning of the end of the Romanov dynasty and the old Russia.

'So Shumayev-Barynin decided to create a haven for the Izgoi away from Russia and away from Europe which, for other reasons, he expected soon to be at war. He had previously visited America and liked it and in 1912 he opened a branch of the Barynin Bank there, and sent his son, Rudolf, to be educated in America.

'In 1917, Shumayev-Barynin and numerous aristocratic Izgoi were murdered in the Revolution. The German Izgoi, themselves involved in European war, saw an opportunity to secure peace and take control of the Revolution by placing their influence and their wealth behind one of the smallest Revolutionary parties, the Bolsheviks. It was the German Izgoi who arranged Lenin's transfer across Germany to what was then St Petersburg. It was they who smuggled arms for the Bolsheviks through Sweden and Finland, they who provided the gold with which the Bolshevik mobs were paid, they who brought pressure on countries outside Russia to recognize Lenin and his Bolsheviks.'

'Was Lenin Izgoi?' Yuri asked again.

'There's no direct confirmation of that. But it's possible some of his lieutenants were. It was one of the reasons put forward by Stalin for the liquidation of the Old Bolsheviks.'

Mrs Dmitrev brought them fruitcake and tea, sat in the armchair opposite her husband and began to sew.

'Meanwhile in America,' Dmitrev continued, 'Rudolf Shumayev-Barynin found himself running the New York branch of Barynin's, and acting as banker to the Izgoi. Because of its Izgoi connections, Barynin's received huge sums of money from Russia, and as the situation worsened, Barynin New York grew in size and prestige, and Rudolf Barynin became a leading international financier.

'Under the direction of the Izgoi, Barynin began to invest heavily in Europe, particularly in war-devastated Germany. He set up a branch of the Barynin bank in Berlin which soon became one of the most prominent financing houses in Germany and a leading representative of American commercial interests there.

'Barynin also involved himself in German politics. He became a member of the Pan-Germanic Thule Society and

128

helped finance their political party, the German Workers' Party which soon became better known as the National Socialist Party. He placed his bank solidly behind Hitler and the Fascists and financially underwrote their rise to power.

'At the same time, Barynin was helping the Bolsheviks. In the late twenties he was a well-known figure in both Berlin and Moscow. He used his influence with Lenin, to arrange for the Wehrmacht and the Luftwaffe to be secretly recreated in Russia. He helped Russian education by creating the Rodina schools, military academies which embodied the teachings of the Russian educationist, Vailan Ostrovensky. He helped finance Stalin's agricultural communes, and syndicated numerous loans for Russian industry. In 1929, Barynin became International Grand Master of the Izgoi.'

'What were Barynin and the Izgoi doing getting involved in the politics of both Russia and Germany?'

'They were fulfilling the Izgoi dream,' Dmitrev said. 'In 1937 — '

There was the roar of a car engine being driven hard, the thump of suspension pitching into potholes. Headlamps weaved across the room. Dmitrev got up and walked to the window accompanied by the sound of brake drums grating on grit. 'Looks like some of your friends,' he called over his shoulder.

Yuri drew his gun and moved to the back of the room near the curtained alcove. The scrape of wheels locking on grass and earth was followed by the sound of an opening door. Feet pounded on the boardwalk. Yuri glimpsed two burly figures in Army anoraks hurry past the window. He slipped behind the curtain.

The door crashed open. The two men stood there for a moment, burly and unshaven, woollen balaclavas pulled hard down over their heads, automatic Kalashnikovs in their hands. One of them shouted, 'Alexander Dmitrev?'

'Yes. Come in.'

From within the alcove, Yuri saw them look round the

room, hesitating. Then one of them reached under his jacket. Too late Yuri saw the grenade dangling at the man's belt, saw him whip it up to his mouth and draw the pin with his teeth.

'Jump out!' he cried as the man lobbed the grenade into the room and slammed the door.

He glimpsed Dmitrev staring curiously at the grenade, saw him move towards Natalya Dmitreva. He heard the sound of feet pounding over rickety wood and grass and as he leapt over the bed and kicked out the window he shouted again, 'Get out!'

The room exploded. Yuri felt his body lifted upwards and forwards. He buried his head in his arms. His shoulder hit the window frame as he was hurled through the gaping window. He felt his body tumble forward. His ears filled with a thunderous slap. His body rose and rolled and then his arms were smashing into his head. Pain streaked up his elbows. His mouth slammed shut and he felt blood spurt into it.

Then nothing.

He couldn't have been out for more than a few seconds. His ears filled with the most awful crackling. He felt heat scorching his legs and opened his eyes. The dacha was burning furiously, flames rising above the tin roof, licking round the wooden supports, throwing up a dark blanket of smoke. He dragged himself across the grass, tasting his own blood. There was no movement from the dacha, no sound except that of the flames.

CHAPTER TWENTY

After what seemed a long while, Yuri dragged himself to his car. Dmitrev's dacha still burned, the flames crackling sharply and sending huge sparks dancing among the trees. He wrenched the car door open and flung himself on to the seat.

His whole body ached. There was a frightening stillness inside his head. His clothes were in tatters and his arms and back felt as if they had been flayed.

There was enough light from the flames for him to insert the ignition key. He started the engine, aware of it only by the vibration of the car. The grenade blast had made him deaf. He pointed the car at the track. The car lurched forward in lugubrious silence.

Each bump, each lurch sent a bone-jarring shudder of pain through him. Trees and a wire fence loomed at him out of the dark. He drove one-handed, crabbing slowly back the way he had come. The silence frightened him.

After five minutes he lurched off the track on to the road. Dark buildings with dismal lights floated past. Yuri concentrated on holding the wheel straight, on keeping his eyes fixed to the yellow scallops of light in front of him. The roadway scudded past. The car wavered. He forced himself to hold the wheel straight. Just keep going, he told himself. Hang on to the wheel. Keep the throttle half open. In an hour you'll be in Moscow.

'Bastards,' Pfc Alvin Marcus thought, wishing he was round the front of the base confronting the demonstrators instead of being stuck here at Narrow End covering the rear of the Cryp Hut and staring at a dark and empty field.

The field was a narrow triangle at the back of the base, accessible only by a narrow farm track which had been sealed off with a troop carrier as soon as the demonstration had begun. There was no way the demonstration could get through to the field, which Alvin thought was a pity. He was raring to have a go at the bastards.

He could hear their cries and the patter of stones against riot shields. Alvin thought the US Army should pull out and leave the peaceniks to be fucked over by the Russians.

The demonstration was one of a series of protests against American bases, a spontaneous prolongation, or so the press described it, of the Easter weekend peace marches. Spontaneous my ass, Pfc Alvin Marcus thought. Every demonstration so far had been organized with nearly military precision.

The demonstrators had arrived at Bad Salzbach around six that evening, about a thousand people in a convoy of VW campers and battered pick-ups. They had ringed the base and chanted. They had tried to prevent traffic and personnel going in or out. As darkness fell they'd tried to rush the base. The sound of stones mingled now with the scrape of rushing feet. The German police were making a charge. Alvin hoped the police were giving them hell.

He picked a fresh stick of gum and looked round the field again. Something moved. He raised his rifle to his face and peered through the night scope. There were people in the field, five soldiers in camouflage jackets. Alvin lowered the rifle. Sergeant Wilson must have arranged reinforcements. Then he thought there was no reason for reinforcements and Sergeant Wilson would not have put in more men without warning him.

He peered through the scope at the spot where he had last seen movement. There were five of them moving crouched close to the ground, wearing camouflage jackets, dark trousers and − that was the giveaway − motorcycle helmets. Alvin unclipped his radio and spoke softly into it. 'I've got five in the field behind Narrow End.'

'Sending you support right away,' Sergeant Wilson answered. 'Can you hold for a coupla minutes?'

'Hold them all night, Sarge.' Alvin could take care of five peaceniks any night of the week. He moved out of the pillbox and crouched beside it.

The protestors came out of the field and up the hill towards him. They were not real protesters, Alvin told himself. They were enemy agents making a raid on a sensitive US installation. They were traitors using the demo as cover to get into the Cryp Hut.

132

The Cryp Hut housed the base's advanced communications equipment and codes. There was no way anyone unauthorized could get into it. Alvin determined to stop the protesters now walking quietly along the perimeter road. He looked around. No sign of Wilson's reinforcements. Never mind. He could handle this. He crawled away from the pillbox and into the ditch opposite the entrance.

The demonstrators approached the gate and stopped, a little confused by the fact that the pillbox was unoccupied. They looked around hesitantly. Alvin emerged from the ditch behind them. He'd got them where he wanted in a nice little group between him and the base. 'Hold it,' he shouted and thrust his M16 at them.

The demonstrators looked as if they might start to run. Alvin fired into the air. They froze. 'Now just keep standing very still,' Alvin said. He listened for the approach of Wilson's men. They waited.

'Yankee, go home.'

A woman's voice. Alvin looked at the smallest figure in the group. One woman and four men.

One of the others said, 'You have no right to hold us here. We are outside your base.'

'You're on the perimeter road,' Alvin said. 'That's base property.'

'German property.' It was the girl again. 'Our property. Our land. Take your nuclear missiles and go home, yankee.'

Alvin shifted his gum to his left cheek. Where the hell were the others? He couldn't hold five people at gun point all night.

'Go!' the woman cried.

One of the demonstrators charged Alvin. Alvin stepped aside quickly and slammed his rifle butt into the man's kidneys, whirled and brought his gun back into the ready position. Two of the demonstrators were heading back to the field, the other two running up the path to the Cryp Hut.

They'd all had to be professionally trained to pull off such a manoeuvre, Alvin thought. 'Halt,' he shouted.

The two figures kept running towards the Cryp Hut.

Alvin raised his weapon and fired, aiming carefully over their heads.

The woman stopped. Alvin drew a bead on her. Through the night he saw her reach under her parka, take out a round, metal object and raise it to her mouth.

Christ! She was going to frag the Cryp Hut! The woman drew her arm back. Alvin pulled the trigger.

Yuri woke in clean bedclothes, sleeping between clean sheets. He allowed the memories of wavering street lights to filter back, remembered driving down into the Special Investigation basement parking lot, voices, and the floor of the parking lot cold against his cheek. He remembered a brightly lit room and people cutting away his clothing, his face and arms being sponged with a lotion that stung. Yuri opened his eyes.

A night light burned. He could make out a window, walls, a table. A burly figure breathed hard by his bed. As his eyes got used to the light, Yuri recognized Boris with the Stechkin grasped firmly between his legs.

'Hello,' Yuri said.

Boris started and grabbed the Stechkin. 'You awake, Captain?'

'Yes. Where am I?'

'In hospital. Don't worry. Andrei and I are looking after you.'

'What time is it?'

A radium dial flashed. 'Just gone quarter past four.'

'I want to see Karelin as soon as I can.'

'He knows you're here. He'll come. How do you feel?'

'Right now, very well.'

'Is there anything I can get you?'

'No.'

'Then go to sleep. They're going to check you out in the morning.'

*

All the next morning they pressed and probed him. They made him listen to recordings of music and speeches. They shone lights into his eyes and made him move every limb. They had him read letters from a chart. At noon the doctor said he was all right, and that he should have plenty of rest. They took Yuri back to his room and gave him something to make him sleep. Andrei sat beside his bed with a Stechkin.

Karelin came in the afternoon. He stared anxiously at Yuri, ploughing long fingers through the greyness of his beard. 'How do you feel?'

Yuri's mouth was sore. His body hurt. His elbows felt as if they had been mangled. But nothing hurt as much as the realization that until he had gone there, Dmitrev and his wife had been happy, and that now they were dead. 'I want to get those bastards,' Yuri said.

Karelin said, 'Dmitrev's assistant, who worked with him on the *Zemschina* file, also died yesterday.'

'How?'

'Apparently, he was walking by a building site when a concrete block fell on him.'

'Two murders?' Yuri asked.

'Two accidents. The local militia have announced that the explosion at Dmitrev's was caused by a gas stove.'

Yuri thought of Dmitrev fishing, of Dmitrev seated in the trees watching the ducks flying home. He told Karelin of his meeting with Dmitrev. Karelin pulled out his recorder and placed it on the bedside table while Yuri spoke.

When he'd finished, Karelin asked, 'How do you feel?'

'I'll live.'

'Boris will drive you back to the apartment,' Karelin said. 'Tomorrow, check out Rudolf Barynin. You should find something on him in the Berlin section of the War Documentation Centre.'

CHAPTER TWENTY—ONE

Monday morning. Along with a hundred or so slightly disoriented passengers, Allison arrived at Zurich's Kloten airport. She felt as if she had been awakened in the middle of the night. She cleared Immigration and Customs without fuss and pushed her luggage trolley into the main concourse where she had the very efficient Tourist Bureau book her into a hotel that was cheap, convenient and quiet. She took a taxi to the hotel and, setting her alarm for noon, dozed fitfully.

The Handel was in a side street off the Bahnhofstrasse. Allison walked there. It was a fine, clear, spring afternoon, and the air felt thin and invigoratingly brisk. Blue trams swished down the middle of the street sending off fat overhead sparks. Sunlight glistened off displays of watches in Omega and Piaget, and on blocks of gold in the shaded windows of the Swiss Bank Corporation. In the windows of the Handel were video screens listing share prices and exchange rates. After the initial horror at her having come all the way from America without making an appointment, Allison was ushered upstairs to meet Herr Direktor Dr Hans Friedmeyer.

Friedmeyer was a sombre-faced man in his mid-fifties, with grey hair cropped close and large, square-rimmed glasses in thin gold frames. He looked inquisitively at Allison before waving her to a chair and sitting down himself. His eyes were very clear.

'I work for the Financial Administration Agency,' Allison said. 'We are a department of the United States Treasury and concerned with any potential abuse of laws or practice in regard to securities, shares, and other economic activities.

'What has brought me here is the fact that your bank has recently bought a substantial amount of cross-defaulted, sovereign loans. We would like to know the identity of the purchasers.'

'I'm sure you would,' Friedmeyer said, tersely. 'However, the identity of the purchasers is nothing to do with the United States Treasury, and the disclosure of that information is, under Swiss law, a criminal offence.'

Allison said, 'In the wrong hands, these loans could damage the entire European and American banking communities. That is why we are interested in knowing who the owners are.'

'I am certain your interest and that of the American Treasury is entirely altruistic,' Friedmeyer said. 'However, we are bound by the law and must obey it.'

Zwingli could not have expressed it better, Allison thought, and asked, 'Why do these purchasers want to hide behind Swiss bank secrecy? After all they are doing nothing illegal buying, selling or owning such loans.'

'People have many reasons for keeping their financial affairs private,' Friedmeyer said. 'And here in Switzerland we respect that. The *raison d'être* for our bank secrecy laws is the genuine conviction of the Swiss people that a man's finances are his own affair, relevant only to his bank manager and God.'

Who, in Switzerland, were pretty much the same, Allison thought.

'It is true that certain misguided people have occasionally abused our laws,' Friedmeyer continued. 'But that is not the fault of the Swiss. Rather it is to do with foreign, less enlightened governments, who seek to impose unacceptable restraints on the financial activities of their citizens. So, Miss Maynard, unless you can give me a very good reason, I am afraid, I cannot reveal to you the names of the persons or organizations on whose behalf the

Handel Kreditbank may or may not have acquired certain loans.'

'Could you confirm that your customers have acquired these loans only as part of a genuine business transaction?'

'Miss Maynard, please understand me. I am not confirming or denying anything. All I can tell you is that if the Handel Kreditbank has bought loans on behalf of its customers, then those customers are persons of the highest integrity and that such purchases would have been made in accordance with the laws of Switzerland and any other country necessarily involved.'

Friedmeyer was getting to his feet. Wouldn't tell you the time from a cuckoo clock, Drewett had said. Drewett had been right.

Allison had lunch at a Movenpick, drank half a carafe of Dole and thought what to do about Friedmeyer. When she'd been investigating the Silicon Valley affair, a Swiss lawyer, Dr Emil Wiederman, had helped her unravel the intricacies of a Luxembourg based company called Sonita SA. Allison finished her lunch and called Wiederman. Wiederman agreed to see her at three. She held two fingers triumphantly over her coffee and thought so much for Swiss bank secrecy.

Wiederman had old and sumptous offices near the Hotel Savoy Baur en Ville. There were faded tapestries on the wall and desks you could kneel at. Everything in the office was genuinely antique except the people who looked young and bright and anxious to please.

Wiederman himself was no exception. But when Allison told him what she wanted, his eyes ceased to dance and he slowly turned the colour of an over-ripe strawberry. 'I think you should return to America, Miss Maynard,' he said, 'before you end up in a Swiss jail.'

Allison walked angrily along the Bahnhofstrasse. She had no intention of returning to America or going to jail. She decided she would have to ask Paul Weiler to find out about the loans.

Even thinking about Paul Weiler gave her the shivers. Weiler was a private investigator with a good business in erring husbands and, Allison suspected, a rather more lucrative one in blackmail. He was fat, sleazy, lecherous and dirty. But on her last case, he had been unprincipled and effective.

Allison phoned him from a café and spoke to an answering machine with dying batteries. Halfway through her message, Weiler came on the line and said, 'Of course I will see you, Allison m'dear. Where shall we have dinner?'

'We will meet in your office,' Allison said. 'As soon as it's convenient.'

'My office it shall be. How long will you be?'

Allison looked at her watch. 'Twenty minutes.'

'I can hardly wait.'

Creep.

Weiler's office was at the less elegant end of the Ramistrasse, reached through a perpetually open doorway between a shop that sold trusses and a café run by Turks. The plastic sign by the door was cracked and the gold lettering on the grimy windows, peeling off. There was a strong smell of burning lamb and decaying food. Allison followed the arrow on the plastic sign to a door on which a second plastic sign said: Paul Weiler, Private Enquiry Agent.

'Paul,' Allison called.

From behind a door between the filing cabinets, Weiler answered, 'Right here. Come on in.'

Weiler was in his early forties, with a large, doughy face, squashed nose, tiny porcine eyes and unkempt greasy hair. He had a petulantly drooping lower lip, coloured a blackish red from too many cigarettes. He padded round the desk to greet her. 'Allison, m'dear.'

Allison turned her head away and took his wet smack full on the cheek. 'Nice to see you, Paul. I don't have a lot of time, so let's get down to business.'

'Business. Right.' Weiler padded back to his own side of the desk.

Allison sat. She told Weiler about the sovereign loans and the Handel Kreditbank.

Weiler smoked and scratched the front of his stomach as he listened. 'What you want me to do is criminal,' he said. He unlocked a drawer in his desk and took out a grey, metal card index, unlocked the index, looked through the cards, locked it, put it away in the drawer and locked that. He sat back in his chair, lit another cigarette and said, 'I can help you, but it won't be cheap.'

'How much?' Allison asked.

'Five thousand dollars and expenses.'

'We can't afford that,' Allison said.

'You'll have to if you want me to break the law.'

'The American government is cutting back on expenditure,' Allison said. 'These days we have to work to a budget. Three thousand, including expenses.'

Weiler said softly, 'You wouldn't have come to me if there was anywhere else to go. It's still five thousand. Take it or leave it.'

'Three thousand,' Allison repeated, trying to keep the helplessness out of her voice.

'I have sources others haven't,' Weiller said and tapped his desk drawer. 'And it will be five thousand.'

'Including expenses,' Allison said.

Weiler's eyes squinted at her through the smoke. 'All right, just for you, five thousand including expenses.' He stubbed out the cigarette in an old typewriter ribbon tin already packed tight with butts. 'Where are you staying in Zurich?'

Allison told him.

'How long for?'

'As short a time as possible.'

Weiler asked for her phone and room number. 'It is usual to have something in advance,' he said.

140

Allison reached into her handbag and signed over a thousand dollars' worth of traveller's cheques.

Weiler stuffed the cheques into his jacket pocket. 'I will contact you at the hotel tomorrow,' he said.

In his office at the Handel Kreditbank, Dr Hans Friedmeyer wrestled impatiently with the phone. Herr Direktor Dr Friedmeyer did not usually make his own phone calls. But this was a call and a phone number he could not entrust to anyone.

This time Kaspar Baur answered. Kaspar Baur was the head of Baur Industrie and the secret conglomerate which controlled the Handel Kreditbank. 'Yes, who is it?' As always, the flat, impersonal tone of the Chairman's voice made Friedmeyer nervous.

'Hans Friedmeyer here, Mr Chairman. From the Handel – '

'Yes, Hans.'

'I had a visitor today from the United States Treasury. One Miss Allison Maynard.' Friedmeyer told Baur about Allison's visit. 'I don't think we have anything to worry about,' he finished. 'It will take the Americans at least six months to get any information from us and by then it will be too late.'

'Where is the Maynard woman staying?' Baur asked. 'How long will she be in Zurich?'

'I don't know, Mr Chairman. I deliberately left Miss Maynard with the impression that we had no further business to discuss.'

Baur said, 'Find out where she is staying in Zurich. If she contacts you again, make an appointment to see her, and let me know immediately. I think we should talk more with this Miss Maynard.'

'I'll do exactly as you say, Mr Chairman,' Friedmeyer said.

Paul Weiler waited outside the Handel Bank. At precisely 5.30 the commissionaire locked back the central revolving

141

door and moments later the staff began to leave. Weiler waited with his back to the wall beside the exit. The Handel employed about forty people and the man Weiler was waiting for was among the last to leave.

Willi Heinitz was the chief clerk of the Handel Kreditbank. He was a severe-looking man in his late fifties and wore a black woollen coat, a chequered black and grey scarf and a grey hat. He had a straight nose, a straight lined face, an erect manner of walking. His mouth curled in distaste as Weiler stumbled against him, muttering at the same time, 'Herr Heinitz, please. A word.'

Heinitz' sensitive nostrils wrinkled at Weiler's smell. He did not recognize the man and he did not like people pushing or standing so close to him. If the man was a customer of the bank he was obviously of no importance. 'If you want to talk to me,' Heinitz said, 'call my secretary and make an appointment.' He tried to step round the man.

Weiler blocked him. 'I don't think you would want me to deliver Monica's message to your secretary,' he said.

Heinitz stopped looking for the commissionaire. The man was smiling at him. His teeth were a muddy brown, and four were missing. 'I know no one called Monica,' Heinitz said.

'Of course I could always deliver her message to your wife.'

Heinitz stopped trying to get past the man. His legs suddenly felt weak and his breathing, difficult. He wanted to lean against the wall. He looked over the man's shoulder and repeated, 'I know no one called Monica.'

'Two Mondays ago,' Weiler said. 'It's always every other Monday isn't it? A little bit of touch and suck. A little bit of the other. Arses turn you on, don't they Herr Heinitz?' He kept raising his voice as he spoke and saw Heinitz' head give a little tremor of anxiety.

The commissionaire was looking at them, and Heinitz hoped he hadn't heard. 'Who are you?' he muttered. 'What do you want?'

Weiler pointed at a café across the Bahnhofstrasse. 'Why don't we go over there and have some coffee and perhaps a brandy. I think you'll need it.'

As head of the Clandestine Division's German Desk at Langley, Alan Hersh had been CIA Director Bill Timmins' only choice when he'd decided to start a discreet investigation into the death of the American NATO officer who had been killed on the autobahn outside Duisburg. Which was just the way Hersh had wanted it.

Since his arrival in Germany, Hersh had met with a Lieutenant Colonel on the staff of East German Army General Kork, taken delivery of a supply of radio controlled detonators and other electronic equipment, and dined with Nino Valdez at his favourite Chinese restaurant in Saschenhausen.

Now he sat in his room at the CP Tower carefully reading the Frankfurt station's files on West German Chancellor Schiller, memorizing every detail of the politician's working and living habits.

The phone rang. It was Kaspar Baur. 'Hi,' Hersh said, 'I've been meaning to call you. Everything's going fine.'

'Who's Allison Maynard?' the Chairman asked.

'Why don't you tell me?'

'She's an Assistant Director of the Financial Adminstration Agency. This morning she saw Friedmeyer at the Handel and questioned him about the sovereign loans.'

'Timmins told me he'd warned off the FAA,' Hersh said.

'If that's so, you'd better find out what she is doing here and who she's working for.'

'Sure,' Hersh said. 'Call you as soon as I know something.' He put down the file on Chancellor Schiller and called Washington.

CHAPTER TWENTY-TWO

The War Documentation Centre was in the former country residence of a sugar merchant, to the West of Moscow off the Enthusiast Schosse. It was protected by four po-faced guards who looked at Yuri with surprise and examined his workpass with suspicion before taking him to meet Alexei Nikitin, the Chief Archivist.

Nikitin was a rancid-looking man in his late forties. He wore an old-style Russian tunic, baggy slacks and worn plimsolls. A scarf was wrapped round his scrawny neck and the frame of his metal-rimmed spectacles was held together with sticking plaster. He squinted at Yuri distastefully. 'You a student?' he asked in a hoarse whisper.

Yuri decided Nikitin did not speak often.

'We don't like students here,' Nikitin said. 'We are not a research institution. When the cataloguing is complete, we will have – '

Yuri thrust his workpass at him.

Nikitin squinted at it through the twisted spectacle frame. 'KGB,' he muttered. 'What does the KGB want with the war? You know there was no KGB till 1953?'

'There was the NKVD,' Yuri said. 'Same thing.'

Nikitin twisted worm-like fingers. 'We don't have facilities for research,' he said, and shrugged helplessly at the walls of shelves sagging under the weight of countless files. 'They have promised that when the cataloguing is complete they will give us more space. They have promised to affiliate us to the university and send students.' Suddenly, his face took on an expression of craftiness. 'You couldn't help us to get – ' Then seeing Yuri's expression he said, 'I suppose not.'

'I'm not in supply,' Yuri explained. 'I'm in political intelligence.'

'And what interests you about the war? Mind you if it is after 1943 October, we cannot help. We haven't got beyond 1943 October — '

'We're interested in a German banker called Rudolf Barynin,' Yuri said.

The name did not make any impression on Nitikin. 'We can't help you with names,' he said. 'You'll have to give me a date. Before October 1943.'

'Try 1937.'

'What month?'

'Why not the beginning? January.'

Nitikin moved a pile of files from a sideboard and took out a dusty ledger. 'A banker,' he said. '1937. I'll look under finance.'

After about twenty minutes of earnest page-riffling he asked, 'The Barynin Bank. Would that be the same thing?'

'I guess so.'

'The file is cross-referenced. Would you want — '

'Yes. All the files.'

Keeping his finger in the ledger, Nikitin sighed. 'This will take some time,' he said. 'Perhaps you'd better come back next — '

'Now,' Yuri said. 'It is a matter of grave importance.' He smiled tightly at Nikitin. 'I may not be able to get you things. But I could certainly stop things getting to you.'

Nikitin scribbled some notes, shut the ledger and walked to the door. 'You'd better go for a walk,' he said. 'We don't allow smoking in here.'

'I don't smoke,' Yuri said.

Nikitin came back an hour later, clutching a pile of files. He put them on his desk and blew dust off them. 'We don't have research facilities,' he said. 'I don't know — '

'This room will do,' Yuri said. 'That way, you can see I don't steal anything.'

'Yes,' Nikitin agreed. 'And you must not write on the files.'

'No,' Yuri said. He placed his pad and pen on the desk and sat down. 'I'll use these.' He held up the pen. 'Ready when you are Comrade.'

It took Yuri two hours to finish reading the files. By then his back was stiff, his notepad full and he hadn't discovered what Dmitrev had been trying to tell him about 1937 or what Barynin had to do with bombings in Munich, organized terrorism in Germany or murders in Russia.

As Dmitrev had told him, Rudolf Barynin had been a leading international banker. He'd set up a branch of the Barynin bank in Berlin which had soon become prestigious and profitable. He had involved himself in German politics and with the support of exiled White Russians had helped the Nazis buy their first newspaper and guaranteed the loan that enabled it to build its impressive headquarters, the Brown House, in Munich's Briennerstrasse.

In 1926, Barynin's had formed a consortium of English and American banks to finance the National Socialists until they came to power and, in 1928, they had persuaded an association of German industrialists, the Ruhrlade, to divert a large part of their political subsidy to the Nazis. In 1932, Barynin's had provided Hitler with a private aeroplane for his use during the election campaign.

At the same time, Barynin had been offering the Bolsheviks their first loans, explaining to Lenin the advantages of allowing the German armed forces to be recreated in Russia, and arranging to finance in Germany *and* Russia, the development of the new weaponry, tanks, armoured carriers and aircraft. He'd built the Rodina military schools in Russia, led a consortium to finance the construction of the Morozov Automobile Works, financed the modernization of the Sherymetev tanning factories and, most touchingly of all,

146

presented Stalin with a Mercedes Benz limousine, like Hitler's.

In 1939, Barynin had been the link between the German Foreign Office, the Chancellery, the NKVD and Stalin. He had met with Hitler and persuaded him to allow Stalin a free hand in the Baltic. He had met with Stalin and convinced him Hitler could be trusted.

In 1945, Barynin had disappeared, together with his wife, the aristocratic Countess de Witt, and his two-year-old son. It was believed they had all been killed in a bombing raid over Munich.

But what had he been trying to achieve? It was no answer that loans to the Bolsheviks and the Nazis were good business. In 1920 the Bolsheviks were tottering and Hitler was barely known, even in Munich. Which meant that right from the outset, Barynin had gambled that the Bolsheviks would last and that Hitler would arrive. Why?

Not political idealism. No two philosophies could be more diametrically opposed than those of Lenin and Hitler. So what was the common ground Barynin had seen?

Not in the countries, not in history or political philosophy. It was in the men, Yuri thought. Lenin and Hitler were the same kind of men, strong, obstinate, determined, magnetic, with a ruthlessness that enabled them to seize power and hold on to it; men with the courage and the will to impose a personal vision upon a nation. Barynin had been enamoured of strong men and strong government. Was that the answer? If so, why had he sought to impose that kind of rule on Russia and Germany? Yuri thought he could understand Russia. Barynin had been Russian. But Germany . . . Barynin had not even visited the place until after the First World War.

Yuri turned his thoughts to what the successors to Barynin were trying to achieve now. Large-scale terrorism in Germany, the murder of archivists who had prepared files on the Izgoi, the involvement of men with identical backgrounds, the provision of secret funds —

The funds were the clue! Above all Barynin had been a provider of funds! Patiently, Yuri went through the files again. When Barynin had created Barynin Berlin, his investment had been channelled through a holding company in Vaduz, Liechtenstein called Skorpion SA. Skorpion SA who nearly seventy years later had paid a terrorist ten thousand dollars to plant bombs at Munich railway station and financed Chernov's secret bank account!

The next step was to find out everything possible about Skorpion SA. Skorpion, Yuri decided, was the key to everything.

He returned to the office, typed out a report for Karelin and went home.

CHAPTER TWENTY-THREE

For the third time that afternoon President Jack Donnelly and his private Advisory Committee watched the shadowy film of Saturday night's shooting at Bad Salzbach. The shooting had unleashed a maelstrom of protest in West Germany. The popular press called for Private Alvin Marcus to be tried by the German civilian authorities. A section of Chancellor Schiller's cabinet wanted an enquiry conducted by the German Bundestag. The anti-nuclear lobby said the killing exemplified the danger of foreign bases and vociferously reiterated their demands for the removal of all foreign troops and nuclear weapons from German soil. Finance Minister Siegfried Lothar demanded that all foreign troops be confined to barracks.

The lights came up. The five men in the room looked around and blinked at each other. President Donnelly said, 'From what we've seen, there's no doubt the soldier did the right thing. He had no way of knowing the woman was only carrying a smoke bomb.'

That afternoon the Advisory Committee consisted of President Donnelly, Secretary of State Max Caldwell, CIA Director William Timmins, Presidential Aide Tom Pierce, and Miles Kingdon.

'Smoke bombs could have damaged some of the equipment in the Cryp Hut,' Tom Pierce said. A slim, alert-looking man in his early forties, Pierce was a former CIA Planning Director turned State Department apparatchik, turned Presidential Aide. It had been Tom Pierce's shrewd electoral analyses that had delivered Big Jack Donnelly to the White House.

Miles Kingdon said, 'Our problem is that as far as the German public are concerned, we murdered an unarmed civilian making a legitimate political protest.'

'She shouldn't have attempted to enter the most secret area of the base,' Tom Pierce said.

'I agree with you,' Kingdon said quickly. 'But if we are going to use that as a defence, then we must be prepared to reveal exactly why that part of the base is so secret.'

'Impossible,' Secretary of the State Max Caldwell snapped.

Kingdon smiled helplessly at Tom Pierce. 'You see.'

Bill Timmins said, 'I think it was a set up,' and sat back in his chair, pleased at having got everyone's attention. He looked at his notes and said, 'The attempt to get into the Cryp Hut was not something that happened in the heat of the moment. It was a carefully planned entry, run separately from the main demonstration. These people, and we know there were five of them, left the main demonstration, cut through a perimeter fence, crawled across a field to the most sensitive part of the base. To do that they must have known where they were going and what they wanted to do when they got there. So my first question is, what did they want?'

'To sabotage our communications equipment,' Max Caldwell suggested.

'And get at our codes and find out something about our communications systems.' That was Pierce.

Miles Kingdon said, 'The woman and her accomplice had no political record.'

'There were three others,' Timmins said. 'When we find them I'll bet they not only have political records, but that at least one of them will turn out to be an electronics expert.'

'It is also possible,' Tom Pierce said, 'that the object of the exercise was to provoke the shooting and stir up anti-American feeling.'

'That's pretty convoluted, Tom,' Miles Kingdon said. 'I mean we're talking about a bunch of pacifists here, people who in their misguided way are trying to protect human lives, not take them.'

Timmins said, 'The second and equally important question is how did they know? The layout of the base is not something they could have gleaned from casual visits, or even from detailed observation. It is something they could only have found out from someone who already knew.'

Max Caldwell said, 'The Army is already holding an enquiry into base security.'

'The source of this leak may well be outside the base,' Timmins said. 'The layout of the base was available to our people and to certain of our German friends. As the demonstrators were German, it seems likely their source was also German.'

'You have suspicions, Mr Timmins?' the President asked.

'Only a premise, Mr President. The person making the most political mileage out of the shooting, the person taking the most anti-American stance and calling most loudly for the withdrawal of our troops is Finance Minister Siegfried Lothar. I'd like to run a discreet investigation into Herr Lothar.'

Max Caldwell said, 'We have enough problems with the Germans without enquiring into a senior member of their government.'

150

Kingdon joined in. 'That is a very paranoid and dangerous reaction, Bill. If the investigation succeeds, fine. But if it fails, if it is discovered — we will only reinforce the Big Brother image of America and the CIA, and make an enemy of a man who could one day be America's greatest and most needed friend.'

Timmins said, 'We have had reservations about Herr Lothar for some time.' He took a file from his briefcase marked LOTHAR, SIEGFRIED CHRISTIAN. 'Lothar,' Timmins said, 'was born in Berlin in February 1937, the same year his father was executed for taking part in an anti-Hitler conspiracy. Lothar was brought up by his uncle Ulrich, a lawyer with a large commercial practice in Berlin. He was educated at the Brandenburg Academy, an old Ordenen style military school, where discipline was harsh, and great emphasis was placed on physical achievement. The physical aspect, as I understand it, was combined with generous doses of Nazi philosophy.'

'Are you saying Lothar is a secret Nazi?' the President asked.

'I'm sure Lothar has already been cleared by the Germans,' Max Caldwell protested.

'I'm not certain Nazism is the issue,' Timmins said and returned to his file. 'Lothar remained at the Brandenburg Academy until 1950, when the family walked out of East Berlin. They settled in Frankfurt where Lothar's uncle recreated the same kind of legal practice he'd had in Berlin before the war, namely a large, commercial practice specializing in corporation law.

'Lothar trained as a lawyer and became a partner in his uncle's firm. The firm expanded. Offices were opened in Stuttgart, Munich and other German cities. Lothar's firm became enormously successful, representing at one time or another almost every major German corporation. In 1968, Lothar's Uncle Ulrich died, and Lothar became head of the firm. Then, suddenly, ten years ago, he retired from the law and went into politics.'

Donnelly asked, 'That seems to surprise you. Why?'

'Because the kind of lawyer who enters politics is usually someone who took to the law to earn a living while advancing his political ambitions, or someone already involved with personal litigation and civil rights. Corporation lawyers, especially those as successful as Lothar, tend to stay with corporation law and become richer.'

Caldwell said, 'Perhaps he had a Pauline vision that compelled him to put the welfare of his fellow man before Mammon.'

'Perhaps,' Timmins said and turned over another page. 'Lothar's party was initially financed by some of his industrial clients. Not surprisingly, its policies were conservative. But then as his party became better known, Lothar began to move across the political spectrum. He embraced ecology and conservation. He made scathing attacks on unemployment, the unfairness of the *gastarbeiter* system and the soullessness of the German economic miracle. He campaigned for equal opportunities and equal rights. In short, he supported a whole range of radical causes.

'At the last election his party held the balance of power between the Democrats and the Socialists. Lothar's price was the Finance Ministry. And the first thing he did was expand trade with East Germany by providing the East Germans cheap loans, and encouraging West German investment. He endorsed Ostpolitik, almost as if he were a reincarnation of Willy Brandt.

'The surprising thing about all this is that despite his change of political philosophy, Lothar has not lost the support of his original backers, and that right now he is being supported by both the left and the right!'

President Donnelly asked, 'What's all this mean? Is Lothar a Nazi, a Communist or what?'

'The answer, Mr President, is that we don't know. And would like to find out.'

Caldwell said, 'I think any investigation should be deferred until things in Germany return to normal.'

'What do you think, Tom?' President Donnelly asked.

Pierce said, 'In the last four weeks, one of our NATO officers has been murdered, there has been an attempted bomb outrage in Munich, and an attempt made to get into the most secret area of our base at Bad Salzbach. Something unusual is happening in Germany and we should find out what. If Bill thinks an investigation of Siegfried Lothar's strange alliances might explain any of this, we should let him go ahead and do it.'

Kingdon turned to the President. 'Such a step is morally and politically outrageous,' he said sharply. 'The United States has no moral right to investigate members of foreign governments.' In a quieter tone, he added, 'German politics does not fall into clear demarcations of left and right, which is why to an outsider, the basis of Lothar's support might appear unusual. I'm certain that if one looks as closely at other German politicians, one will find the same pattern.'

'We should be ever watchful,' Tom Pierce said.

The President turned to Max Caldwell. 'Max, I want you to convey our regrets to Chancellor Schiller for what happened. Inform him that we will not permit an enquiry into the shooting, nor will we allow Private Marcus to be tried by the German civilian authorities. There is also no question of our troops being confined to barracks or withdrawn from Germany.'

Secretary of State Max Caldwell said, 'We must show some token appreciation of Schiller's problems. We must not make him feel he is being dictated to.'

'In that case, tell him nicely.'

'The important thing,' Miles Kingdon said, 'is that we should not only be seen to be strong, but be seen to be just and fair. The shooting, our actions, the German reaction are all forming opinion. We cannot simply act in a high-handed manner. We must show the Germans we were right. And the best way to do that is go along with their demands, at least a part of the way.'

President Donnelly looked keenly at his former tutor. Between the wars, Kingdon had lived in Germany, and walked through most of it. He'd been a *wandervogel*, one of those semi-mystics who travelled with only a walking stick and a small back pack, living on what he could find or what the people would provide. President Donnelly believed that experience had given Kingdon a unique insight into the German psyche. 'Tell us why.'

Miles Kingdon said, 'Germany is changing. If we do not recognize and accommodate those changes, we will make enemies where there should only be friends. A new Germany is emerging, a Germany unaware of its past and free of the guilt caused by the excesses of the Third Reich. These new Germans are at the halfway stage now. In a few years they will be running its government, its schools, its corporations, its banks and all its institutions. This generation shorn of its past will not accept that their fate and that of their country should be permanently determined by a history they were not part of. They will make changes. They will have the power to demand changes. That is the Germany which is emerging now, and that is the Germany we should be preparing ourselves to deal with.'

Tom Pierce asked, 'Are you recommending that we deliver Marcus to the civilian authorities and restrict our troops to barracks preliminary to withdrawing them from Germany?'

'I am recommending that whatever we do should be done in consultation and cooperation with the German government, that we should not ride roughshod over the feelings of the German people.'

'What exactly do you suggest we do?' the President asked.

'Firstly, we should not investigate Siegfried Lothar or any other member of the German government. Secondly, we should agree to a joint investigation of the shooting. Thirdly we should agree to discuss with the German government the confinement of American troops to barracks until this matter blows over.'

Tom Pierce said, 'If we confine our troops to barracks then we might as well withdraw them.'

Kingdon asked, 'How long do you think people with a common culture, language, history and heritage can be kept apart by the armed might of two foreign powers?'

'As long as we and the Russians have that power,' Tom Pierce said.

'Yalta was forty years ago,' Kingdon remarked quietly. 'It may not be our decision in the end.'

The President gathered his papers together and stood up. 'There will be no German investigation into the shooting,' he said, 'nor will we tolerate any interference with our troops in Germany.' He looked across at Timmins. 'However, given the present uneasy situation in Germany, Bill, I think we should put any investigation of Lothar on the back burner.'

A perfect compromise, Tom Pierce thought.

CHAPTER TWENTY-FOUR

There was a week-old copy of *Pravda* in the apartment, together with six copies of lesser known works by Lenin and a volume of Brezhnev's speeches. On television there was folk dancing on one channel and there were white-coated doctors discussing the evils of drink on the other. Yuri watched while he alternated mouthfuls of sausage and raw tomato. By the time he'd returned to Headquarters from the War Documentation Centre, the special KGB food store had closed, so he'd had to make do with what there was in the apartment; sausages, tomatoes and vodka. He thought the worst thing about living alone in Moscow was there were no TV dinners.

Correction. Second worst thing. The worst thing about living alone in Moscow was being alone. He thought of Stefan and Galina and wished he could go home.

He finished eating, made some tea and wrote out a shopping list. He thought about Barynin and wondered how to find out who owned Skorpion? He'd heard that lawyers in Vaduz were as close-mouthed as those in Zurich. He settled in front of the television and drank more tea.

The folk troupe was replaced by the news. West German Finance Minister Lothar appeared with subtitles, declaiming the callous murder of a girl protestor at an American base the previous Saturday and demanding the confinement of all foreign troops to barracks. A news commentator piously endorsed Lothar's hopes for peace and freedom. A second news reader announced that General Secretary Timochek had begun a campaign to stamp out corruption and the sale of *na levo* goods. Four illegal traders had that afternoon been arrested outside the Rossiya —

There was a brusque knock on the apartment door. Yuri went and peered through the tiny spyhole. In the curved lens was the distorted image of a Special Investigations workpass. He couldn't read the name. 'Who is it?' he demanded.

He didn't hear the name either as a muffled voice said it was a set of photographs from Karelin.

Photographs? What photographs? Something must have cropped up. Yuri unlatched the chain and opened the door. The man came in very fast, shouldering the door into Yuri's face and pinning him against the far wall. His fist grabbed Yuri's shirt front, his elbow was rammed against Yuri's chest, and with his other hand he pressed a Makarov against Yuri's throat. Too late, Yuri recognized the KGB Colonel who had thrown them out of Chermassov's office.

'What the hell do you want?' Yuri asked as the Colonel kicked the door shut. Fool! He should never have let the man in. He should never have answered the door without his gun. The Makarov felt like ice against his jugular.

'Tell me how you found out about Munich.' Underneath his leather overcoat the Colonel was wearing a brown civilian suit.

If the Colonel wanted information, he wouldn't kill till he'd got it, Yuri thought. 'What's it to do with you?'

The Colonel tapped Yuri's jaw bone with the gun. 'Talk before I break your jaw.'

The Colonel wouldn't kill him but he would break his jaw. And perhaps blind him with the gun sight. Yuri cursed his carelessness. His gun was in the bedroom. If he ever got out of this one, he'd take up religion.

The Colonel tapped Yuri's jaw again. 'Talk.'

'Karelin,' Yuri said. 'Karelin got the information.' The Colonel was a big man and very solid.

'Who from?' The Colonel's whole face seemed to ripple when he talked.

'I don't know.'

Another tap. Harder this time. The gun sight scraped flesh. 'C'mon. You can do better than that.'

It was obvious the Colonel was no amateur. His arm was wedged tightly against Yuri, keeping him pressed against the wall with the weight of his body. 'Who was Karelin's source?'

'You'll never believe it. Valdez.'

The Colonel didn't believe it. He pulled back slightly and drove his elbow into Yuri's middle. At that distance and that angle it didn't have much power, but it still managed to crush air out of Yuri's lungs. A few more of those, Yuri thought, and he'd stop breathing. 'Karelin turned Valdez three years ago.'

'Liar!'

The Colonel tried it with the elbow again. As he pulled back, Yuri edged sideways. He drove his knee into the Colonel's crotch, whipped his arm up and deflected the gun. The Colonel gasped and hung on to him. Yuri heaved sideways and punched the Colonel in the stomach.

The Colonel doubled up trying to pull Yuri down with him. Yuri grasped him by the coat collar and swung him into the wall.

The Colonel's grip broke. He slid along the wall, came upright and braced himself. He lifted his gun hand and forced his body into the classic position, feet apart, gun held straight out in front of him.

Yuri flung himself towards the lounge, cartwheeling on to his elbow and back. He rolled through the doorway, regained his feet and slammed the door shut. A bullet smacked into it a split second before he heard the shot. He heard the Colonel run across the lobby.

Yuri ran to the cupboard and took out Boris' Stechkin. The safety was on. There was a full magazine. He flicked off the safety catch and turned. The Colonel came through the door, saw Yuri and the Stechkin, stopped and skidded, tried to run back.

Yuri fired, the burst of automatic fire like giant drumbeats. The Colonel flung up his hands. The gun bucked against Yuri's middle. The folds of the Colonel's overcoat vibrated as if tugged at by tiny darts. He staggered backwards into the wall of the lobby, slid sideways along it and sat.

Yuri went after him. The Colonel slumped against the wall, his arms spread out on either side of him, one hand still gripping the Makarov. The body slipped sideways as Yuri felt for the pulse at the throat. The Colonel was dead.

Yuri put down the Stechkin and went through the pockets. No ID's except the SI workpass in the name of Alexandrov, a handkerchief and forty roubles. Yuri picked up the phone and called Headquarters. He asked for Emergency and was put through to Mark, who asked him to wait till he got there, and not to let anyone else in.

Yuri brought a sheet from the bed and threw it over the body. He put the chain back on the front door, switched off the television and waited. He kept the Stechkin by him.

He wondered how the Colonel had found out where he lived? He hadn't been followed, and his movements had kept to no regular pattern. Which meant the KGB hadn't found out. They had been told.

The only people who knew of the apartment were Karelin, Mark, Boris and Andrei. They were hardly likely to go blabbing to — Galina!

He sat petrified by the realization. Galina had decided going to the KGB would be easier than divorce and there would be no arguments. Then he thought, she couldn't have! She wouldn't have! On the other hand, why the hell not? Yuri poured himself some vodka and drank it slowly until Mark came.

Mark came with four other men, one of whom he introduced as Captain Andreyvich and who took scrupulous notes while Yuri told them what had happened. They examined the body, searched the pockets, stood around drawing lines, collecting spent bullets and taking measurements.

Mark helped himself to the vodka. 'Where are Boris and Andrei?'

'Assigned to other duties. This morning Karelin decided I was fit enough to look after myself.'

Mark said, 'You can't stay here. They might send someone else.'

'Right,' Yuri agreed.

The room danced as the men photographed the body.

'You'd better come with me. We'll find you somewhere with guards.'

'I could go to my apartment,' Yuri said.

'When the gunman doesn't report back, don't you think they'll come looking for you there?'

'Karelin's got a permanent guard on the apartment,' Yuri said. 'If you're worried, you could double it.'

'OK. I'll drive you there.'

Mark came into the janitor's office with Yuri and spoke to the Special Investigations man on duty. The man gave Yuri a wary look as he went upstairs.

Oleg Polyakov opened the door. For a moment Yuri felt his

stomach lift, his arm tense. The shock was mutual. Polyakov backed away from the door. Yuri pushed past him into the lounge and asked, 'Where's Galina?'

'In the bath.' Polyakov had on a burgundy warm-up suit. 'I took her running,' Polyakov said. 'We did fifteen kilometres. She's getting in shape again. She wants to get back into competition.'

Yuri felt Polyakov was talking to ease his embarrassment. He was a big man, about three inches taller than Yuri, with thick shoulders, a strong neck, flat stomach and a tapered waist. Polyakov was all hard muscle. His face was squarish, with deep-socketed eyes, dark, straight eyebrows, and brown hair cut so short the scalp showed. Yuri said, 'Galina is twenty-five and a mother. She's been away from the sport for five years. Kids that weren't even born when she started, are winning now.'

'But she has the determination,' Polyakov said. 'In sport determination is just as important as muscle and stamina.'

Give her that kind of hope and you'll break her heart, Yuri thought. Then, whatever the hell Galina did with her body was her business. He said, 'Gymnastics is a sport for nymphets.'

Polyakov sat, more relaxed now. 'Not necessarily. Nelly Kim and Ludmilla went on till their early twenties.'

'But not Comaneci and Korbut. And none of them took five years off and raised a family and came back.'

'Still she must have the chance. You never know what might happen. You never know what you can do till you try. Besides,' he leaned forward, confidentially, 'she needs to do it, Yuri. For herself, you know what I mean? She still blames herself for getting hurt, for not being in the team.'

'We did not take part in the Olympics that year,' Yuri said.

'But the Olympics is only one championship,' Polyakov said. He leaned back in his chair and crossed his legs, now really at home. 'The most prestigious championship, perhaps, but there are others. The European championships, the World championships, the — '

Yuri wasn't listening to Polyakov. He was staring at Polyakov's crossed legs, and his feet clad in imported, impossible to obtain in Russia, New Balance running shoes. Size 10.

Yuri got to his feet. He was at once hot and cold. 'Stand up,' he said.

Polyakov looked at him. 'What?'

'Stand up.'

Polyakov stood.

Yuri kicked him in the balls.

Polyakov doubled up, bringing his hands to his middle. Yuri chopped him on the side of the neck. Polyakov's neck was like wood. He tried to bring his knee into Polyakov's face, but Polyakov moved his arms and blocked it. He straightened and tried to grab Yuri.

Yuri hit him on the nose. Polyakov fell backwards over his chair. Yuri leapt over the chair and punched him again. Polyakov grabbed Yuri's arm, and pulled their bodies together, holding Yuri close, so he had no room to swing another punch.

'Have you gone mad?' he gasped.

'Bastard,' Yuri grated as he struggled in Polyakov's grip. They rolled over the carpet, bumped against the sofa and knocked over a small table.

Polyakov was stronger than he was. Go for the soft spots, Yuri thought, the eyes, the underside of the nose. From behind and above him, he heard Galina scream, 'Yasha!' He felt her hands clawing at his jacket. 'Stop this! Stop this at once!'

Polyakov pushed him away and wriggled out from underneath. Galina hung on to him. Yuri struggled up, lifting Galina with his shoulders. He heard Stefan cry 'Daddy.'

Galina shouted, 'Have you gone crazy or what?'

In front of him Polyakov got to his feet and stood warily.

161

There was a puffy spot on his cheek, where he'd hit the sofa.

Stefan rushed into the room between them. Yuri shrugged Galina off and picked up the child.

'Daddy, daddy,' Stefan cried and put his arms about Yuri's neck.

Yuri pressed the boy to him. 'Get out of here,' he said to Polyakov.

'No,' Galina shouted. 'This is my house as well. I won't have you — '

Yuri stroked Stefan's head and turned to his wife. 'That bastard almost made you a widow,' he said. He looked at Polyakov. 'What did you tell them, you son of a bitch? What did you do to get those shoes back?'

Galina looked perplexedly from Yuri to Polyakov. 'What the hell is all this?'

'It wasn't only the shoes,' Polyakov said. He looked at Galina. 'The KGB arrested me. They were going to put me in jail because of the shoes. They threatened to take away my residence permit and my card. When I got out of jail I was being sent to work in a factory.' He looked angrily at Yuri. 'What have you done, Orlov? Why do the KGB want you?'

Galina said, 'If you had to come back why did it have to be like this?'

Yuri looked at Polyakov. 'I think you'd better leave,' he said.

'Perhaps I should.' Polyakov looked from him to Galina. 'It's better you resolve your problems between you.'

He went.

Stefan brought a toy car. Yuri pushed it over the carpet. It bounced over a bump and turned over. Stefan laughed.

Galina said, 'I'm going to have dinner. Have you eaten?'

'Not well.'

She brought him a glass of wine and went into the kitchen. Yuri asked Stefan about school. Stefan had a new friend called Alex who came from Georgia. He brought out a set of building bricks. From the kitchen Galina called out to Yuri not to excite the child too much.

They played with the blocks and from time to time Yuri reached out and hugged his son. Galina came from the kitchen and watched them. 'You'd better put him to bed,' she said. 'The food will be ready in fifteen minutes.'

Yuri collected the car, the blocks and his son and went into the bedroom. He lifted Stefan into his bed and read him a story. Stefan kept asking him where he'd been and if he was going back to Germany.

'No,' Yuri said. 'Not for a long time.'

'You will be here tomorrow?'

'Yes.'

'And the next day? And the one after that?'

'Yes,' Yuri said.

'Promise.'

'Promise.'

Stefan slept.

Yuri and Galina ate in silence. Galina drank her wine in large gulps and refilled her glass, sloshing the wine from the bottle and filling the glass to the brim.

Yuri asked, 'Why did you tell Polyakov?'

Galina shook her head. 'I didn't know he would be picked up by the KGB.'

Yuri asked, 'Why him?'

'I don't know. I was worried. I thought when we met something would happen. And it didn't. I didn't know if I loved you or not. I didn't know if we should stay together or not.'

'But why talk to Polyakov?'

'I told you. He knows me best.'

'What did you tell him?'

'That you were back. That we'd met. That we'd made love like strangers. That I didn't know . . .'

'Polyakov's in love with you,' Yuri said. 'Did you know that?'

163

Galina sipped her wine and coloured. 'Yes. I suppose so.'

'You should make up your mind,' Yuri said.

'You, too.'

The phone rang. Galina took it quickly before the ringing could disturb Stefan. 'It's for you,' she said.

It was Karelin. He told Yuri the man he had killed in the apartment was Colonel Alksnis, a Deputy Director of Special Services.

'Holy shit!' Yuri breathed.

'Exactly.' Karelin told him he'd asked his men to leave the body in the apartment. 'That'll buy us time. The moment they know you killed Alksnis, they'll want you suspended, perhaps even held in jail till they find out what happened.'

'I don't want that,' Yuri said.

'Me too. I want you out and running.' Karelin added, 'I read your report on Barynin. I think checking out Skorpion will be a good idea.' He told Yuri he was sending an escort for him right away and wanted him to leave for Europe first thing the next morning.

Yuri said, 'Pick up Polyakov and find out who he talked to. He's the one who told the KGB about the apartment.'

'No!' Galina gasped. She ran from the table and tried to take the phone from him.

Yuri brushed her aside. 'Find out who picked him up and who interrogated him.' He looked at Galina. 'Then let him go.'

'We'll do that,' Karelin said. 'Mark's on his way to collect you.'

Yuri put the phone down.

Galina cried, 'How could you? How could you abuse your position — '

Yuri said, 'Whoever Polyakov spoke to sent someone to kill me.'

She looked at him horrified.

'That's why I'm here. That's why Karelin has reinforced the guard here.' Yuri told her what had happened at the apartment.

'How long are you going to live like this?' Galina cried, 'Running, shooting, being shot at. For your sake, for our sake, when does it stop?'

'Soon. I go back to Europe tomorrow.' He gave a wan smile. 'You'll have some peace.'

'That isn't what I meant.'

He said, 'I don't know when it will end. But it will be soon.'

She started to pile dishes in the sink. He went round behind her, took her by the elbows and turned her round. 'It isn't safe for me to stay here. Karelin's sending an escort for me. I'm going to Headquarters now.'

She lowered her head.

'I wish I could stay. There is a lot we have to say to one another.'

She fought back a sob. 'Maybe another time.' A tear broke and rolled down her cheek. 'If there is ever time.'

Tuesday April 15

CHAPTER TWENTY-FIVE

It was four o'clock the following afternoon before Willi Heinitz finally brought himself to act. He had been blackmailed. He had been forced to betray his employer and breach the law of bank secrecy. He had been forced to become a coward. He felt angry and disgusted with himself, angrier and even more disgusted with the sordid mother-raper who had compelled him to behave in such a despicable way.

For the sake of his own self-respect, for the sake of the bank, he had to do something about Weiler, even if he, Willi Heinitz, was exposed and dismissed from his job — Heinitz put such thoughts out of his head. He had worked out a more delicate way. He finished entering his ledger, went upstairs and knocked on the door of Herr Direktor Dr Friedmeyer.

'What is it?' As he did more frequently these days, Friedmeyer sounded harassed and tense.

'I would like a word, Herr Direktor. If you have a moment.'

Friedmeyer looked at his watch and decided he had a moment. 'All right. Come in. Sit down.'

Heinitz sat and tried not to slump. He clasped his hands between his thighs. He cleared his throat. Friedmeyer was looking at him impatiently. 'Yesterday,' Heinitz began, and cleared his throat again.

'Go on, Herr Heinitz. Do go on.'

'Yesterday afternoon,' Heinitz began again, 'a man called Paul Weiler met with me here at the bank on the pretext of opening an account. I now believe that the sole purpose of Weiler's visit was to meet a senior official of the bank. Last evening, when I was leaving the bank after work, I was accosted by Weiler.

'Weiler said he had a couple of minor queries concerning the account he'd proposed to open. Knowing how important all accounts are to the bank and as I had a few minutes to spare, I accompanied Weiler to the Sport Café for a cup of coffee. It then transpired that Weiler hadn't the slightest interest in opening an account. What Weiler really wanted was information about the bank's customers.'

'What information?' Friedmeyer's voice sounded strained.

'He wanted to know on whose behalf we had been buying sovereign, cross-defaulted loans. He offered me 5000 francs for the information.'

Friedmeyer's stare had become glassy. 'And what did you tell him?' His voice seemed trapped at the back of his throat.

'Nothing of course. I warned Weiler of the illegality of his action and walked out of the café.' Heinitz looked directly at Friedmeyer. He wasn't sure if Herr Direktor believed him or not. 'Today, I ran a check on Weiler. I discovered he is a

166

private enquiry agent with an office in the Ramistrasse. And so I thought I'd better inform you.'

'Why did you not come to me with this earlier?'

'It was only when I discovered Weiler's occupation that I realized he had a professional interest in the information, and that he might approach others.'

'You have a record of his application for a bank account?'

'No. I shredded it this morning. Even if his application was genuine, Weiler is not the kind of customer we want.'

'How did Weiler take your refusal?'

'He got very angry. As I persisted in my refusal, he threatened to tell the bank scurrilous lies about me. When I still refused, he swore he would ruin me.'

'Are you sure you didn't tell Weiler anything at all?'

'Nothing. I swear.'

Friedmeyer stared at Heinitz thoughtfully for a long time before dismissing him. He picked up his phone and dialled. Almost immediately, he heard the flat, neutral tones of Kaspar Baur. 'Yes. What is it?'

'It's Hans Friedmeyer again, Mr Chairman. I have some news to report.'

Weiler called Allison at five that evening. 'Allison, m'dear, I've got everything you want. Have you got everything I want?'

'Yes,' Allison said. Last evening she had spoken to Drewett, who had telexed four thousand dollars from the FAA's slush fund. She had collected it that afternoon from the Union Bank with no more formality than the production of her passport. The money now lay in four separate packets in her handbag. 'Where shall we meet?'

'Let's have dinner.'

'Honestly, Paul. We've both got — '

'We must have dinner,' Weiler said. 'I'm in Vaduz, right now. I won't be back in Zurich till about seven. And I'll want to eat.'

'All right. Where?'

Weiler gave her the address of and directions to a lakeside restaurant just outside Zurich. 'You can take a cab there,' Weiler said. 'I'll drive you back afterwards.'

Not bloody likely, Allison thought. She wasn't getting into any wrestling matches with Weiler. She went down to the desk and rented a car.

Yuri reached Zurich's Kloten airport on an Austrian Airlines flight from Vienna at seven that evening. Karelin had ordered him to lay a false trail and he'd flown first to London, where he'd changed his identity and then flown to Vienna. In Vienna he'd destroyed the false identity papers and flown to Zurich under his own name.

Yuri cleared Swiss immigration and moved into the gleaming terminal with its bright electric signs and glittering shop windows. He changed money at a bank window and walked past a supermarket with more cold cuts, fruit and vegetables than he'd seen in the whole of Moscow. At a self-service cafeteria he bought himself a sandwich and a cup of coffee and carried it to a stand-up counter. He stood watching the terminal while he ate.

No one was watching him. No eyes turned abruptly away; there were no hurriedly put down newspapers. No one walked suspiciously towards or away from him.

A small, moustached man wearing a black homburg carried a cup of coffee over to where Yuri stood. He placed a battered leather briefcase between them. Yuri wondered if with most of the cafeteria empty, two men standing at the one counter would look odd, then decided even if it did, it was too late. .

'Yuri.'

'Herbert.'

Herbert Schwering was a lawyer in Zurich who handled financial transactions for Sovexport and Electronorgtecknica.

'You have the information?'

'Skorpion SA is a private corporation registered in Vaduz. Its resident director is Gerhardt Hausmann. Skorpion is run

168

from his offices.' He gave Yuri the address. 'You will have no difficulty finding it. Vaduz isn't very big.'

'Thanks,' Yuri said.

Leaving his coffee unfinished, Schwering left. He'd also left the briefcase behind. Yuri carried it to the men's room and opened it. Inside was a Swiss-made SIG 9mm pistol and two boxes of ammunition.

CHAPTER TWENTY-SIX

The restaurant was outlined with fairy lights and there were a few cars parked beside it under a row of brighter arc lamps. There were tables set in cosy alcoves, a small bar at the back, and beyond it a wide patio from which a lawn ran down to the silvery grey lake. Resplendently gruesome in a red bow tie and a suit of blue shadow checks, Weiler sat at th only occupied table on the patio.

His hair was plastered down and he was freshly shaved. He had a pink carnation in his buttonhole. There was an empty glass in front of him and an ashtray with three cigarette ends. A bottle of champagne protruded from an ice bucket beside him. He got to his feet. 'M'dear, how lovely to see you.'

A waiter poured. Weiler offered her a foaming glass, picked up his own, clinked. 'To a marvellous evening.'

Allison sipped the champagne. Weiler looked like a bookmaker on a dirty weekend. 'How did it go in Vaduz?'

'I found out who's buying the loans.' He looked at her damply. 'Have you brought the money?'

Allison took the four packets from her bag and placed her hand over them. 'Who's buying the loans?'

Weiler looked at the packets greedily, smiled and fizzed more champagne into their glasses. 'First we'll work and then

169

we'll play,' he murmured. 'The Handel's customer is Liechtenstein corporation called Skorpion SA.'

Allison suppressed a buzz of excitement. 'Is Skorpion the only buyer?'

'I believe so. Skorpion owns forty per cent of Handel. And it is buying the loans with money Handel is borrowing from other banks.'

A mirror image of what Barynin's were doing. If the loans went belly up then it would be the other banks that would be left holding the baby. But why the obsession with sovereign loans? 'Who owns Skorpion?' she asked.

'I don't know. Skorpion is administered on behalf of its true owners by a lawyer in Vaduz called Gerdt Hausmann.'

'Hausmann would know who owns Skorpion?'

'Yes.'

'What can you tell me about Hausmann?'

'He's a man in his late sixties or early seventies, very prosperous and influential. He's been running companies like Skorpion for many years.'

'How do I get to meet him?'

'First you go to Vaduz. Hausmann's address is − '

Allison came aware of Weiler staring past her and turned. A man had come on to the patio from the side of the restaurant and was standing in the shadows thrown by the lights of the main room. He had his hands raised in front of him and was gripping something that glinted.

'Oh God!' Weiler cried and jumped to his feet, kicking over the table. Plates and cutlery smashed to the floor. Knocking over a chair, Weiler ran towards the restaurant.

As Weiler moved the intruder moved too. There was a bright yellow flash, a sharp crack.

Weiler stumbled. A hole appeared in the middle of his forehead. As he fell, his outstretched hands wrenched at a tablecloth, pulling plates, knives, forks and glasses to the floor. There was another flash, another crack. Weiler's body jerked.

Allison saw the man turn towards her and threw herself behind the fallen table. There was a rush of feet, a loud buzz from the restaurant. People rushed on to the patio. Someone screamed. Allison peered over the table and rose to her feet. The man had gone.

She picked up her handbag and stuffed the four thousand dollars back into it. Weiler was lying on his back, a thin spiral of blood worming from the hole in his forehead. His eyes were open and staring. Below the flamboyant carnation was another blotch of red.

Allison edged slowly back through the crowd. Her body felt like ice. To stay would mean getting involved with the Swiss police, would mean explaining why she was carrying four thousand dollars and the business she had with Weiler.

Clutching her handbag, she walked through the restaurant as if remotely controlled, went down the steps and got into her car. No one took any notice as she turned out of the car park and took the road to Zurich.

She drove like a robot, her mind numb, her body reacting automatically to the stimuli of road patterns and traffic. She'd never seen someone being killed before. She thought of Weiler with his flower and his — She tried not to think of Weiler. She had to think of herself. She had to think of getting away from Zurich and from Switzerland before the Swiss police traced her.

She crunched the car on the raised pavement as she parked outside her hotel. It took her only minutes to pack. The porter on duty expressed little surprise at her checking out so abruptly and so late. She threw her bags in the car and drove out of Zurich in the direction of Kloten.

She would find a small, nondescript hotel, she decided. Transatlantic flights left in the afternoons. Tomorrow afternoon she would get the first flight back to America. She drove through small, tidy villages, with neon-lit shop signs and bright window displays, signs advertising banks and beer kellers and hotels garnis. She wondered who had killed Weiler.

Weiler had been a shady, sordid character. He had been lecherous and corrupt. He had specialized in divorce with a sideline in blackmail. Any of his victims could have killed him. Weiler's murder could have had nothing to do with Skorpion.

She thought about that as she drove. If Weiler had been killed because of Skorpion, they would have done it *before* he'd returned to Zurich and *before* he'd contacted her. If it had been because of Skorpion, they would have killed her and Weiler. Allison shuddered.

Her headlamps illuminated blue and white signposts. Chur, Sargans, FL Liechtenstein 100 km. One hundred kilometres was roughly sixty miles. The road was good and she could be in Liechtenstein in little over an hour.

No one would expect her to go straight to Vaduz, she thought. And Vaduz would be as good a place as any to stay in. If she went to Vaduz she could see Hausmann in the morning and return to Zurich in time to catch the first flight to the States.

She followed the sign and held the car tight on to the banking that curved on to the expressway.

Herr Direktor Dr Friedmeyer was in a panic. He smoked dark cigars as he dialled repeatedly. Financial juggling was one thing, but murder — in Switzerland they still executed people for murder and he had no doubt that he was an accessory to the fact.

'Who is that? What is it?'

'It is Friedmeyer, Mr Chairman.'

'Yes, Hans. What's happened?'

Lapsing occasionally in his panic into the more familiar Schwytzer dialect, Friedmeyer told him. He had, as instructed, had Valdez' friend, Chico, go after Weiler. Chico and another man had staked out Weiler's office and Weiler had finally come there at about seven o'clock in the evening, dressed as if going to call on a fancy lady. He had stayed in his office only long enough to deposit an envelope he'd been carrying, and left.

Chico had broken into Weiler's office and found that Weiler had spent the day in Vaduz investigating Skorpion.

'What!'

For the first time Friedmeyer could recall, the Chairman's voice betrayed some emotion. 'Skorpion,' Friedmeyer repeated disconsolately. 'According to Chico, Weiler had traced a lot of connections, Skorpion Handel, Skorpion Hausmann, Skorpion and the loans.'

'What did Chico do?' Baur demanded, impatiently.

'Chico radioed his assistant who said that Weiler was at a restaurant outside Zurich, the Hummer am See.'

'When Chico got there, Weiler was already talking to a woman and there were packets of money on the table. Chico had no alternative but to kill Weiler.'

'And the woman?'

'By the time Chico had finished with Weiler it was too late to get a clear shot at her.'

'Who was she?'

'From the description Chico gave, it could have been the woman from the American Treasury, Allison Maynard.'

'What happened to her? Is she with the police?'

'No. There has just been a police radio alert for the woman who was with Weiler at the restaurant.'

'Do you know where she is now?'

'I found out she was staying at the Bristol. But when I called there a few minutes ago, she'd checked out.'

Friedmeyer heard the Chairman sigh. Then he asked, 'What's happened to Chico and Uwe?'

'They're on their way out of Switzerland.'

'Good. Keep tabs on the police, Hans, and keep in touch.' The Chairman rang off.

*

The first call Baur made was to Alan Hersh. He told Hersh
what had happened in Zurich and what he wanted to do with
Allison Maynard.

'She's American,' Hersh said. 'There'd be fewer com-
plications if we handled it.'

'As you like.'

'You'd better get things straight with Hausmann.'

'I'll do it now.'

Baur phoned Hausmann. 'Gerdt? Yes I know it's late. I am
expecting an American lady called Allison Maynard to call
you tomorrow for an appointment. I want you to see her.'

'I'll do that. What does she want to see me about?'

'Skorpion.'

'Look here. I'm not — '

'Relax, Gerdt. This is what is going to happen.'

Wednesday April 16

CHAPTER TWENTY-SEVEN

Yuri sat on the hotel terrace with rolls and coffee. As
Schwering had said, Vaduz was small; just two linked streets
lined with shops, banks, small cafés and hotels. In the space
between the streets there were a parking lot and two office
blocks. Yuri had woken up early that morning and covered the
town in twenty minutes. Hausmann's office was on the
ground floor of one of the blocks in the parking lot. It had its
own entrance and a row of bronze plaques set in rosewood.
The biggest said Dr Gerdt Hausmann. One of the smaller
plaques below read Skorpion SA.

Yuri wondered how to confront Hausmann. Should he
phone for an appointment and say he was a Russian defector
with a fortune in hot roubles? Or should he simply barge in

like a KGB thug? Either way, what was he going to ask Hausmann?

The girl who had checked in last night came on to the terrace. He'd noticed her in the hotel lobby when he'd returned from dinner, not only because she was worth noticing, but also because of the typically raucous American manner in which she'd been demanding a phone directory.

She was tall, about five foot eight in medium heels, with shoulder-length brown hair, a nice firm mouth framed with tiny laughter lines at the corners and steady, level brown eyes that Yuri thought in some lights would turn green. Her skin was tanned and beneath the tan, freckles. She wore a mannish brown jacket and a skirt, a blouse with tiny polka dots. Her chin was as if anything a trifle too rounded and aggressive. But when she smiled at the waiter, Yuri noticed she had a dimple on her right cheek.

They were the only guests on the terrace and Yuri wondered if he should walk across and join her. Then he thought he had enough problems with Hausmann. Besides the girl had begun to read a thick paperback book.

He wondered what she was doing in Vaduz. There was an air of compact efficiency about her. Perhaps she was an executive of some kind. Yuri looked at her hands. She wore no ring.

The girl left her book, marking her place with her room key, the bulky disc marked '7' protruding from the pages, and walked to the terrace rail. She stood there looking down at the street and the parking lot. A black Mercedes stopped sharply between a set of white lines outside Hausmann's office. The driver was a short man about five foot six or so, with wide shoulders, grey and black hair combed back over a broad head. He wore a blue, shadow-striped, double-breasted suit and could have been any age from fifty to seventy.

A second grey-suited man climbed out of the front passenger seat. He looked in his mid-twenties. He reached into the back of the Mercedes and took out a briefcase, raincoat and hat. Carrying them before him like some precious relic, he followed the older man up the steps and across the wide patio. The doors of Hausmann's office opened. The two men disappeared inside. The doors shut. Yuri thought, so that was Hausmann. As Schwering had said, a prestigious and important man.

Allison went to her room and called Swissair. There were no direct flights to Washington, so she made a reservation on the 1.35pm Swissair flight to New York. She thought about Hausmann. He had looked like a typical Swiss lawyer, prosperous, self-important, successful, conservative. He had not looked at all like the kind of man who shot people. Besides, Paul Weiler had been killed in Zurich, not Vaduz. She told herself again Paul's death had nothing to do with Skorpion. Which meant that she could safely meet Hausmann before returning to the United States. She picked up the phone beside the bed and dialled.

Yuri sat on the terrace and contemplated Vaduz. The morning had grown pleasantly warm. He draped his jacket over a chair and rolled up his shirt sleeves. If he tilted his chair back he could look at the castle on the mountain overlooking the town. In the cool shade behind Hausmann's windows, faint figures moved. Yuri ordered more coffee and wished all surveillance was as comfortable.

The American girl came out of the hotel and walked along the street towards the stamp museum. Yuri watched her veer across the parking lot towards Hausmann's office. It seemed a strange detour. Having examined the exterior of Hausmann's office, the girl strolled back to the centre of the lot, crossed the road and came back in to the hotel.

Intriguing.

The American girl came out of the hotel, crossed the street and went down the steps to the parking lot. She walked briskly as if she knew where she was going. She turned right after the steps, skirted the cars, tripped up the steps and across the patio of the office building into Hausmann's office.

Gypak! Yuri stared fascinated. He waited five minutes. The girl did not come out. So she had been expected. He went downstairs to the lobby, smiled at the concierge and asked for the key to room number seven.

Her room was identical to his, except it had a good view of the hotel's parking lot. The girl was travelling light. One case containing a miracle of a portable computer with a telephone attachment, transformer and batteries, a second case small enough to be carried on board an aircraft, with clothes, toilet articles, no nightclothes Yuri noticed, and a luggage tag which gave her name as Allison Maynard and her address as care of the Financial Administration Agency, Washington.

What, Yuri wondered, was an American government financial agency doing with the likes of Gerdt Hausmann? Certainly not laundering the budget or asking for a loan. Yuri smiled and thought he knew the answer.

Allison Maynard worked for the CIA.

Yuri went back to the terrace. There was a sudden spurt of activity from Hausmann's office. Doors opened. The office staff emerged, walked to their cars and drove away. Behind them the blinds were drawn. The young man who had arrived with Hausmann strung a notice on the door. Yuri was just able to read it. GESCHLOSSEN.

Now what the hell was going on? If Hausmann was having a meeting with the CIA why did he have to close his office and send his staff home? And the girl had been packed and ready to leave, obviously not anticipating a long meeting.

Yuri went to his room and collected the SIG. It seemed as good a time as any to call on Hausmann.

Shortly after eleven o'clock that morning, swaddled in his coat and looking, as always, on the verge of freezing, Karelin sidled into the office of Director Mikhail Gamalrik like a ghost. He took off his fur hat, revealing a high forehead and shiny dark hair combed back and stuck flat with brilliantine.

Even the great Karelin had his vanities, Gamalrik thought.

Karelin lit one of his *papyrosi* and put the match carefully away in its box.

Gamalrik, who had never been in the field, remembered Karelin had written the training manual. He asked, 'What can I do for you, Comrade Director?' his politeness hiding his resentment at Karelin turning up with only a few minutes' warning.

'I wanted to talk to you about Munich.' Karelin's tone and expression was that of an old friend who'd dropped in for a chat.

'What about Munich?' Gamalrik tried to keep the tension out of his voice.

'Chernov worked for you?'

'Chernov worked for Directorate K, yes.'

Karelin nodded encouragingly, as if he appreciated the difference. 'And when you heard what had happened in Munich you sent Colonel Alksnis to investigate?' Karelin's gaze was approving.

'Yes. That's correct.'

'And the conclusion Alksnis reached was that Chernov had intervened to stop the bombers and was himself killed?'

'Given the facts available that was a reasonable conclusion. Are you aware of any other facts, Comrade Director?'

Karelin waved an inconclusive hand. 'Do you agree with Alksnis' conclusions?'

'I repeat, on the basis of the available facts it was a reasonable conclusion. Also given the whole context of Munich, it was a satisfactory conclusion.'

'I like pragmatic solutions,' Karelin said. Carefully he put the ash from his cigarette into his matchbox.

'You're not in enemy territory, now,' Gamalrik said and pushed an ashtray across.

Karelin gave him a thin smile. 'Force of habit.' He looked

178

directly at Gamalrik. His eyes were like flat, polished stones. 'Did you know Chernov committed suicide?'

'Did he?'

'That conclusion is also possible from the facts.'

Gamalrik felt the pressure of Karelin's stare as if it was something physical. 'If you say so.'

'If it is a reasonable conclusion, why do you think Chernov killed himself? Were you aware of any personal problems he had? Was there any difficulty with his work?'

Gamalrik shook his head. 'No.'

'Do you know of *any* reason why Chernov should have killed himself?'

'No.'

'What was Chernov's relationship with Nino Valdez?'

'Routine, I believe. In fact Chernov's files show very little association with any underground movement. That is in accord with Directive 3243.'

'Of course,' Karelin said, thoughtfully. 'How was Chernov financed?'

'Through the Residency. He would forward his accounts to us for approval, and we reimbursed the Residency.'

'Chernov had no accounts of his own?'

'That would have been irregular. If we needed to spend money without Residency knowledge, we would have arranged disbursements from here. If for any reason a separate account was necessary, Petrov would have run it, not Chernov.'

'And Petrov's dead?'

Gamalrik composed his face into an expression of mourning. 'Yes. It was very sad. The pressure of the last few days got to him.'

'His medical reports showed no sign of heart trouble.'

Gamalrik shrugged. 'He was fifty-nine. At that age these things frequently happen without warning.'

Karelin asked, 'What is the relationship between your Directorate and Valdez?'

'The same as that with any other underground group sympathetic to our cause. We give them encouragement and limited support. Mostly encouragement.'

'What kind of support?'

'Money, materials, and training. It's during the training stage that we acquire their loyalty.'

'Did the Directorate authorize the supply of radio controlled detonators to Valdez, Chernov, Raspe or the East German SSD?'

'Not as far as I know.'

'We have traced the supply of this equipment to Chermassov.'

'It's nothing to do with us. We have not authorized the issue of that type of equipment since Directive 3243 was made.'

Karelin passed Gamalrik Chernov's note. 'This would seem to indicate that far from being the hero of Munich, Chernov was one of its organizers.'

Gamalrik fought to keep his face expressionless. He adjusted his glasses and read the note.

Karelin put copies of the bank statements on the table. 'Did you know Chernov was paying terrorists and running a secret bank account?'

'No. Where did you get these?'

'From Chernov's safe. Does that signature mean anything to you?'

Gamalrik frowned at the note. 'I can't say it does.'

'It is the sign of the Izgoi,' Karelin said, his eyes fixed on Gamalrik. 'An ancient secret society, dedicated to the control of Russia.'

Gamalrik looked away. 'Are you telling me that Chernov was a member of this Izgoi? That he was financed by them? That Munich was his idea?'

'Based on that note and the bank statement it is a reasonable conclusion,' Karelin said.

'I shall commence an immediate investigation into this,'

Gamalrik said firmly. 'In cooperation with your own investigation, of course, Comrade Director.'

Karelin asked, 'Your father died in June 1937?'

The colour drained from Gamalrik's face. He blinked furiously. 'Yes . . . that is so.'

'The same time as the father of Colonel Alksnis?'

'I — I wouldn't know.'

'Did you know Colonel Alksnis before you came to Moscow?'

'No.'

'What about Chernov or Chermassov?'

Gamalrik shook his head. 'I was brought up in Omsk. It is far from everywhere.'

'And you know nothing about the Izgoi?'

'Nothing whatsoever.'

Karelin got to his feet and smiled. 'I'm most grateful for your time. I would like very much to continue our discussion. My office, tomorrow at eleven o'clock?'

It was a summons not an invitation. 'Yes — yes of course,' Gamalrik said.

CHAPTER TWENTY-EIGHT

Allison stared angrily at Hausmann over the gag. Her wrists were bound firmly to the chair behind her. She resolved she would not give him the pleasure of watching her struggle uselessly.

Hardly fifteen minutes ago she'd been admitted into the building by an elderly woman clerk, and ushered into Hausmann's office by the young male secretary. Hausmann had seemed pleased to see her. He had offered her coffee and made small talk about Vaduz, Switzerland and America. Then

181

Allison had asked why Skorpion was purchasing cross-defaulted, sovereign loans.

Hausmann had seemed totally unfazed by that. 'Simply good business,' he'd said. He'd pointed out that sovereign loans were undervalued, a consequence of the American habit of alternating over-confidence with panic. The fact of the matter was that the international community would never allow any large sovereign borrower to go under. So while the Americans were panicking it seemed a good time to buy sovereign loans.

'History has shown that the international financial community does not always bail out countries,' Allison had said. 'History has shown that sometimes countries refuse to be bailed out.'

'A fair commercial risk,' Hausmann had said. Then he had asked, 'What is the interest of the American Treasury in these loans?'

'Because they are sovereign and cross-defaulted,' Allison had replied. 'And we do not know who owns them.'

Hausmann had smiled and poured coffee. 'Now you know. How did you find that out?'

'You know I wouldn't tell you that.'

'And I wouldn't insist. Here we respect confidentiality.' Hausmann had sipped his coffee and talked about the value of confidentiality and how it was misunderstood by many people, especially the American Treasury. He told her how in 1945 the Americans had seized the Swiss gold reserves that had been sent there at the outbreak of the war for safekeeping, and how Treasury agents had stomped all over Switzerland afterwards looking for assets of the Third Reich. 'The end was desirable,' Hausmann said, 'but the means were despicable. Your colleagues acted as if Switzerland was an American colony and not an independent country with laws, traditions and customs of its own.'

Allison had interrupted Hausmann's rambling by asking why Skorpion hadn't bought the loans direct.

'It was more convenient to use Barynin and the Handel,' Hausmann had said and talked about the difficulty of establishing lines of credit abroad.

But why two banks and two lots of commission, Allison wondered. And if Skorpion could lay out a few tens of millions in cash, what was the difficulty in establishing a line of credit? 'What kind of business does Skorpion do?' she'd asked.

'Investment.'

'And the source of its capital?'

'Profit from investments.'

A nice tight circle that. She'd asked if he'd done business with Barynin's before.

'Quite often,' Hausmann said. 'We've been dealing with Barynin since before the war.'

'Then you must have known Rudolf Barynin?'

Hausmann's face had clouded. 'Not very well. We were never large enough to be intimate with the senior management of Barynin's.'

'But you know Ellesmere Wentworth?'

'Yes, of course.'

Allison had found herself looking round the office for a sign of Ormus. She'd thought of asking Hausmann about it, then told herself that she was almost in Switzerland where things were solidly rooted in money. 'What do you propose to do with all these loans?' she'd asked.

'Earn interest and then hopefully a capital profit.'

'And who makes that profit?' she'd asked. 'Who owns Skorpion?'

'You know I couldn't tell you that,' Hausmann had smiled and looked at her cup. 'Please have some more coffee.'

'No thanks.' Allison had decided she had got all the information she could from Hausmann. She would have to think of another way of finding out who owned Skorpion. She picked up her bag.

Hausmann had begun talking about the Swiss gold

reserves. 'Quite naturally the blacklist hurt Switzerland. At the time, America was the only country that had trading reserves. So . . .'

Allison had felt a twinge of nervousness. It had seemed that Hausmann was talking for the sake of talking, that for some reason he wanted to keep her in his office. She'd got to her feet. 'I must leave now,' she'd said. 'I have a plane to catch.'

'Stay, stay,' Hausmann had almost implored. 'Have some more coffee. Have an apéritif.'

'Thank you, no. I must go now.'

Finger archly raised, Hausmann had come round his desk. 'One moment please. I have something you might like to see concerning Rudolf Barynin and the old Barynin bank.' He had gone to the outer office.

Allison had waited. She had heard the sound of drawers being shut, of hurried conversations and equally hurried footsteps. Hausmann had returned looking somewhat tense. 'My assistant is looking for the document. Will you have some coffee?'

'No thanks. I must leave now.' Her nervousness had intensified. Behind Hausmann the outer office was dark. A door had slammed. 'I'm running late. Why don't I call you — '

Hausmann's assistant had appeared in the doorway.

'I must be going,' Allison had said and walked towards him. Hausmann had stepped aside and walked to his desk. His assistant had covered her with a gun.

Allison had stopped horrified.

'I'm afraid you'll have to stay,' Hausmann had said.

She'd turned to Hausmann fighting both anger and fear. Hausmann had been standing behind the desk. He'd also had a gun.

'What is this?' Allison had cried. 'What do you want?'

'Sit down,' Hausmann had ordered. His assistant had walked up to her, forcing her to step back into the room. She'd felt the chair press against the back of her knees. She'd sat.

184

'What's the meaning of this?' Allison had demanded.

Hausmann had said, 'Please place your hands behind your chair.'

While Hausmann had covered her with his gun, his secretary had tied her wrists to the chair. He'd then placed a gag across her mouth.

'You aren't the only one with questions,' Hausmann had said. 'There are some people who want to talk to you.' He'd looked at his watch. 'They should be here soon.'

Yuri walked up the steps at the side of the office building. White blinds blanked out Hausmann's picture windows. There was no light behind the frosted glass of the door. Hausmann's was definitely *Geschlossen*. Except his Mercedes was still in the parking lot below. Yuri jabbed his finger on the bell.

A shadow appeared behind the glass, followed by the click of an expensive lock sliding. Hausmann's male secretary half opened the door.

There was a light beading of sweat on his hollowed cheeks. A hank of dark hair fell across his forehead. The grey suit looked rumpled and his tie had slipped two inches down his shirt front. 'What do you want?' He stared at Yuri with large, surprised, dark eyes.

'I want to see Herr Hausmann,' Yuri said. Behind the secretary the office was dark, the desks cleared, the type-writers hooded.

'He's busy.' The secretary made to shut the door.

Yuri jammed his foot against the door and pushed. The secretary pushed back. Yuri waited with braced hands till the man's effort was expended, then threw all his weight at the door. The door swung open. The secretary staggered backwards. Yuri rushed in.

The secretary recovered his balance, fumbled in a bulging pocket.

Yuri chopped him on the right arm, drove his palm with the

185

fingers folded into the secretary's face. Yuri hit him hard in the solar plexus, chopped down viciously on the exposed neck. The secretary's legs splayed out like a rubber giraffe's. Yuri caught him as he fell, reached into his pocket and took out a German Luger, then lowered him to the floor.

The office he was in had three doors leading off it. Yuri tried the furthest. It opened on to a corridor with more doors, a small kitchen and a barred emergency exit at the end. The first door on the right was a bathroom. Yuri went back to the main office. From behind the third door on his left a voice called, 'Werner, who is it?'

'Me,' Yuri said and flung open the door.

Hausmann was crouched frog-like behind a large, leather-topped desk. Opposite him the American girl sat, gagged and bound to a chair. Yuri saw Hausmann move sideways, pulling at a desk drawer. Yuri leapt on to the desk and kicked Hausmann in the face.

Hausmann kept going sideways. His chair tilted. He sprawled across the floor.

Yuri jumped off the desk, pulled open the drawer and took out the gun Hausmann had been reaching for. He covered Hausmann with it. 'On your feet,' he snapped. 'Untie the girl.'

Hausmann stared up at him, uncomprehending. His glasses were broken, and there was the beginning of a huge weal along his jaw and neck. Blood trickled out of the corner of his mouth. Hausmann pressed a hand to it and stared disbelievingly at the red wetness.

Hausmann muttered, 'Who are you? You don't . . . You're not the − ' He shambled towards the girl and stood behind her, his fingers fumbling with the gag. Above the gag, the girl's eyes were green.

Hausmann removed the gag. The girl rubbed her mouth against her shoulder and said, 'Whoever you are, thanks.'

'You're welcome.'

Hausmann freed the girl's wrists. 'Thanks again,' she said,

rubbing her hands together and standing up. 'Now we'd better get out of here. He's expecting company.'

'In a moment,' Yuri said. He went up to Hausmann and grabbed him by the jacket lapels. He pressed the gun against Hausmann's left nostril. He said, 'Mr Hausmann, I have some questions and not a lot of time. Now tell me, who ordered Munich? On whose orders did Skorpion pay $10,000 to Raspe?'

Hausmann looked at him, terrified. 'I don't know anything.'

Yuri took the pistol away from Hausmann's nostril and hit him across the face with it, turning his wrist so that the gun sight gouged flesh. 'Who had Skorpion pay Raspe? Who had Skorpion pay Chernov?' A white stripe appeared on Hausmann's face, filling rapidly with blood.

'Who are you?' Hausmann asked.

Yuri drew the gun back. 'Raspe. Chernov. Barynin. Skorpion. The Izgoi. Tell me about them.'

'I don't know what you're talking of.'

Yuri hit him again. Blood spurted on to his hand. 'Tell me about Rudolf Barynin,' he said. Hausmann's legs were going. He was beginning to slump against Yuri. 'Tell me about the Izgoi? Tell me what they're planning in April? Tell me what's happening on the thirtieth?'

Hausmann shook his head.

Yuri held him at arm's length and clubbed him in the chest. 'Talk, damn you, or I'll break every bone in your body.'

Hausmann swayed. 'No,' he gasped. 'It is too much. I know nothing.'

Yuri hit him again and let him stagger against the wall. Pocketing the gun he went after him and punched him three times.

An arm grabbed his. The American girl cried, 'Stop it, for Chrissake, before you kill him!'

She was right. But he had to get the information. He yanked Hausmann up and held his fist in front of his face. 'I'm going to break your nose,' he said. 'And then shatter what

187

teeth you have left. After that I'll start on your fingers, one by one.'

From behind him the girl said, 'If you want to find out about Skorpion, get the keys to his safe.' She came and stood beside him.

'Check his pockets,' Yuri said. Hausmann wriggled feebly. The girl took a bunch of keys from his pocket and walked over to the safe.

'No,' Hausmann gasped. 'Please, no!'

Yuri hit him.

The girl opened the safe. Inside was an open steel drawer with about a dozen files. She selected three. 'I think I've got what you want.'

'For God's sake,' Hausmann gasped. 'You don't know what you're doing!'

The door burst open. Two men stood there with Colt Detective Specials in their hands. Yuri recognized one of the men. Sam Costa, a CIA heavy out of Frankfurt. 'Freeze, buster,' Costa said.

The girl flung the tray of files at them.

Yuri fired. The shot flew high. The men ducked back into the main office, shutting the door. Yuri emptied Hausmann's gun at it.

There was another door leading from Hausmann's office to the corridor. Beckoning to the girl to pick up the files, Yuri opened it. The corridor was empty. He threw the empty Luger into the room and they rushed into the corridor. Yuri pointed to the emergency exit, grabbed a fire extinguisher from the wall and jammed it against the lock of Hausmann's door. They ran down the corridor to the emergency exit secured by a metal bar. The girl pushed the bar and swung the door open.

'Wait,' Yuri shouted.

It was too late. A man stood in the open doorway, gun in hand. As the girl tried to swerve round him, he grabbed her.

Yuri ran up to them. The man turned, undecided whether

to take Yuri, the girl or the files. Yuri hit him in the throat, then on the temple. The man fell. He took the girl's hand and raced down the side of the building.

'What now?' she panted.

'The hotel.'

They'd emerged on a different side of the building, which now stood between them and the car park. Ahead of them was the junction where the two Vaduz streets met and joined a third leading out of Vaduz. They sprinted along the side of the building to the junction. A policeman with a whistle was on traffic duty. Ignoring his irritated bleating they darted between the vehicles and across the road.

They raced across the far pavement, past an old hotel and a row of shops. Between the shops and their hotel was the tiny ramp of the hotel car park.

'You have a car?' she asked.

'No. You?'

'The white Mercedes 190.'

They ran into the hotel. The girl took an envelope from her handbag and counted out two hundred dollars. 'Rooms seven and — '

'Eleven.' He took the files from the girl.

She left the money with the receptionist and they ran up the stairs.

'I'll come down to your room,' Yuri said as he left her at the second landing. 'In two minutes.'

He raced into his room, flung clothes, toilet articles and the files into his grip and was back down the corridor in under sixty seconds. The girl was waiting for him just inside her door. He picked up one of her cases and they ran down the stairs again and out through the rear entrance. They hurried past kitchens and head-high metal rubbish bins. The girl sprinted ahead and unlocked the Mercedes. They got in.

The girl accelerated down the ramp, stopped at the street. Across the road, the three men and Hausmann's secretary were standing outside the office looking in all directions. One of them spotted the white Mercedes and pointed. They ran down the steps and climbed into a red BMW sedan with German plates.

The girl turned right into the one-way system and drove out of Vaduz.

'Straight ahead is Austria,' she said. 'If I go left we head back to Zurich.'

Yuri was looking back. The BMW had to turn left out of the car park and follow the one-way system all the way round. 'Try Austria,' Yuri said. 'And if you hurry we'll lose them.'

CHAPTER TWENTY-NINE

Feldkirch had wide, curving streets thick with traffic, buildings with steep, triangular roofs and houses with exposed timbers. They passed an ornate tower whose clock face had Roman numerals painted in gold.

Allison looked at her rescuer out of the corner of her eye. A tall man whose height made him look almost bony, with wide, flat shoulders like paving stones. An unremarkable dresser. His grey, lightweight suit, pale-blue, striped shirt and narrow tie could have been bought in any department store. His shoes were black lace-ups with rubber soles. He wore a cheap digital watch. His pockets bulged with guns. Her warrior, Allison thought, her saviour. But why had he barged into Hausmann's office?

He was obviously some kind of policeman. But who did he work for? His English had a strong European accent and his German was fluent. A Swiss or German cop? No, not Swiss. A Swiss policeman would have summoned reinforcements by now. So German. What was the interest of the German police in Skorpion, the Izgoi, Barynin and the men he'd said had been paid by Skorpion, Raspe and Chernov? Time to get to know each other, Allison thought. She looked directly at him. 'My name's Allison Maynard. Who are you?'

Yuri started. His assumption that the girl was CIA and Hausmann a CIA conduit was wrong. Hausmann had grabbed the girl and kept her bound and gagged in his office till the CIA had come to collect her. He said, 'My name is Orlov. What business did you have with Hausmann?'

'I work for the United States Treasury.' He was owed an explanation, Allison thought. 'We're interested in why Hausmann is buying sovereign, cross-defaulted loans through Skorpion SA.' She eyed him carefully. Skorpion was why *he* had come to see Hausmann.

'What is the US Treasury's interest in sovereign — what you said?'

'Cross-defaulted loans.' Allison explained what they were.

'And you came all the way here to talk about that?'

Allison gave him Drewett's Domesday scenario. A loan was defaulted and all a country's cross-defaulted loans were called in. The country having difficulty meeting the repayments on even one loan, declares a moratorium on all its loans, thus forcing the lending banks to treat all their loans to that country as bad debts; which in turn reduces the amount of assets the banks have and the amount of money they can lend and forces them to cut back on lending and to call in existing loans. At the same time, the banks' shareholders, worried by the depletion of the banks' assets begin to sell their shares, forcing down share prices. Depositors fearing the banks might go under, begin withdrawing their money, forcing the banks to lend less and call in more loans, causing more shares to be sold, more deposits to be withdrawn. Soon, Allison said, everyone was on a downward spiral to bankruptcy. 'First it's the banks. Then it's industry and commerce. Before long we are facing the biggest financial crisis the world has ever seen and the collapse of our entire economy.'

If America went, Russia went, too, Yuri figured. 'And Skorpion can do all this?'

191

'Technically, yes.'

The Izgoi plans were bigger and wider-reaching than he had imagined. He would have to contact Karelin. 'Why did Hausmann attack you?' he asked.

'He wanted me to stay till those people came. They wanted to question me.'

Yuri looked at her closely. She was telling the truth. 'Those men were CIA,' he said.

'CIA? What do you mean CIA?'

Yuri thought her puzzlement was genuine. 'The first man who came into Hausmann's office, the bronzed one with the moustache and the gun was Sam Costa. He's a CIA minder who works out of Frankfurt.'

'I don't believe it. I'm an American. I work for a government agency. I'm − How do you know this man, Costa?'

'That's part of my job. If you want to check on Costa, call your representatives in Frankfurt.'

'What were you doing in Hausmann's office?'

'We too are interested in Skorpion,' Yuri said. The financial plans of the Izgoi had put a new aspect on everything. He would have to work with the girl. He needed her financial expertise to understand the files, and warn the Americans about the Izgoi. 'Skorpion financed the recent attempt to bomb Munich station.'

The attempt had merited two columns in the *Washinton Post*. Allison remembered reading that the bombs had been timed to go off at the height of the rush hour. She winced in horror. Hausmann had arranged that and she'd thought he was nothing more than an elderly, respectable lawyer.

'Raspe and Chernov were both involved in that bombing,' Yuri said. 'They were paid by Skorpion.'

Hausmann had probably arranged the killing of Paul Weiler, too. 'And what is the connection between Skorpion, the Izgoi and Barynin?'

'The Izgoi are the people behind Skorpion. Rudolf Barynin was a Grand Master of the Izgoi.'

192

'The Barynin who . . .' So that was the link between Skorpion and Barynin! 'Tell me about this Izgoi,' Allison said.

They were approaching a fork in the road. He said, 'Go left and follow the signs to Konstanz.'

'Why?'

'We're going to Germany. That'll give your CIA friends three countries to search instead of two.'

'They're not my friends,' Allison said. She turned left.

The BMW streaked down the autoroute, swaying slightly as it reached one hundred and twenty miles an hour. The roar of the engine was muted by the rush of wind. Outside Vaduz the road had divided, left to Switzerland, straight ahead for Austria. Knowing the girl had come from Zurich, Costa had opted for Switzerland. Now he said, 'Fuck it. They must have gone to Austria.'

The driver checked his mirror, braked and spun the car round in a tyre-shredding handbrake turn.

'Fucking brilliant,' Costa said. 'All we fucking need now is to be slammed for reckless driving.'

They raced back to Vaduz.

They stopped outside the hotel and the driver tooted the car's horn twice. The man who had tried to stop Allison and Yuri outside Hausmann's left some money on a café table and ran to the car.

'The woman was Allison Maynard, all right,' he said as he got in.

'And the man?'

'A Russian called Yuri Orlov. Maynard paid both their bills, and didn't stop to collect her change.'

'You're sure he was Russian?'

'Sure. I checked his registration.'

They drove into the parking lot. Costa walked to the Post Office and made a call to Frankfurt. He told Hersh everything.

CHAPTER THIRTY

They skirted hills covered with vineyards and drove through towns with castles and defence walls and tight-set old houses that pressed close to the lake. 'The Izgoi,' Yuri said, 'are an ancient Russian secret society.' He summarized Dmitrev's account of the Izgoi for her and told her how Zakhar Shumayev-Barynin had founded a branch of the Izgoi in America, how Rudolf Barynin had involved himself in Germany and Russia and become involved in German and Russian politics.

'A secret society,' Allison said. 'Planning something mysterious, infiltrating its members into high places — that's incredible.' She had another thought. 'If they're a secret society how do you know they exist?'

'We found a letter Chernov had written. It was signed with the mark of the Izgoi, a curiously drawn letter M — '

'Enclosing the letters OR and US?' She felt the excitement bubble within her. It was difficult to concentrate on the road.

'How do you know?' His tone was both curious and suspicious.

'I have seen that sign in America too. It is the sign of a college fraternity called Ormus.'

'Ormus converted the early Izgoi to Christianity,' Yuri said. 'Tell me what you found in America.'

Allison told him about Wentworth, Berle and Clairvaux.

Yuri listened in a stunned silence. 'So Stalin did not eradicate the Izgoi,' he muttered, almost to himself. 'The seed of Zakhar Shumayev-Barynin has flourished. The Izgoi are in America and in Russia. They have infiltrated the administration, the KGB and the CIA.' He raised his voice. 'That explains why Costa was sent after you.'

'You mean Costa is Izgoi?'

'That's possible. What's certain is that the people in the CIA behind Costa are.'

'You don't really mean . . .' Allison stopped. Of course he did mean it and she believed it. The Izgoi existed. They were behind Skorpion. They had infiltrated their people into high positions in America and Russia. 'How do you know so much about Russia?'

'I'm Russian.'

Allison fought to keep her hands steady on the wheel. In a strained voice she said, 'I suppose the next thing you'll be telling me is that you work for the KGB.'

'I do,' Yuri said.

'Jesus H. Christ!'

They were driving through a town with medieval towers and gates and a castle overlooking a ravine. Yuri said, 'Turn around and drive back to the lake. Stop at the last hotel we passed.'

'Why?'

'To eat and read the files.'

Allison stopped the car in the middle of the street and turned to look at him. 'Listen, we can't go on like this. You're Russian and I'm American and — '

'Suit yourself.' He grinned at her. It was a nice grin and made him look a lot younger. 'But if you don't work with me, you'll never know what's in those files.'

It was lunch time in Germany and breakfast time in Washington. Brad Drewett met CIA Director William Timmins at a Hot Shoppe on Connecticut Avenue. Timmins' aerial-festooned black CIA Ford was parked outside. Inside, Timmins was eating ham and eggs, hash browns and coffee. 'You're a goddam stupid sonofabitch,' he said.

Drewett ordered coffee.

Timmins took another mouthful of egg. 'I warned you to lay off Barynin's. Lay off means keep off, do not touch, do not

195

get involved. And what do you do? You send that cookie, Allison Maynard, to Switzerland.'

Drewett sipped his coffee. 'Allison Maynard is in Switzerland conducting an investigation for the FAA. What she is doing in Switzerland is nothing to do with the CIA.'

'Like hell it isn't! I was woken up at five o'clock this morning and told that Allison Maynard had raided the office of a Swiss lawyer and removed certain documents including the details of certain clandestine payments to a number of CIA agents.'

'Raided the office of a Swiss lawyer! Hang on, Bill! You're not talking of Dirty Harry here, you're talking about Allison Maynard. She's a woman, remember, a cookie.'

'Your Dirty Harriet,' Timmins continued, 'was accompanied by a KGB agent positively identified as Yuri Orlov, a Political Intelligence officer working out of Munich under journalist cover.'

'No! That's impossible!'

'They stayed at the same hotel in Vaduz and Allison Maynard paid both their bills. That fact is corroborated not only by our people, but by hotel registers and independent witnesses.'

'Allison Maynard's no Russian agent,' Drewett said. 'It's a frame-up.'

'It's no frame-up. The facts are beyond dispute. The lawyer's name was Gerdt Hausmann. He contacted our people immediately. Like it or not, believe it or not, Allison Maynard is a Russian spy.'

'I won't belive it,' Drewett cried. 'Allison Maynard is not some screwed up radical. She is — goddam it, she's an accountant. When did you hear of an accountant working for the Russians?'

'At five o'clock this morning,' Timmins said.

'Bill, we've known each other twenty years! We've trained together and worked together. And I swear I'm not bull-shitting you. Allison Maynard's trip to Switzerland was something we both planned. She went because we both felt it was the only way to investigate Barynin's without getting involved in whatever the CIA were doing.'

'Looks like she screwed you, Brad.'

'I've worked with Allison three years. I persuaded her to join the FAA. She's no spy.' Drewett pushed away his coffee, angrily.

Timmins sighed. 'It's always difficult to believe that someone you work with, someone you personally selected, works for the other side. But it happens. Money, love, sex, we know all the reasons. We've both seen it happen before.'

'Allison Maynard is not a spy,' Drewett insisted, fiercely. 'Two weeks ago she exposed a KGB plot to take control of an American producer of strategic software.'

'That may have been arranged by the KGB to give her credibility.'

'That's nonsense!' Drewett said, angrily. 'I worked with Allison on that case. It wasn't a set-up. And she's been twice positively vetted by the FBI. There's not been the slightest trace of political involvement. Christ! She's not even a registered voter!'

Timmins said, 'That isn't the point, Brad. The point is that she has stolen vital information and is working with the Russkis. That information could expose a lot of agents. We could lose men and we could lose networks.' He paused and looked directly at Drewett. 'Before I left to come here, I approved a termination order. She's got to be stopped, Brad. That's definite and that's final.' Timmins left some money on the table. 'Best get her back, Brad. Have her contact any American Embassy in Europe and offer to return to Washington. If she does that the termination order will be cancelled.'

'A clear case of infatuation,' Alan Hersh was saying. The person at the other end of the line was Karl Augustin, Chief Liaison Officer of the German BND. 'It is not the kind of thing we usually concern ourselves with, but in this case, the woman is a senior Treasury employee and privy to certain highly sensitive economic information.'

'And you want us to find and collect her for you?'

'Simply find her. It may be best if one of our counsellors were to talk to her and persuade her to return voluntarily to the United States.'

'The name is Maynard, first name Allison?'

'Yes. And we believe they could be staying somewhere within a hundred-mile radius of Vaduz.'

'That's a lot of hotels,' Augustin said. 'By the time we get a trace they would have moved on.'

'Why don't you talk to the telecommunications people?' Hersh suggested. 'Check for any calls to the Soviet Union. I wouldn't imagine many people from around there call Moscow.' Hersh finished the call and dialled the number of the Liaison Section of Austrian Intelligence.

CHAPTER THIRTY-ONE

They got adjoining rooms, had sandwiches and coffee sent up and went through the files. There were two bulky folders containing accounts, letters and other documents, a third containing letters from one Casimir Heilbron setting out details of his escape from Germany and life on an *estancia* outside Buenos Aires. The file had a different reference from the other two folders and obviously had been taken by mistake. They concentrated on the folders.

The information in them was complex and detailed. Allison and Yuri went through them very slowly, Allison working through the figures, Yuri helping with the German, both of them scribbling laborious notes. It was after seven o'clock when they finished.

Skorpion had been incorporated in 1920. It had owned all the Barynin banks, and still controlled Barynin New York through a charitable foundation in Geneva. Its shares were bearer shares, which, Allison explained, meant that the names of the owners were never registered, and whoever physically possessed the shares was deemed to be the rightful owner.

Up to 1937, Skorpion had merely received and invested its profits from the Barynin banks. In 1937, however, it had begun to trade actively. The accounts for that year showed millions of dollars spent and lost. Thereafter it had devoted itself to charitable activities. The accounts for the next twenty years showed substantial payments to the Barynin Foundation and to unidentified educational charities and child welfare organizations. Judging from the profits and losses on exchange, however, Allison deduced that the charities had been situated in America, Germany and Russia.

In January 1945, Barynin Berlin had made a substantial transfer of funds to Skorpion, followed by two similar transfers in February and March. In September that year, following the formal closure of Barynin Berlin, Skorpion had bought itself the Bank Europe-Sud America in Buenos Aires.

Thereafter Skorpion had remained virtually dormant, accumulating profits from its Argentinian and American banks, and distributing largesse among its charities. Then in 1963, it had bought forty per cent of the Handel Kreditbank.

The company had continued to accumulate profits until three years ago, when it had again begun to trade actively, lending moneys to various unidentified companies and borrowing heavily from Baur Industrie, Barynin's and Handel.

There was a list of the last three months' receipts and payments in the files. Most of the payments were marked as loans, and the recipients were private companies located in tax havens. There were other payments identified only by account numbers and without any indication of their purpose. There were also two names, Aug. Weinrich and Niebury.

The payment to Niebury had been $75,000 and had been made at the beginning of February. That to Weinrich, $100,000 at the end of March.

'Why August if the payment was made in March?' Allison mused. 'Would that be a repayment date, or — '

'It's a name,' Yuri said.

Allison looked at him, puzzled.

'Not August as in month, but August as in August Weinrich.' He told Allison that August Weinrich was the West German Minister of Defence.

'And Weinrich is — he's been — in any case he's on their side.'

'Right. And Niebury?'

They both looked at each other, frowning while they thought, then shook their heads in unison. 'It could be a place,' Yuri said.

Allison went over the accounts again. There were no more names. 'If Skorpion is financing terrorism,' she said, 'then channelling funds through tax haven subsidiaries is as good a way as any to do it. But these sums of money are enormous.' She made a rapid calculation. 'Excluding the loans, they've spent about eight million dollars in the last three months. This isn't terrorism. It's war.'

A war that could begin in the third week of April, next week. Yuri summarized what he knew. A secret organization had for centuries attempted to control Russia. It had set up a branch in America, and had supporters in both Germanies. Its former leader, Rudolf Barynin, had been concerned with the politics and finance of Russia and Germany. It was thought that the Izgoi had been eliminated by Stalin, but that was not so. The Izgoi had emerged in Munich. Their members were in positions of influence everywhere. Their plans involved a major event or events next week, with everything culminating on the thirtieth of April. At the same time, the Izgoi had, through secret subsidiaries, bought a considerable sum of sovereign loans, which they could use to

200

shatter the banking and economic systems of the West. That too, presumably, would happen by the thirtieth.

What he had to do was obvious. He had to find the leaders of the Izgoi and stop them. And to find them he would not only have to go after terrorists and the KGB, he would have to look among businessmen and bankers; he would need the help of an organization with financial knowledge and skills, one which was based in America. He asked Allison, 'Can your organization stop the Izgoi using the sovereign loans?'

'If we could find out who they are and what they are doing, yes.'

'We should work together to stop the Izgoi,' Yuri said. 'The Izgoi is working against both our countries.'

She said, 'I'll need to talk to Brad Drewett. He's my Director.'

'Can you trust him? Can you be sure he is not Izgoi?'

'I trust Brad completely.'

Her statement was one of fact, not emotion. Yuri decided to accept her judgement. He said, 'You'd better talk to your Director.'

Allison half smiled. 'If I am going to do that, I'll need to know the whole story. I'll need to know who you are and what you are doing and everything you know about the Izgoi.'

Yuri didn't like that, but saw the sense of it. 'I am a KGB officer,' he began. 'I work for a special unit which keeps a check on the KGB itself. Two weeks ago, a former contact saw me in Frankfurt. He told me . . .'

When Yuri had finished, Allison thought, that was some story. She looked at his face with its healing scratches and fresh bruises. Yes, she could believe Yuri Orlov had done all those things, and she found a strange excitement in the fact. Watch it, she told herself. Your more emancipated women friends wouldn't approve and remember he's Russian. 'I guess I'd better go and call Brad,' she said.

'You also had better tell me everything.' He gave her

another of those grins. 'I've also got to make a call.'

Allison hesitated momentarily and did. When she'd finished she went to her room and called Brad.

'Alli, I'm so glad you called. Where are you? The first thing I want you to do, is to get to an Embassy and have them get you on the first flight back to Washington.'

Why an Embassy, Allison wondered. She could get a flight just as easily herself. 'I can't leave just yet,' she said. 'There's a lot happening here. Barynin's and the sovereign loans are part of something much, much bigger. They're linked to the murder of the NATO commander a few weeks ago, and the bombing incident in Munich.'

'Allison, I want you to call your nearest Embassy, tell them where you are and arrange for them to fly you back.'

Drewett hadn't even listened to what she'd said. 'I can't do that, Brad. I need to stay here and I need some help. How much, you can decide once you've heard what I've got to tell you.'

'Fine. Get back to Washington and I'll fix you up with all the help you need.'

'I haven't the time for that. Whatever's going to happen will happen here in Europe in the next two weeks. And it could be catastrophic, Brad. It could even be war.'

'All the more reason for you to get back here as soon as you can.'

'Why can't we talk now? Why do you want me back in Washington?'

There was a moment's silence while Drewett chose his words. 'Allison, the CIA have orders to get you back. They believe you're working for the Russians.'

'That's crazy! I may be working with a Russian, but that's because it's necessary. The CIA are not to be trusted, Brad. They have been infiltrated.'

'The CIA say that you and a KGB agent raided a lawyer's office this morning and removed some files containing highly secret information.'

'That's disinformation, Brad.' Quickly, she told him what had happened at Hausmann's.

'And what was Orlov doing in Hausmann's office?'

'The Russians are also investigating Skorpion and the people behind Skorpion, a group called the Izgoi. The Izgoi have infiltrated their people into important positions in Russia. And, I think, in America.'

'You have proof of this?'

'No. But I've got some damned good evidence.'

After a moment's silence, Drewett said, 'Allison, come back.'

'No.'

'If you don't, the CIA have orders to terminate you.'

'And you want me to walk into an Embassy . . .' The realization stunned her. She couldn't speak.

'Don't worry, Alli. I'll speak to the Ambassador and arrange for you to be in his care all the way. I'll – '

Brad! The CIA! She didn't know whom to believe or trust. In a small voice, she said, 'Goodbye Brad. I'll call you another time. And I'll send a message to your mailbox.' She put the phone down. What on earth was she to do?

Yuri spoke to Karelin. 'Have you any news?'

'Nothing at all.'

Which meant it wasn't safe for him to tell Karelin what had happened. He read off his telephone number backwards.

'I'll have to change that code,' Karelin said. 'You'll have an alternative by noon tomorrow.'

Which meant that Karelin would arrange a contact through another source, probably Otto. 'Or earlier. I'll need a full code.'

'I'll fix that.'

So Yuri's contact would be high enough for Yuri to tell him everything he knew. Yuri put the phone down. He wished he could have asked how Stefan and Galina were.

Allison came in with sagging shoulders and lowered head. She told Yuri of her conversation with Drewett.

'You were right to refuse to go back,' he said, and saw relief in her eyes at his confirmation. He wouldn't abandon her, Yuri thought and told himself it was because of his ingrained loyalty to agents. But what use was she if she couldn't involve her department or her government? And if the CIA was after her wouldn't she be more a liability than an asset? Immaterial, Yuri told himself. He couldn't allow her to be killed. Besides, he didn't have the faintest idea about finance and needed her to talk to Weinrich. 'We'll work together,' he said.

She looked pensive. 'But all the CIA cannot be Izgoi.'

'If they have a termination order on you, the ones who matter are.'

'So what do I do? I can't go back and I'm not sure if we should — '

'Right now,' Yuri said, 'I need a financial expert and you have nowhere to go. Let's go down and have dinner and decide how we start finding the Izgoi.'

CHAPTER THIRTY-TWO

They had dinner in the hotel restaurant. Yuri got them a secluded table and ordered drinks. Scotch and soda for himself and gin and tonic for her. Allison forced herself to stop thinking about the weird illogic of her situation and concentrate on the Izgoi. After all, that was why he'd wanted her to stay with him, wasn't it? Because she was useful. 'What do the Izgoi want?' she asked.

'Originally, control of Russia. Now, I think their plans are more ambitious. They're seeking to influence both Russia and America.'

'And Germany?'

'Germany, too. I wish I knew what was happening.

Terrorism and sovereign loans don't fit or make sense. Yet, they must.'

The waiter brought their food, grilled fish from the lake and Weissherbst, a dry, slightly pinkish local wine he'd suggested she try.

Yuri said, 'It all comes down to what exactly Skorpion is doing now, and who owns it?'

'Those charities must be connected to the owners?'

'Most definitely. But we don't know who they are.'

'And the tax haven companies, the loans and why the activity of 1937 is repeating itself now.'

'1937 was a significant year for the Izgoi,' Yuri said. 'I don't know why.' He frowned. 'We could speculate forever.'

'We only have those names, Weinrich and Niebury.'

'So we'll start by seeing Weinrich.'

Allison raised her glass. 'To our partnership and détente!' The wine was light and smooth. Good choice.

'To détente!' He touched his glass to hers.

Allison asked how he was so familiar with Germany.

Because he'd lived and worked there, he said. Until Munich happened, he'd been expected to take over the German desk.

Allison was surprised at his frankness. She'd expected a KGB officer to be less direct. She asked him what he'd done in Germany, and he told her he'd been a Political Intelligence Officer, a gatherer of information from publications and contacts. He asked Allison about her work at the FAA and Allison found herself telling him about her work, her family, her married former lover, and her more recent unmarried accountant. She looked at the photograph he showed her of a strong-faced blonde woman and a little boy, telling herself that it was not a twinge of disappointment she felt at the fact he was married. The boy had his father's long lashes and his mother's hair. 'That was taken last year,' Yuri said. 'When Stefan was two. He's nearly three now, much taller and not so chubby.' She like the way his face softened when he looked at the picture and the pride in his voice when he spoke about his son.

The evening passed quickly. The events of the day began to feel comfortably distant. A waiter approached and said, 'Herr Orlov, there is someone in the lobby who wishes to speak with you.'

They both felt the same, sudden shock. Instinctively, Allison felt herself reaching for his hand. Yuri said to the waiter, 'Wait for me by the door and show me the person.'

He turned to Allison. 'It may be one of my people. On the other hand, it may not. Reach your hand out under the table and rest it on my knee.' She looked at him, puzzled, but did as he asked. 'I'm going to give you a gun,' Yuri said.

'I know nothing about guns.' Their hands brushed, then Allison felt the cold, hard metal of the weapon.

'Listen carefully. On the left hand side of the gun is the word "Gesichert". Below that is a thumb piece. Before you use the gun, push this lever forward and up. Then hold the butt with both hands, point and pull the trigger.'

'Yuri, I can't shoot a person.'

'Don't worry. You won't hit them. You'll only frighten them.'

'Where will you be?'

'I'll be in the lobby talking to whoever is waiting to see me. Now take the gun and put it into your handbag. Then go up to your room, lock the door, release the safety on the gun and wait there till I come for you. Do not let anyone in. If someone tries to force his way in, shoot at the door.'

He pressed the gun into her hand.

'I'm not sure — '

'Don't worry. You'll be fine.'

'Will you be all right?'

'Sure. Now go.'

Allison slipped the gun into her handbag and went.

The waiter showed Yuri a man seated in a low chair by the reception counter. In his early thirties, the man was short and thick-set with a downy patch of light-brown hair. He carried a dark-blue gaberdine topcoat over one arm and wore a blue-striped, double-breasted suit. He had a professional's air of resolute patience.

Yuri studied the topcoat and the line of the suit for suspicious bulges. There were none he could see. Opening his own jacket so that the SIG was easily available, Yuri pushed through the doors into the lobby.

The man's gaze swivelled, then his head. He was a pro all right. He rose easily to his feet. He had a policeman's level, impassive stare. 'Captain Orlov?'

'Who're you?'

'My name is Gunther Roth.' He quoted the phone number Yuri had given Karelin.

'I was told noon tomorrow. How did you get here so quickly?'

'I was nearby.' He looked round the wood-panelled, low-ceilinged lobby with its dusty prints and plaques from Touring Clubs. Having made sure they were unobserved he slipped Yuri a matchbox. 'Your codes and phone numbers.' He held up a piece of paper. 'Can you remember those?'

Yuri relaxed. That was typical Karelin procedure, half the information written, half memorized. He studied the numbers. 'I've got them.'

Roth carefully crumpled the paper and slipped it into his pocket. 'You ask us for any help you require. Otto is a very busy person. You should not therefore bother him unnecessarily. All routine material should be channelled through me. Now you have something to tell me?'

'Sure. Let's take a walk.' Outside, the lake was a vast expanse of black, spotted with the lights of boats. They went through the hotel's parking lot across the road and along an empty pier where a darkened steamer was moored. Yuri told Roth everything that had happened since he'd arrived in Vaduz and what he proposed to do.

'I don't know about the girl,' Roth said. 'I'll have to check with Otto.'

'She's necessary.' Yuri's tone was suddenly terse. He caught a sudden wariness in Roth's glance.

'She's also American.'

'And the only one with the right background and experience to talk to Weinrich.'

'You'll still need authorization from Otto.'

'We only have days,' Yuri said. 'It is important we see Weinrich as soon as possible.'

'I know. Call me when you get to Bonn.' He turned and led the way back to the hotel.

After Roth left, Yuri spoke with the receptionist, then went upstairs and knocked on Allison's door. 'It's me, Yuri.'

She came to the door, gun in hand. Her face was pale and her breathing tremulous. Behind her the computer screen glowed. 'Oh God! Am I glad to see you! I've never been so scared before.' Abruptly she threw her arms around his neck and hugged him.

Yuri liked the feel of her body against his. He put his arms around her and said, 'It's OK. The man was my contact.' Then he felt the cold steel of the gun at the back of his neck, and thought he could just about get his head blown off if she got too grateful. 'Put your arms down slowly,' he whispered, 'stand back and put that gun very gently on the bed.'

'Oh shit!' Allison said. She did as she was told. 'Did I do it right?'

'That was great. Now come back and hug me again.'

CHAPTER THIRTY-THREE

There were no hugs a second time around. Instead she walked over to the computer. 'I managed to log on to a German financial data base,' she said. 'I've got us some information on Baur Industrie.'

Allison sat and tapped the keyboard of the computer. 'Baur Industrie was founded by Albert Baur, a chemical engineer with IG Farben who had developed certain industrial processes to do with plastics. In 1926, Baur broke away from Farben and, supported by Barynin Berlin, set up on his own. By 1930, Baur Industrie became one of the most profitable chemical companies in Germany, and by 1935, through amalgamation, acquisition and Barynin finance, one of Germany's largest.

'Like every other German company, Baur's was severely damaged by the war, but by the 1950s it was again large, successful and prosperous. In the mid-1960s Baur began to diversify into defence, banking, electronics and high technology and this was accelerated after 1969 when Albert Baur died and management of the company had passed to his son-in-law, Kaspar Baur.'

'How come he had a son-in-law named Baur?'

'It is a German business tradition. When an important industrialist does not have any sons to succeed him, then the son-in-law takes on the family name.'

'Strange tradition.'

'A very practical one. A certain amount of good will usually attaches to a firm's name, and it would be most disconcerting to deal with Baur's one day and Schmidt's the next.'

'Didn't Albert Baur have any sons?'

'Yes. But Michael Baur seems to have been nothing more

than a figurehead. He played little part in the company's affairs, and the company's reorganization seems to have been carried out by Albert and Kaspar. Michael Baur was killed in a car crash in 1972.'

Allison tapped the keyboard. The characters on the screen scrolled upwards. Yuri stared at twenty rows of figures. 'Baur's last published accounts,' Allison said. 'The only interesting thing about them is the amount of Baur's loans to Skorpion, and the fact that it has not only subscribed hugely to the recent $330 million loan to East Germany but sold most of its European and American investments and re-invested the proceeds in East Bloc paper.'

'Very strange.'

'Especially when right now Baur's appears to be stretched to the limit. If Skorpion goes under, it could pull down the whole of Baur Industrie.'

'Everything comes back to Skorpion,' Yuri said. He picked up the pillows from the spare bed and placed them lengthwise on Allison's bed.

'What are you doing?'

'Making a dummy.'

'Why?'

'I've got us a third room.'

'Us? Aren't you reading too much into a friendly hug, Captain Orlov? Knights did not always bed the damsels they rescued.'

'That was because by the time they got their armour off it was morning.' He drew the covers back, pulled at the pillows and stood back studying his efforts. He said, 'There are people who have other designs on your body.'

'What do you mean?'

'The CIA are a very efficient organization. There's a good chance they'll find us here.'

Allison felt a spasm of panic. 'So what's the point of taking another room? Let's get out of here.' Her voice was shrill.

'It's late and most hotels will be shut.' Yuri adjusted the pillows and asked Allison to turn off the lights.

She did so and asked, 'What are you going to do?'

Yuri looked at the pillows in the light thrown from the computer screen. 'I want to see who they send after you. Also, I want to send a message to Langley.'

'Why not call them. The operator will get the number for you.'

Yuri adjusted the pillows till he was satisfied they looked like the figure of someone asleep. 'Pity we couldn't have a looped taped recording of someone snoring,' he said.

'I don't snore.'

'Snorers are always the last to know.' He turned on the lights. 'I'm going back to my room. I'll call for you in ten minutes. Then we'll go upstairs.'

Allison stood uncertainly by the bed. 'Why don't we just leave?'

He gave her a small smile. 'Don't worry. It will be better this way.' He walked to the door.

'Better make it twenty minutes,' Allison called after him. 'A girl's got to look her best sharing a bedroom with a strange man.'

The room was on the third floor immediately beside the stairway that ran up one side of the hotel. It was identical to the rooms two floors below, with the same light, modern furniture finished with a dark, wood veneer to give an impression of age. There were twin beds, a shared bedside table, a telephone, a large wardrobe with thin, brass door handles, a desk, chair and small armchair covered in a roughened brown fleck. There was a picture window and a door leading to a balcony that overlooked the lake and the front of the hotel. Allison picked the bed furthest from the door.

Yuri was wearing a sports jacket over a warm-up suit and trainers. He went out on to the balcony and arranged two chairs. Then he came back and picked up a blanket and pillows.

Allison said, 'Look, there's no need to be such a gentleman. You can sleep on that bed.'

'Who's being a gentleman? I'm just getting ready for your friends.'

'You're sure they'll come?' Underneath the jacket, Allison saw he was wearing a gun.

'No. But if they do, I don't want them to feel unwelcome.' He leaned forward and kissed her lightly on the cheek. 'Now you get some sleep. You've had a long, hard day.'

Allison didn't know what made her do it, but she took his face in her hands and kissed him lightly on the mouth. 'Goodnight, Yuri,' she said. 'Thank you for taking such good care of me.'

'No problem. I'm looking after me too.' He pressed her to him briefly, patted her on the shoulder and went out on to the balcony. She heard the scrape of chairs and saw him spread out the blankets and pillows. Then he called to her to draw the curtain and turn off the light.

Bloody romantic!

His makeshift bed was all right to rest in but not to sleep. Yuri dozed fitfully, watching the lights die in the lake, wakened by the occasional blare of a car horn, and the roar of a racing exhaust. The breeze from the lake pulled at his blanket and his face felt cold. He smiled at the memory of Allison's lips against his. Her body when he'd hugged her had been lithe and strong and responsive. Much better to have . . .

He put such thoughts out of his mind. He had to be prepared for men who would kill both of them. Yuri waited. His back grew stiff. He stretched. He adjusted the chairs. The gun dug into his armpit. He dozed. His right foot grew numb. He pulled it out from under the blanket and massaged it. His neck and shoulders felt tense and stiff.

It was nearly three o'clock when they came, drifting quietly into the parking lot on dimmed lights. Two men got out, hats pulled down and coat collars turned up. Yuri stretched and flexed his arms and shoulders. The driver was staying with the car.

The men walked beneath the balcony to the front of the hotel. Yuri did three knee bends and three back stretches. He went quietly across the bedroom and slipped into the corridor.

The corridor was dark, the stairway to his right. The steps were cement, eight to a flight, zigzagging against the interior wall. At the end of each flight was a landing with heavy fire doors leading to a T-shaped corridor along which were the rooms. Yuri slipped between the first set of fire doors and stood on the landing.

He heard the hum of the elevator and the sliding of metal doors. He drew his gun. Moments later the fire door on the floor below him squeaked.

They were following standard procedure, he thought. The driver with the car, one man working the rooms, the other keeping watch outside. Yuri peered down the stairwell. In the faint light from the exterior window he could make out a shadow standing by the fire door on the floor below. He put a foot on the first stair.

The man was looking through the fire door along the corridor. Gradually allowing it to take his weight, Yuri placed a foot on the second stair. The third stair. Very gently, very lightly, he moved to the fourth stair. His breath wafted shallowly through his half-open mouth. Five. He could see the man very clearly now. The man had his hands in his pockets and was chewing gum.

Bracing himself with his left hand against the banister, Yuri took another step. He held his breath. He was so close now he was sure the man could hear him breathe. In one movement Yuri took the seventh step, reached forward and placed the barrel of the SIG against the man's neck. 'One move and you're dead.'

The man went still as a door post.

Yuri stepped on to the landing behind the man and wrapped his left arm around the man's neck, pressing it right against the gun barrel. He pulled the gun barrel away and smashed it down behind the man's ear. The man's knees buckled, his body became a dead weight. Yuri dragged him sideways and lowered him to the floor.

Yuri took the man's Colt Detective Special. Then he lifted up the man's right hand and dislocated two of the fingers. He pushed past the fire door into the corridor.

From behind the door of his room came the sound of two muffled coughs. Yuri took the key from his pocket and opened the door of Allison's room. The bathroom was to the right of the minute entrance lobby. He went in and waited.

Moments later he heard a scrabbling in the lock. The door opened and a figure came in, silent and fast, moving quickly past the open bathroom door. It stood at the end of the entrance way. There were two muffled coughs followed by a strong smell of cordite. Yuri came out of the bathroom and jabbed his gun into the man's kidneys. 'Better drop your gun,' he murmured. 'Unless you want to piss blood the rest of your short life.'

The man dropped the weapon on to the carpet. Yuri shoved him into the room and turned on the light. 'Go and sit in that armchair. Keep your hands where I can see them.'

The man did as he was told. There was an angry flush under his tan and a faint sheen of sweat on his cheeks.

Yuri said, 'You tried to kill me. By rights I should kill you. An eye for an eye and all that.'

Costa said, 'Don't be stupid. You know how it is. It's just a job. There's nothing personal to it. What have you done with Deke?'

'Put him to sleep. Don't expect too much from him. Even if he does wake soon, he won't be using a gun for a while.'

'So, what do you want from me?'

'Who put out the termination order?'

214

'You know I couldn't tell you that.'

Yuri pointed to the bed with its punctured and blackened sheets and pillows. 'Why her? She's American.'

'Because she's one of you.'

'But you don't kill every American who's a Russian agent. Why this one?'

'I don't know. I just follow orders.'

'Whose orders?'

'I can't tell you.' He raised his palms two inches off the chair. 'OK if I smoke?'

'Go ahead.' Costa was too much of a professional to try anything stupid. He reached into his jacket, brought out a pack of Marlboro and a lighter. He lit up.

'It's not your policy or ours to kill foreign agents. We use them, we drain them of all they know, we turn them. So why a termination order on this one?'

'I don't ask for reasons. I just do what I'm told.'

'When did you first know Maynard was a Russian agent? Think carefully, was it before or after Vaduz?'

Costa breathed twin streams of smoke. 'What difference does it make.'

'What were you sent to Vaduz for? Did you have orders to kill her then?'

'No. We were sent to Vaduz to collect her. The termination order came after you got away.'

'Why afterwards and not before?'

'I reckon it's because of the information you took.'

'If you had collected her from Hausmann's office, where would you have delivered her?'

'Frankfurt. Then Washington.'

'Were you supposed to give her a hard time, rough her up a bit, scare her?'

'Yeah. We were asked to soften her up.'

'Whose orders?' Yuri asked again.

Costa gave a small smile. 'Can't tell you. Sorry.'

'What do you think is in the files?'

'I wouldn't know.'

'Go on. Have a guess.'

'Vital information of some kind, I suppose. Military secrets, political secrets, something like that.'

'Would you like to see the files?'

Costa's eyes widened in surprise. 'Yeah. Sure.'

Yuri passed him one of the files. Costa stubbed out his cigarette and looked through it. 'This is all money stuff. It's about fifty years old!'

'You see. No vital political or military secrets. It isn't information that will end the world. These files deal with the financial history of a company called Skorpion, founded in 1920 by a man called Rudolf Barynin. How does that fit in with your orders to kill Maynard?'

'Look, I don't know. I was just told − '

'By whom? Was it your regular channel of command?'

'No. The orders were special.'

'And a special case officer?'

'Yeah. Someone from Langley.'

'What's his name? And don't make trouble for yourself hiding it. You know I can get the information from our people in Frankfurt.'

Costa thought for a moment. Then he shrugged and said, 'His name's Alan Hersh.'

'Could you bypass him and go direct to Langley?'

Costa frowned. 'What the hell are you talking about?'

'I want to send a message to Langley, as high up as you can get. It must not pass through Frankfurt and must not go through Hersh.'

'I can demand a personal channel of communication with my Head of Ops in Langley.'

'OK, will you give him this message? Allison Maynard is not one of ours. Whatever she is doing, she is doing for America. She is not a spy and the termination order must be cancelled.

'Two, sovereign loans − got that, sovereign loans − are

linked to the killing of the NATO officer and the attempted bomb outrage in Munich. There will be more events in Germany over the next few days, and whatever is going to happen will happen by the thirtieth of this month.

'Three, we will share what information we have with the Americans, but we will only deal with people we trust. Until acceptable contacts are established we will only deal with Brad Drewett, Maynard's superior at the FAA. You got all that?'

'Sure. I got it.'

Yuri had Costa repeat the message and said, 'That's great.' He took the file back. 'Put your hands on the chair.' When Costa had done that he swivelled the SIG and smashed its butt across the fingers of Costa's right hand.

'You bastard!' Costa writhed and twisted away. He held up his hand. His second and third fingers were twisted at an unnatural angle.

'Just in case you had second thoughts and wanted to come back,' Yuri said. 'Nothing personal.'

Thursday April 17

CHAPTER THIRTY-FOUR

Yuri woke Allison. He told her. 'They've come and gone. And we're leaving.'

She yawned and stretched and slid out from under the bedcovers. She'd slept in jeans and a blouse. Her hair was rumpled and her eyes slightly puffy. Without make-up she looked like a lazy schoolgirl. 'Where are we going?' she asked.

'To Stuttgart. Later tomorrow we'll fly to Bonn.'

'Why leave now if they've gone?'

'Because they might send their friends.'

'What happened?'

While they walked downstairs, Yuri told her. Her face went pale when she saw the sheets and pillows. 'Oh my God!' she whispered, as the possibility of being dead hit her. She stared horrified at the jagged holes and the scattered filling.

'Don't think about it,' Yuri said. 'Think about getting your things together and going.' Now that the action was over and the adrenalin had ceased pumping, he could feel the fatigue. His chest was tight, and his legs felt jointless. His whole body ached. There was grit in his eyes and he wanted to sleep.

'That,' Allison said, still staring at the bed, 'that could have been me.'

'Well, it wasn't. And isn't.' Yuri went to his room and packed.

Ten minutes later, having paid their bill and left a generous amount to cover the ruined bedclothes, they were driving along empty roads in faint, silvery dawn light.

Allison asked, 'What would you have done if they hadn't come?'

'We'd have met up somewhere.' He pushed the seat back and stretched out his legs. He wanted a bed. He wanted sleep.

Allison said, 'I can't believe how in one day my life has changed. I am running like a criminal. I even feel guilty.'

'You've done nothing wrong.'

'True. But I find myself thinking I must have.'

'You cannot rely on other people's judgements,' Yuri said. The smooth motion and gentle rush of wind was very soothing.

'I also feel angry. I'm trying to do what is right and my own people are trying to stop me. I can't believe that, if not for you, I could have died.'

'That's the trouble with being American,' Yuri said. 'You expect the guy in the white hat to win.'

Allison asked, 'How do you cope?'

'I don't look for reasons. I only think of what I have to do.'

'And what's that?'

'For the present, find the Izgoi and stop them.'

'Don't you think of why you do it?'

'Sometimes.'

They reached the autobahn and headed towards Stuttgart. The road was wide and empty. From time to time Yuri looked around and studied the cars behind them and the cars they passed. No one seemed to be following them. He pressed his legs against the floor of the car. Images of Galina and Stefan mingled with those of Karelin and Costa. His mind was drifting.

Allison said, 'How old are you, Yuri?'

'Thirty-three.'

'Are you frightened of dying?'

'I want to live.'

The road stretched endlessly. Polyakov was saying, 'She needs to do it for herself. You understand?'

Allison said, 'I'm scared, Yuri. I'm so scared I can hardly drive.'

Beside her, Yuri slept.

'Where are we? What's happened?'

'We're near Stuttgart. I've checked us into a motel. You need to sleep properly.'

Yuri slipped the gun back into its holster and looked at his watch. Half past five. He buried his face in his hands, rubbed his eyes and got out of the car. The morning was cool, with just a hint of mist.

'They only had one room,' Allison said.

The one room was at the end of a corridor, sparse and functional, with a large lumpy-looking bed, a convertible divan, a table, chair and a curtained-off alcove strung with coat hangers. Yuri dumped the cases and started to pull out the divan.

'You're too tired to be chivalrous,' Allison said. 'Just get into bed.'

He stripped to his underwear and did.

When he woke again, light was streaming into the room. She was asleep beside him, her breath fluttering against his shoulder. Her lips were slightly parted. Yuri spent a while looking at them before he kissed her.

Her mouth opened, accepting him, moved, kissed him back. He opened his eyes and found her looking at him. Her eyes were definitely green. He brought his arms around her, ran them down her back. She was wearing blouse and knickers. No jeans. He stroked the backs of her thighs. They were firm and smooth and very long.

She moved on to her back; pulling up her knees, put her hands to her waist and rolled the knickers off her legs. He unbuttoned her blouse and kissed her breasts. Her nipples sprouted against his tongue.

She stroked his head. Slowly he brought his face up between her breasts and kissed her throat. She twisted her head and brought her lips to his. They pressed against each other and kissed, mouth writhing upon open mouth, heads twisting, hardly able to breathe.

She gasped as he entered her and closed her legs tight round him, holding him to her, in her, opening her body to him. She was all around him. Her body enveloped him. He was surrounded by her firmness and her strength and molten moistness. She was all, she was everything. His palpitating breath caught in his throat, and he heard her cry out as he cascaded into her in wave after wave after wavelet.

First thing that Thursday morning, Brad Drewett saw Tom Pierce in his office in the Executive Wing of the White House. For a short while at Langley, Pierce had been his assistant. He told Pierce about Barynin's, the sovereign loans, Allison's trip to Switzerland and his meeting with Timmins the previous day. 'Allison Maynard may be mistaken,' he finished, 'but she is no Russian agent.'

Pierce said, 'I'll talk to Timmins, but I won't promise

much. It's a field decision, Brad. I can't interfere.'

'Timmins could be wrong,' Brad said. 'It won't be the first time the Director of the CIA has made a mistake.'

'He's got to call the shots as he sees them.' Pierce's expression was neutral. 'To issue a termination order he must have a good reason to believe Allison Maynard is dangerous.'

'I've spoken with Allison,' Drewett said. He told Pierce about the conversation. 'Perhaps there is a good reason why she is working with the Russians.'

'It's still Timmins' decision,' Pierce said. Then in a softer voice, he added, 'We have to live with the facts as we see them.'

'Stop being so goddam pious,' Drewett snapped. 'You're not going to let an innocent woman be killed without even hearing what she has to say?'

'As I understand it,' Pierce said, 'no one's going to kill her, if she returns to Washington.'

Zhukovka, twenty miles from Moscow, was where the elite had their dachas. Super-elite, Mikhail Gamalrik thought as he drove through the dappled forest, catching fascinating glimpses of large timbered houses with fretted eaves and long, low, modern bungalows of glass and brick, with two-car garages and artfully tangled gardens running all the way down to the river.

The General's dacha was of the older brick and wood type and stood about six kilometres in from the main gate. There was a khaki-coloured Zil limousine outside, and a jeep in camouflage drab, both vehicles sprouting a forest of radio aerials. A smart young lieutenant in STF uniform opened the door and led him to a vast lounge whose broad-beamed, polished, pine floor was covered with rugged scatter rugs.

The General came in at a brisk pace with a smartish stamping of heels. His skin glowed from his customary early morning cold shower, and his grey hair was spikily erect. He wore uniform today and his chest was covered with medals. 'You said it was urgent,' he snapped.

'Yes. Karelin saw me yesterday. He knows about Chernov and he knows about Munich. Chernov left bank statements and a letter signed with the symbol.' Gamalrik gulped and added, 'Karelin even asked about my father. He knows about 1937.'

And most of all, the General thought, he knows about you.

'Karelin has summoned me to SI headquarters this morning,' Gamalrik said. 'What do I do?'

'You put off the appointment for the same time tomorrow. Between now and then I will have sorted out Comrade Karelin.' The General smiled encouragingly. 'Go to your office now. Act normally. I will speak to you first thing tomorrow morning.'

Gamalrik took the General's hand. 'Thank you.'

'Goodbye, Mikhail.' The General watched Gamalrik leave. You are like my son, he thought. You are my son. But even you cannot be allowed to prejudice Skorpion. Not when everything is so close . . . so close.

CHAPTER THIRTY-FIVE

The two men lunching at the Frankfurter Hof had a close physical resemblance. Both were in their early forties, lean, with tautly handsome faces and clad in expensive English suits. The man with the shock of prematurely grey hair and pale actor's face was Finance Minister Siegfried Lothar. His tanned, dark-haired companion was the Chairman of Baur Industrie, Kaspar Baur.

Lothar toyed with his steak and sipped mineral water. His eyes were clouded, and his face so drawn with worry that the corners of his eyes and mouth seemed permanently furrowed. 'We must abort,' he said, despondently. 'There are no other alternatives.'

'We will not abort now!' Kaspar Baur's voice was low and angry.

Lothar pushed away his plate and lit a cigarette nervously.

Baur told himself he couldn't allow Lothar's nerve to crack now. He forced a confident smile. 'Don't worry, Siggy. Between my people and Hersh's, we'll get the files back.'

'It's too late,' Lothar pointed out, glumly. 'The files will have been read.' He leaned forward, lowering his voice. 'Do you realize there are people walking around now with that information in their heads?'

'Two people,' Baur said and held up the first and second fingers of his right hand. 'Just two people, and it doesn't matter a damn what they have in their heads. The Maynard woman has been isolated from all official American contact. The Russian's control in Moscow is about to be neutralized.'

'How do you know?'

'Hersh has got a termination order on the woman and right now she's on the run, too scared to talk to any American official. The General told me about neutralizing the Russian. He insists we carry on. Nothing must be allowed to stop us now. Those were his very words. Nothing must be allowed to stop us now.' He stared intensely at Lothar.

Lothar shook his head. 'I still think it is too dangerous. I still think we could all be exposed.'

'That's nonsense. Those files only contain means of information, account numbers, names of companies, lists of financial transactions with no stated purpose. No one can find anything in those files.'

'There's always Hausmann. They could go back to Hausmann and break him.' Lothar's voice cracked and he began to speak with increasing rapidity. 'Hausmann knows all the connections. If he talks Skorpion is finished and we are finished, now and forever. We will all be disgraced, exiled, jailed, even killed. We will lose any chance of repeating Skorpion at a more favourable time.'

'There will never be a more favourable time,' Baur said. 'And Hausmann won't talk. I promise you that.' There was a frightening heat in his eyes that made Lothar look away. Abruptly, Baur smiled. 'Don't worry, Siegfried, by this time next week you will be Chancellor of Germany.'

'What about Hausmann?'

'The General has ordered me to take care of him.'

'You!' Lothar stared at Baur in horror. 'Hausmann has been like a father to you!'

Baur's smile remained rigid. 'Second father,' he said, flatly.

Below the glittering chandeliers men in evening dress and women in smart dresses moved in a formal quadrille among scurrying waiters carrying trays of canapés and drinks. Allison in a hurriedly bought cocktail dress and new shoes, and Yuri in a hired tuxedo, moved slowly through the crowd. Allison hoped they didn't look out of place.

That morning they had copied relevant portions of the Skorpion files and deposited the originals in a safe deposit in Stuttgart, each of them giving the safe deposit company a secret password and instructions that the files were to be released only against both passwords. In the afternoon they had flown to Cologne and been met by Gunther Roth.

Roth had spoken to Yuri in Russian, and then explained in English that his superior had approved Allison working with Yuri. Still speaking English, Roth had told them Weinrich's calendar for the next ten days was full. However, that evening, Weinrich was giving a cocktail party at his home in Bad Godesburg and Roth had arranged two invitations. He had given them invitation cards, money, the names of a couturier and dress hire firm and suggested they rented a car in Allison's name from a little-known agency in the centre of Cologne.

Allison had not been to a diplomatic party before. She felt

inadequate surrounded by all these people, so well coiffed, articulate and urbane. And such a tastefully decorated room! The painting over the marble fireplace was a genuine Cranach and the walls were lined with huge tapestries of battle scenes. 'You do this so well,' Allison whispered to hide her nervousness.

'It used to be my job.' Yuri smiled politely at the wife of the Peruvian Ambassador and lifted two glasses of champagne from a passing tray. He looked very elegant in his tuxedo, would have looked better if the jacket fitted.

Yuri talked to the Bulgarian Chargé d'Affaires about wheat and to the Canadian consul about the forthcoming Commonwealth conference. Smiling, he moved Allison towards the far end of the room, where a portly August Wienrich stood, with some African diplomats, a covey of Army officers and a slim, dark-haired man in a dark-grey lounge suit who Yuri figured was Weinrich's principal secretary.

They spoke to the Australian representative and the diplomatic correspondent of *Stern*. Yuri backed Allison into the circle around Weinrich. He waited for one of the periodic conversational lulls and said loudly, 'Of course the Izgoi were never completely eradicated by Stalin.'

'You mean there are Izgoi now?'

They were rewarded by a startled glance from Weinrich. 'We know they have spread through Europe and America. They may even be here, in this room.'

Matching Yuri for loudness, Allison asked, 'Did you say the Izgoi once controlled Russia?'

'Attempted to control. They had great influence over the last Tsarina.'

A figure loomed behind Allison's shoulder. 'I couldn't help overhearing — ' August Weinrich was smiling at them. 'I once read about the Izgoi when I was at university. I was doing a paper on ancient secret societies. It's the first time I've heard anyone mention them since.'

'Really,' Yuri said staring directly at Weinrich. 'You surprise me.'

225

'And why is that?'

Yuri thought he detected a shadow of wariness flit across Weinrich's face. 'Three weeks ago. A hundred thousand dollars,' he said.

The blood rushed to Weinrich's cherubic face and the whites of his eyes showed in clear circles around his pupils. 'I don't know what you are talking about.'

'The payment from Skorpion,' Allison said. 'On the twelfth of March.'

'We have proof,' Yuri said.

'The actual account books of Skorpion.'

Weinrich looked from one to the other of them. 'Who are you? Who sent you?' Then his voice dropping hoarsely, 'What do you want?'

'We want to know why,' Yuri said.

'Now,' Allison said.

'Not here,' Weinrich gasped. 'Come upstairs to my office.' He led them out of the room and up a flight of wide, curving stairs with heavy, dark, wooden furniture. He flung himself down behind a massive oak desk. 'You don't know what you're asking.' He pulled out a chequebook. 'Perhaps we can come to some arrangement.'

'No,' Yuri said. 'Just tell us why.'

Weinrich looked from one to the other of them. 'Who are you? Are you journalists?'

'No questions,' Yuri said. 'Just tell us why.'

'All right.' Weinrich opened the drawer and replaced the chequebook, whipped his hand out clutching a small pistol. 'Now you will tell me who you are.'

'Don't be absurd,' Yuri said. 'You think we would have come here without arranging a backup.' He looked at his digital watch. 'If I don't make a phone call in the next quarter of an hour, my colleagues will be calling a press conference.'

'Who are you?' Weinrich asked again. The gun in his hand was unsteady. His eyes flicked nervously about the room.

'Thirteen minutes,' Yuri said.

With his left hand, Weinrich pulled a phone to him and punched out a number. When a man's voice answered, he cradled the receiver into his shoulder and said, 'I have two people here who want to know why I was paid $100,000. What do you suggest I do, bearing in mind you assured me of total confidentiality?' He stopped and listened. His eyes wandered over Yuri and Allison as he described them briefly. 'You *know* about them. You *will* collect them in ten minutes. Fine. No, I won't worry.' He put the phone down. 'My friend promises to explain everything to you.' He sat back in his chair and smiled.

Yuri stood up. Weinrich's gun jerked nervously. 'You forget I have to make a phone call,' he said.

'You can do that, after my friend gets here. Now sit.' Yuri knew he could take Weinrich, but if he did that, he might not find out who Weinrich had telephoned. He looked at Allison, sitting very erect with her hands on her lap, her face stony and pale. No problem there. Yuri decided to wait.

With a brusque knock at the door Weinrich's secretary came in. Weinrich looked at him in annoyance. 'What is it, Ulrich?'

'I'm sorry, Minister. I've just had a message from the Chairman.'

'I've just spoken with him. He's coming here shortly.'

'But before that, he wanted me to settle some business.' The secretary's tone changed. His hand darted from his pocket. Yuri stiffened as he saw the shiny black Mauser appear in the secretary's hand.

'Don't!' Yuri cried, getting to his feet, dropping his hand to the SIG in his pocket.

'Ulrich — what — ' The Minister swivelled his own weapon at Ulrich.

Ulrich fired, the sound of his shots mingling with the harsh, staccato barks of the gun in Yuri's pocket. The secretary flung up his hands, wheeled and fell. Weinrich slumped sideways in his chair. Allison was on her feet, her hands covering her face.

Yuri pulled her hands away and backed out of the room. They raced down the stairway and out of the house.

It was after nine o'clock when Gamalrik finished work and took the elevator to the basement parking lot. Karelin had been most amenable to a postponement of their meeting. And by tomorrow Karelin would have been neutralized. Gamalrik felt relieved.

Except for his Zil and the duty men's vehicles, the parking lot was empty. The pool chauffeur came to collect his briefcase and edging between the concrete pillars, opened the rear door. Gamalrik threw himself into the rear seat. 'The dacha,' he said, 'as fast as you can without killing either of us.'

Obediently the driver pulled out of the park and accelerated up the ramp. The security guards recognized the car, and with a cursory glance into the rear and a brisk salute, raised the barrier. They circled the centre of Moscow and drove East along Enthusiast Schosse. The lights and the buildings fell away. Gamalrik turned on the Sony cassette player. He'd always found listening to Rachmaninov very relaxing.

In a few days he thought, it would all be over. The ambitions of a thousand times a thousand lifetimes would be achieved and he would have helped bring it about, he, Mikhail Gamalrik from Omsk on the Manchurian border. His father would have been proud. This was what Captain Gamalrik of the First Armoured Corps had lived and died for. This was what his son had trained for all his life. The car jerked convulsively, twice. The driver cut the engine and drifted to the side of the road.

'What's wrong?'

'A gas block, I think.' The driver ground at the starter.

Two men moved off the street, looking curiously at the car. The starter whined. The men approached as if to help. Even though it was only a cool spring evening, they wore bulky overcoats and balaclavas under their caps. One of them

228

opened the front passenger door and the other the rear. From under their overcoats they produced guns. Gamalrik had the presence of mind to throw the radio switch before he said, 'I don't know who the hell you are, but I am a Director of the KGB.'

One of the men got in beside the driver, the other beside Gamalrik. Miraculously, the engine fired. The car moved away. Gamalrik stared at the masked faces. 'I am Mikhail Gamalrik, Head of Directorate K. Who are you and what do you want?'

The man in the front seat spoke. 'We're from Special Investigations, Colonel. You're under arrest.'

Damned, duplicitous Karelin, Gamalrik thought.

'You fool,' the one beside Gamalrik said. 'He's transmitting.' He leaned forward and switched off the radio.

Gamalrik said, 'You realize you cannot arrest me without the written authority of the KGB Director-in-Chief?'

The men said nothing.

'Could I see the authority, please?'

The driver made an unscheduled turn and sped down an unlit road. Gamalrik repeated, 'Could I see the authority, please?'

The man beside him said, 'That isn't how we work.'

So Karelin was looking for a swift, illegal solution. Gamalrik would – Gamalrik realized that there was nothing he could do. The men were taking him to an SI safe house where they would pump him full of drugs and make him talk. Once he talked, the illegality of Karelin's methods would be of little interest. He could not let that happen. He knew too much. He would reveal too much. He would ruin everything. He reached into his pocket. 'I have a heart condition,' he said. 'I have to take a pill.'

The man beside him jabbed him with the gun. 'Keep still.'

The man beside the driver lunged over the seat. He was carrying something thick and wet in his hand. He pressed it into Gamalrik's face.

Gamalrik gasped and inhaled ether deeply. One man was holding his head, the other was pressing down on his body, pressing the anaesthetic to his face. He tried to struggle. He tried to hold his breath. He felt his lungs bursting with the pressure. He opened his mouth and gasped. He felt his body start to sag.

Allison and Yuri reached Cologne an hour after the shooting. Yuri had kept the car radio on all the way, but there had been no reports of the killings. As if from way outside herself Allison watched him summon Roth and get rid of the SIG and the car. He was so normal, so calm, as if it had been just another day at the office.

She knew he'd killed the men in Munich, but seeing him kill was somehow different. She shuddered as she recalled the sudden lifelessness of Weinrich's secretary. Life. Death. It was all so sudden and so very final

Yuri was standing by her holding a large gin and tonic. 'Drink that while you have a long, hot bath.' She was suffering from shock. She'd hardly spoken a word on the drive back, and in the light of the hotel lobby her eyes were rigid and dark. He went with her to their room. 'Try to relax.'

Easier said than done. But she tried.

Afterwards, they went down to the bar and waited for Roth. Allison thought she felt more of a piece, till photographs of Weinrich and pictures of his house flickered on the TV screen above the bar. She felt her hands tremble.

Roth came. Keeping one eye on the TV screen, Yuri told him everything that had happened. According to the news the police had no idea who the killers were. 'They'll be a while identifying you,' Roth said and told Yuri that their invitations had been issued in false names and that even those names had not been on the official guest list.

Allison asked, 'Shouldn't we leave Germany before they find out?'

'If they know about you the border guard will already have

been alerted. If they don't know about you, there's no point in leaving.'

'But we wouldn't know they know till it's too late.'

'Right now you have nowhere to run,' Roth said. 'And there is work to be done here.' He told them that a computer trace in East Berlin had thrown up a reference to a forty-two year-old Colonel in the Belgian army called Niebury, who was stationed in Germany. 'He could be your man,' Roth said. 'I'll have more details tomorrow. Perhaps you'll get more out of him than Weinrich.'

Not another meeting, not another killing, Allison thought despondently. Then with despair, what the hell else can I do?

Friday April 18

CHAPTER THIRTY-SIX

A night's sound sleep made a world of difference. The next morning she persuaded Yuri to take her to the cathedral, one of the most splendid in Europe. She thought about Niebury. The meeting would have to be arranged more carefully, perhaps more officially. She asked Yuri about it.

'We'll have to deal with it as it happens,' he said. He was thinking the Izgoi knew they had visited Weinrich, and if they knew what was in Hausmann's files, they would be expecting them to call on Niebury.

'There must be no more killing.'

'It isn't up to us. For my part, I'd rather be alive than dead.'

'How long will the killing go on?'

'Until we stop the Izgoi or they stop us.'

'But don't you feel anything? Doesn't it worry you?'

'I try not to think about it,' he said.

Roth met them for lunch with photographs of Niebury and more details. Niebury was a Colonel in the Supply Corps, a widower — his wife had died recently — and childless. His army record was excellent as was evidenced by his rank at such a comparatively young age. He came from a military family, which made it all the more unusual for him to be involved with the Izgoi. Roth gave them Niebury's office and home phone numbers. They decided Allison would make the contact and set up the meeting. It was more likely that Niebury would talk to an American official than a Russian who knew nothing about finance.

Friday afternoon and for Gerdt Hausmann the weekend was just beginning. He drove his Mercedes carefully up the mountain overlooking Vaduz. Beside him sat Kaspar Baur who had come to Vaduz to find out what had happened to the Skorpion files and who had spent all day questioning Hausmann.

Despite what he had told Lothar, Baur knew the whole structure of their operation lay in the files. If Maynard and Orlov were able to read the clues, if they were able to get behind the companies in Luxembourg and elsewhere, everything would be exposed; the names and bank accounts of everyone who supported them and everyone who had been bought, the names of politicians, businessmen, army officers, television commentators and journalists. For probably the hundredth time that day he asked Hausmann, 'You sure the only names you used were Weinrich and Niebury?'

'I'm positive, Kaspar.'

Fools, Kaspar thought. Why did they have to be different?

Hausmann darted a quick sideways glance at Baur's narrow, high-cheekboned face. He was relieved that Kaspar had been so reasonable and accepted that there was little Hausmann could have done when faced with a lunatic brandishing a gun.

Kaspar had mellowed, Hausmann thought. He remem-

232

bered the boy he had met, nearly a quarter of a century ago, a wild, impulsive, wilful, arrogant, cruel boy on his way to Russia to learn of the Izgoi and his destiny. That boy of twenty years ago would not have accepted a mistake. That boy would have unleashed his Argentinian thugs on Hausmann. That boy would have ordered his death. The General, Hausmann thought, had done his job well. When Kaspar had arrived that morning, Hausmann had never imagined that they would end the day driving to his home so that Kaspar could pay his respects to Frau Hausmann. They were halfway up the mountain when Kaspar asked Hausmann to stop.

'We aren't home yet,' Hausmann said.

Kaspar gave him a small smile. 'I know. I wanted to smoke a cigarette.' He took out a pack of Gitanes. 'And I didn't want to fumigate your nice car.'

How considerate, Hausmann thought. The boy of twenty years ago, even the man of five years ago would have done as he'd damn well pleased. Then he remembered something. 'I didn't know you smoked.'

Kaspar laughed. 'Only rarely, when I'm totally relaxed.' He pointed through the windscreen. 'I remember the first time we stopped here. It was the day we met. I was on my way to Russia, and had never been to Europe before and you invited me to stay at your home. I remember you stopped here and showed me the view. It's still as beautiful as I remember it.'

'Yes,' Hausmann said. 'Like in a picture book.'

Kaspar opened the door. Turning to get out he dropped his cigarettes on to the floor behind the seats. 'Santa Maria!' he swore, bending over the seat. Then he unlocked the rear door and climbed into the back seat. 'It's right under the seat.'

Hausmann turned and saw him crouching with one knee on the floor and the other on the rear seat. Kaspar smiled at him and said, 'It's been a long time, Gerdt, and now we're near the end. In a few days all our ambitions will have been achieved. We couldn't have done it without you.'

Kaspar *had* changed, Hausmann thought and turned away, smiling.

Kaspar took the knuckle-duster from his pocket and clubbed Hausmann on the back of the head. Hausmann grunted and slumped forward against the steering wheel. Kaspar reached over and pulled Hausmann sideways. He hit Hausmann again.

Then he went round to the front of the car and opened Hausmann's door. He walked to the edge and looked down the mountain. Below him Vaduz lay placid and tranquil, pretty as a doll's village. The sun glinted off a car being driven fast up the mountain. Kaspar recognized his own BMW coupé.

He took the keys out of the ignition and a rag out of his pocket. He unlocked the fuel tank and soaked the rag thoroughly with fuel. As the BMW drove up, Kaspar went back and started Hausmann's car, leaving the engine idling quietly in neutral.

He stood by the open driver's door while one of his companions ignited the trailing rag. When the rag was burning freely, Kaspar reached across Hausmann's body, released the handbrake and put the car into drive.

The car moved forward slowly and tumbled over the edge. It hit a rock and rolled, slid down on its roof, rolled once more, bumped and clattered, hit a tree and exploded in an orange ball of flame.

Kaspar walked quickly back to his own car. It was right that he and not a stranger should have done it. Hausmann after all, was among the last of the old council and had been like a second father to him. As they drove back to Vaduz, he told Nino Valdez, 'You'll have to send someone right away to take care of Colonel Niebury.'

The half-finished apartment blocks stood out like gaunt skeletons against the evening sky. The development was new, on the edge of Moscow. Gamalrik's body had been found in one of the finished apartments, so new that it had not yet been allocated.

234

When Karelin got there militia vehicles and an ambulance were mixed among the builders' trucks and the heaps of bricks and wood piled under dirty tarpaulins. There were two gleaming black KGB Volgas bristling with antennae, and uniformed chauffeurs leaning against the bonnets purposefully picking their teeth. Karelin parked his Zhiguli, showed his workpass to the militia man beside the scarlet ribbons suspended in front of the building and went in. Gamalrik's body had been found in an apartment on the second floor.

The apartment was crowded with men. a group squatted before a windowsill dusting it with fine powder, a man in a leather jacket and jeans was taking photographs with an old Rollei. There were uniformed militiamen and officers from Homicide and Forensics in plain clothes, a doctor with the inevitable brown bag and Konstantin Valichek, Director-in-Chief of the KGB.

'A bad business,' Valichek said. He was a large man with a mournful face, sagging jowls and heavily ringed eyes. His hair was a speckled crew cut. 'Gamalrik was one of the best.' He put his hand on Karelin's sleeve and led him outside the apartment. Valichek was a fellow survivor of Stalingrad.

'What have you been doing, Anatoly?' he asked.

'Working too damned hard.'

'You know I can't protect you on this one. The murder of a KGB Director is a very serious matter.'

'I agree. You want me to find the murderer?'

'Don't be clever with me. I'm going to have to order your arrest and suspension. If there is anything you want to say, you'd better tell me now.'

'What have I got to do with this?'

'You and whatever happened in Munich. That was your problem with Gamalrik wasn't it? Munich?'

'Tell me what happened?'

Valichek told him that the body had been found that afternoon by workmen investigating a smell from the apartment. Gamalrik had been found strapped to a chair, with cigarette burns on his hands and chest and the marks of crudely administered injections on his arms. Pathology was of the opinion that Gamalrik had died from a drug overdose.

'And you think I arrested Gamalrik?'

'Abducted,' Valichek corrected. He pulled out a pocket recorder and switched it on. 'This is a copy of a transmission received from Gamalrik's car at 9.29 pm last night.'

The tape whirred. There was a shrill crackle of voices. Karelin recognized Gamalrik's voice. 'I don't know who the hell you are, but I am a Director of the KGB.'

Two soft metallic clangs followed. In the background something mechanical whined.

Gamalrik's voice said, 'I am Colonel Gamalrik, Head of Directorate K. Who are you and what do you want?'

'We're from Special Investigations, Colonel. You're under arrest.'

'You fool! He's transmitting.' A click. Silence.

Karelin looked up at Valichek. 'Those weren't my people. I did not have Gamalrik arrested. I did not have him brought here. I did not have him interrogated. I did not torture him. I did not have any drugs administered to him. I did not kill him.'

'Then who?'

Karelin thought whoever had killed Gamalrik had cut his last contact with the Izgoi. He said, 'I was playing Gamalrik with a long lead. There was no reason for me to arrest or kill him.'

'So who?'

'I don't know. I need your help. I need to keep control of the SI for a little longer.'

Valichek sighed. 'I'll do what I can, but I can't promise it'll be much. Gamalrik was an important man. He was a Director of the KGB.'

The phone rang with its now familiar empty peal. Allison was about to replace the receiver when it was picked up. A slurred voice said, 'Niebury.'

'Colonel Niebury, I would like to talk to you about the $75,000 you received from Skorpion in February.'

The silence that followed was so long that Allison wondered if the line had been disconnected. Then Niebury said, 'Noon tomorrow. The same place.'

'Which is where?'

'The self-service cafeteria at Medenbach service station, east side.'

'How will I recognize you?'

'I don't give a shit whether you do or not.' The phone crashed down.

Allison repeated the conversation to Yuri and Roth. 'He sounded very drunk.'

Roth said, 'We'll call him tomorrow when he's sober.'

Yuri said, 'No. We'll meet him. Niebury will come. He thinks we are Izgoi.'

Saturday April 19–Monday April 21

CHAPTER THIRTY-SEVEN

Shortly before noon, Allison parked a rented beige Opel near the self-service cafeteria at Medenbach. They had decided to use two cars, Yuri and Roth preceding Allison and checking out the service station, Allison following in time for the meeting.

If Niebury came, Allison would wait five minutes to make sure he wasn't being followed, then go and join him in the cafeteria while Yuri and Roth remained outside watching the parking lot, the service station and the cafeteria. She talked. They fought. It was the most sensible arrangement.

A few minutes after noon, Niebury's six-year-old

Mercedes coupé — last night Roth had found out the make and registration number of Niebury's car — weaved rapidly across the service area and parked untidily before the cafeteria. Niebury got out, a stocky figure in dark trousers and an olive-green lightweight anorak. He went in to the cafeteria leaving his car unlocked.

A couple in motorcycling leathers were at the counter, a family of four already seated. There was another group of three men, two more groups, a single man reading a newspaper and Niebury alone at a Formica-topped table staring at a cup of black coffee and a large brandy. He was unshaven, red-eyed, and puffy-cheeked. Little trace here of the exceptional Army officer, Allison thought as she walked towards him, and he looked a good deal older than his photograph. 'We spoke last night.' She sat on the chair opposite him.

Niebury's expression of bored disinterest was replaced by a momentary alertness as he looked at and then past her. 'You've come alone?' He sounded disappointed.

'Who else did you expect?'

Niebury's eyes roved the café. Then he laughed and took a sip of brandy, raising the glass with his left hand. 'Never mind. You can tell them I won't do it. And tell them they can't have their money back. It's gone. All gone!' He laughed and drank more brandy.

Allison smiled encouragingly. 'What should I tell them you aren't going to do?'

'Don't you know?' He stared at her suspiciously before lighting a cigarette one-handed.

Allison shook her head.

'I'm not going to bugger up the NATO supply lines. That's what I'm not going to do. Tell them that.'

'Why? Won't the plan work?'

'Oh it works all right. Bloody NATO all dressed up and unable to get anywhere because there's no gasoline for their tanks.' He laughed furiously. 'Oh yes it works. But I won't do it. I'm a soldier.' He pronounced it shoulder.

238

'Why bugger up the NATO supply lines?'

Again that flash of suspicion, followed this time by a shrug. 'To put you damn Yankees in your place. The Russkis too. You've made a right fuck-up of the world, haven't you? Both of you. Superpowers, shit! Spend more on fucking nuclear arms than people. You know, with half your countries' annual defence budget we could have found a cure for cancer.'

There was a dampness in his dark eyes. Cancer was important to him. Allison remembered his wife had recently died. 'Was that what your wife died of? Cancer?'

Niebury drank his brandy and nodded.

That had happened a month ago. Which explained why the brilliant army officer was drinking his way to oblivion. And that had been the reason for the money. 'You gave her the best?'

A proud nod. 'Special clinics in Switzerland and Austria. Private rooms. Doctors from America. Yes I gave her the best. I wanted her to have the best.' He choked and beat at the table with his fist. 'I wanted her to live.'

'What would she have said if she'd known how?'

Niebury stared at her angrily. 'Mind your own damned business.'

'And now you won't do it?'

Niebury shook his head.

'Because you're a soldier?'

'Because there's no reason to.' Niebury lifted the glass and drank.

'Who wanted you to bugger up the supply lines?'

An expression of wariness flitted across Niebury's face. 'Don't you know?'

Allison said, 'I work for the US Treasury. We know about you and we know about them. We're going to stop whatever it is that you're doing.'

For a long while Niebury stared at her. Then he looked away saying, 'Do what you like.'

'Aren't you interested in how much we know, in how we found out?'

Niebury gave an indifferent shrug and stared into the amber bottom of his glass.

Allison showed him the photocopy of Hausmann's account. 'We understand *why* you did it. The important thing is what you are going to do about it now, what *she* would have wanted you to do. You're still a damned fine soldier you know. She always believed that. Are you going to walk away or are you going to help us stop them?'

'What makes you think I care what happens?'

'Otherwise why come here to deliver a refusal?'

Niebury remained silent for a long time. Finally he pushed away the brandy glass. 'The West Germans are going to make a pact with the Soviets,' he said. 'A pact which will be opposed by the USA and NATO, who in order to prevent the effectuation of that pact will order NATO troops to move against the Bundeswehr. That's what I was paid to stop.'

'You and who else?'

'Others in supply. For forty-eight hours from the thirtieth of April most of NATO will be paralysed.'

'Who else was paid?'

Stubbornly Niebury shook his head. 'I won't tell you that.'

'Who paid you?'

'Hausmann. He handled all the negotiations.'

'Who's behind Hausmann? Who is the Chairman?'

Niebury shook his head. 'I don't know.' Then he told her that once when he'd needed more money, Hausmann had called someone in Frankfurt for authorization. 'I made a note of the number.' He scribbled it on a paper napkin and passed it to her. 'That's all I have to say.' Abruptly he got up and hurried out of the cafeteria.

Two hours later they were back in the centre of Cologne. The phone number Niebury had given Allison was that of Kaspar Baur.

Roth said, 'Baur will be difficult to reach.'

Allison said, 'Not if we use the files as bait.'

240

'We will have to be very careful about that,' Yuri said. 'Baur is a very important man with powerful connections. We cannot just walk in on him and talk about files.'

'So what do we do?' Allison asked.

'First, we find out everything we can about Baur. Gunther, you too. Talk to Otto and get us everything you have on Baur. Allison and I will return to Stuttgart tonight and go through the Skorpion files again, and see if we can find a safe way to approach Baur.'

They spent all the next day, Sunday, reading the files. Allison said it would take months and a lot of court orders to unravel the account numbers. There was nothing new about Baur, there were no new leads and no new names. She linked the computer to a magazine data base and pulled out some biographical information on Baur, most of it from gossip columns and none of it new or useful. Baur was simply the ageing whizz-kid businessman who had married Albert Baur's daughter and transformed Baur Industrie into a highly successful conglomerate. He was occasionally photographed with models and starlets, he skied at St Moritz, raced powerboats at Cowes and played polo practically everywhere. Nothing to tell them how they could set up a safe confrontation.

Only eleven days to the thirtieth and the third week of April had already begun.

Roth came the next afternoon. According to East German records, Kaspar Baur had been born Kaspar Herlingen in Dresden in 1942. His father had been distantly related to the Baurs. After his father's death, Baur had lived with his mother in Dresden, qualified as an engineer, moved to Berlin and in 1962 emigrated to the West.

'That easily?' Yuri asked. Twenty-year-old engineers with all their working lives before them weren't the sort of people the East Germans allowed to emigrate anywhere.

'That easily,' Roth said. 'The officer who processed Baur's

application was Ernst Feldmann, the present head of the East German SSD. And Russian approval to the application was given by Mikhail Gamalrik, then head of the KGB's 11th Department in East Berlin.'

Gamalrik and Feldmann. Yuri recalled his debriefing in Moscow. Gamalrik's Directorate K had been responsible for Munich, and the SSD bomb expert had been part of Feldmann's handpicked SSD Special Operations Group.

Roth said, 'That isn't all. Otto carried out a verification of our records on Baur.'

'Verification?'

'A physical check that the facts recorded on the file are correct. We checked the school and the technical college Baur attended, and two of the three factories where he'd worked. While all the records confirm that Baur attended those schools and worked at those factories, we could not find one single person at any of those schools or at any of those factories who remembered meeting Baur or what he looked like.'

'You're talking of twenty or thirty years ago,' Yuri pointed out.

'There were still people in those places who'd been there the same time as Baur.' There was a note of satisfaction in Roth's voice.

'What are you saying, Gunther? That Baur might be a legend?'

'According to Otto there is no record of a legend involving Baur being created by the SSD.'

'But Baur obviously is a legend.'

'Created by Feldmann, Gamalrik and others, for a purpose contrary to that of the East German state.'

So how did *they* get to Baur safely? They went through the files again. Nothing. In frustration, Yuri picked up the file of letters from Casimir Heilbron to Gerdt Hausmann.

The letters covered a period of eighteen years. They described how Heilbron had escaped from Berlin with the help of a Russian general, got to Argentina and set up a bank in Buenos Aires.

'Yuri,' Allison cried, reading over his shoulder. 'The name of the bank! The Banque Europe-Sud Amerika!' She left him and hurriedly riffled through the Skorpion accounts files. 'That is the bank that Skorpion bought in September 1945!'

With, Yuri remembered, money that had been provided by Barynin Berlin. They read on. The letters described Heilbron's growing success in business, the arrival of his wife and three-year-old son. Heilbron seemed obsessed with the child. Every letter detailed the boy's activities, and even when his wife died, Heilbron's only thought was the effect it would have on the boy.

The boy, Cassian, had grown up spoilt and undisciplined. At eleven, he'd been expelled from an exclusive German school and compelled to attend an Argentinian school in Buenos Aires. At sixteen, he had got drunk with some school friends, picked up a teenage prostitute from the waterfront, raped her repeatedly and then assaulted her so brutally that the police had got involved. One of Cassian's accomplices had been Nino Valdez.

Heilbron had used all his influence and a considerable sum of money to settle the matter. He'd grieved that the boy would never realize his destiny.

That same year, 1959, the mysterious General who had helped Heilbron escape from Germany, had visited Argentina. Heilbron had been in raptures over the visit. The General had told him their dream *would* be realized, but not for another twenty or thirty years. Most of the children were now of age and the General was infiltrating them into positions of future authority within Russia. The General had the support of a new man in the Troika, and was creating an elite body of troops. In twenty or thirty years the network would be complete.

The same thing, Heilbron wrote, was happening in both Germanies. The young men had their feet firmly placed on the lower rungs of the Party, the Army, the Security services, the civil service and the professions. The Americans with their drive and money had already opened six academies from whose pupils they were selecting the elite.

In twenty or thirty years, everything would be ready, the General had said. The children would be middle-aged and in positions of influence and power. Germany would have achieved the necessary political and economic stability. And the era of Izgoi triumph and Izgoi domination would begin.

Heilbron had told the General about his problems with Cassian, and the General had wanted Cassian sent to him in Russia. A year later, Cassian had gone, visiting Hausmann on his way through to Europe.

In 1963, Heilbron had sold his bank and returned to Germany to create the economic base for the Izgoi. He had asked Hausmann to remind Albert Baur of his obligations to Barynin Berlin and of the undertakings Baur had given. He had asked Hausmann to arrange the transfer of Baur's controlling shares in Baur Industrie to Skorpion, and told Hausmann that Cassian's time with the General had changed him beyond all recognition. The General now felt he was a suitable successor, and Cassian was returning to the West through East Germany. Heilbron wanted Albert Baur to take Cassian into Baur Industrie and give him the financial training necessary to play his part in the plans of the Izgoi.

They put down the letters, stunned. They had no doubt that Casimir Heilbron was Rudolf Barynin, that Barynin and his family had not died in a bombing raid over Munich but had escaped to Argentina and helped recreate the Izgoi. Kaspar Baur was Rudolf Barynin's son and the most likely owner of Skorpion. But who was the General, the architect of the Izgoi?

Yuri thought, whatever the risk, they had to take Baur and get the truth from him. He told them his plan. Allison would set up a meeting with Baur on the pretext that she was tired and frightened and wanted to surrender the files for a sum of money large enough to enable her to disappear. She wanted a meeting with Baur to discuss terms. She would insist that Baur should come alone.

Meanwhile, Roth would bring some heavies from East Berlin. They would grab Baur, take him to a safe house, drug him and get the truth.

'It's crude and nasty,' Yuri admitted, 'but it's the only thing I can see working.'

'Will Baur come?' Roth asked.

'He will not be able to pass up a chance to get the files. Even if he doesn't believe Allison he cannot afford not to see her, just in case she is telling the truth.'

'In that case he'd probably arrange a secret backup.'

'Which your people will spot. If we spot them before the meeting we change the venue. If after, your boys will have to run interference as well, so you'd better make sure they're very good.'

'They'll be good,' Roth promised.

It was early evening before Allison got through to Baur. He listened to her very carefully, concentrating on every inflection. When she'd finished, he said he would like a meeting and he had no objection to coming alone. He had only two conditions. The meeting would have to be in Frankfurt — Allison could pick the place and the time — and Yuri Orlov must be present.

Yuri had whispered, 'Ask him why?'

'Why do you want Orlov?'

'I want to be sure I am getting all the files and I don't want Orlov taking the files off me after I've paid you off.'

Allison looked at Yuri and Roth. Yuri nodded.

Tuesday April 22

CHAPTER THIRTY-EIGHT

Allison kept swallowing heartbeats as she waited in the hotel conference room. They had arrived in Frankfurt that afternoon and met with Otto's protectors, three burly, leather-jacketed men who'd arrived in a ropy-looking Wartburg which they'd said had a tuned engine and two machine pistols under the spare tyre in the boot.

They'd examined the hotel, Roth had produced photographs of Baur and they'd finalized their plan over a late lunch. Yuri and Allison would meet Baur in a conference room on the fourth floor at seven o'clock. One of Otto's men would be stationed in the hotel lobby, checking Baur's arrival and that he was unaccompanied; a second man would cover the stairway to the fourth floor, the third would be outside the rear of the hotel covering the service entrances, and Roth would sweep the outside of the hotel for anyone following Baur. They all had personal radios and would communicate a warning in case of trouble.

If Roth's sweep confirmed that Baur had really come alone, they would all converge on the conference room, seize Baur and take him to a house near the Palmengarten where they could interrogate him. If Baur had brought protectors, Yuri was to use his gun and his fists to get Baur out of the conference room to Roth's room on the fifth floor. It was, as Yuri had said yesterday, a crude and nasty plan.

Yuri's personal radio crackled briefly. Baur was on his way through the lobby, alone. Moments later he came in, a slim, wiry man with a thick head of tight brown curls, an even suntan and a dazzling smile. 'Miss Maynard, Mr Orlov.' With a brisk nod he sat at the end of the table opposite them.

The table ran the length of the room, four chairs on either side, one at each end. Baur was now separated from them by the length of the table and nearer to the door than they were. Mistake number one, thought Yuri.

Baur looked at a bulky digital watch and said, 'Let me explain why I want the files. I am the executor of Gerdt Hausmann who was killed in a car crash last Friday.'

Car crash! Allison felt the blood drain from her face. Another death. Another murder? She heard herself ask, 'What happened?'

Baur sighed. 'Gerdt should have stopped driving years ago. He was rich enough to afford a dozen chauffeurs, but there you are. He liked driving himself, and he frequently drove too fast.'

Yuri looked at his own watch. Thirteen minutes to go. Too long, he thought, worriedly. They should have cut the time needed for Roth's sweep down to ten minutes. But Roth had insisted that was the minimum time he required.

Baur was saying, 'The business of Hausmann and Skorpion, like so much other business, in Vaduz consists of representing other people. It is my understanding that the business of Skorpion's clients is being severely prejudiced by the absence of these files. In order to prevent those clients suffering further damage and seeking recompense from Skorpion and Hausmann's estate, I am prepared to arrive at a settlement with both of you in exchange for the files. What sum do you have in mind?'

Allison thought once a sum of money was agreed the meeting would end. Roth's men still had twelve minutes to go. She said, 'In order to satisfy my curiosity, Mr Baur, tell me, what is Skorpion doing with sovereign loans and the recirculation of funds among companies in tax havens?'

Baur laughed. 'The truth is I don't know.'

'But Baur Industrie has lent substantial funds to Skorpion.'

'True. But the relationship between Baur Industrie and

247

Hausmann is not strictly commercial. It is a relationship that goes back many years, long before you were born, and a little while before I was.' Baur smiled sadly at each of them.

Yuri wondered why Baur was being so garrulous. Eleven minutes to go.

'Albert Baur, my late father-in-law, who founded our company and Gerdt Hausmann were very close friends. I believe that Hausmann was of great help to Albert when he was founding Baur Industrie, and since then there has always been a very special relationship between Baur Industrie and Hausmann.

'It is a relationship I decided to continue after I became Chief Executive of Baur, because of the respect I had for my father-in-law and because the Hausmann deals have always been good business. Every pfennig Hausmann borrowed has always been punctually repaid. As we say here in Frankfurt, good business makes good friends.'

'Who owns Skorpion, Mr Baur?'

'To be perfectly honest, I don't know. I'm sure you must find that difficult to believe when we have lent so much money to Skorpion. But as I've just said, we weren't really lending money to Skorpion. We were lending it to Gerdt Hausmann, the friend of Albert Baur.' Baur's watch gave an instrusive beep. He pressed a button on its case. 'Now tell me how much you want for the files.'

Allison and Yuri exchanged glances.

'Come, come, you must have a figure in mind. What is it? Fifty thousand dollars, a hundred?'

Baur wasn't really dealing, Allison thought. No one with his business experience would have raised an offer by fifty thousand dollars unprovoked. Slowly she said, 'I need enough money to build a new life.'

'How much does that cost?'

'I will also need guarantees that no action will be taken regarding the original removal of the files.' Eight minutes to go.

'That wouldn't be a problem.'

Baur waited for her to tell him the sum of money she required. Strange, she thought, he hadn't wanted to check that the files were there and had not been tampered with.

There was a tread of feet in the corridor outside. People going into one of the other conference rooms? Voices. Seven minutes. The footsteps paused outside the door. Roth's people were early.

Yuri reached under his jacket for his gun. The door burst open and smashed against the wall. Uniformed men crowded in the doorway, rushed into the room. Yuri hesitated.

'Police! Don't move!' There were five of them, four of them carrying machine pistols, standing now with their backs to the wall, machine pistols covering Yuri and Allison, the fifth a more senior man carrying a Heckler and Koch automatic, also pointing directly at them.

Baur calmly clicked the buttons on his watch. 'Perfect recording, I think, Inspector.' He gave Yuri and Allison another of those dazzling smiles. 'Blackmail, you see, never works.'

The Inspector reached forward and took Yuri's gun. 'Stand up slowly, both of you. Keep your hands raised.'

There was nothing else they could do but obey. Yuri looked at his watch. Still five minutes to go. By the time Roth's men came — why hadn't they spotted the police? Or like him had they been concerned about shooting policemen?

The Inspector stepped back and nodded to one of his men, who put down his machine pistol and stepped forward. He went up to Allison, put his hands on her shoulders and turned her round. 'Please, put the hands behind, the wrists together.'

Allison looked at Yuri.

Yuri nodded. The one thing they hadn't expected was that Baur would go to the police. The fact that he had gone to the police could only mean he was not implicated with the Izgoi.

The man was tying Allison's wrists behind her. Rope, Yuri thought. Police didn't use rope, they used handcuffs. The

249

man was walking up to him. Yuri looked at the machine pistols and the Inspector's automatic. There was nothing fake about any of that.

'Please,' the man said.

Yuri put his hands behind him while the man tied them firmly together. It was too late to do anything else.

'We will leave from the service entrance,' the Inspector said. 'For your sakes, I suggest you be quiet.'

The men surrounded Yuri and Allison and walked them to the elevators. As they went out, Yuri heard Baur say, 'Thank you, Inspector. You know where to find me if you want me.'

There was no sign of Roth's men as they were led down to the rear entrance. They were bundled into a police car between two policemen. As they drove away, Yuri saw the Inspector and the other policemen draw topcoats over their uniforms and walk towards the street.

CHAPTER THIRTY-NINE

Yuri tried to see where they were being taken. They crossed the Friedens Bridge, went past the Telefunken building and along Streisemann Allee. 'It'll be OK,' he whispered to Allison.

'No talking, please,' the policeman on his right said.

The policeman pushed their heads down against their knees. Yuri felt the car sway over tram lines. He twisted his head and looked as they passed beneath a railway bridge.

After a while the policemen got tired of holding them and allowed them to sit up. The road was narrower and the houses were fewer. They were driving to the south of the city, heading towards the Stadtwald. After a short distance they turned off into the forest.

A solitary light to the side of a house illuminated a wood and glass door. They stopped. The policeman got them out of the car, shepherded them down three small steps and opened the door. Inside was a narrow, bare corridor and a smell of resin and embrocation. A very special police station, Yuri thought. If it was a police station.

One of the policemen opened a door on the far side of the corridor and pushed them into a brightly lit gymnasium, with tumbling mats on the boarded floor, a corner stacked with *tatami*, punch bags, climbing frames, metal weights and the lathes used in kendo. Standing by a bench used for abdominal exercises were Nino Valdez and three of his men. They weren't doing sit ups.

No doubt now the police were working with Baur. The policemen left. Valdez walked across to Yuri and punched him in the face, stomach and body. Yuri flexed his stomach muscles and let his body sway with the blows. Valdez wasn't a trained fighter and his blows carried no weight. Valdez' knuckle caught him on the mouth and he felt the inside of his lip split. Beside him Allison gasped.

Valdez stood back panting, his forehead and hair damp with sweat. 'That's for starters,' he panted.

Yuri swallowed a trickle of blood. He did not want Allison to become more frightened than she already was.

Valdez strutted back to the bench and sat, placing his hands, elbows outwards, on his thighs. 'All right, you two,' he said. 'You can make this easy or you can make it difficult. We want the Skorpion files. Tell us where they are and once we've got them, we'll let you go.'

Yuri knew that once Valdez had the files, he would kill them. He said, 'The files are in Moscow. With the KGB.'

'Don't fucking lie, man.' He gestured with his head towards Allison. 'She'd never have let you give those files to the KGB.' He came back and stood in front of Yuri. 'The KGB are looking for you, Orlov. Shall I give you to them?'

'Why don't you call the Centre and check?'

'No need, man. I know you've got the files. Now tell me where.'

Yuri thought as long as he kept Valdez' attention, they would leave Allison alone. 'The files are with the KGB,' Yuri repeated. 'And very soon the KGB is going to come looking for you, Nino. They have some unfinished business to settle with you.'

'Balls,' Valdez said, and hit him with a short swing to the mouth. The blow hurt. As Yuri swayed, one of the men punched him in the kidneys. His right side exploded with pain. He arched and twisted sideways. Valdez hit him in the stomach. Yuri staggered. A swinging foot crashed against his thigh. He staggered across the middle of the room with the four men punching and kicking at him. He must not go down, he thought, he must not go down where they could get at him with their feet.

He tried to weave. A fist caught him on the cheek. Another blow bounced off his shoulder. They were playing a game with him, moving him around the floor, punching and kicking. All of them were laughing. Their laughter had an excited, cruel sound. He gasped. A punch caught him on the side of the head and sent him staggering. The blows rained at him from all directions. He couldn't move fast enough. His body felt stiff and heavy. He staggered and swayed and someone kicked his feet from under him and he fell on his shoulder across the floor.

For a moment he lay there terrified, staring at the gleaming shoes poised around him. He tried to get his legs underneath him. He could feel the blood trickling out of his mouth and his shirt clammy with sweat. His cheek was swelling and there was a sharp aching pain from his right ribs, a duller one in his back. Bile rose to the back of his throat.

Valdez stooped and pulled his head up by the hair. His pudgy face drew level with Yuri's. Without the glasses his eyes were small, porcine and bright with excitement. His thick, rubbery lips moved. 'Where are the files, Orlov?'

'Moscow.'

Valdez slammed Yuri's head on the floor. Yuri felt the room cave in, the light go. Then there was confused, blurring illumination and he was halfway across the room. Valdez was dragging him by the hair. He tried to struggle and felt the skin of his scalp lift. He flexed his knees and lurched after Valdez. Valdez reached the wall and released Yuri's head.

The others pulled him up by the shoulders, dragged him against the climbing frame and lashed his body to it. Yuri tried to stand upright, not to allow his body to sag against the ropes.

Valdez jerked the heel of his hand under Yuri's chin. The back of Yuri's head jarred against the bars of the frame. 'Where are the Skorpion files?'

'At the . . . KGB Centre . . . in Moscow.'

Valdez slammed his head against the bars. Again the room seemed to collapse on him. The men began to hit him with their fists. There was no way he could avoid the blows. Blood streamed from his nose and mouth. An eye began to close. The entire front of his body was a single, desperate ache. He felt his breath stop.

And heard Allison scream, 'Stop it! For God's sake, stop it before you kill him!'

There was a patter of heels. Yuri opened his eyes and saw her run across the room, towards him. One of the men hit her across the face. She reeled, recovered her balance and came on. A second man came up behind her and grabbed her. She struggled furiously and then went helplessly still.

Valdez went up to her. 'If you want to stop him getting hurt, tell us where the files are.'

Allison's wide, frightened eyes looked into Yuri's. Deliberately, Yuri shook his head.

'They're in Moscow,' Allison said.

Valdez said, 'Bitch' and slapped her. He stood back and looked from her to Yuri. Then he asked the men to take Allison over to one of the benches.

253

The men pushed Allison face down on the abdominal bench and passed the support strap over her ankles. They roped her waist to the bench and one of them took off her shoes. Valdez pulled her skirt up and rolled down her stockings. He went into the equipment store room and returned with a weight lifter's belt. He swished the belt lightly against the soles of Allison's feet. 'We begin softly, and gradually the punishment gets worse. We will find out what we want to know, because the effectiveness of this treatment lies in its duration, not necessarily its pain.' Valdez swung the belt a little harder. It wrapped around Allison's ankles with a light smack. Allison jerked and her body sawed at the ropes. Valdez looked at Yuri. 'Where are the files, Orlov?' he asked.

Yuri kept his gaze on Allison's frightened face. 'Moscow.'

The strap swished again. Allison's body quivered. Her eyes widened, her teeth clamped down on her lips. A pale red mark appeared against the back of Allison's calves.

'The files are in Moscow,' Yuri shouted.

Valdez hit Allison across the thighs. The bench vibrated with the blow. A tiny streak of blood followed the mark of the belt. Allison's face went white then red.

The belt swished down again. This time Allison cried out. Valdez was raising the belt again, slowly, deliberately. Allison's face was screwed up in fear. Yuri said, 'Stop it, Valdez, and I'll tell you.'

Swishing the belt in front of him Valdez came over and stood in front of him. 'All right, Orlov. Talk.'

'The files are in a safe deposit. They can only be released against the delivery of – '

He heard the sound of a door opening, the rush of feet across the corridor.

Valdez wheeled as the door to the gymnasium flew open. Two of Roth's men stood there, leather jackets flying open, machine pistols chest high. There were tiny flashes and a deafening crackle as they fired. Valdez' men didn't have time to get their guns out before they were hit. They staggered, and wheeled and fell.

Roth pushed past the men into the room, Walther in his hand. Yuri saw the door of the equipment room still open. 'Valdez,' he shouted. 'Through there.'

'Where?' Roth rushed up to Yuri.

Yuri pointed with his chin.

There came the sound of a door closing.

'Outside, quick.'

One of Roth's men sprinted for the corridor. They heard the sound of a car starting. Roth reached forward and began to free Yuri.

Roth rushed them from the house where a doctor he knew examined Allison's bruises, gave her a sedative, warned her she would be sore and that she should wear jeans for a couple of days. He inspected Yuri's cuts and bandaged him up tight, and told him to move very carefully until he could be X-rayed.

They drove back to the hotel. The policemen had been in the hotel before Baur arrived, Roth said, most probably in a room on the fourth floor. They were, Roth thought, genuine, one or more of them Izgoi or under obligation to Baur. They had obviously not wanted to get involved in making the procuration of the files official.

The first Roth had known of their arrival was the warning by the man on the fourth floor landing. Unwilling to get into a shoot out with the police, they had covered the rear entrance and watched the police take Yuri and Allison away. Then, their suspicions alerted by the fact that the Inspector and the remaining men had covered up their uniforms and driven in the opposite direction to which Yuri and Allison had been taken, they had collected the Wartburg and gone after the police car. Unfortunately, the Wartburg had poor lights and they had lost the police car in the Stadtwald, then spotted it driving out of a side turning, examined the houses along the street and after two false leads, found the one where Yuri and Allison were being held.

They had to leave Frankfurt straightaway, Roth said. His men were in danger because of the shooting, and who knew what further influences Baur had with the authorities in Frankfurt?

'Where do we go?' Yuri asked.

'Home. To East Berlin,' Roth said. 'Both of you will be safe there. And Otto wants to meet with you.'

Wednesday April 23

CHAPTER FORTY

Wednesday morning in Bonn was typically misty. Watching the pale-grey curtain outside the windows of his dining room Chancellor Helmut Schiller hoped it would lift quickly. He'd lived and worked in Bonn for over twenty years and still hadn't got used to its insidious mornings. He turned his attention to his guest, Colonel Brian Martins, Deputy Chief of Staff of the British Army on the Rhine. 'No one seriously wants any changes,' he told Martins. 'All they're looking for is a convincing reason to keep things as they are.'

Schiller had thought of an unusual way to persuade his Cabinet colleagues of the impossibility of yielding to the extremist minority demanding that foreign forces be expelled from Germany or at least have their role so circumscribed as to make them virtually useless. Schiller had invited a senior officer from each of the NATO forces to talk to his Cabinet about the political, military and strategic consequences.

'The American presentation was a winner,' he said. 'Films, cartoons, mobile models.'

Brian Martins sighed. All he had were facts and an overwhelming argument. He sipped the last of his coffee and pushed his cup away. He was a man in his late forties, bristle-haired, moustached, very alert and very military-looking even in civilian clothes.

Schiller was saying, 'Many of them remember the war and few of them have any great fondness for or trust in the Russians. Their problem is that they are politicians, and the nature of a politician is not to lead, but to follow what he thinks will be a popular idea. And right now, there is no doubt that the ideas of this Revolutionary German Army are fashionable.'

Martins lit a cigarette. 'The whole point is that unlike the troops across your border we are not an occupying army. We are friends joining together against a common peril. We are here because the German people want us to be here.'

'I wouldn't place too much emphasis on that,' Schiller warned. 'If you're here because the German people want you, then they will expect you to leave if the German people demonstrate they do not want you.'

The door to the breakfast room opened and Schiller's five-year-old daughter came in wearing a neat, brown school uniform and carrying a satchel. Schiller took her on his knee. 'This is Colonel Brian Martins from England.' He smiled at Martins. 'My daughter, Helga.'

Helga cuddled up to her father and murmured, 'I want to go to school in Papa's car.'

'Papa can't take you to school today,' Schiller said. 'Today, Papa has a lot of work to do and has to go with Colonel Martins.'

'Colonel Martins can come with us.'

The Chancellor and the Colonel laughed. 'No, sweet-heart,' Schiller said. 'Today you go to school with Mama.'

'I like Papa's car better.'

'Tomorrow,' Schiller promised. 'I'll take you to school in my car tomorrow.'

The Chancellor's wife came in and collected Helga. Schiller enquired about Martins' family. Martins said he had two sons, both at school in England. Schiller picked up the internal telephone and ordered his car to be made ready.

Transporting the Chancellor of West Germany the four kilometres from his residence to the Chancellery required three sedans equipped with bullet-proof glass and specially strengthened suspension and chassis, three drivers, five police bodyguards armed with Walthers and automatic weapons, and today, because of the presence of a senior NATO officer, a motorcycle escort.

The procession left ten minutes after the Chancellor's wife had taken their daughter to school. As they raced through the damp, quiet streets, Schiller said he regretted travelling like this. But what could one do when there were lunatics everywhere? Even poor Weinrich had been gunned down by his own secretary.

'Better safe than sorry,' Martins said. He patted the attaché case on his knee and wished he had ten minutes alone to run through his speech once more.

They raced past the University and through the Markt. They were speeding along Sternstrasse to the main road that would take them out of the centre of Bonn across Kennedy Bridge, when Martins saw the blue Ford Transit. It jerked down Wenzelgasse and accelerated towards them.

'Watch out!' he shouted as the van sped across the street and then his scream froze in horror. The van had no driver.

Martins felt his body thrown back in his seat as the driver spun the wheel and kicked down on the accelerator. But it was too late. A motorcycle smashed against the car door, its rider cartwheeling above the squat, onrushing blue hood. There was a deafening crash. Martins saw his door buckle, the glass shatter. There was a savage pain above his right knee, then a horrible, blinding flash.

And an explosion that shook the whole of Bonn.

*

Allison slept fitfully and woke sore and tired. Last night they had flown to Tegel and crossed into East Berlin at the U-Bahn checkpoint beneath the Friedrichstrasse. Inside there had been guards and massive grilled gates, outside arc lights, wire, concrete blocks, a boundary of freshly swept sand and the Wall. She remembered the sick fear she felt at the realization that she was going into the country from which she might never get out.

On the flight from Frankfurt she had thought about staying behind in West Berlin, decided against it because there had been nothing she could do without Yuri and Roth, because West Berlin was a large CIA station and the CIA had orders to kill her. Travelling underneath West Berlin she'd had plenty of time to reflect on the irony that her only allies were two Communist intelligence officers.

They had been collected outside the subway station and driven along progressively more dimly lit streets to this apartment, small, square and functional, with a strong smell of disinfectant and stale cooking.

Roth had said, 'You will stay here till we come for you,' seeming somehow more formal now that he was back home.

'When will that be?' Allison had asked.

'I will come tomorrow morning.' He'd led her to the kitchen and checked there were enough meat, eggs, bread and milk. He'd warned them against leaving the apartment. Their presence in East Berlin was unofficial, and if they were questioned by a policeman they would be in serious trouble. Also they were not to make any phone calls until they'd met with Otto. He'd hoped they'd get a good night's rest.

Roth came at eleven and told them of Chancellor Schiller's assassination.

'The Izgoi,' Yuri said. 'That's what they had planned for the third week of April. They're taking over West Germany.'

'Schiller's successor hasn't been appointed yet,' Roth said. He took them to a hospital where Allison was examined again and Yuri X-rayed. The doctor told Yuri that nothing was broken and that he needed his dressings changed regularly and plenty of rest.

They returned to the apartment. Otto Dietrich came shortly afterwards, a short, stumpy man with a rough peasant strength about him and a face as crinkled as a raisin. He walked straight up to Allison, bent over her hand, clicked his heels and said, 'Dietrich.' He shook Yuri's hand and clapped him lightly on the shoulder. Then saying 'Excuse me, we have to discuss something regarding the KGB,' he switched to Russian and told Yuri that Karelin had been accused of killing Mikhail Gamalrik and was suspended from duty. 'The enquiry is tomorrow,' he finished, and shrugged. 'Then we'll see.'

'Did Karelin do it?' Yuri asked.

Otto shook his head angrily. 'You should know that isn't his way. I believe someone thought Karelin would break Gamalrik and moved to stop them both.'

If they succeeded in nailing Karelin, Yuri thought, everything was finished. 'What about my family?' he asked.

'For the present they're safe. There are still SI guards at your apartment.'

Otto got Roth to fix up a tape recorder and had them sit together on the lumpy sofa facing it. 'Both of you had better tell me everything,' he said. He and Roth made notes while they did, and from time to time interrupted to request confirmation and elucidation. Two hours later when they had finished, Roth wound the spools and put them away in a small case. He disconnected the recorder.

Otto said, 'I have run some more checks on Baur. As you know, his company has invested heavily in East Germany and I have here a record of his visits and the people he met with.' He handed Yuri a typewritten paper. 'You can read German?' he asked Allison.

'Enough,' she replied. They read.

Baur had first returned to East Germany five years previously and been welcomed as an honoured guest by the then Finance Minister and current President, Konrad Blucher. There had been three other visits that year and SSD surveillance had reported nothing unusual. Then Baur had come to East Berlin shortly before Christmas, and spent the weekend with General Werner Kork, present Chief of the East German General Staff, whose other guests had been Franz Eidemann, head of the East German Special Forces, Ernst Feldmann, Director of the SSD, and Mikhail Gamalrik, then in charge of KGB-SSD liaison.

In April the following year Baur had attended a reception at Eidemann's country home, and spent the weekend with Feldmann. In July he had been visited at the Metropol by Gamalrik. He had met with Blucher and spent a weekend with Feldmann. He had met eight more times with Kork and Eidemann. His visits over the subsequent years had followed a similar pattern. Every time he came to East Germany, he'd seen Kork, Blucher, Feldmann or Eidemann.

'There is a definite pattern,' Yuri said.

'But not evidence of a conspiracy.'

'Aren't all these people Izgoi?'

'We have no proof of that. We have no proof that the Izgoi exist, and even if we had that proof we could not move against Blucher, Feldmann and the others until we know what they are doing and are certain of success. To move prematurely will only reveal what we know and then *we* will be eliminated.'

'The Izgoi assassinated Schiller,' Yuri said. 'Their plan is scheduled for completion by next Wednesday.'

'If you are right, it is even more necessary that we proceed with caution. There is no one to take over from us if we are eliminated.'

'But what do we *do*?' Allison cried.

'For the present, recover from your injuries, while I find out more about Baur and his connections.'

'What about Barynin and this Russian General?' Yuri asked.

'You will have to investigate that in Russia after Karelin is cleared,' Otto replied.

If Karelin is cleared, Yuri thought.

Eating hash browns and scrambled eggs, President Donnelly watched Siegfried Lothar being sworn in as Acting Chancellor of Germany. He'd been woken at four o'clock that morning with news of the assassination and at half past five, Bill Timmins had reported that the terrorists had used a sophisticated radio-controlled vehicle to carry out the killing. Both Timmins and the President had wondered how the terrorists had got the equipment and discovered the Chancellor's route and schedule.

The television screen filled with a close-up of Lothar's face. Weak, Donnelly thought, spiteful, over-emotional. Definitely not the kind of man you want on your side in a tight situation. Or for that matter, on the opposing side. Donnelly finished his second cup of coffee while Lothar paid the usual tributes to his predecessor and vowed that no effort would be spared to bring the killers to justice.

'However,' the President put down his coffee, as Lothar's face took on a peculiar expression, 'the legitimate demands of the German people *can* and *will* no longer be ignored. It is an insult to the German people that their countries should still be under occupation.'

Countries, Donnelly thought. Is he speaking for East Germany too?

'Germany will cease to be the garrison town of Western Europe. It will cease to be an occupied country and Germans everywhere will be able to hold up their heads with pride and for the first time in fifty years be free men. America and Europe have imposed similiar constraints on Germany before and we all know what happened then. It will not happen again!'

It was happening now, the President thought.

Lothar said his first act as Chancellor would be to demand the immediate withdrawal of all foreign troops from Germany. It was not true that without the protection of the

American army the Russians would march into Bonn. That was simply propaganda spread by America and its Allies. Lothar would prove it. In a few days he was meeting with East German President Konrad Blucher to discuss the creation of a neutral and allied Germany.

The President reached for a phone and spoke to the Chairman of the Joint Chiefs of Staff. 'Tell me, General, what is the status of our European Strategic Reserve?'

'Right now, green.'

'I want that changed to blue.' Blue was the second highest status below red. It meant that the four Army divisions presently held in reserve in America could be moved into Germany in less than a week.

The President's second phone call to the General Secretary of the Soviet Politburo took a little longer to connect.

'Mr General Secretary, I wanted to check your reaction to Chancellor Lothar's speech. It seems that he is considering a reunification of Germany.'

General Secretary Timochek did not wait for the interpreter to finish translating the President's words. 'Never,' he said.

Thursday April 24

CHAPTER FORTY-ONE

It was a grey morning in Moscow, damp and cold. Karelin had his chauffeur drop him right by the steps of the central courtyard inside KGB Headquarters in Dzerzhinsky Square. He went down into the basement. A guard checked his pass, saluted, and led him along a bare corridor to a room with a plain wooden door. They were on the same level as the prison, and a smell of crowded humanity permeated the thick walls.

Inside the room five men were seated behind two of three tables arranged facing each other. At the central table were Director of the KGB Konstantin Valichek, and two Deputy Directors of Administration. With their backs to the door were Afram Yurevich, Gamalrik's replacement at Directorate K and a black-suited, bespectacled man Karelin did not recognize and assumed was some kind of lawyer. With a nod that embraced everybody, Karelin walked across the room and sat at the third table.

KGB Director Konstantin Valichek coughed. 'Comrade Karelin, are you alone?'

'Yes.'

Valichek looked surprised. 'You are not being represented?'

'No.'

Valichek hesitated. Then he cleared his throat and said, 'In that case we can begin.' He fiddled with a pair of half-framed spectacles and looked at the papers in front of him. 'Comrade Karelin, charges have been laid against you that on − the seventeenth of April − '

Karelin got to his feet. 'Comrade Director, I am fully aware of the charges made against me. May we save time and take the charges as read.'

Valichek peered at him over his glasses. 'It is most irregular, but if you agree and no one else objects . . .' He looked round the room.

'I plead not guilty,' Karelin said. 'I also move that in order to save time I accept the prosecution evidence regarding the circumstances of Director Gamalrik's abduction. What I deny, despite the evidence of the radio transmission from Director Gamalrik's vehicle, is that Director Gamalrik's abduction was authorized directly or indirectly by me or that it was carried out by members of Special Investigations.'

The black-coated lawyer was on his feet. 'Is it not true, Comrade Director, that you were investigating Director Gamalrik? That you in fact interviewed him shortly before he was abducted?'

'It is correct that I saw Director Gamalrik the day previous to his abduction,' Karelin said. 'The matter under investigation was one over which I believed I was receiving the Director's full cooperation. In fact, I believe that the reason for Director Gamalrik's abduction and murder was *because* of his cooperation. I also believe that the abduction was structured in such a manner as to falsely implicate Special Investigations and hinder us in completing the more serious investigations we were working on jointly with Director Gamalrik.'

The lawyer said, 'From the evidence of the radio transmission it is clear that the men who abducted Director Gamalrik were from Special Investigations. It is — '

'The only thing clear from the radio transmissions,' Karelin interrupted, 'is that the men said they were from Special Investigations. We have no evidence that was true.'

'Or false,' the lawyer said.

Karelin turned to Valichek. 'Comrade Director, I would like to make a full explanation of the circumstances leading to my interview with Director Gamalrik.'

'Yes,' Valichek said. 'Of course.' He gestured to the lawyer to sit.

'My department,' Karelin said, 'is presently concerned with investigating certain breaches of Politburo Directive 3243 prohibiting the involvement of Soviet agencies in terrorist acts. It is my Department's belief that certain members of the KGB have conspired with other persons and organizations to breach that directive.'

'Have you any proof?' Acting Director Afram Yurevich asked.

'We have enough evidence to justify continuing these investigations.'

'Are you going to present that evidence to this enquiry?'

'Not in any detail. I would not want our investigation prejudiced.'

The lawyer was on his feet again. 'Comrade Valichek, while we all appreciate the confidentiality of an ongoing investigation, I submit it cannot be used as a defence to the very serious charges that have been made without a sufficiently detailed account of the investigation being given. Otherwise I am afraid the defence of an ongoing investigation will be brought to every charge.' The lawyer looked quite upset at that thought.

Karelin said, 'Perhaps it may be better that my evidence be heard first. If that is inadequate, then we can consider what further evidence is necessary.'

'Agreed,' Valichek said quickly. He waved impatiently at the lawyer.

'A few weeks ago,' Karelin began. 'We were informed that there would be a KGB-supported attempt to bomb Munich railway station.'

The lawyer was on his feet again. 'Who was your informer? Mr Chairman, the enquiry has a right to know.'

'All that matters is that the information was accurate,' Karelin snapped. He looked at Valichek, who indicated he should continue. 'I placed one of my most trusted officers, Captain Yuri Orlov, who was already in Munich, in charge of the investigation. Orlov intervened to prevent the bombing, and while doing so, shot and killed Gunther Raspe, a member of the so-called RGA, and an East German defector from the SSD, one Sigmund Heller. Orlov was then interrupted by Vasili Chernov, of Directorate K. Upon Orlov attempting to arrest Chernov, Chernov commited suicide.'

Yurevich and the lawyer were both on their feet. 'That is untrue!' Yurevich cried. 'Chernov prevented Munich!'

'We demand that the enquiry be adjourned until Orlov's evidence can be heard.'

'Colonel Alksnis conducted a thorough enquiry into Munich!'

'Mr Chairman, may I please continue?'

'Order. Please be seated, comrades. Let the defendant finish his statement!'

When Yurevich and the lawyer had seated themselves, Karelin went on. 'Orlov subsequently searched Chernov's offices and discovered that Chernov had access to a secret bank account, copies of which I will now present to the enquiry.' He handed out copies of the Trepart SA bank account and said, 'That bank statement was found in Chernov's desk at the Residency. Orlov's discovery was witnessed by Chernov's superior, Vladimir Petrov, who unfortunately is now dead.'

'So we have no independent evidence that this statement was Chernov's?' the lawyer asked.

'No. What we do have is this intriguing note in Chernov's handwriting.' Karelin passed copies of the note round. 'We believe this note was addressed by Chernov to Nino Valdez, the head of the terrorist group, Centrale, which is run by Directorate K.'

Karelin allowed that information to sink in and gave everyone time to read the note before he continued. 'Colonel Alksnis, as you all know, conducted an enquiry into Munich and concluded that Chernov had somehow discovered the plot and was killed trying to stop it. The purpose of my interviewing Director Gamalrik was to ascertain if Alksnis had any facts to support that conclusion, or whether that conclusion was merely being used by Alksnis as publicly credible disinformation.

'At the same time, I wanted to present my own evidence to Director Gamalrik. My interview with him was extremely cordial. He gave me his impressions of Chernov, and voluntarily made Chernov's files available to me. He agreed to a further meeting with me. Originally this was to have been held the day he was abducted, but it was changed at his request to the next day. So you see, far from wanting to arrest Director Gamalrik, I was working with him. In fact Director

Gamalrik was a vital part of my investigation into the extent which Directorate K has been penetrated by those allied with Chernov.'

The lawyer was on his feet again. 'All we have had so far, Comrade Director, is your unsupported version of events. If Special Investigations did not abduct Director Gamalrik, who did?'

'I think that is a matter for a different kind of investigation,' Karelin said. 'If you want my opinion, it is the same people who attempted to kill my key investigator, Captain Orlov.' Karelin explained how after Yuri had returned from Munich, he had been kept isolated until he could be debriefed. 'Then,' he added, 'this happened.' He took out his personal radio. 'With your permission, Comrade Director . . .'

Valichek nodded.

Karelin spoke into the radio. A few minutes later there was a measured tread of feet in the corridor outside followed by a knock on the door. Four men entered carrying a large wooden box on their shoulders. They put it down in the centre of the room.

'Open it,' Karelin ordered.

A strong smell of putrefaction filled the room. Everyone put their hands to their noses and tried not to breathe.

Karelin said, 'That, Comrades, is the body of Colonel Alksnis, who was killed while attempting to murder Captain Yuri Orlov here in Moscow.' Karelin looked directly at Yurevich and bowed. 'Perhaps you would like to confirm the identification, Comrade Director? Colonel Alksnis was on secondment to Directorate K was he not?'

'For goodness' sake, man, close the box!' the lawyer shouted. 'We have no confirmation that this man attempted to kill Orlov. In fact no one knows where Orlov is. If the so-called attempt on Orlov's life is relevant to the enquiry, then the least we can ask is that Orlov himself be present to confirm the facts.'

'Captain Orlov's presence will not be necessary,' Karelin

said. 'I have here affidavits from Lieutenant Mark Kutsov who visited the scene immediately after the incident, Captain Vadim Andreyvich who recorded Orlov's statement, and a former international gymnast, Oleg Polyakov, who is a family friend of the Orlovs and who was arrested by Alksnis and compelled to reveal where Orlov was living.'

The lawyer sat down. 'We will consider those statements,' he muttered, but Karelin knew that was just a formality. The lawyer would not press further for fear of more facets of KGB involvement being revealed. He looked directly at Valichek. 'Comrade Director, I deny that I authorized Director Gamalrik's arrest, interrogation, torture or the administration of drugs. I deny that such matters were carried out on my behalf or on my direct or indirect orders or that any members of my department carried out this arrest with my authority. I demand that the charge against me be dropped, that I be reinstated forthwith and that I be permitted to continue with this investigation into this very grave conspiracy which is aimed at destroying Russia.'

Valichek looked round the room. 'Do I hear any opinions to the contrary?'

No one in the room said anything.

The atmosphere in the apartment that Thursday morning was strained. Ever since Otto had left yesterday, Yuri had been depressed and silent, while Allison had worked at the computer, preparing a detailed report for Drewett. At four in the morning he had told her about Karelin and the consequences to his family if he were convicted. Allison had felt angry. She still didn't know whether it was because he'd taken so long to tell her, or because he cared so much for someone else.

Allison tapped furiously at the computer. Yuri stayed in front of the television, switching between West German channels, to catch opinion on Chancellor Schiller's assassination and Lothar's new moves. 'Worrying isn't helping anything,' she'd told him at breakfast. 'You must force yourself to snap out of it.' She'd been about to tell him to go for a walk, when she'd remembered they were not supposed to leave the apartment.

Roth came around ten. Otto was caught up with the West German Chancellor's assassination and wouldn't come today, Roth told them. But Otto had sent some more information about the East German conspirators. Feldmann, Blucher, Eidemann, Kork and West Germany's new Chancellor, Siegfried Lothar, had all been educated at the same school, the Brandenburg Academy.

'What kind of school is that?' Allison asked.

'An Ordenen castle,' Roth replied. He told them that the Ordenen castles had been special Nazi schools reserved for the Aryan elite of Germany. 'They were a combination of military school and ancient academy,' he explained. 'Using strict discipline and physical fitness to reinforce academic ideas, and I suppose, Nazi philosophy.'

'A kind of brain washing?' Allison asked.

Roth smiled. 'All education is a kind of brain washing. Otto says, the basic idea underlying the Ordenen castle goes back to the ancient Greeks. Their ideas were developed by a Russian educationist — '

'Vailan Ostrovensky?'

Roth looked at her in surprise. 'Yes.'

'That's it!' Allison cried. 'The schools! *The Rodina schools in Russia, Clairvaux Academy in America, the Brandenburg Academy in Germany, they're Izgoi schools!*' She rushed to the Skorpion files and went through the accounts. She showed them the figures for 1938 and 1939. 'Look! These payments to educational charities in Germany, Russia and America must have been for the schools. The Izgoi have used those schools to indoctrinate their children, and infiltrate them everywhere.' Rapidly, she told Roth about Clairvaux. 'I must get this information to America,' she finished. 'If Drewett can get the Clairvaux records we will know who the American Izgoi are.

270

And you, you must get hold of the records of the Brandenburg Academy.'

'Those records were destroyed,' Roth said, 'soon after
Blucher became President.' He walked over to the computer
and looked at the report Allison had been typing. When
Allison had finished explaining how it would be transmitted,
he said he would talk to Otto and be back shortly with a
telephone engineer to make the necessary connections.

He was back an hour later and watched fascinated as the
report was transmitted. It was noon in East Berlin and in
Washington Drewett wouldn't even have woken up. Please do
something, Brad, Allison wished silently. Do something and
help all of us to stop running. Help us to stop the Izgoi!

CHAPTER FORTY-TWO

First thing that morning, the German Ambassador had
informed Secretary of State Max Caldwell that unless American
forces in West Germany were immediately confined to their
barracks, Chancellor Lothar intended serving notice of West
Germany's withdrawal from NATO, and since then Tom
Pierce had been shuttling between the State Department and
the White House. He'd had joint and several meetings with the
President, the Secretary of State, the West German Ambassador, the Director of the CIA and the Joint Chiefs of Staff. He
had discussed everything from Lothar's psychological profile (on
record with the CIA) to an embargo on West German goods.
He had listened to the President alter the status of the European
Strategic Reserve to orange and have Bill Timmins prepare a
prognosis of how each member of Lothar's cabinet would react
to an American withdrawal from Germany, and to the offer of
becoming an American-supported Chancellor.

271

'No German will want to become an American puppet,' Miles Kingdon, summoned in desperation by the President, had announced firmly. 'You have little to worry about. In a couple of months when his position has been more firmly established, Lothar will undoubtedly make concessions.'

'Concessions, my ass!' the President had said. 'We're in there and we're staying there.'

'And what will you do if Germany walks out of NATO? Rely on the French?'

'Invade the bastards,' the President had said, but without conviction.

'And risk a nuclear war? This is a time for patience and diplomacy, Jack, not threats.'

Leaving the President with his former tutor, Pierce returned to his own office and asked his secretary to get him a mug of black coffee and two aspirins. His secretary told him Mike Karas, a CIA Director of Special Operations, was waiting to see him, together with Agent Sam Costa, who had his right hand in a cast.

Pierce asked his secretary to show in Karas and his companion, but to bring his coffee first.

In his office at the FAA, Brad Drewett kept staring at the decoded contents of his electronic mailbox. He'd re-entered the material in clear, transferred it on to the same disk as the original message, printed out both the original and the decoded messsage, and read both twice.

Allison was incredible! Her report was incredible! And Allison had been more than brave!

He went over the report again. Weiler, Weinrich and Niebury murdered. Hausmann, perhaps murdered. Chancellor Schiller's assassination part of a much larger plot. Allison and Orlov kidnapped after a meeting with the German industrialist Kaspar Baur, who Allison believed was the son of Rudolf Barynin and the owner of a company called Skorpion SA which had financed the attempted bombing of Munich railway station *and* used the Handel Kreditbank and Barynin New York as a front to purchase sovereign loans.

The sovereign loans, the murders, the campaign of terrorism in Germany were all orchestrated by a secret society called the Izgoi. Like his father, Rudolf Barynin, Baur was a member. Also, East German President Blucher, SSD Chief Feldmann and Army CIC Werner Kork. In West Germany, Siegfried Lothar — that accounted for a lot — in America, Ellesmere Wentworth, Cowdrey Berle and Miles Kingdon.

The Izgoi had infiltrated the KGB and important positions in Russia, East and West Germany and the United States. They had been trained in special schools financed by Skorpion and the Barynin fortune, Rodina in Russia, the Brandenburg Academy in Germany and Clairvaux in the United States. Clairvaux, Drewett thought, Miles Kingdon.

I do not know what the objectives of the Izgoi are, but I do know that it involves the USA, Russia and both Germanies, and it is for this purpose that they have mounted a campaign of terrorism in Germany and are buying sovereign loans. Whatever the Izgoi is planning comes to fruition on the 30th.

Before then we must act to stop them.

Yes, Allison, don't worry, we will. Drewett called a friend in the American Embassy in Zurich and had him check the past week's papers for reports of Paul Weiler's death. He had his secretary collect newspaper reports of Weinrich and Niebury's murders. He did not require independent confirmation of Allison's report, but others would.

When his friend called back and confirmed the manner and location of Paul Weiler's death, Drewett taped the call and telephoned Tom Pierce.

In Tom Pierce's office, Karas was saying, 'I thought you should hear this yourself. It's strictly a political matter.'

Karas was round-faced and graceful, with a crew cut and pale, rimless glasses. He was forty-seven, six foot tall, a damn fine analyst and had once been Pierce's deputy.

Costa was obviously one of Karas' heavies, shorter, wider, harder looking, with a receding hairline, drooping moustache, a good suntan and a hand in plaster.

Nine days ago, Costa said, on the instructions of Special Agent Alan Hersh he had attempted to carry out a termination order on an American woman, Allison Maynard. He had traced Maynard and her Soviet lover, KGB Captain Yuri Orlov, to a hotel near Lake Constance, where he had been attacked, disarmed and confronted by Orlov — quite a character this Orlov, Pierce thought — who had then wanted Costa to deliver a message to Karas, bypassing Hersh.

Costa said, 'This is the message. Allison Maynard is not one of ours. Whatever she is doing she is doing for America. The termination order on her must be cancelled.'

Standard KGB cover-up, Pierce thought.

'The sovereign loans are tied to the killing of the NATO officer and the attempted bomb outrage in Munich. There will be more terrorism in Germany and whatever is going to happen will happen by the thirtieth of this month.'

The sovereign loans? How did Orlov know of the sovereign loans? And tied to —

'Three, and I think here Orlov was speaking for the KGB, they will share their information with us, but they will only deal with people they trust. Until acceptable contacts are established, they will only deal with Brad Drewett, Maynard's supe —'

'I know,' Pierce snapped. He looked from Costa to Karas and back again. 'How do you know this is not a Soviet disinformation operation, that you people haven't been suckered?'

Sam Costa held up his cast. 'I got no reason to love Orlov, Mr Pierce, and the next time I see him I'll break his balls. But I reckon he was telling the truth.' He told Pierce how Orlov

274

had shown him the Skorpion files. 'It was all figures and accounts going back to before the war. If that's why someone wants Allison Maynard killed, then we're the ones that are being suckered.'

As soon as Karas and Costa left, Pierce had his secretary call Brad Drewett. 'Tell him it's K-One,' he said.

'I was just about to put Mr Drewett through to you,' his secretary said. 'He's just come on the line for you. He too says it's K-One.'

At Drewett's insistence they met at the FAA offices. He showed Pierce Allison's report, played back the message from Zurich and let Pierce read the press cuttings on the murders. Pierce told Drewett about Costa's visit.

'That's all the independent confirmation we need,' Drewett said. 'We'd better move and move fast.'

'Agreed. Let me have West Berlin station get to Allison, collect her evidence and give her support.'

'You must be out of your skull,' Drewett said. 'You think after what she's been through, she'll trust anyone from the CIA? Besides,' he pointed to Allison's report.

Before you take any action on this report or even discuss it with anyone, it will be vital for you to know that they are not Izgoi. The FIRST thing you must do is obtain the records of Clairvaux and ascertain who their graduates are and what they are doing now. This is VITAL.

Pierce said, 'Raiding Clairvaux could be tough. The President was there. He's close to Miles Kingdon. For Chrissake, Kingdon was at the White House all morning advising the President to lay off Lothar and Germany!'

'We don't need the President,' Drewett snapped. 'All we need is a sympathetic judge.'

'I can fix that,' Pierce said.

'And some support from the FBI.'

'That too. We could go in tonight.'

'Great. And Tom. You'd better do something about that termination order.'

'As soon as possible,' Tom Pierce promised.

CHAPTER FORTY-THREE

Allison moved restlessly about the kitchen. Her limbs felt cramped and her head thick, as if stuffed with cotton wool. She looked out of the window at the dismal, empty streets. She wished she could go out and walk in the rain. It seemed such a simple, natural thing to do. But not for her. She was a prisoner in a tiny apartment in East Berlin.

All evening Yuri had sat in the lounge, drinking endless cups of tea and watching television.

'You want more tea?' Making tea would give her something to do, take her mind off wondering if Drewett had got her report, if Drewett would do something, if she'd end up spending the rest of her life hiding in a tiny apartment in a craphole like East Berlin, if the Izgoi would succeed.

Yuri said, 'Five days. In five days the Izgoi plan could have succeeded and we could all be dead.'

'For Chrissake! That's just the sort of cheerful conversation I need. You want some tea or not?'

'We can't just sit here recovering,' Yuri said. 'We've got to do something.'

'What?'

Yuri held out his hand. 'Come and sit by me.'

Pressing her hands to her face Allison went and sat on the sofa beside him. 'I'm sorry. I didn't mean to sound off at you. You've got problems too.'

She felt Yuri's arms round her shoulders. 'We both have.' She pressed her head against his.

'I was also thinking about us.'

'What about us?'

Yuri said, 'When this is over, we're over. I don't want to let you go, Allison. I'd like us to go on. Not like this. Differently. Not running, not in a place where we're frightened, or unhappy or lonely.'

Allison stroked his hand. 'I'd like that, too. But it's impossible.'

'I always thought if we tried hard enough we could make the impossible, possible.'

'Then let's try.' She couldn't find a Kleenex. Yuri passed her his handkerchief. She wiped her eyes and blew her nose. 'Maybe something will happen. Maybe we'll never find the Izgoi and we'll become a kind of Pandora and a Flying Russian, condemned to roam the world forever and hide out in crummy apartments and be together always.'

He kissed her cheek gently. 'Maybe.'

With a cursory ring of the doorbell, Otto let himself in. He hesitated in the doorway, then strode in unbuttoning his coat and flinging his hat on the table by the sofa. 'Karelin's been exonerated,' he cried. 'He's back at SI and wants to talk to you.' He turned to Allison. 'Have you heard from your people yet?'

'No. It's too soon for a reply.'

'But they are acting? They will keep you informed?'

'I believe so.'

Otto sat opposite them on one of the lumpy armchairs. 'I've got more information on Feldmann and the others. All their fathers were in the German army. And all of them died in 1937.'

'1937! That's when the fathers of Gamalrik, Alksnis, Chermassov and Chernov died! What happened in 1937 to kill all these people?'

Otto smiled grimly. 'In May 1937, there was an attempt by

277

the German army to overthrow Hitler. The plot was led by Field Marshal Erwin Lothar whose son is now the Chancellor of West Germany, Colonel Horst Feldmann who was Deputy Commander of the Abwehr, General Wilhelm Kork who was Commander of Wehrkreis III and the fathers of President Blucher and Colonel Eidemann. The plot was discovered and all of them were executed. In May 1937 also, Marshal Tukachevsky, one of Stalin's favourite officers, attempted to overthrow Stalin. The dual conspiracy was called Skorpion.'

Yuri repeated incredulously, 'You mean that at the same time as Lothar and the others were trying to overthrow Hitler, Tukachevsky was attempting to overthrow Stalin?'

'At exactly the same time.'

Allison said, 'I can't believe Germans and Russians would have worked together like that.'

'Germans and Russians have worked together more often than not. In any case, since the Radek-von Seekt pact of 1920, the German and Russian armies trained together. Tukachevsky, for instance, did most of his armoured training in Germany.'

'What was the object of the coups?' Allison asked.

'The public reason was the destruction of two evil dictatorships. The private reason was a union of Russia and Germany and the creation of a Central European Federation, which would have dominated Europe, dwarfed the British Empire and become as wealthy and powerful as the United States.'

'How were the conspiracies discovered?' Yuri asked.

'They were betrayed by a French banker who was part of a consortium put together by Rudolf Barynin to underwrite the coups.'

'That explains why Skorpion lost so many millions in 1937,' Allison cried. 'Because of this parallel conspiracy.'

'And why did this Frenchman betray Barynin?'

'At the last moment he realized the political and economic consequences of the Federation on France and discovered he

278

was a patriot. He betrayed the conspiracy to the French authorities who in turn leaked it to Reynhard Heydrich, Chief of the Nazi Secret Service, who in turn passed the information to Stalin through the Czechoslovak intelligence service and that country's Prime Minister, Edward Benes.'

It was all starting to make sense, Allison thought. The creation of a Central European Federation meant the creation not only of a military and political unit, but also of an enormously wealthy economic unit, potentially more powerful than the United States or the Soviet Empire. Which was why America and Russia would both go to war to prevent it. Which was why Europe had really gone to war fifty years ago. She said, 'So that's what the Izgoi are planning now. A union of Russia and Germany. A repeat of 1937.'

Otto said, 'The world has changed a lot since 1937 and neither America nor Russia will give up their Germanies. The Izgoi could involve us in a nuclear war.'

Yuri asked, 'If all the conspirators were executed why were the sons of the Germans sent to the Brandenburg Academy? Ordinarily such children would have been executed or exiled.'

'In this case,' Otto said, 'Hitler was persuaded to do otherwise. In 1937, Hitler was both preparing for war and trying to maintain the German recovery, an impossible task which made Germany heavily dependent on foreign financing. Rudolf Barynin warned Hitler that execution of the conspirator's families would arouse grave international disapproval, and bring about the withdrawal of foreign financial support for Germany. It was far better that the children be schooled in the ways of National Socialism. That way they would be living proof of their fathers' errors, and Hitler's foreign credits would be safe.'

'But didn't Hitler know about Barynin?'

'No. The financial plot was never revealed. It wasn't in fact discovered till long after the war.'

'Barynin financed the upbringing of the children of the conspirators through the charities Skorpion secretly funded,'

Allison said. 'What happened to the schools after the war?'

'They were allowed to continue.'

'And teach Fascism?' Yuri asked.

'Of course not.' Otto looked at both of them. 'When the war ended Germany had been under a Fascist dictatorship for twelve years. All its administrators and civil servants, the people who ran things, were Fascist or Fascist sympathizers. When we took over we did not have the people with the training, knowledge or experience to replace them. And without those Nazi administrators, we could not have run a town council, let alone a country.' Otto grinned. 'So we created programmes for rapid indoctrination.' He shrugged and added, 'I have never ceased to be surprised at how small the pragmatic differences between Leninism and Hitlerism turned out to be, and how easily these former Fascists adopted the mental attitudes of ardent Communists.'

'And the same thing happened with the schools?' Allison asked.

Otto nodded. 'Yes. After all, the system was there. Only the doctrine needed to be changed.'

Yuri asked, 'Didn't the Russians object?'

'On the contrary, the Soviet Administrator increased the number of schools. You see, fundamentally, the schools were a good idea. The Academies have produced many brilliant individuals. The civil service and Army are full of them and not all of them are Izgoi.'

'Who was the Soviet Administrator?'

Otto smiled. 'Marshal Maxim Iakir, who is now one of the most powerful men in Russia.'

'Is Iakir Izgoi? Could he be our mysterious General?'

'I hardly think so,' Otto laughed. 'Iakir has always been too close to the establishment. He was a devoted Stalinist, and after Stalin's death was one of the people who brought Khrushchev to power.'

Allison asked, 'What about the children of the Russian conspirators?'

'It seems Stalin was prevailed upon to spare them by what was left of his Army. By the time the executions were over, Stalin was becoming concerned about Hitler's ambitions and had become more reliant on his troops. The children were spirited away by surviving members of the Izgoi, sent to Rodina schools, and then infiltrated into positions of influence and power.'

'Who arranged that?' Yuri asked.

Otto shook his head. 'You will have to find out who in Moscow. Karelin is arranging for you to make a search of the Archives. He wants you to return and brief him and General Secretary Timochek.'

'When do I leave?' Yuri asked.

'Now.'

Allison felt her heart sink like a stone.

CHAPTER FORTY-FOUR

Shortly after six o'clock that evening a police car and a Chevrolet sedan raced in convoy up the short gravelled drive to the gates of Clairvaux College. The guards moved in a line before the locked gates. The Police Chief climbed out of the squad car and spoke to the guards. After an argument, during which the guard telephoned Dean Miles Kingdon twice, the gates were opened and the cars rushed to the main building.

Chief Haskins, the two FBI men, Pierce and Drewett went up the steps into the building. The room they entered was large and sprawling with a splendid view of the grounds. Kingdon sat before a micro computer, sideways to one of the desks. He swivelled round as they entered. 'What is the purpose of this intrusion?' His gaze was flat, his voice was neutral.

Chief Haskins strode towards him. 'I have here a court order impounding the records of Clairvaux College.'

'Yes,' Kingdon said slowly. 'You said that when you spoke to me from the gate. May I know the reason for this order and why the College wasn't given an opportunity to oppose it?'

One of the FBI men said, 'The order is an interim one. Your representations can be made at the final hearing which will rule whether the interim order stays or not.'

'Then perhaps I should keep the records until the hearing.'

'We keep the records,' the FBI man said. 'If the court so orders, they will be returned to you.'

Kingdon studied each of the men in turn. 'There are no records,' he said. He indicated the computer with a tilt of his head. The screen was blank.

Drewett walked up to the computer and pressed some keys. The screen remained blank. 'Have you erased all the records, Mr Kingdon?' he asked.

Kingdon said, 'I was trying to get the records for you. There was an accident.'

The FBI man rushed up to the wall safe. He pulled the door open, cried 'Sonofabitch!' and jumped back, flicking at his suit with his hands. A stench of acid filled the room. Drewett ran past the FBI man and peered. The safe contained a large tray of still bubbling acid, in which a few scraps of burnt paper floated. 'Why have you destroyed the College records?' he turned and shouted at Kingdon. 'Why?'

'Because the College records are nothing to do with you. Those records are confidential.'

'Why?' Drewett asked.

The FBI man marched up to Kingdon. 'I'm going to arrest you,' he said.

'On what charge? I wasn't aware of the court order when I destroyed the records.'

'That isn't what it looks like,' the FBI man said. 'Please stand up, Mr Kingdon.'

From beneath his desk Kingdon pulled out a long-barrelled .45. The FBI man froze.

Chief Haskins said, 'Even if you managed to shoot the six of us, there's more of my men outside. Let's not be silly, Mr Kingdon. You're better off coming quietly.'

Kingdon looked up at him and smiled. 'You're too late,' he said, quietly. 'There are too many of us, and more Academies like Clairvaux. You will never find us in time.' With a swift, blurring movement he raised the gun, put it to his mouth and fired.

Karelin was waiting for Yuri in the Immigration area at Sheremetyevo, together with Mark Kutsov, Boris and Andrei whose Stechkins were in full view.

'You look as if you've been in the wars,' Karelin smiled.

'On the losing side,' Mark added.

They shook hands and exchanged hugs. Karelin told Yuri he had taken Yuri's information to General Secretary Timochek who had given them unrestricted powers to find the Izgoi and the mysterious General who had met with Barynin in Argentina. They could interrogate anyone they liked, Karelin said, handing Yuri an authority on embossed Kremlin notepaper, they could go anywhere and do anything, including Yuri noticed, enter Russia without clearing Customs or Immigration.

Karelin had a Zil limousine parked outside the terminal. Boris drove back to Moscow as if possessed, while Karelin debriefed Yuri.

'This General is the key to everything,' Karelin said. 'Do you have any idea who he could be?'

'The only General I've come across is Maxim Iakir,' Yuri said. 'The one who authorized the continuance of the Brandenburg schools.'

Karelin said, 'Iakir is not a General, he's a Marshal. He is also a senior member of the Politburo who has loyally served every Russian leader since Stalin. Since Khrushchev, Iakir has been part of every General Secretary's inner circle. In fact, he made Khrushchev.'

'The General was close to someone in the Troika,' Yuri said.

'Not Iakir,' Karelin said. 'Iakir began his rise to power by bringing out his tanks *against* Tukachevsky.'

'I can't think of anyone else,' Yuri said.

Minutes afterwards the car turned into Dmitrova. 'I think you should stay with your family tonight,' Karelin said. 'Tomorrow, you will begin work at the Archives.'

'Are the guards still there?' Yuri asked.

Karelin nodded. Then he peered closely at Yuri and asked, 'What's the matter, Yasha? Aren't you glad to be home?'

'It's such a shock,' Yuri said. 'I must be jet lagged.'

The room President Jack Donnelly liked to call his rumble room was long and narrow and filled with comfortable chairs and soothing prints. It was a room, Tom Pierce knew, the President liked to relax in. Not much relaxation tonight, Pierce thought.

Pierce and Drewett had raced back to the White House from Clairvaux, and Pierce had demanded to see Donnelly as a matter of grave urgency. Without a word of explanation Pierce had given Jack Donnelly Allison's report. Now he and Drewett stood watching the President as he read it.

The President finished reading and looked up at them. As he'd read the report his face had seemed to sag, the muscles holding his jaw and mouth had gone softer. He'd looked ten years older and Pierce saw that beneath his tan, the President's face was ashen.

'Who's Allison?' the President asked.

Drewett said, 'Allison Maynard is my assistant director at the FAA.'

The President leaned sideways for a phone. Tom Pierce stepped forward quickly and placed his hand on the receiver.

Donnelly stared angrily up at him, his eyes narrowing.

'What the hell's this? I want to talk to Timmins.'

'You don't talk to Timmins,' Pierce said. 'You don't talk to anyone till we're through.'

Slowly, the President moved upright away from the phone and sat erect in the middle of the sofa. 'Do you mind telling me what the hell is going on?'

'Earlier this evening we got a court order from Judge Stevens and had the FBI raid Clairvaux College,' Pierce said. 'We wanted the college records.'

'And?'

'Miles Kingdon destroyed the records and then shot himself.'

'Jesus wept!' The President looked as if he had been rabbit punched. 'Miles shot himself! I won't believe that! Miles!' He ran his hands across his face. 'He was here only this morning. Miles wasn't one of these . . .' His hand beat angrily at the report. 'This is true . . . But I can't believe Miles. He was so wise, so brilliant, so clever. He taught me . . .' The President looked up at them. 'And you think I − you think − it's a reasonable conclusion, I suppose.' He put Allison's report down on the sofa beside him and visibly straightened himself.

'I am not one of these Izgoi,' the President said. 'I did not know about them nor did I have anything to do with them while I was at Clairvaux. I was only at Clairvaux for two terms, while my father was working in what is now Saudi Arabia. And the first I heard about the Izgoi was when I read Allison Maynard's report.

'Miles Kingdon was one of my tutors at Clairvaux. I liked him. No it was more than that, I hero-worshipped him. Miles Kingdon was no ordinary person. A few years older than me, he was a Rhodes Scholar, he'd travelled all over Germany, he'd fought Max Schmeling, the only man who beat Joe Louis in his prime, he'd boxed for America, he'd finished sixth in the last of the great trans-American runs. To me Kingdon was everything I wanted to become, scholar, teacher, aesthete, fighter. I believed he was the nearest a human being came to being superhuman.'

The President shrugged and grinned wryly. 'You know I wasn't one of Clairvaux's successes. It wasn't the military marches or the sport, but the discipline and the cramming that I couldn't take. At the end of my second term Clairvaux decided I didn't have whatever they required for a Clairvaux man and asked my father to remove me. To be honest, I was relieved.'

Drewett remembered that the President had gone from Clairvaux to a small college in Texas, then graduated in law from Columbia, joined the family oil business and used the family oil fortune to launch him into politics.

'I never returned to Clairvaux,' the President said. 'And I didn't see Kingdon again till ten years ago, when I met him by accident at the Senate cafeteria. He told me he'd come up to see someone over an education matter, and I invited him to stay over for dinner. It was strange. There was I, an adult, a fully fledged Senator, someone looked up to, respected and admired, but with Kingdon I was a schoolboy again, a schoolboy privileged to walk and talk and eat with his hero.

'We saw each other regularly after that, and though the relationship became less adolescent, I never lost my respect and admiration for Miles Kingdon.' The President ran his hand over Allison's report. 'Even now, I find this difficult to believe.'

'Do you think Kingdon was using you, Mr President?' Drewett asked.

The President slapped the report again. 'That seems to be the inescapable conclusion.' He looked from Drewett to Pierce. 'Everyone who was at Clairvaux couldn't be Izgoi, you know. If that was so, it wouldn't have been a secret for so long.' The eyes narrowed, the scar tissue on the edges of his lids seemed to mould together. 'What are you two guys going to do? It seems to me you have a decision to make. Are you going to fight me or do we work together on this?'

Pierce said, 'We're not sure.'

The President said, 'Face the fact, Tom. There isn't a hell

of a lot you can do without me. If you're going after the Izgoi, you're going to need all the authority of this office. Otherwise,' he slapped Allison's report for emphasis, 'they'll bury you.' He looked directly at Pierce. 'You armed, Tom?'

Slowly Pierce nodded. 'I thought if Kingdon was Izgoi, if you were at Clairvaux . . .'

'Then you'd better get ready to use that gun, Tom, because I'm not going to sit on my ass till you make up your mind. I'm going to start doing something about the Izgoi right now.' He picked up the phone. 'What's the status on the termination order on Allison Maynard?'

'I was hoping to clear that with you once we'd got the Clairvaux records.'

'Let's clear it now,' the President said. He called Timmins and ordered him to cancel the order.

Pierce and Drewett sat. The President put down the phone and said, 'As we didn't get the Clairvaux records, how do we find out who these American Izgoi are and neutralize them?'

Pierce and Drewett shook their heads. The records of Clairvaux College had been their only lead. Then Pierce said, 'Why don't we begin by standing down everyone involved with Maynard? Bill Timmins, Karas, Costa, Cowdrey Berle and that special agent of Timmins' investigating Duisburg, Alan Hersh?'

The President frowned thoughtfully, before he nodded. 'All right. As things stand, the only people I trust right now are both of you and me.' He looked at Drewett. 'How do we make contact with Maynard? Brad, could you get to East Germany tomorrow?'

'I could. But I think Tom had better go.'

Pierce said, 'I don't know Allison Maynard and she doesn't know me. Right now she'd probably run from any American, except Brad.'

Drewett said, 'I could tell her you were OK.'

'That still wouldn't make her trust me. You saw the message from Orlov. You're the person they want.'

Drewett shook his head. 'But you're the person they need. Once you get there, some tough decisions will have to be taken. You'll have to talk with the Russians and the East Germans, you will have to bring in other people and other agencies. Things will happen more effectively if they are being handled by a Presidential aide rather than a Director of the FAA.'

'Brad's right, Tom,' the President said.

'Nothing will happen unless Maynard agrees to talk to me.'

Drewett said, 'I could send a message to her electronic mailbox telling her of your arrival, who you are, what — '

President Donnelly interrupted. 'How secure are these messages?'

Brad explained that Allison's mailbox was in Washington, that she accessed it by linking her computer to a phone line and using certain codes known only to her.

'Phone lines are too risky,' President Donnelly said. 'Give Tom a code name,' he said. 'And tell her that anyone contacting her through her mail box using that code name is to be trusted.'

'That means I'll need access to a computer, and I don't know the first thing about them.'

Drewett said, 'I can show you all you need to know in twenty minutes. I'll also let you have a disk with the appropriate codes and procedures. That way, if you forget anything, all you have to do is load the disk and it will tell you what to do.' He smiled and added. 'And I'll let you borrow my portable.'

'You're hurt,' Galina said.

'I *was* hurt. I'm all right now.' Yuri peered round Stefan's head as he spoke. Feeling those tiny arms around his neck, that tiny body pressed to his chest was the most magnificent thing in the world.

'You're thinner. And you look tired.'

'Now that I'm home I can rest.'

'Are you back for good, this time?'

Yuri kissed Stefan's hair. 'I think so.'

He looked round the apartment. No sign of Polyakov's warm-up suit or running shoes.

That night, he told Galina about Allison.

'You're a damned fool,' Galina said, hurt but not angry. 'She's American.'

'I know.'

Galina thought for a while and asked, 'Are you going to live there?'

'I don't think so.'

'So she will come to Moscow?'

'I haven't asked her. I don't think she will like Moscow.'

'And what are you going to do about Stefan and me?'

'I won't abandon you.'

'You're still leaving us,' Galina said.

Friday April 25

CHAPTER FORTY-FIVE

That morning Yuri went to the Archive Records Centre on Barrikadnaya. He was met by a senior archivist and shown into a small partitioned room with a computer terminal and screen. The archivist showed him how to operate the computer.

Yuri sat down and punched 'Skorpion' into the computer.

NO SUCH FILE, the screen flashed.

He tried again. Same result. He felt foolish and thought if Allison were with him she'd know what to do. He put Allison out of his mind and typed in 'Skorpion 1937'.

SKORPION/12 JUNE 1937. CROSS REF: TUKA-CHEVSKY, the screen blinked.

Yuri typed in 'Tukachevsky.'

Details of the life and career of Marshal Tukachevsky scrolled over the screen. On 12 June 1937, Mikhail Nikolai-vitch Tukachevsky, Marshal of the Soviet Union, had been executed for participating in the Skorpion Conspiracy.

Heart pounding, Yuri keyed in 'Skorpion/12 June 1937.'

Again the information moved across the screen. Skorpion had been a conspiracy by a group of Russian and German officers simultaneously to overthrow both Stalin and Hitler. The Russians had been led by Marshal Tukachevsky, the Germans by Field Marshal Lothar.

Over 5000 officers and men of the Red Army had been involved. And all of them had been executed. Yuri watched the names roll past, Tukachevsky, Gamalrik, Kuryakin, Svyatoslav, Alksnis, Primakov. Yuri stared fascinated. So many men. Impossible, he thought. Then, not impossible. It had happened! It was true! These men had been part of the double conspiracy called Skorpion and their sons now held positions of power! So many sons. He asked the archivist for a print-out of the list.

He went over to the Ivushka Café on Kalinin, had a *kotolet* and tea, bought Galina an Abba record from the Melody Music Shop and returned to his cubicle on Barrikadnaya. At last everything was making sense, everything was coming together.

Given normal Soviet practice, the sons of conspirators would not have been allowed within a thousand miles of Moscow. He pulled Alksnis' file and cross-checked it to Skorpion/12 June 1937.

DELETED the screen flashed, OCT 12 1958, BY ORDER OF GENERAL SECRETARY TO THE POLITBURO.

He tried Gamalrik, Svyastoslav and Kuryakin. All deleted, all dated October 12, 1958, all ordered by the General

Secretary to the Politburo. Yuri sat back in his chair and stared at the screen. The General Secretary in October 1958 had been Nikita Khrushchev. And Nikita Khrushchev, Yuri remembered, had been made by Maxim Iakir.

He got Iakir's file. Maxim Iakir had been born in 1909 and had been a professional soldier all his life. Top student of his time at Moscow Staff College, Iakir had joined one of the new armoured brigades, and soon became a leading theoretician on tank warfare. He'd spent much time in Germany and had trained at a German Armoured School. He'd lectured at Staff College, written books, and by the time he was twenty-eight, had been the youngest tank commander in the Red Army.

He'd been posted to Lyublino, just outside Moscow, in command of the 1st Armoured Corps. In 1937 he'd been personally commended by the Generalissimo for his resolution and courage, and the next year transferred to Stalin's personal Military Advisory Staff at the Kremlin. He'd remained there till the Nazi invasion, when he returned to active service. He'd been involved in the defence of Moscow, and had led the break-out afterwards. He had hounded the Germans all the way back to the Dneiper.

Repeatedly decorated and commended, his tanks had played a vital part in the counter-attack at Minsk, and he had led them all the way through Poland to Berlin. He'd stayed on in Germany as a Soviet Military Administrator and then returned to create the Special Task Forces of which he had remained Commander in Chief until he'd become a chief strategist at the Ministry of Defence.

Iakir had risen in rank, Lieutenant-Colonel, Colonel, General, Marshal. He had been C-in-C Warsaw Pact forces, and Red Army Chief of Staff. He was now Minister of Defence, elder statesman of the Politburo, and friend of Valentin Timochek.

It was lunacy to even imagine that he could be Izgoi.

In New York, Drewett sat in Ellesmere Wentworth's office

and said, 'You're not doing yourself any favours.' He had arrived three hours previously with a team of FAA auditors and two FBI men, and since then he had been trying to get Ellesmere Wentworth to cooperate.

Wentworth wiped his face with a crushed Kleenex. 'I've already told you. I know nothing about any conspiracy.'

'It's over,' Drewett said. 'Kingdon's dead. We know everything.'

'I only knew Kingdon vaguely,' Wentworth said.

'You're forcing us to take away your banking licence. You're going to end up over your head in criminal charges and lawsuits. Why not make it easy on yourself?'

'There's nothing I can tell you.'

Drewett nodded to the FBI men. They pulled Wentworth to his feet and led him away. Drewett went round Wentworth's desk and quietly and methodically went through its drawers.

Two hours later, Jameson, the head of the FAA audit team, came in. 'Think we're about all wrapped up now, Brad.' Jameson was a clerkly man in his mid-forties. He placed a bulky file on Wentworth's desk and took out a notebook. 'I've got a list of the tax haven companies, but it'll take us a few weeks to check them out. Barynin's present position is very iffy. They're right on the limit now. Almost all their reserves are in sovereign loans, about ten million dollars' worth. They've also got options on another eighty million, exercisable on the twenty-eighth – next Monday.'

'Why the options?' Drewett asked.

Jameson shrugged. 'I don't know, unless it's part of the attack on the dollar.' He told Drewett that all day the dollar had taken a bashing in Europe.

Drewett switched on Wentworth's computer terminal.

Because of speculation that at the bankers' conference in Zurich next Monday, at least one sovereign loan would be defaulted, the dollar had closed 10 cents down in London, 60 pfennigs down in Frankfurt and 2 francs down in Zurich.

Drewett took Jameson's notebook and said, 'OK. You'd better take your boys home.'

After Jameson and his team left, Drewett remained in Wentworth's office studying Jameson's notes and thinking. Already the Izgoi control of sovereign loans was proving effective, and if on Monday a sovereign loan was defaulted, it would be the beginning of the end. Why, Drewett wondered, had Barynin's taken options when they could default a loan just as easily with ten million as with ninety?

He looked at the notes again and made a call to the Chairman of the bank selling the option. Yes, the bank had granted another option exercisable on the twenty-eighth. The grantee was a Luxembourg company, Cremid SA.

Here we go again, Drewett thought, and asked the banker who owned Cremid. The banker didn't know, but he said the company's performance had been personally guaranteed by Kaspar Baur and five others. He gave Drewett the names. Drewett asked if the banker knew of any other options exercisable on Monday? The banker didn't. He suggested Drewett phoned around.

Drewett did, and by three o'clock had a list of nearly two billion dollars' worth of options on sovereign loans taken out by Cremid, all exercisable on Monday the twenty-eighth, and all guaranteed by Baur and his group of investors.

Drewett studied the investors' names and checked their backgrounds. None of them were in first-line banking and all of them were mavericks. They controlled their own companies and had reputations for shrewdness and riding away from the herd. He wrote out the list of names:

Avery Cartwright	USA	Commodities
Michael Henley	UK	Securities
Ingmar Sundstrom	Sweden	Shipping
Carlo Aguita	Italy	Construction & Hotels
Hugo Hendrik	Switzerland	Pharmaceuticals & Electronics

Drewett made more phone calls. None of the men were available that evening nor would they be available for the whole of the next week. They were all, Drewett gathered, attending the bankers' conference in Zurich.

Drewett made one more call and reached Tom Pierce just as he was leaving for the airport.

'If all of them are Izgoi,' Tom said, 'we're finished.'

'If they were, they'd have bought the loans, not wasted money on options.' Drewett told Pierce what he thought Pierce and Allison should do.

'Good idea,' Pierce said and told Drewett the President was meeting with the Secretary to the Treasury and the Chairman of the Federal Reserve Board at noon the next day. Pierce wanted Drewett to be there, and asked him to get to the White House fifteen minutes early and brief the President.

In his suite at the CP Tower, Alan Hersh stared perplexedly at the phone. Bill Timmins had called him at five o'clock that morning and informed him that the termination order on the Maynard woman was cancelled. Now, just twelve hours later, Timmins was ordering him to return to Washington. 'What exactly do you mean, "stood down"?' Hersh asked.

Bill Timmins said, 'Your work there's over. You're to return to Washington.'

Hersh felt a twinge of panic. Returning to Washington could be a precursor to interrogation and arrest. 'But why?'

'It's nothing to do with you, Alan. It's something political. A lot of people are being stood down here. I've been stood down, too.'

'You! For Chrissake, why?'

'I don't know. It was a request from Donnelly himself.'

'This is lunacy, Bill. What do the politicians think they're doing?'

'Ours not to reason why,' Timmins said quietly. 'I believe there have been some new developments on the German situation and they want to move fresh teams in.' He told Hersh Pierce would be on a Pan Am flight arriving in Frankfurt at ten-fifty the next morning. 'Meet him, hand over to him and have a nice holiday,' Timmins said.

Hersh put the phone down, thoughtfully. A nice holiday was the one thing he would not have, yet.

Saturday April 26

CHAPTER FORTY-SIX

Tom Pierce came wearily out into the main concourse at Frankfurt International Airport. He'd dozed only fitfully on the flight over and he'd had a full day before leaving Washington the previous night. In addition to helping with the West German diplomatic crisis and supervising the stand downs, he'd had to prepare carefully edited briefing papers for the CIA Station Head in Germany and Supreme Allied Commander Europe.

Pierce wished he felt more alert. If his arrangements with Allison Maynard permitted, he was meeting with the CIA Head of Station that afternoon and Supreme Allied Commander Europe early the next morning and at some time he would take over the Duisburg file from Hersh. He clutched Drewett's computer a little tighter as he walked. Thank heaven Drewett had given him that disk. With all he had on his mind, he would have forgotten his own name, let alone codes and computer protocols.

He became aware of a heavily moustached man in a pale-brown corduroy suit striding towards him, with a wide smile and an outstretched hand.

'Hi there, Tom!'

'Alan Hersh! What are you doing here at this time of the morning?'

'Well, I thought I'd give you a ride into town and brief you on the way. The sooner I hand over, the sooner I get home.'

Pierce looked quickly at Hersh. There was no hostility there, no sarcasm. Perhaps Hersh really wanted to go home. He forced himself to concentrate. He would need all his faculties for his meeting with Allison, the Head of Station and SACEUR. Better to go to his hotel, catch up on some sleep, shower and arrange to see Hersh another time. 'That's very nice of you, Alan, but – '

'No trouble,' Hersh smiled and took the computer from Pierce's hand.

Karelin studied Yuri's hastily typed report. 'It's good,' he said. 'But we have to find this General. He is the key to everything and I don't want Timochek dithering about after I see him, and the only way to do that is to give him a complete report.'

'I've checked,' Yuri said. 'There is not one of the conspirators I can tie to someone who was a General in 1945.'

Karelin said, 'Have Army Records give you a listing of Generals in 1944, 1945, 1956, 1957, 1958 and 1959. Then check them off against the Skorpion conspirators.'

'All five thousand of them?'

'Yes. If you have any trouble with Army Records, have Mark speak to his father. His father is head of the GRU.'

'I won't have any trouble,' Yuri said. 'Timochek's letter works miracles.'

'I want your information by three,' Karelin said. 'I'm seeing Timochek at quarter past.'

Yuri thought it would take more than Timochek's letter to work that miracle.

Timochek's letter produced the information he wanted. Copying it out and checking it took two hours. He was struggling with his lists when the archivist suggested he could load the information into the computer and have it compare names. The archivist showed him how. It still took time and by half past two he had exhausted the list. No son of a conspirator had made it to General.

But there had to be a General somewhere. He considered running the comparisons again and decided that would take too long. He wondered if Barynin's visitor had really been a General. Heilbron-Barynin had been a banker not a soldier. Perhaps to him all senior army officers had been Generals. Or perhaps all officers from whatever service. Yuri wondered if he should go back to Army Records and check out colonels and then perhaps Navy Records for submarine commanders.

He looked at his watch. No sense in delaying reporting to Karelin. He'd know as much in fifteen minutes as he knew now. He went out, found a call box and dialled.

Mark took the call. 'You've missed him. He had a contact to see on the way and left ten minutes early. He asked me to call him at the Kremlin if you found anything.'

'Save your breath,' Yuri said. 'I found nothing.'

He went back to the Archives. The computer fascinated him and he wished he had one of his own. A little one perhaps, like Allison's. He tried not to think of Allison. He wondered what she was doing now in East Berlin. He looked at the computer. Better do some work.

What work?

Try Iakir.

He pulled Iakir's file and punched 'Skorpion/12 June, 1937.'

His characters remained embedded at the top of the screen. Below it a narrow, green stripe flashed. SEARCHING, SEARCHING, SEARCHING. Suddenly the screen went blank. He'd screwed up the main computer, Yuri thought.

Words appeared on the screen.

In 1937, Iakir had been twenty-eight years old and Commander of the 1st Armoured Division stationed at

Lyublino. On 27 May 1937, the day of the Skorpion coup, he had moved his tanks with lightning speed to defend Moscow. Afterwards he had been commended for the speed of his move and been personally thanked by Stalin.

So much for Iakir's being Izgoi. Yuri stared at the screen almost willing it to produce an answer. If not Iakir, who? Or just who?

Yuri read the screen again. The speed of his move, the lightning speed . . . Yuri thought tanks did not move quickly. He read the file again. Within forty minutes of receiving the order, Iakir had ringed Moscow. Forty minutes, to get his men out and into the tanks, to have engines started and get the huge beasts trundling, forty minutes to cover the distance between Lyublino and Moscow.

Impossible! Unless Iakir's tanks had already been ready, Yuri thought, to take Moscow, not defend it! He stared at the screen for a moment and then rushed out to call Karelin.

Karelin had not wanted his visit to the Kremlin to attract any attention, so he'd driven himself in one of the pool Zhigulis. The sentry at the Nikolsky Tower took his workpass and studied it carefully, looking from the workpass to Karelin and back again. It must be because he was driving himself, Karelin thought. The guard was probably more used to KGB Directors swanning through in limousines. The guard returned his pass. Karelin shifted into gear and drove into the Kremlin.

On the roadway in front of the Arsenal a squad of soldiers were drilling. Karelin stared at them with surprise. The men were STF not Kremlin Guard. Perhaps a detachment on special duties or ceremonial training, he thought.

He stopped before the flight of steps at the far end of the courtyard. There was a squad of soldiers on the steps. Karelin looked for Timochek's secretary. Still waiting for an elevator, he thought, got out of the car, locked the doors and walked to the steps.

298

Still no secretary. Never mind. He knew the way to Timochek's office well enough. He went up the steps. Where was — Karelin had a definite feeling something was wrong. The soldiers had formed a loose semi-circle by the doorway and an officer had come out to stand between them and the door. They were all looking at Karelin with a frozen hostility, and again he noticed the men were STF.

The officer took his workpass. 'Comrade Timochek is expecting you?'

'Yes. I have an appointment.'

The officer looked at the workpass, then at his watch and returned the workpass to Karelin.

'Where's Secretary Suslov?'

'He's ill.' The officer snapped his fingers. Two of the soldiers fell in behind Karelin. 'Come, I will take you to the General Secretary's office.'

'You don't really need to. I know the way.'

The officer turned on his heel and led the way into the building.

The room inside was vast. Along one side, tall windows looked on to Red Square. To the left, French windows opened on to a balcony. Before one of the windows was a large desk, handsome and intricately carved, a quarter of its tooled-leather surface covered by an armada of telephones. Behind the desk sat the sturdy, grizzled figure of Marshal Maxim Iakir. 'Do come in, Comrade Director,' the Marshal said. 'I have been expecting you.'

'I am sorry,' Karelin said, preparing to retreat. 'I wanted to see General Secretary Timochek.'

Iakir smiled. 'General Secretary Timochek is indisposed. I am afraid you will have to put up with me.'

Karelin took two steps back. 'In that case, I will return when he is better.'

'Wait!' Iakir's voice was almost a parade ground roar. He held out his hand. 'General Secretary Timochek is likely to be indisposed for a very long time.' Iakir looked down at the diary on his desk. 'I understand you have a report for the General Secretary on the Izgoi. Let me have it please.'

'That report is private to the General Secretary.'

'I am sure he wouldn't have wanted to exclude me,' Iakir said. The veined hand reached across the desk. The thin lips curled into a cruel smile. 'Yes, Comrade Director. Everything you are thinking is exactly right. I am the leader of the Izgoi and we have taken over the Kremlin. A new era has dawned for Russia and the world!'

Behind him Karelin heard the soldiers slide the bolts of their rifles.

CHAPTER FORTY-SEVEN

At precisely three o'clock that afternoon, Allison sat in the bar of a small hotel near the Kufürstendamm. A curved counter took up half the room, four Formica-topped tables and fitted plush benches the rest.

Late last afternoon she'd heard from Brad. Action was being taken on her report and an emissary from the White House was on his way to meet with her. He would fix a rendezvous through her mailbox and identify himself as Loanshark.

At eleven o'clock that morning she'd received a message from Loanshark suggesting a meeting at sixteen hundred hours in Room 232 of the West Berlin Hilton.

Never meet in a hotel room, Otto had said. Always arrange your *treffs* somewhere public and not too open. The bar of the Hotel Savigny was ideal. It was public, not visible from the street and so small that any backup would fill it.

Otto had also wanted her to alter the time. 'Make it earlier. Give them less time to prepare surprises. And have him bring the computer as a recognition symbol.'

300

'In a bar that size I think I could spot an American easily enough,' Allison had said.

'I'm not worried about your recognizing each other,' Otto had said. 'Carrying something will occupy one of his hands and give him something to think about.'

When Yuri returned to Special Investigations Headquarters, Mark was in Karelin's office, his face clouded with worry. He had five short-wave radios and a transistor going simultaneously. They had traffic, fire, accident, militia, the KGB and Radio Moscow. 'I can't understand it,' Mark said to Yuri, 'Karelin hasn't reached the Kremlin yet.'

'Who did he take with him?' Yuri asked over the sound of Radio Moscow's daily half hour of pop music.

'He went alone. I hope he hasn't driven into something.'

Yuri dumped his notes on the desk and told Mark about Iakir.

'He wasn't seeing Iakir. He was seeing Timochek.' Mark called the Kremlin again.

They waited ten minutes, then got into Mark's MG and hurried towards the Kremlin. Flags still fluttered. The red walls still stood. Red Square was empty of traffic and workmen were erecting stands.

They drove back to Headquarters. In Karelin's office the radios sounded like a disc jockeys' convention.

'Something's happening,' Mark said. 'The Kremlin guard is all STF.'

At that moment the radio programme cut out and was replaced with the sombre opening of Mozart's Funeral March.

Something had happened.

An announcer interrupted the music. In hushed tones, he said that Russia's dynamic young leader Valentin Timochek had been suddenly taken ill in the Kremlin that afternoon. Kremlin and Army doctors were with him at that very moment and a further bulletin would be broadcast as soon as more news was available. Meanwhile the Politburo urged the people to remain calm and go about their normal business. Marshal Maxim Iakir, Minister of Defence and senior member of the Politburo, would take over the General Secretary's duties until he recovered.

Mark looked at Yuri white-faced. 'It's begun,' he said.

Allison sipped coffee and waited. She could look out of the bar into the reception area with its photographs of the bombed Hotel Savigny on its walls. She wondered what she was going to do. She couldn't keep running. She wanted to go home. The meeting with Loanshark could be the first step, she thought.

She thought about Yuri, wished he was with her and wondered if they would ever meet again. Perhaps she could visit him in Moscow. She'd never been to Moscow, but would they be allowed to meet? To stay together? Then she remembered Yuri was married and had a son. Shit! As if she didn't have enough problems.

A man hurried past the reception desk and came into the bar, pausing to allow his eyes to adjust to the murkier light. He was carrying a case with the brightly coloured logo of an apple. Allison recognized Drewett's case.

He walked over and dumped the case on a vacant chair. 'Hi there, Miss Maynard,' he said cordially. 'Sorry to be a little late.' He sat down, smiling. 'I'm Alan Hersh.'

Allison felt her heart stop. Alan Hersh with his moustache and matching corduroy coordinates was CIA! Alan Hersh was the man who had ordered Costa to kill her and Yuri! In a small voice, Allison said, 'Hello.' She tried not to look at Roth and Hans for reassurance.

Hersh tilted his chair and placed a foot on the plush-covered bench. He put his foot down and waved to the barman. 'Your report was excellent. Bill Timmins was very impressed and also the people at Sixteen Hundred.' He ordered a beer and asked Allison what she wanted.

Allison ordered another coffee.

'Yes, even the President was impressed. When you get back home, Allison, you could become Director of the CIA.'

Allison said, 'You're CIA, Mr Hersh. I was expecting someone from the White House.'

'That's right. Tom Pierce should have been here.' He threw her a helpless smile. 'Tom's sent me instead. Tom's had to go to Berne.'

The waiter brought Allison's coffee. The specially drawn beer would take longer. Hersh said, 'Now let's begin stopping the Izgoi and start getting you home.'

Allison couldn't believe it. How could Brad expect her to work with the man who had tried to kill her? Of course at the time they had thought she'd gone over to the Russians. But to kill? Then she thought, rules change, circumstances change . . . or did they?

The waiter brought Hersh's beer. A line of froth stuck to his moustache as he drank it. He said, 'Right now Tom's talking to the Swiss government. We feel that our best chance is to open up Skorpion from the Swiss end, which is why he sent me to collect the files. Before we can persuade the Swiss to act we will have to convince them Skorpion is acting illegally.'

That made sense. Then Allison thought opening the Skorpion files would only provide more evidence, that what they needed now was not more evidence but a lot of action. Action to stop Baur, to stop Feldmann and the East Germans, to stop the Izgoi in Russia. Instead of charging off to Switzerland, Tom Pierce should have spoken to her and Otto. They had much more vital information than anything he could get from the Swiss.

Pierce had made a big mistake, she decided. And if Pierce was bumbling along like that, giving him the files could only lead to a big, bureaucratic whimper. She said, 'The Skorpion files were illegally obtained.'

'That doesn't matter. When the Swiss see what's in them they won't give a damn how they were obtained.'

Allison still hesitated. She didn't trust Hersh and now she had grave reservations about Pierce. And Brad. Brad had boobed. She said, 'I'd like to see Tom Pierce.'

'Believe me, Tom is looking forward very much to meeting you. You shall deliver the files to him, personally.' Hersh laid some more froth on his moustache and asked, 'Where are the files?'

Allison stared at him. 'They aren't here in Berlin.'

Hersh brought his head close to hers. 'We need those files urgently, Allison. This whole thing is beginning to break and the pressure on us is increasing. Lothar is driving everyone mad with his demands for us to get out of Germany, and yesterday in Frankfurt, Paris and London, the dollar dropped seven per cent because of rumours that at the bankers' conference in Zurich several major international loans would be defaulted.'

So that was what the Izgoi were doing with the Skorpion loans, Allison thought, neutralizing America by weakening the dollar. She said, 'I'd like to talk to Brad Drewett.'

Hersh leaned back, surprised. Then he sipped his beer and said, 'Sure.'

They made the call from a telephone box in an alcove opposite the reception desk. A door beside the telephone box led to the gentlemen's lavatory. Hans went in ostentatiously unfastening his fly. Hersh stood by the lavatory door while she spoke.

'Brad,' Allison said, 'I'm in West Berlin with Alan Hersh. He wants me to deliver the Skorpion files.'

'Alan Hersh! You should be talking to Tom Pierce!'

'Hersh tells me Pierce is in Switzerland.'

'Could you put Hersh on the line and listen in?'

'I think so.' Allison went and spoke to the girl. The girl invited her round the counter and handed her a phone from the desk. 'Where's Tom Pierce?' Drewett was asking.

'Berne, I believe.'

'What's he doing there? He was supposed to be meeting with — '

'The Head of Station and SACEUR,' Hersh said.

'That's right. He didn't show,' Drewett said. 'When did you last see Tom?'

'When he got in this morning. I met him at the airport. I wanted to hand over my files and get back home, but Tom wanted me to stay on and work with Allison.'

'Why was that?'

'Tom had this idea of using the Swiss to expose Skorpion, and right there at the airport he made two calls to Berne.'

'Did he give you the codes for Allison?'

'Sure. How else do you think we met? And I've got your computer too, Brad.'

Drewett asked, 'Did Tom leave a contact number?'

'No. He wanted me to check back with Frankfurt when I'd got the files.'

'OK,' Drewett said. 'We'll try and locate him in Berne. Give me Allison.'

Allison put back her receiver and walked to the phone box.

'Where are the files?' Brad asked.

'They're not with me in Berlin.'

'How long will it take you to get them?'

'I could be back with them in twenty-four hours.'

'Good. Get the files and arrange to meet Hersh at the same time tomorrow. But do not deliver the files to anyone until you have spoken with me.'

'All right.'

'How are you otherwise? Are you OK? Are you being looked after?'

'I'm fine, Brad,' Allison said, 'but I'd like to come home.'

She put down the phone and went back to the bar and told Hersh she would meet him at the Savigny the next day with the files.

'Wouldn't it be quicker if we went together and got the files? That way, you'll be on your way home and Tom and I — '

'I couldn't get the files if anyone else was with me.'

'I see.' There was a hard edge to Hersh's tone. 'Where are the files, Allison?'

'Safe.'

'Aw come on, sweetheart. We're both on the same side.' He peered at her and asked, 'You're not sharing information with the Russkis, are you?'

Allison said, 'You'll have the files tomorrow.'

Hersh kept staring at her. Suddenly he grinned and lifted his glass. 'To us. And the hell with the Izgoi.'

'The hell with the Izgoi,' Allison said and picked up her handbag. She paid for the call and left.

Hersh quietly finished his beer. The two men at the next table left money by their glasses, called cheery good afternoons and left. Hersh looked at their clothes and the bigger man's boots. East German, he thought. The Maynard bitch had come to the meeting with minders. Just as well he hadn't tried anything. He walked quickly to the door and watched the men leave.

Hans and Roth caught up with Allison at the Café Mohring. Allison filled them in on what had happened. They found a post office near the Europe Centre and called Otto. Otto said Hans should return to East Berlin and Allison go with Roth to Stuttgart and collect the files. He told her Yuri's password and warned them about being followed. He said that before delivering anything to Hersh they should make copies.

Allison and Roth took the U-Bahn to the Friedrichstrasse, said goodbye to Hans and returned to the Ku'damm. Roth made Allison change trains twice without warning and then, certain they weren't being followed, took a bus to the airport.

Allison bought plane tickets and an hour and a half later was renting a car in Stuttgart. While she completed the hire documents, Roth got them a newspaper. As they walked to the car park he showed her the front headline. SOVIET

LEADER SERIOUSLY ILL. MARSHAL IAKIR TAKES CHARGE.

In his suite at the Baur au Lac in Zurich, Kaspar Baur stiffened to attention as he heard the voice of Marshal Iakir. 'Things are moving a little quicker than expected,' Iakir said. 'We are now waiting on you.'

'There are no problems here,' Baur said. 'Everyone will be here on Monday to sign the agreements. Once that's done its all over.'

CHAPTER FORTY-EIGHT

Yuri fidgeted restlessly while Colonel Mikhail Kutsov carefully went through the SI files on Munich and the Izgoi. When, half an hour after the news of Timochek's illness had been broadcast, they'd had no word of Karelin, Mark had collected their files and driven with Yuri to GRU Headquarters where he had insisted on speaking to his father.

Colonel Kutsov had listened carefully to what they'd had to say and was now just as carefully going through the files. Yuri looked at his watch. It was nearly three hours since Karelin had left for his appointment with Timochek.

Colonel Kutsov finished reading the files. He pulled off wire-rimmed reading glasses and blinked at Yuri and Mark, stroking the bridge of his nose where the glasses had pinched. 'A hell of a business,' he breathed. 'A hell of a business.' He stared past Mark and Yuri at the wall. Colonel Mikhail Kutsov had the same narrow features and pale-blue eyes as Mark. His tight blond curls were sparser and mixed with grey. One day Mark would look like that, Yuri thought. If Mark or he or any of them lived that long.

Colonel Kutsov reached for a phone and barked orders. Minutes later, four heavily armed soldiers entered, one of them carrying two Stechkins. Colonel Kutsov ordered the soldier to hand the weapons to Mark and Yuri, then posted two of the men at each end of the corridor, and the other two outside the door of his office. 'You will wait here till I return,' he told Mark and Yuri. 'You will not leave this room on any account.' He made one more phone call, then checking his Makarov had a full magazine, he left.

Mark produced a chess set from his pocket. 'You play?'

'Of course.'

'We might as well.'

Drewett got to the White House at twenty to twelve and told the President about Allison's phone call and what he had discovered at Barynin's bank the previous day.

'I wonder what's happened to Tom,' the President said, worriedly. 'It isn't like him − '

'Perhaps Tom is trying to get the Swiss to intervene in the bankers' conference in Zurich,' Drewett said.

'Perhaps,' the President said, dubiously. At that moment his secretary informed them the Secretary to the Treasury and the Chairman of the Federal Reserve were waiting.

The meeting dragged on through the afternoon, moving hesitantly in convoluted spirals as each man tried to avoid the stark reality that there wasn't a thing they could do to save the dollar.

The Chairman of the Federal Reserve feared that when trading opened in Europe on Monday, the European banks, led by the Germans, would cut short-term credit lines to American banks.

The Secretary to the Treasury expounded on the effect a further fall in the value of the dollar would have on foreign-owned short-term dollar deposits and bank shares. Yesterday, American bank shares had dropped eight points.

President Donnelly suggested they printed more dollars.

308

The Treasury Secretary said that even a temporary increase in money supply would increase both inflation and the budget deficit to impossible levels.

'Why don't we simply pay off the defaulted loans?' the President asked. 'Surely we can match these speculators dollar for dollar?'

Brad pointed out that the speculators were about to corner the market with two billion dollars' worth of loans. 'We repay those and they'll only use our money to buy more loans and repeat the cycle till we run out of cash. And can you imagine the effect on the borrowing countries if they knew their loans were guaranteed by us?'

They discussed approaching the IMF, and selling American assets abroad. They discussed instituting exchange controls, pumping reserves into supporting the dollar and speculating against the mark. At three o'clock they heard that Chancellor Lothar had announced a meeting with Marshal Iakir and East German President Blucher the following Wednesday, to discuss turning West Germany into a neutral zone.

'No way,' the President cried. He called his Chief of Staff and put the European Strategic Reserve on Red alert.

At five o'clock the worst news came. The American Ambassador in Germany informed the President that Tom Pierce's body had been found under a rubbish heap in Frankfurt. He had been tortured, drugged and shot twice in the head. The RGA had claimed responsibility and described it as a blow against American economic imperialism and a step towards the freedom of Germany.

The President adjourned the meeting and asked everyone but Brad to leave. 'I want you to take Tom's place,' he said. 'I want you to get over there right away, contact Allison Maynard and stop Baur pulling the plug on us.'

'I'm going to need the same clout Tom had.'

'You have it.' The President gave Brad a letter describing him as the President's personal emissary and a phone number on which he could be contacted at any time. He told Drewett he should take a gun.

Brad thought about Tom and hesitated. He'd never liked carrying guns.

It was after nine o'clock when Colonel Kutsov returned, accompanied by two other men. The older man with the wispy hair, thick-lensed circular glasses, and sunken-cheeked face, was senior Politburo member and Chairman of Party Control, Pavel Aliyev. The short, dark-haired man with straight black eyebrows and tortoiseshell eyes was Vladimir Borodin, Head of Soviet Ground Forces.

They crowded uncomfortably along one side of Kutsov's desk. Kutsov enquired if Yuri and Mark had eaten, had the guards bring them pies and tea and while they ate, had them go over their story again. 'Everything is confirmed by the files,' Colonel Kustov said. He leaned forward to get a better look at Borodin. 'The question is whether we move now or later. My information is that all Iakir has are the STF and two tank regiments from the provinces who don't know their way around Moscow.'

'Typical Iakir,' Borodin smiled. 'Relying as always on tactical surprise and pressure at key points.' His smile faded. 'To bring my troops out could plunge Russia into civil war.'

'Unacceptable,' Aliyev snapped.

Yuri felt his heart sink. Borodin and Aliyev weren't going to do anything.

Colonel Kutsov said, 'I'm sure General Borodin is only talking of a skirmish. Iakir has no depth and we have an overwhelming superiority of numbers.'

'Still unacceptable,' Aliyev said, curtly. 'The Revolution was started with a skirmish.'

Borodin said, 'I will not have Russians firing on Russians. Who knows how many Izgoi there are in the Army? Who knows in which units they are and what positions they hold? We march on the Kremlin and before we know what's

310

happening we'll have our Army fighting each other.' He turned to Yuri. 'Your report indicates a similar situation in Germany?'

Yuri wished he could deny it. 'That's correct, sir.'

Borodin turned to Colonel Kutsov. 'You see. We start fighting in Moscow, and immediately begin a civil war in Germany. Our forces get split and the loyalty of our Army gets divided.'

'And can you imagine the consequences that will have in Poland and Hungary?' Aliyev asked. 'The consequences of even a brief skirmish at this particular point in our history is unthinkable. Certain people may see in such a disturbance a sign of weakness, and take it as a signal to start a struggle for so-called independence.'

Leaning forward and turning sideways, Colonel Kutsov was finding it difficult to address both men. 'In that case what do we do?'

Aliyev said, 'As I see it, the Americans are our only salvation. They have as great an interest in a divided Germany as we have. They must warn Iakir that if he persists in this folly, they will intervene.'

'That still leaves us with Iakir in the Kremlin,' Colonel Kutsov said.

And the Izgoi controlling their lives and Karelin in Iakir's hands, Yuri thought.

'Better a Russia run by Iakir, than no Russia,' Aliyev said.

Sanctimonious arsehole, Yuri thought.

'Yesterday, the American dollar fell substantially against all other currencies on rumours that a number of sovereign loans were going into default.' Colonel Kutsov's voice was edged with despair. 'I think we are going to find the Americans too busy with their own problems to think about resolving ours.'

'Not if they know the attack on the dollar is part of the Izgoi plan.' Aliyev turned to Yuri. 'Tell me, Captain Orlov, how many dollars' worth of sovereign loans have the Izgoi bought?'

'I'm not certain. Perhaps, fifty million.'

'Treble that,' Aliyev said, 'and you have one hundred and fifty million dollars. The Americans could match the Izgoi purchases dollar for dollar. And they *will*, if they know what is at stake.'

'What happens if the Izgoi have more than one hundred and fifty million dollars' worth of loans?' Colonel Kutsov enquired. 'What happens if they have a billion?'

'One default leads to a number of other defaults,' Yuri said. 'A country unable to pay one loan, could be forced to default on all its loans.'

'I'm aware of that,' Aliyev snapped. 'It alters nothing.' He leaned forward, placing scrawny elbows on the desk. 'Our only solution is to involve the Americans. The alternative of plunging Russia into civil war is unacceptable. Where are the Skorpion files, Captain?'

'In Stuttgart.'

'I want you to get to Stuttgart as soon as possible and arrange for the publication of those files. I am right, am I not, in saying that in your days as a political intelligence officer you used the cover of a journalist and are familiar with journalistic practices?'

'I have worked as a journalist,' Yuri said, despondently. Aliyev and Borodin were worse than useless.

'Good. I want you to liaise with your American friends and have the details of your investigation and the Skorpion files published.'

'What good will that do?' Yuri asked. 'Iakir will deny everything. Everything will be suppressed.'

'Publication will serve two purposes,' Aliyev replied. 'Firstly, it will provide the Americans with the evidence they need to take action. Secondly, it will stop Iakir becoming Chairman of the Politburo. For years Iakir has connived and manipulated and schemed with his Izgoi. And what is he now? A stand-in for the General Secretary. If he kills Timochek, if Timochek dies, Iakir does not automatically become General Secretary. He has to be elected. And what chance do you think he would have if every member of the Politburo knew what we know, if every member of the Politburo knew and believed everything that Captain Orlov has just told us?'

'No chance at all,' Colonel Kutsov said. 'If it comes to the vote.'

'It has to come to the vote,' Aliyev said. 'The Izgoi are not strong enough or numerous enough to take over Russia by force. Their strength lies in anonymity and in secret manipulation. If the story of Iakir and the Izgoi is made public, the basis of their organization and their strength is broken. For a putative leader of Soviet Russia to be accused of not being a Marxist is the most serious charge you can make.'

Yuri felt a faint stirring of hope. He said, 'Iakir must know this already. They will be looking for me.'

'But they won't find you,' Borodin said. 'Accompanied by a heavy military escort, you will be taken as soon as possible to an Army airfield from where you will be flown to Finland. From there you will take a civilian flight to East Berlin.'

'Is East Berlin safe?' Yuri asked.

'I will confirm that myself with Otto Dietrich,' Aliyev replied. He peered closely at Yuri. 'Well, Captain, will you do it?'

'What news of Karelin?'

All three men immediately looked more gloomy. Colonel Kutsov did his best to sound reassuring. 'No news, I'm afraid. But don't worry. In these circumstances no news is frequently a good thing.' He leaned across the desk. 'There is little else we can do. I want you to understand that. This is what Anatoly himself would have wanted you to do. It is the only way we have of saving him and stopping the Izgoi.'

Yuri said, 'There is also the question of my family.'

'They have already been moved out of Moscow,' Colonel Kutsov said. 'I shall take personal responsibility for them until you return.' He looked at his watch. 'I think we had better move you now, Captain. We want you airborne before dawn.'

CHAPTER FORTY-NINE

Allison and Roth returned to Berlin shortly after noon. Roth said if they had to hang around till three they had better get the files into a safe deposit. They found one near the Ku'damm and used the same split password system Allison and Yuri had used in Stuttgart. They went to a Post Office and Roth called Otto. Allison called Washington.

Otto was away from the office, and Roth told his secretary they were back and where the files were. The FAA told Allison that Brad was on his way to Berlin.

'Isn't that great!' Allison cried to Roth. 'Brad's going to be here.'

'Maybe he'll be at the meeting.' Roth suggested they have lunch.

Yuri reached East Berlin shortly after noon. Otto was there to meet him with a retinue of SSD bodyguards. They drove to an inn outside Berlin where four other men waited.

Otto introduced them as former East German President Wilhelm Dietmark, a frail-looking, bespectacled man in his late sixties, General Franz Koller, a light-haired, light-eyed, pale man with a Prussian haircut, Politburo member Meissner who reminded Yuri of former Soviet leader Andropov, and Reynhard Fiedler, a stocky, tough-looking professional soldier with a craggy face and deep-set eyes.

Yuri told them what had happened in Moscow and of his meeting with Aliyev and Borodin.

'Publicity,' Meissner mused. 'That won't help us.'

Koller said, 'What we need is military support. Can you get back to Moscow and tell Borodin that?'

'No,' Otto snapped. 'There's no question of Orlov flying back and forth to Moscow. The Izgoi plans will be completed in three days, and we're better off accepting the fact that our Russian friends have chosen to take care of their problem and left us to take care of ours.'

'Typical,' Fiedler grunted.

Koller said, 'The Russians have 380,000 troops in East Germany. There's no question of my troops attacking the Soviets.'

'And heaven knows how many East Germans are Izgoi,' Dietmark said.

'Our only hope seems to be to go along with Borodin. As I see it, what Borodin hopes to do is to force Iakir's abdication by publishing or threatening to publish the Skorpion files. Then once proper order has been restored, they will deal with their Izgoi.'

Koller said, 'That still leaves us with our Izgoi, and the difference is that our Izgoi, men like Blucher, Eidemann and Feldmann, are already in power and cannot be ousted without a revolution which the Russians will suppress so that it will not be an encouragement to others.'

Yuri asked, 'Why don't you arrest the Izgoi leaders, Blucher, Feldmann, Eidemann – '

Otto said, 'And be hanged for treason. You forget, Yasha, that these people are in control, have been in control for a while.' He looked at the others. 'We cannot use the East German army without destroying all we have gained in the past forty years. We cannot arrest our Izgoi leaders. And we cannot rely on our Russian friends to resolve our problems. I suggest we take another approach. Let's examine how we can stop the Izgoi achieving what they want.'

'Or delay it,' Koller said, 'until Borodin's plan is effective.'

Otto said, 'What the Izgoi want is a union of Russia and the old Germany. Already, Lothar has called for a conference ostensibly to declare West Germany a neutral zone, but in reality to set the basis for the union of our three countries.'

'The Americans will never permit that,' Dietmark said. 'They will go to war.'

'Right now the Americans are too busy protectinng their precious dollar to fight anything.'

'It's a problem, with some help, they can resolve,' Otto said. He looked at Yuri. 'Allison understands these things, doesn't she? Do you think with the help of the files she can stop Baur?'

'Right now the Americans will do anything to stop Baur. And if there is anything at all in those files — yes, I would say definitely yes.'

Otto told them that even now Allison was on her way back to Berlin with the files for a meeting with the Americans. 'We can get there,' Otto said, looking at his watch, 'if we leave right away.'

All that day there had been an air of crisis about the White House. Limousines arrived and departed in a continuous stream. Newsmen seemed permanently camped on the lawn.

President Jack Donnelly felt as if all the blood had been drained out of him. Germany was unifying. A new man was running Russia. On Monday the dollar would go through the floor. Tom Pierce had been murdered and his own establishment was infiltrated by the Izgoi.

With an effort, he forced himself to concentrate on the meeting. The Secretary of State, the Joint Chiefs of Staff, the Secretary General of the Nuclear Defence Affairs Committee, the Assistant Director of the CIA and the Secretary to the Treasury were all gathered to discuss the viability of rushing the American NATO reserves to Germany. As the arguments ebbed and flowed around him the President felt like a spectator watching a lengthy rally at a tennis match. He looked at his watch. If he didn't intervene, the arguments would go on for ever.

'I want our reserves to start moving into Germany as soon

as possible,' he said. 'And the hell with how Lothar feels about it.'

Treasury Secretary Don Sturgis shook his head. 'In that case I cannot take responsibility for what will happen to the dollar.' He explained that on Monday, European banks and American corporations with foreign currency commitments would start switching out of dollars. 'Even think of starting a war,' he said, 'and the Arabs will start pulling out, which will mean a massive compulsory cut in our budget deficit and a dollar worth about twenty-five English pence. And that, Mr President, will only be the beginning.'

'But can't we − ' the President began.

'We are a debtor nation,' the Treasury Secretary said. 'We must be mindful of the whims of those whose money we have borrowed and on which we have chosen to rely.'

'Besides,' Sturgis said waspishly, 'the American people would not support a President who took them to war while their savings were being lost and their real wealth depleted.'

The President sighed. He wished Tom were there to give him some encouragement. 'I still want our European Strategic Reserves over there,' he said. 'It will be a sign we're prepared to fight. If things get too bad, we can always pull back.' He sighed and thought Tom would have called it a typical political decision.

The receptionist at the Savigny was the same girl who'd been on duty the previous afternoon. She recognized Allison and said her friend had left a message. Allison was to bring the files to the Intercontinental. She gave Allison the room number. Mr Hersh was there with Mr Drewett.

'Great!' Allison said as they walked back towards the Kurfürstendamm. 'Brad's here! Let's collect the files.'

'No,' Roth said. 'First we go to the Intercontinental and meet him, then we get the files.'

They were at the Intercontinental in fifteen minutes. Allison asked at the reception for Brad Drewett. The clerk gave her a room number. Same room as the one she'd been told at the Savigny. Allison picked up an internal phone and dialled. 'Brad?'

Hersh said, 'Hello.'

Allison asked, 'Where's Brad?'

'He's taking a shower. Come on up.'

'We'll meet you in the bar on the top floor,' Allison said. 'Both of you.'

Hersh hesitated, 'I don't know. Brad's expecting some calls – OK, I'll tell him.'

They went to the rooftop bar. Berlin spread below them. They could look right over the Wall. Allison ordered coffee and Roth pointed out the Potsdamer Platz, Checkpoint Charlie, Tempelhof and Treptow Park. 'Doesn't it make you nervous,' Allison asked, 'knowing anyone can look over your wall?'

'Not my wall,' Roth said. 'And it wasn't built to prevent people looking.'

Allison wondered if she should talk about the Wall with him, but a certain hardness in his glance discouraged her. With a softly tinkling bell a page boy advanced towards them bearing a large placard: MAYNARD. Allison beckoned him over.

'Miss Maynard?'

'Yes.'

'Your friends are waiting for you in the lobby.'

Allison frowned. She had definitely told Hersh they were in the rooftop bar. Then she thought maybe Drewett and Hersh had another appointment, that they were on their way out and wanted to make other arrangements. 'Fine,' she said. 'Thanks.' She paid their bill and walked out on to the landing before the elevators.

A door was open. Two swarthy-looking men were standing before the elevator, about to get in. They saw Allison and waited, allowing her to precede them. They followed her and Roth into the lift, acknowledged her smile and pressed a button.

318

The doors closed. The elevator whooshed down. As it braked for the third floor, both men pulled out guns. 'This way please, Miss Maynard,' the one nearest the door said. His English had a light, lilting accent and he wore pale, blue-lensed spectacles.

As the elevator stopped, the men pocketed their guns, making sure they were pointed at Allison and Roth. Allion looked across at Roth. His face was expressionless. He shrugged and nodded.

One of the men backed out of the lift. Allison and Roth followed. The bespectacled man came behind them. They went a few yards down the corridor before the man facing them stopped before a door and gave it a coded knock.

The door opened. The man backed in. Hersh stood in a small lounge, a gun drooping from his hands.

'Brad couldn't make it,' he smiled. Then his smile went. He looked at them and at the men. 'Where the hell are the files?'

CHAPTER FIFTY

It was nearly half past three when Otto, Yuri and Hans stopped outside the Savigny. The road down from the inn had been slow and cross-town traffic in West Berlin heavy. Otto waited behind the wheel while Hans and Yuri went in.

There were only two salesmen in the bar. Hans described Allison and Roth to the receptionist. The girl said the American had come earlier and asked them to come to the Intercontinental. He'd left a room number but the girl had given the paper to Allison.

'How long ago was she here?'

'About half an hour.'

They thanked her and went outside. Otto drove to the Intercontinental. Yuri went in and checked. No Allison in the lobby or the downstairs bar. No one registered in the name of Hersh. The clerk remembered a young lady who had come in about half an hour ago and thought she was in the roof garden bar.

Yuri rode to the top of the Intercontinental and down again. He went into the underground parking lot and joined Otto and Hans. Hans had taken an Uzi out of the boot and had folded it under his jacket.

Otto said, 'Roth wouldn't go to a meeting in a room, but there's always a first time.'

Yuri's mouth was dry. His heart was beating fast. 'We could start searching the rooms.'

'By the time you've finished, it'll be tomorrow.' Otto frowned. 'There are two possibilities. They could be with friends or with enemies.'

'Hersh was no friend,' Yuri said.

'They could be somewhere in the hotel, or they could have met here and gone elsewhere.' Suddenly, he started up the car and drove out of the parking lot back towards the Kurfürstendamm. He told Yuri about Roth's message. 'Whatever's happening, no one's going anywhere without those files,' he said. He told Yuri what he thought they should do.

'Where are the files?' Hersh swung furiously at Allison. His fist, still clutching the gun, caught her on the side of the head and sent her sprawling against the wall. A violent shaft of pain stabbed through her brain. She felt herself slipping down the wall, and fought to stay upright. Out of the corner of her eye she saw Roth lunge forward and one of the men swipe viciously at him with his gun butt. The side of Roth's face turned bright red. He turned to face the men. One of them kicked him in the stomach. The other hit him again on the head with the gun butt. Roth went down.

Allison pulled herself erect. 'Where's Brad?' she asked.

'Never mind Brad. Where are the files?' Hersh was advancing across the room towards her. She hoped he wouldn't hit her again.

Hersh stopped. 'I want those files, Allison. Those files are important. We need to talk to the Swiss.'

Allison stared at him in horror. 'You're not going to talk to the Swiss,' she said. 'You're Izgoi. You killed Tom Pierce. What have you done with Brad?'

'Tom had to die. He got in the way. Don't make us kill you, Allison. Don't be foolish. You can't stop us now. No one can stop us now.'

Behind Hersh the men had turned Roth on to his face and were lashing his hands behind his back.

'The files will only be delivered to Brad,' Allison said.

Hersh stood in front of her, a strange vacancy in his stare.

The men had finished binding and gagging Roth. They put him into a closet. Hersh stood away and nodded to the men. They advanced towards Allison.

'What are you going to do?' she asked. 'You won't get the files this way. The files are being held in a safe deposit. Only Brad can collect them.'

Each of the men took one of her hands.

Allison screamed.

Hersh hit her and, holding her by the hair, dragged her to the centre of the room. He pulled her head down, making her bend forward. The men pulled her hands behind her and bound them. Hersh pushed her on to one of the beds.

A pillow was thrust over her face. When it was taken away she saw Hersh standing over her, squirting liquid out of a small syringe.

'Allison, my dear,' he said, softly. 'Tell me, where are the files?'

Allison stared at him horrified. She wouldn't speak. She wouldn't tell him.

Hersh leaned forward. The other men pressed her to the

bed while Hersh jabbed her with the needle. Allison felt a steady trickle of warmth flow up her arm, flow gently over her body. She struggled. She tried to pull her arms and legs free. Concentrate, she told herself, do anything, do something, don't let it get to you. She felt the first wave of fatigue.

'Allison, where are the files?' Hersh's voice, distant, soothing.

'I don't know.'

'You've been a very foolish girl, Allison. You've been very bad. Now why don't you tell me where the files are and we'll let you go.'

She wished Hersh would stop talking. She wanted to sleep. She tugged at her bonds, aware that her struggles were weak.

She was drifting, drifting, the bed was engulfing her in warm, soft waves. From a long way beyond the clouds a gentle voice asked, 'Where are the files, the Skorpion files?'

The safe rental was in a narrow street off the Kurfürsten-damm, a small room with thick plate-glass windows and a narrow door. A clerk sat behind a polished counter. Otto went in and checked. The files had not been collected.

While Hans covered the Ku'damm end of the alley and Otto loitered before grilled windows containing videos of sex and violence, Yuri waited in a mini supermarket opposite.

Twenty minutes later they came, two men in identical shiny, blue, lightweight suits walking quickly from the Ku'damm, one dark and wiry, the other pudgy and wearing blue-tinted glasses. Valdez!

Yuri went to the supermarket exit and signalled the others. Valdez and his companion went in. Through the net curtains of the safe deposit window Yuri could see them talking to the clerk. The clerk tapped something into the computer on his desk.

Yuri darted across the road and stood with his back to the plate-glass window of the safe deposit. He heard the sound of a door opening and footsteps. Valdez and his companion came out on to the street, Valdez carrying a shiny, new briefcase, his companion looking warily about him, his hand close to his unbuttoned jacket. They turned right towards the Ku'damm.

Yuri hurried behind them and unloosed his gun. In front of them, Hans stepped on to the pavement, bringing the Uzi from underneath his jacket. Yuri shouted, 'Drop the case, Nino!'

Instinctively, Valdez and his companion turned. Valdez' companion went for his gun. Yuri fired, aiming for the arm. The man whipped back against the wall. His gun clattered on to the pavement. Valdez lifted the case protectively in front of him, his free hand darting beneath his jacket. 'You!'

Yuri saw the barrel of the gun over the top of the briefcase and levelled his own gun at Valdez. There was a sharp, stacatto clatter. Valdez' body jerked. Blood drained from his face. He released the briefcase and fell.

Otto came from across the pavement, looking very serious and officious. He flashed a card in the face of a startled bystander. 'Police,' he said and took the case.

Yuri rushed past Otto to Valdez' companion and thrust his gun against the man's head. 'Where are they?'

The man's eyes rolled. He tried to look away.

Yuri cocked the weapon. 'Tell me, you bastard, where are they?'

'The Intercontinental.' The man told him the room number.

'How many men?'

'Only Alan Hersh.'

Hans was pulling him by the shoulders. 'Let's go, let's go.' Yuri dragged the man to his feet and ran with him to the car. Otto was already behind the wheel, the engine running. 'The Intercontinental,' Yuri cried, as Otto snatched the car into gear.

Leaving Otto covering the man, Hans and Yuri went into the hotel. Hersh's room was on the ninth floor.

They took the elevator. The rooms were set off long corridors with a slight curve to them. Hersh had a room four doors down from the elevator in the centre of a block. They walked cautiously past the room. No sound came from it. They walked to the end of the corridor and back again. Yuri spoke briefly to Hans. Hans smiled and nodded. They walked back down the corridor, singing loudly.

Outside Hersh's door they stopped and laughed. Yuri pounded on the door and drunkenly yelled, 'Klaus, Klaus where are you?'

There was no reply.

Then Hans cried, 'Klaus, whom have you got in there? We know what you're up to, you miserable bastard.'

Yuri shouted, 'We know you're with that little tart from the coffee shop. Come on, Klaus, open up and let's have a look.'

'Or we'll tell Ingrid,' Hans shouted.

From behind the door an American voice shouted, 'There is no Klaus here. Go away. You have the wrong room.'

Yuri cried, 'Don't make jokes. We are going to make music here, while you make love.'

'Such things we do for our friend.'

They sang. Hans shouted, 'Has she got bigger tits than Ingrid?' Yuri pounded on the door.

Hersh opened it.

Yuri jabbed the gun into his stomach and pushed him into the room.

Hersh staggered and twisted. He had been holding a gun behind his back. Yuri, still moving, hit him in the throat. Hans came in fast, kicking the door shut and whipping out the Uzi.

Yuri ran past Hersh to Allison. Her eyes were closed. There was an ugly bruise on her cheek. But she was still breathing. Hans pushed Hersh forward at the point of the Uzi.

Yuri turned to Hersh. 'What have you done to her?' he asked softly.

'Why don't you wait and see?'

Yuri reversed the SIG and hit Hersh across the nose. The bone cracked. Hersh reeled against Hans who jabbed him in the kidneys. 'And where's my friend, Gunther?'

Hersh looked from one to the other and nodded towards the wardrobe.

'Cover him,' Hans said. He opened the wardrobe and dragged Roth out.

'Who are you?' Hersh asked.

'Yuri Orlov. Valdez is dead. We have his friend. We're going to take both of you back to East Berlin for interrogation.'

'No!' Hersh screamed. 'You will not!' Lowering his head and bellowing, he charged at Yuri.

Yuri shot him twice.

Hans was still freeing Gunther. 'You'd better go down and have Otto bring in a body squad,' Yuri said. He went over to Allison and began to unfasten her wrists.

Otto's men were brusquely efficient. They got a doctor to Allison and sent Roth back to a hospital in East Berlin. They took Hersh's body away in a laundry basket, and spirited Valdez' goon back to East Berlin. The doctor said that Allison had been drugged and the effects would soon wear off, that she'd have no ill effects apart from a sick headache. They waited in the room till she was able to sit up, then moved her to the Savigny where Otto had booked her a room.

Allison woke to the sound of low voices and the taste of bile at the back of her throat. Her cheek felt stiff and it ached, but it was nothing to the nausea that racked her. She remembered the sight of Hersh's bloodstained body and felt her stomach twist. She forced herself to be still.

Almost at once Yuri was beside her lifting her off the bed, dragging her one-armed across the room, kicking open the door of the bathroom and holding her as she retched. He gave her water and helped her back to bed.

She was sick twice more and then she slept again. When

she woke her clothes were soaked with perspiration, but her head felt clear and her limbs, light. 'What time is it?' she asked.

'Getting on for seven o'clock,' Otto said. 'How do you feel?'

'Exhausted, but alive. What happened at the hotel?'

Otto told her. She told him what had happened to her and Roth. She asked about Roth. Otto told her Roth was back in East Berlin and would be out of hospital tomorrow. Allison sat up. 'Have any of you seen or heard from Brad?'

'You're sure he's in Berlin?'

'He was coming to look at the files and stop me giving them to Hersh.'

Otto reached for the phone and said, 'No problem, we'll find him. You Americans are so predictable.' He called the Kempinski, the Palace, the President, the Ambassador and the Schweizerhof. None of them had a Mr Drewett staying with them.

Puzzled, Otto called the Savoy and the Parkhotel. Same answer.

Allison asked for the phone and called Washington. The office told her that Brad's flight had been delayed in London, that he had been looking all over Berlin for her and that he was staying at the Excelsior.

One phone call and twelve minutes later, Brad was round at the Savigny. Allison clung to him. 'Christ, Drewett, am I glad to see you.'

'Take it easy, kid. Take it easy. I'm here and nothing more is going to happen to you. We're going to wrap this up and I'm going to take you home.'

'It's still good to see you.' She introduced Brad to Yuri and Otto. Otto said, 'I'd better get some food sent up. It's going to be a long evening.'

CHAPTER FIFTY-ONE

In Washington the President was having breakfast with Treasury Secretary Don Sturgis. Early that morning had come the news that the Bundesbank, on the direct orders of Siegfried Lothar, had begun to sell large amounts of dollars. Sturgis feared that when New York opened, the dollar and bank share prices would crash, that by evening at least one major bank would have had to close its doors. Sturgis wanted the foreign and stock exchanges closed.

'That will let the world know we're not only panicked but also that we're powerless,' the President said.

'Mr President, we are already bleeding to death.'

The white phone, the President's direct line to communications, rang. With a sinking heart, President Donnelly answered.

'It's Walt Grivens, Mr President.'

'Go ahead, Walt.' Grivens was the President's senior communications aide.

'The Acting General Secretary to the Politburo is on the red line. The transmission has been confirmed.'

The President indicated to Sturgis that he should leave the room.

Walt Grivens said, 'The interpreters are patched in and the call is wired to your confidential secretary and the recording system. Are you ready for the transmission, sir?'

The President took a deep breath. 'I'm ready,' he said.

Donnelly had never spoken or met with Marshal Iakir. All he knew of the Marshal was the briefing that State had given him and the photographs he'd seen of a stocky, bemedalled officer standing on the podium at ceremonial occasions. 'Good morning, Mr General Secretary,' he began. 'How is Comrade Timochek?'

He heard his phrases being repeated in Russian, then a deep, arrogant voice also speaking in Russian. The President's interpreter said, 'Good afternoon, Mr President. The General Secretary will unfortunately be incapacited for some time.'

'I am sorry to hear that.'

Again the pause while the translations were made.

The next translation was brutally direct. 'We have learned, Mr President, that a massive move of American troops to Germany is being planned.'

'Mr General Secretary, the deployment of American tactical forces between NATO allies is not a matter for discussion between us. However, let me give you my personal assurance that, should the movement you mention occur, it is in no way directed at the Soviet Union.'

'I do not agree, Mr President and must warn you that the Soviet Union will view any increase of the American presence in Germany as a deliberate act of provocation.'

'Mr General Secretary, any movements of NATO forces within NATO territory is as innocuous as any of your military exercises.'

'There is no comparison. The movement of your forces is not a military exercise but an attempt to intimidate an ally who has expressed a desire to move outside the warmongering capitalist clique of NATO. It is an act of aggression, Mr President, and the Soviet Union must react to it as it sees fit.'

'What precisely do you mean?' the President asked. State had told him that Iakir had been a highly adventurous tank commander, and he wondered if Iakir was hankering for a replay of World War II.

'I mean that if by noon tomorrow the United States has not issued a denial of its intention to land forces in Western

Germany, we shall take such steps as we consider necessary to defend ourselves. We shall begin, Mr President, by calling up our own reserves.'

'You mean you will declare war?'

The President heard Marshal Iakir laugh. 'I don't think it will come to that. In your position, Mr President, I would contemplate seriously the effects of Russian mobilization on your already sinking dollar.'

The President put the phone down. Iakir was right and Iakir was blackmailing him. Even the hint of Russian mobilization would force whatever foreign money there was left in America, elsewhere. Treasury Secretary Sturgis had already spelt out the consequences of that withdrawal, and once the money left, it would only come back after confidence was regained, which meant only after the President had announced that under no circumstances would America involve itself in a European conflict.

Which announcement would give Iakir and Lothar and Konrad Blucher a free hand to create the kind of Central European Federation which America had always opposed and which would destroy world peace.

But what alternative did he have? If he moved US forces into Germany, Iakir's announcement would sink the dollar and the American people would certainly not support a President in a European war while their banks were collapsing, their homes and cars being repossessed, and their jobs being swallowed up. Whatever he did, he would lose, unless Brad Drewett achieved something in Berne.

In Berne, Drewett was finding the Swiss unexpectedly cooperative. Last night after talking with Allison, Yuri and Otto and reading the Skorpion files, Drewett had worked out a strategy. He would seek the cooperation of the Swiss government while Allison and Yuri stopped Baur's syndicate. Drewett had spoken to the President who had ordered a military plane to fly them to Switzerland and had the

American Ambassador arrrange a meeting first thing that morning with the Swiss Ministers of Finance and Justice.

The Swiss listened with growing surprise and indignation to Drewett's revelations of the financial manipulations of Skorpion and Kaspar Baur. The Swiss franc was the world's healthiest currency and the Swiss Ministers of Finance and Justice intended keeping it that way. Switzerland was a small country with a narrow industrial base and its prosperity depended on Swiss investment outside Switzerland — especially dollar investments. 'Switzerland needs the world,' the Finance Minister said, piously quoting a former Chairman of the Swiss National Bank, and summoned the head of his legal department, a large, beefy-looking lawyer called Bernd Rossner to the meeting.

Rossner listened carefully to Drewett and just as carefully went through the documents he had brought. An hour later Drewett and Rossner were on their way to Zurich in a Swissair executive jet where a chauffeur-driven limousine and a police escort waited to rush them to Vaduz.

Avery Cartwright was a large, solid, well-scrubbed man, with a bald pate, a sallow complexion and the bushiest eyebrows Allison had ever seen. He'd just finished breakfast in his suite at the Atlantis Sheraton in Zurich when Allison and Yuri arrived. 'I can't imagine what the FAA could possibly want with me,' he grumbled. 'I'm not a banker. I deal in commodities, copper, tin, chromium, azmium — '

'Money,' Allison snapped.

Last night Drewett had told them of the syndicate and Baur's attempt to prevent the Americans matching any default of the sovereign loans, dollar for dollar. 'These men must be stopped from supporting Baur,' Drewett had said. 'Without their support he cannot succeed.'

'What if they are Izgoi?' Allison had asked.

Drewett had told her what he'd told Pierce. If they were Izgoi they would have bought the loans instead of taking options.

330

Which meant that some members of the syndicate could still be Izgoi, Allison thought. The syndicate consisted of Baur, an American, a Swiss, a Swede, an Italian, and an Englishman. They had decided to break the American.

Flying to Switzerland last night on a military aircraft they had gone through all the Skorpion documents and selected material summarizing the plans and criminal activities of the Izgoi, the personal histories of Rudolf Barynin and Kaspar Baur and the 1937 Skorpion plot. With the help of the American Consul in Zurich, his secretary and photocopier, they had compiled the material into a bulky dossier and made ten copies, one of which Drewett had taken that morning to Berne, and a second of which they'd brought to their meeting with Cartwright. Allison wished the appointment could have been later. They'd only had three hours to sleep.

'Money is a commodity, like everything else,' Cartwright said.

'What are you and five other gentlemen planning to do with the sovereign loans you are about to buy?' Allison asked.

'Corner the market,' Cartwright said. 'It's a legitimate business.'

'And smash the dollar?'

'In business the dollar is a neutral currency, just as tin is a neutral metal.'

'The dollar is *your* country's currency,' Allison snapped.

'If the government had a strong dollar, then people wouldn't speculate against it. It's the government's job to protect the dollar. That's what I pay my taxes for.'

'It is also the government's job to prevent financial manipulation — '

'Now look here, young lady, don't you come here trying to scare me because the government doesn't like what I'm doing. I'm dealing straight and above board speculating against a weak currency, and if the US Government doesn't like it, because that currency happens to be the US dollar, tough.'

'It is also the government's job to protect the dollar from

conspiracy and fraud. It is also the government's job to seek out and punish the perpetrators of murder and treason.'

'Treason! Come on, lady, there's nothing treasonable about buying or selling dollars or sovereign loans.'

'Why don't you read this and see if you agree?' Allison passed him the dossier.

Cartwright read. When he finished, his face was ashen. 'Sweet Jesus,' he muttered. 'Honestly, I had no idea. Hey look, I want no part of this. Soon as I finish packing, I'm getting out.'

'We'd like you to stay and participate in the syndicate,' Allison said.

'Stay! Participate! You've just been telling me it's criminal, larcenous, treacherous — '

'We want to know when and where the meeting will take place,' Allison said. 'We want to attend the meeting.'

In Vaduz, Drewett and Rossner were met by more police and more lawyers. They went to the office of Gerdt Hausmann where a cowed-looking secretary helped them go through Skorpion's books.

Apart from office rent, salaries and a few general expenses, most of Skorpion's money had been redistributed to other tax haven companies, the payments indicated only by a date, amount and company name. There was no indication of why the payments had been made, and Drewett thought it would take months and an investigation of all the companies before the reasons were found.

'There is another company,' Drewett said. 'Trepart SA.'

One of the lawyers protested that Rossner's permissions did not cover the records of Trepart. After twenty minutes argument and several phone calls, Rossner informed them that he had sequestered the records of Trepart SA, also incorporated in Vaduz, formerly administered by Hausmann and wholly owned by Skorpion.

Drewett and Rossner went through the books. The cash

book was similar to Skorpion's, except the entries were fewer. All Trepart's income had been derived from Skorpion, and the moneys had been disbursed among a number of bank accounts in Vaduz, the Cayman Islands and Switzerland.

'The same routine,' Drewett said in disgust. 'Skorpion collected the money and disbursed it to corporate shells. The identities of whoever the corporate shells ultimately paid, are hidden in numbered accounts.'

Rossner turned to the back of the cash book and produced a list of sixteen bank account numbers eack linked to a name. 'Hausmann had to have a quick way of knowing who he'd paid what to, and who owned each account. He obviously wasn't expecting his records to be inspected by outsiders.'

Drewett looked at the names and checked them back to the payments at the front of the books. Nino Valdez had received money from Trepart, as had Centrale and the RGA. So had the terrorists Gunther Stochiawak and Wolfgang Raspe, as well as Siegfried Lothar and his New Social Democrats.

Drewett spoke to Rossner who listed out the payments to Lothar and his political party. In the past five years, they had received over fifteen million Swiss francs. There seemed to be little doubt that Lothar had been financed by Skorpion and controlled by the Izgoi.

Rossner had the list photocopied, then called the President of the bank in Zurich to which the money had been transferred and made arrangements for the account to be inspected as soon as they returned to Zurich.

Drewett urged Rossner to hurry. If they did not get back to Zurich soon, they would be too late to help Allison and Yuri.

CHAPTER FIFTY-TWO

When, by quarter past two, Drewett hadn't returned, Allison and Yuri went to the hotel in the Dolder where the bankers' conference was being held. They wore the plastic tags Cartwright had given them and carried three briefcases with copies of the Skorpion dossier, a Colt Python Drewett had procured for Yuri and a transmitter channelled to the US Consul's office.

Cartwright had told them that Baur's syndicate was meeting to discuss the options at three o'clock in room 507. The bankers' meetings were being held in the Gassner and Rudwiger rooms on the ground floor. Allison and Yuri mingled briefly with the delegates and shortly after three took the elevator to the fifth floor.

The room was at one end of the corridor which had been partitioned off by a desk behind which sat two of Baur's Argentinians. Allison told them they were Cartwright's assistants and had brought documents for the meeting. The guards checked the identity tags, looked into one of the briefcases and phoned. Moments later Cartwright hurried down the corridor towards them, his face shiny with sweat. 'Alice, Simon,' he greeted them hoarsely, reading the names off the plastic tags, and told the guards, 'Let them through.'

They followed Cartwright to the conference room. Cartwright flung open the door. Allison entered. Baur gasped, 'You! What are you doing here?' his hand darting beneath his jacket. Yuri whipped out the Colt Python and stepped from behind Allison. 'Don't anyone move,' he said. 'Especially you, Mr Baur.'

Baur looked at Cartwright, his hand clutching the lapel of

his jacket. 'What is the meaning of this, Avery? These people are government spies.'

'Miss Maynard represents the US government,' Cartwright said, walking nervously round the table to his seat. 'I think we should all hear what she has to say.'

Allison surveyed the men seated round the table. Baur and Cartwright she knew. The languid-looking blond man with the bored expression and regimental tie was the Englishman, Michael Henley, the small, wiry, dark-haired man next to him Carlo Aguita. She recognized the severe looking man in his mid-fifties from newspaper photographs, Sundstrom. The earnest-looking man with the spiky hair and horn-rimmed glasses next to Sundstrom had to be the Swiss, Hugo Hendrik. All present and correct, Allison thought. Whether she and Yuri left that room alive or not would depend on how many of them were Izgoi. She tried not to worry about what had delayed Drewett and to keep the nervousness out of her voice. She said, 'My name is Allison Maynard. I work for the American Financial Administration Agency which is concerned with preventing acts of economic sabotage.'

'Very interesting,' Henley drawled. 'But no acts of economic sabotage are being planned here. Now will you please leave. We are busy men and have a lot to discuss.'

'What you are discussing here is the exercise of an option on two billion dollars' worth of sovereign loans,' Allison said.

'A perfectly peaceful and legal enterprise,' Sundstrom said. His startlingly jet-black eyes were fixed on Yuri. 'Business which does not require the attention of people with guns.'

'When you have read the dossiers you will see that the guns are necessary.'

Sundstrom switched his gaze to Allison. 'I don't care who you are or what department of the American government you represent. But until your colleague puts away that gun, no one will read anything and there will be no discussions.' He placed his palms flat on the table in a gesture of finality.

From across the table Cartwright looked helplessly at her

while Henley smiled quietly to himself and Aguita grinned sarcastically. Hendrik doodled on the pad in front of him while Baur leant back in his chair, his glance alternating warily between her and Yuri.

'Yasha.'

'Yes.' Yuri didn't understand precisely how, but he knew that if these men were stopped from exercising their options, the whole Izgoi plan would crumble. And he had decided they *would* be stopped, even if it became necessary to kill all of them, even if in killing them Allison and he died.

He kept watching Baur. Baur was the leader, Baur would make the first move, Baur was the man he wanted to kill. He kept thinking of the Stadtwald, of Petrov and Karelin. Try something, Baur, he wished silently, please give me an excuse.

'Put the gun away,' Allison said.

Yuri looked round the table. No one other than Baur appeared armed. Before Sundstrom got any ideas of what he should do with the gun, Yuri put the weapon in his pocket, walked up to the table and sat.

'Could we talk now?' Allison asked Sundstrom.

Sundstrom nodded.

'Your business has already considerably weakened the US dollar,' Allison said.

Aguita said softly, 'In business some win, others lose.' The expression on his face belied the softness of his tone. His fists were clenched on the table before him.

'In this case winning and losing is not a matter of chance or skill,' Allison said. 'It is a result of deliberate manipulation for a purpose that has nothing to do with profit. You are gathered here to approve the exercise of certain options on the purchase of sovereign loans, and I believe it is your intention to use those options to default certain of those loans. You then hope to take advantage of the fact that you have already sold the dollar short and make substantial profits.'

'There is nothing illegal in any of that,' Hendrik said.

336

Henley said, 'The simple fact is that American banks should never have got involved to the extent they have in sovereign loans. And I for one will certainly not permit them to avoid the consequences of their actions because of the FAA or a Russian carrying a gun.'

Allison said, 'But the real object of your consortium is not to attack a weak dollar, not even to make a substantial profit by attacking an artificially weakened dollar. The real purpose of your consortium is to paralyse America while you make certain political changes in Europe.'

'That is a false and malicious slander,' Sundstrom snapped. 'I am a businessman, not a politician.'

'You will not frighten us with lies!' That was Hendrik.

Allison looked at them. Were they Izgoi or simply good actors? She said, 'Wittingly or unwittingly you are working to achieve the political ends of a group known as the Izgoi, whose former head was Herr Baur's father, Rudolf Barynin.'

Everyone at the table turned to Baur.

'This is nonsense,' Baur cried. 'All of you know I was born in Dresden to the family of Herlingen.'

Allison tapped the dossiers. 'Here you will find a report by East German counter-intelligence which casts some doubt on that. You will also find a series of letters between Casimir Heilbron, which is the name Rudolf Barynin took after he escaped from Germany in 1945, and Gerdt Hausmann, the lawyer who ran Skorpion SA in Vaduz, evidencing the fact that Herr Baur was not actually born in Dresden, but in Berlin, that he emigrated to Argentina and was brought up as Cassian Heilbron, that he was trained in Russia under the auspices of Marshal Iakir, and was smuggled back to the West with the help of Izgoi friends in East Germany.'

'Lies!' Baur shouted. 'Every word is a CIA fabrication aimed at preventing us capitalizing on the weakness of the dollar!'

'Even if it were true,' Henley interrupted smoothly, 'what difference does it make? What we are about to do here has nothing to do with who Kaspar Baur is or was.'

Allison said, 'All of you have been persuaded to participate in this venture by Kaspar Baur. You have been induced to participate by the promise of enormous profits. But what you are really doing is helping Baur achieve the ambitions of the Izgoi.'

'Shut up, woman,' Baur shouted. 'We have had enough of your propaganda. Leave us to continue with our business.'

'I know nothing of the Izgoi,' Hendrik said.

'Who are the Izgoi?' Sundstrom asked.

'The Izgoi are an ancient secret society, founded in Russia, who for centuries have been attempting to unite Russia and Germany. Their last attempt was made in May 1937 when members of the German and Russian Armies attempted simultaneously to overthrow Stalin and Hitler.'

'Rubbish,' Henley snorted.

'The plot was financed by the Barynin bank and was called Skorpion. The plot was discovered and the conspirators killed. The children of the conspirators are now attempting to fulfil the ambitions of their fathers. Mr Baur here is the son of Rudolf Barynin. The leader of the German conspirators was Field Marshal Erwin Lothar whose son became Chancellor of Germany after Chancellor Schiller was assassinated by the Izgoi. Also involved in the conspiracy was Lieutenant Colonel Jurgen Blucher, the father of East German President Konrad Blucher, and behind it all is Marshall Maxim Iakir, Acting General Secretary of the Communist Party of the Soviet Union .'

'A ridiculous fable,' Aguita snorted.

'Quite unbelievable,' Sundstrom said.

'The true purpose of your venture,' Allison continued, 'is not to make a profit out of the dollar, but to achieve the economic and military paralysis of America while the Izgoi fulfils its political objectives, the creation of a Central European Federation embracing Russia and the two Germanies.' Quickly Allison placed the dossiers on the table. 'All the evidence you need is here. I suggest you read these before you make a final decision.'

The men looked at each other. 'She's right,' Cartwright said, 'I've already read the dossier.' Hendrik reached out and pulled a dossier to him. So did Sundstrom, then Henley, Cartwright and Aguita. There was silence while they read, cursorily at first, then with more attention. Yuri watched Baur, willing him to try something. Baur sat immobile, then pulled a pad towards him and made some notes.

'This is a deliberate ploy by the US Government to interfere in private business it considers prejudicial to its interests,' Aguita cried.

No one paid him any attention. Softly, Baur began to speak. 'Look at the world today. Two power blocks confronting each other, threatening to blow up all of us, even neutral Switzerland. Gentlemen, you are being given an opportunity, a rare opportunity, to change all that. You are being given an opportunity to create a whole new world, to shape it according to *your* design, *your* principles. Imagine, a new United States, stretching from the Atlantic to the Pacific, a vast territory with huge untapped resources, a country that will dominate the world peacefully, the way Russia and America do not and never can.

'Think of it, gentlemen, domination without confrontation, control without conflict, a world run according to economic principles. Imagine the vast resources of Russia harnessed to the genius of Germany, think of the opportunities you will create, the new order you will help form. Think of changing the lives of four hundred million people and making them wealthier and happier.'

'Think also,' Allison said, 'of the means taken to achieve such an end. Murder. Conspiracy. Incitement to treason. Betrayal of whole nations.'

'You talk nonsense, woman. Gentlemen, we are not children. We have all had to take unpleasant and uncomfortable decisions to achieve our ends.'

'I've never killed anyone to achieve my ends,' Hendrik said. He gathered his papers together and stood up. 'I'm sorry,

Kaspar. I won't go on with this. Even if none of this is true, it is not the kind of involvement I seek.'

'Hugo, may I remind you that we have an agreement to work together. The essence of all business is that agreements are honoured.'

'We had an agreement to agree.'

'Then at least let us be democratic. Let us put the matter to a vote.'

'All right.' Hendrik hesitated and sat.

Baur looked round the room.

Hendrik said, 'I vote against it.'

'A minority of one to five,' Baur said, softly.

Allison looked slowly round the table. She could only count on Cartwright. And if all the others were Izgoi . . .

Sundstrom said, 'I will vote . . .' He looked directly at Baur. 'No.'

Allison sighed softly.

Avery Cartwright said, 'I think you're nothing but a mobster, Baur. The answer's no.'

Three and three, Allison thought. They couldn't pass the resolution. She and Yuri could walk out of here with the Izgoi plan in ruins.

'Three and three,' Baur said. He smiled. 'Let me try to persuade at least one of you to change his mind. You are all practical men, and what you have read is true. You have now to face the reality that the Izgoi plans are too far advanced to be stopped. Whatever decision you make here, we already have Russia and the two Germanies. On Wednesday when Chancellor Lothar meets with President Blucher and Marshal Iakir, the foundation of the new union will formally be laid, a union, my friends, that will dominate Europe and present numerous opportunities for its friends, a union that will not forget those who opposed it.'

'Whatever you achieve now is only temporary,' Allison cried. 'Don't forget America! America will fight – '

'As Miss Maynard has *not* told you,' Baur interrupted

340

smoothly, 'the Izgoi have also infiltrated America. Right now America cannot fight the Izgoi. In a short time it will not want to. And whoever controls America it will have to come to terms with the reality of the new Federation . . . as you gentlemen must. So what is it to be?'

'Without your consent the Izgoi cannot go ahead,' Allison cried. 'They need vast amounts of loans to prevent America buying off the loans. Without you there will be no Federation.'

Slowly Hendrik shook his head. 'I am Swiss,' he said. 'I do business, not interfere in other countries.'

Allison looked at Sundstrom and Cartwright. Cartwright said, 'My vote's still no.' Sundstrom stroked his chin and stared into space.

Her voice shrill with desperation, Allison cried, 'After you have voted they will eliminate you. Remember what they did to their own when they ceased to be useful. Remember Hausmann and Weinrich!'

'You don't know what you're talking about,' Baur snapped. 'The Izgoi always have room for their friends.'

Sundstrom spoke. 'That may be so.' He looked from Baur to Allison and back to Baur again. 'My vote is still no.'

Allison felt her shoulders sag with relief. It was over. They had —

Baur said, 'So I must use my Chairman's casting vote. I vote in favour. The resolution is carried. You will all sign accordingly.'

'No.' Cartwright, Hendrik and Sundstrom cried together.

Hendrik got to his feet. 'I will sign nothing. I am leaving.'

Baur said, 'The meeting has been called, the votes have been taken and the resolution has been passed in accordance with the articles of our company. No one leaves this room until the agreements are signed.'

Hendrik gathered up his papers and walked to the door. There was a sharp crack. Hendrik dropped his briefcase and stared disbelievingly at the blood trickling through the fingers he'd instinctively pressed to his chest, looked white-faced and disbelieving round the room. 'No,' he gasped, staggering. 'No.' He reached out a hand for the table, missed and fell.

'Leave him,' Baur snapped, as Henley moved his still smoking gun to cover Yuri, Sundstrom and Cartwright. 'It looks as if we have a clear majority now.'

'No,' Allison cried. 'You cannot achieve a majority through murder.'

'All that matters is if these gentlemen sign or not.' Baur took out his own gun.

Yuri's hand dropped to his pocket. Baur, Henley and Aguita all had their weapons drawn covering him, Allison, Sundstrom and Cartwright. He would have to take the gun from his pocket, clear the table and shoot three men before they could get a shot in. Damn Sundstrom, he thought. Damn him for being a fool and letting Sundstrom tell him what to do. Henley and Baur were looking at him now. At any moment they would ask Yuri to get his hand back on the table. Yuri knew being practical men they would shoot him first. Any moment now, they would fire.

'You're a stupid, interfering bitch!' Baur told Allison. 'If you'd handled this right you could have been rich! You could have worked with us, instead of against us.'

'You'll never understand it, Mr Barynin,' Allison said. 'But there are some of us who don't care about being rich.'

There were shouts in the corridor outside and the sound of racing footsteps, the sound of firing and a tremendous hammering on the door.

'Bitch!' Baur snarled, his lips drawn back, his amethyst eyes blazing.

Yuri slid forward and downwards off his chair, tugging at the Python as he went. He felt the barrel clear his pocket, entangled feet kick at his legs and body, the chair hit him in the back. He reached up and pulled Allison down. His finger squeezed the trigger and his body twisted with the recoil. The sound of the shot was deafening. A foot kicked him in the ribs. He heard Baur cry out and saw a pool of red spread across the middle of his shirt. There was the sound of a door shattering and booted feet thumping the carpet. Baur's torso twisted. His head hit the table. Someone shouted, 'Police! Put down your guns!'

Two heavy objects were thrown on to the table. Cautiously Yuri dragged himself up, past Allison's head. The room was full of uniformed men. Aguita and Henley stood away from the table, their hands in the air, their guns on the notepads in front of them. Baur lay slumped across the table, his head turned sideways, his amethyst eyes open, staring and glazed.

Brad Drewett pushed his way past the Swiss police. 'Oh Jesus, I thought we were too late. We got back from Zurich an hour ago and heard your recording and Rossner got the police and — Oh hell!' He put his arms around both their shoulders. 'Are you all right?'

'Just about,' they said, together.

Tuesday April 29

CHAPTER FIFTY-THREE

It took them the rest of the evening to settle matters with the Swiss police and early the next morning, Drewett flew to Bonn with Rossner and the Swiss Minister of Justice where they met with Lothar's coalition colleagues. The party leaders were horrified, angry and frightened at the information they were given, and decided immediately to strip Lothar of all offices and take steps to ensure his permanent hospitalization.

At the same time, from a hotel in West Berlin, Otto Dietrich called General Franz Koller in East Berlin. His message was convoluted in content but simple in meaning.

Otto wanted Koller to contact Colonel Borodin and have him come to West Berlin as soon as possible.

At three o'clock that afternoon, West German radio and television announced the resignation of Siegfried Lothar. In a broadcast statement, Lothar's successor, Dr Antonius Bosch, said that Siegfried Lothar had been under immense strain and that every commitment he had made had been reviewed by the Cabinet, which had decided to postpone the Alternative Détente indefinitely. He was also pleased to announce that a serious conspiracy involving a large number of terrorist groups had been uncovered by the BND. All the leaders were incarcerated but in order to ensure that there would be no threat to the independence of Germany, he had invited President Jack Donnelly to send American NATO reserves to Germany.

An hour later, Colonel Borodin demanded and got an audience with Marshal Iakir. Iakir asked him about the readiness of Soviet forces. All that day, he said, American troops had been massing for departure to Germany.

'We're not going to war with America,' Borodin said. He pulled out copies of the Skorpion dossier and left them on Iakir's desk. 'I wouldn't advise you to treat me as you did Karelin,' he said. 'If I am not back in my Headquarters in forty-five minutes, Colonel Rublov is taking command. His tanks are already moving on Moscow and his forces are ready to march on the Kremlin.' Borodin pointed towards the papers. 'Copies of these have already been delivered to your colleagues on the Politburo and the Director General of the KGB. I believe that by now most of your Izgoi colleagues have been arrested.' He placed a piece of paper on Iakir's desk. 'Lothar has resigned. Franz Koller's East German troops are currently preparing to oust Blucher, Eidemann and Kork. We don't want a civil war that would damage Russia and Germany. I suggest you resign immediately and announce the miraculous recovery of General Secretary Timochek.'

'And if I refuse?'

'You are only delaying the inevitable. It is over for you and your Izgoi. Your only choice is how you choose to end it. You cannot bring Russia down with you but you could damage it, you could create a crisis from which the Americans and the enemies of Communism can profit. Or you can be a patriot and go quietly.'

'And if I do that?'

'What happens next has nothing to do with me. It's political.'

Iakir thought for a long while. Ever since he'd heard the news of Baur's death and Lothar's resignation he'd known the game was over. He had done his best, and the choice now was whether to prolong a battle he had already lost, or go honourably, leaving the other undiscovered ones to take over as he had done after Lyublino.

He thought back to that Thursday in May 1937. It had been a surprisingly warm day and he had been in his command office at Lyublino listening to the patient throb of tank engines outside. He had been twenty-eight years old then, the youngest Lieutenant Colonel in the Red Army and commander of the Moscow Armoured Brigade.

The phone had rung. It had been Rudolf Barynin from Berlin wanting Marshal Tukachevsky.

Wondering if his phone was tapped, Iakir had said, 'The Marshal isn't here. You should try Headquarters or his dacha.'

'I've tried both places.' Barynin's tone had been abrupt. 'If you do see the Marshal — well never mind — '

'What is it?'

'Tell the Marshal, Joint Exercise Skorpion has been aborted.'

Iakir would never forget the shiver that had run through him, colder than death. 'If I see him,' he'd said and put the receiver down with a shaking hand, knowing then that everything had gone terribly wrong.

Immediately, the phone had rung again. General Marensky had cried, 'I want your tanks in defensive formation round Moscow. Now!'

The throb of the tank engines outside had seemed deafening. Mechanically, Iakir had acknowledged the order. Then he had reached into his desk drawer, taken out his revolver, and placed it against his temple.

His finger had stopped on the first pull of the trigger. He had been ordered to bring out his tanks, he'd thought. Which meant Marensky didn't know. Which meant he was safe.

It was a portent, he'd decided. He had to go on. The torch had been handed to him. It was his duty and his privilege to pass it on.

And he had tried and he had passed it on. There were others. There always would be others. Iakir signed the paper and pushed it across the desk to Borodin. Then, as he had done nearly fifty years ago in Lyublino, he reached into his desk drawer.

He looked across at Borodin and nodded.

Borodin stood, saluted and walked out of the room.

Iakir took out his revolver and raised it to his temple. His finger tightened on the trigger. This time it did not stop against the first pull.

Wednesday April 30

CHAPTER FIFTY-FOUR

That Wednesday, order came out of chaos. The dollar firmed against all other currencies, aided by the Bundesbank which began buying back most of the dollars it had sold. Bank shares halted their downward slide and the bankers' conference in Zurich ended without anyone being defaulted.

In Moscow, a newly recovered General Secretary Valentin Timochek announced that he would shortly be seeking a summit meeting with President Donnelly to discuss matters of mutual concern.

That same day's *Pravda* carried a small announcement stating that the Soviet hero, Anatoly Karelin, had been put in charge of the KGB's Directorate K, and in order to assist him in his continuing duties at Special Investigations, Captain Yuri Orlov and Liutenant Mark Kutsov had been appointed Deputy Directors.

In East Berlin, the Russian troops who had turned out to welcome their new commander, Colonel Rublov, stayed on the streets, the heaviest detachments arranging themselves around the Party offices in Alexanderplatz.

Soon after his arrival, Colonel Rublov saw President Blucher. An hour later it was announced that at a Politburo meeting that morning, former President Wilhelm Dietmark had replaced Konrad Blucher as both President and General Secretary.

As soon as the news of Dietmark's appointment was broadcast in West Berlin, Otto crossed over. He was met by a Russian staff car and rushed to the Party offices in Alexanderplatz where his old friend Dietmark told Otto that his first task was to execute the warrants ordering the arrests of Generals Eidemann and Kork, SSD Chief Feldmann and a number of other persons.

At Charles de Gaulle airport Allison and Yuri walked round one of the linked hubs from which corridors to waiting aircraft radiated like spokes from a wheel. They walked slightly apart from each other, staring unseeingly at coffee shops, and showcases full of jewellery, cameras, perfumes, cigarettes, alcohol and souvenirs.

'I can't believe it's over,' Allison said. 'No more fighting, no more running, no more shooting.'

'No more us,' Yuri said.

'I wish you would live in America,' Allison said.

'I'm a Deputy Director of the KGB.' He forced a smile.

The previous night Drewett had told Yuri if he'd wanted it, a nicely cushioned defection could be arranged. 'No,' Yuri had said. Now he told Allison, 'That would work as well as your coming to live in Russia.'

'We could try. You once said nothing was impossible.'

'I am Russian. I would miss my family too much.'

Allison bit her lips. 'Perhaps I'll get to Moscow sometime.'

'If the Izgoi come back. Or the Moscow Narodny steps out of line.'

They reached a departure gate. A green bulb flashed beside a sign with a flight number and a destination. Moscow.

Allison said, 'For a little while, I think, I loved you, Yasha.'

'I loved you too,' he said.

They stared at each other for several moments, trying to find something all-encompassing to say. 'It's not so bad,' Allison said. 'We're both going home.'

A coy French voice announced the last call for Air France's flight to Moscow. They looked at each other for a moment. Then Yuri bent down and kissed her lightly on the lips. 'Goodbye, Allison. Take care.'

'You too, Yasha. Take very good care.'

Their hands touched. Yuri turned away and strode down the corridor.

Allison wouldn't watch him walk away. She turned and walked around the terminal, forcing herself to look at shop windows, concentrating on not crying.

Drewett came up and put a friendly arm around her shoulder. 'Some things end and others begin,' he said, consolingly. 'That's how life is. In a few hours, you will be home, and everything will be different. You'll be different. You'll feel better.'

Yes, Allison thought, numbly. Different, better. It was like not drowning.